CHASING DIETRICH

MICHAEL MEARS

Copyright © 2010

by Michael Mears

Contents

July 1941

I have a hunch that childhood ends when kids first realize their parents can't always bend the world to their liking. Or worse yet, that bad things happen to good people.

I will always remember the young Liz whose life was a stream of curiosity and wonder. She was a fabulous child although at first I watched her closely, half fearing something God-awful.

Only fireworks frightened Liz. It was the noise. She would hide behind me, peeking over my shoulder at the exploding light as if I were somehow shielding her from harm. I felt proud about my protective power even if it was as fanciful as her fear was unfounded. An entirely rational man would have missed the pleasure. Too bad for him, although I understood the flip-side risk.

Then came the afternoon when Liz sensed the world was not benign and I lost my magic. She was seven. She walked into my study, and for the first time hemmed and hawed as if she wasn't sure what she wanted. She wasn't quite on the verge of tears, but she was troubled as never before.

"What's going on, kiddo? It looks like the dog ate your Milky Way."

"Dad, you know Bailey hates candy." She sounded exasperated with my ignorance and rolled her eyes to prove it.

"Well, I'll be. I thought she'd eat anything from old shoes to cotton candy."

"Daaaad, don't be redickolus."

I loved it when she used words that were a little big for her tongue.

She crossed her arms and pursed her lips.

"Hey, I'm sorry. Come over here, Honey."

She climbed on my lap and rested her head on my shoulder. After the fact it seemed that she was giving me a last chance at working magic. Or maybe she was already beyond that and was taking a moment to gather herself. Eventually she sat up and looked at me with adult-like seriousness.

"Did Momma ever have a brother who died? Seth?"

"What gave you that idea?"

"I heard Momma and grandpa talking."

I didn't like lying, but Liz wasn't ready for Seth's story and all its baggage. She would never be ready for that.

"Gosh, your uncles look pretty healthy to me," I said.

That was the truth but a dodge.

She looked relieved but confused.

"Sometimes Grandpa looks sad when he looks at me."

"No way. He's just getting older."

I rolled my eyes as if getting old was something strange that we had to put up with.

She wasn't ready to challenge me, but I could see she wasn't convinced. To her credit she wasn't quitting either.

"Cain was in the Bible, right? Didn't he kill his brother?"

I had to think about that. I'd left bible reading behind in high school with the priests.

"Honey, according to the Bible, Cain and Abel were brothers. Cain killed Abel, jealous over God accepting Abel's offerings while rejecting his. I think that's the story. We have a Bible around here someplace. We could look it up. But what does Cain have to do with your mom?"

I knew the answer but I wasn't going down that road if Liz was thinking about something else. Her hair was in pigtails that day and she was fiddling with one as if she could tug her concern straight from her mind.

"Liz, talk to me. And ease off the pigtail or you're gonna yank out some brain."

She gave me a you-are-impossible look but was undeterred.

"Did God hurt Cain for being bad?"

"The mark you mean?"

Liz nodded.

"I think it was for his protection."

That didn't make much sense to me, or to Liz from the look on her face.

"That's how I remember the story," I said.

"So, Momma isn't bad?"

"No, of course not."

"Then why does she have a mark like Cain?"

The scar, Seth's story, and Liz's own story were cut from the same cloth. The truth about the scar would lead to the rest. So I told the lie we had planned for the long anticipated question. Some baloney about boiling water - a cooking accident from before the war. The scar predated the war but there had been no accident.

Had I told Seth's story that afternoon, I would have gotten it wrong. Only some years later did I discover the folly at the heart of the story. It could have been a bitter pill for the person who had the most right to anger. That she saw the story in a different light was the measure of her character.

PART ONE

SARA

1934

NEW YORK AND BERLIN

Chapter One

The smell of aviation fuel permeated the cramped cabin. It mixed with our perfumes, colognes and perspiration, making the air a retched brew. Our faces were ashen, matching the clouds that shrouded the Junker's windows. As the tri-motor bounced through the turbulence, the airframe's rattling seemed to signal the plane's looming disintegration.

If this was aviation, it could keep slugging the mail. I would stick to the train.

Behind me sat Frau Gerta Oster. She was repeating the Our Father at breakneck pace, as if the incantation could keep the Junker airborne. She, her husband, and five other couples had been visiting Vienna. The Strength Through Joy program was subsidizing vacations for workers. After all, if Jews and industrialists could travel, why not the workers who really created the country's wealth? Hitler understood that. The wives each wore their motherhood Cross of Honor. They were color coded with braids. Blue meant three kids; green, four; yellow, five; and red, six or more. Party pins flickered from the suspenders of their husbands' lederhosen. Did these otherwise normal looking couples believe the Nazi rigmarole or did their medals and pins signal opportunism or fear?

I knew this much: Gerta Oster believed. Before taking off we had talked at Vienna's Nallion Field.

In 1934 flying seemed a chancy proposition even in good weather. Only daredevils flew in bad weather and it was that kind of day. Morning storms had everything grounded. The few travelers in the terminal were an antsy bunch, looking to kill time. Gerta spotted me for an American by the week-old Paris edition of the *Chicago Trib* I was reading. She asked if I spoke German.

When I responded "ein kleine", she asked what Americans thought of Hitler. Did I look like George Gallup? Despite Zukor's warnings, I wasn't sure whether the man with the funny moustache frightened or amused me. I decided to be flattering and told her that he scared the shit out of me.

Her pudgy face tightened in protest, and she launched into a tribute. Hitler was more than inexpensive vacations. He brought Germany order and jobs. He was the leader the Fatherland needed after years of Weimar decadence, inflation, and chaos. The surrender of 1918 had been a stab in the back. The humiliation and reparations of Versailles needed to be redressed. Hitler would do that, peacefully. He could do no less as a soldier who had been wounded in battle. As she spoke rapture spread across her face.

I wasn't buying.

"In the states we hear the Nazis are thugs with crazy ideas. Aryan superiority. Jewish conspiracies. What's with all that?"

She didn't miss a beat.

"The communists, the Weimar traitors, the elders of Zion. That's who frighten me. Hitler needs to be strong. I say God bless him. And you should watch your tongue in the Fatherland."

"We also hear that people like Goebbels and Goering are stealing the country blind."

Gerta gave the lobby a furtive scan, then asked to see my passport. It apparently passed muster.

"Some of us are concerned about the Brownshirts. And the little Fuhrers fatten themselves but not at our expense. The Fuhrer himself lives in modest rooms at the Kaiserhof. He is an ascetic. He doesn't even eat meat so that we may have more. So what is the rest to us?"

"At whose expense do the little Fuhrers fatten themselves?" I asked.

"Why the," she began, only to be interrupted.

"Gerta, enough of this talk, come here! Excuse my wife, sir.

Like all women she rattles on. She means no offence to the party. Excuse us. Heil Hitler."

As quickly as he had appeared Herr Oster escorted his wife to a remote corner of the terminal where he proceeded to lecture her. About what I couldn't hear. Shortly her great chest began to heave as if she were sucking back tears.

As if their privacy was my responsibility, I looked away and noticed a man sitting on the bench across from me. His eyes moved from the Osters to me. Their blue intensity and his shy grin gave him a certain allure. He looked older than he likely was, as if he'd seen too much or lived too hard. Unlike the Osters and the rest of the Strength Through Joy crowd, he was expensively tailored and decidedly composed. It would take more than bad weather to ruffle him.

"What's that all about?" I asked in German, inclining my head toward the Osters.

"They and their friends are worried."

"I'm not keen on going up in the soup myself."

"That is part of it. However, you needn't worry. I see our plane landing safely."

"You must make a killing on the horses."

He nodded as if acknowledging a compliment.

"Unfortunately I have no time for the races. But I sometimes see what the future will bring."

"Well, take me along if you ever go to the track. Last time out I lost my shirt."

"Perhaps if you drank less."

I gave him a phony laugh. "What makes you say that?"

"I am a clairvoyant. But even if I were only a shyster, I could smell the alcohol and see the stains on your tie and cuffs. The rest is no great leap."

"So are you Sherlock Holmes or the guy from the Opera last night? Hanson, I think."

"I am, in fact, Eric Jan Hanussen."

"No kidding. The morning paper said you gave some performance. Read a few minds, hypnotized a few suckers, had the audience in the palm of your hand. Then pissed off everyone by refusing to predict the future."

"Strange, isn't it? I do things not easily faked only to have the audience grumble when I don't give them predictions of grand tomorrows."

"So why didn't you give them what they wanted?

"They don't want the future I really see. Besides the future was not on the playbill."

"You can make more dough doing private readings?"

"You are a cynical man."

"You've read my mind?"

"Perhaps I only listened to you talk."

"So you're only Holmes, making inferences."

"No. I am Hanussen."

As if thinking something over, he paused, and then continued, "Shall I prove it to you?"

"We're not going anyplace."

"What if you could see the future, if only for a moment? Not necessarily yours or mine, but something from the days ahead. If you saw a fragment of some tomorrow, you might understand why I prefer entertaining to prognostication. Shall we try?"

He spoke quietly with sweetness in his voice. His eyes lost their intensity and became pools of inviting liquid. A mantle of innocence fell over his face. The guy was a mesmerizer. But spell-casting wasn't something I believed in.

"How about a look at the next Kentucky Derby?"

"Concentrate with me. We shall see what we see."

He took a deep breath, closed his eyes, and held his hands before my eyes. Palms up, he rhythmically fingered the air as if trying to touch the unseen.

What do I see?" he said.

Damned if I knew. I looked past his busy hands. His eyes were now open, fathomless pools of inviting serenity.

"Relax. Let your eyes close if they become heavy. Then come and look through mine. Watch my hands through my eyes."

His voice caressed me, as smooth and warm as a summer

breeze. He kept talking. *Watch out*, I thought. I suppose I did, but I can't remember what all he said. However, I became convinced he was about to pluck a phantom from the future and make it materialize on his fingertips. And he did.

A mass of red meat pulsated between us. Blood coursed down his hands onto his forearms and was absorbed into his sleeves. It oozed through his clothing eventually falling from the summer wool of his trouser cuffs to the wooden slats of the terminal floor.

His eyes were gray with grief. A flood of tears washed the innocence from his face leaving it not wise but lost in hell looking for help. A manic laugh twisted from his mouth. Then his face transmuted through a parade of expressions that played like the dance of the seven deadly sins. I wanted out but couldn't escape his vision. I seemed condemned to be a spectator in another man's nightmare.

Then suddenly it was over. Hanussen and I sat on our benches, ordinary men waiting for the weather to clear. He regarded me with a coy smile.

"Did your horse lose?" he asked.

Before I could tell him he was an asshole, Hanussen stood, bowed slightly, clicked his heals, and walked toward the gate. Just as he reached the gate, our flight was called.

It was inevitable. Between the Junker's bouncing and Hanussen's gory vision, the specter of my war returned. I was back driving my ambulance, bouncing across bomb-ravaged roads with bloody kids dying in the back. At seventeen I'd gone to Europe for the adventure of war. Ambulance driving seemed like an honorable way to participate. It was both more and less than I had bargained for. I did my job well enough, but there was no glory in helping the wounded. And the anguish of those dying boys still festered within me.

To chase my old demons, I thought about what Hanussen had done to me. Fortune tellers and hypnotists were fashionable in the early '30s. When selling apples seemed like a decent job, a little mystery from the other side could be as diverting as a good ball game. But I was a tough guy who usually recognized bunk for what it was. What had I seen? Certainly not the future. Hanussen had managed to hypnotize me and then fill my head with garbage. Strange times. Bunk seemed real; and I was just another not-so-tough sucker.

The Junker broke free of the clouds twenty miles east of Berlin. It landed at Tempelhof in the twilight of a late spring day. Walking across the tarmac to the terminal, I listened and breathed deeply. The air was pure, light, dry, and alive with the songs of countless birds. Not surprising. More than half the city was covered with farms, forests, parks, and gardens.

I fell in at Hanussen's side as we walked into the terminal. I asked if he wanted to share a taxi.

"No." he said and upped the tempo of his step.

As he walked off, he looked back at me and said, "We will meet again and more than the weather will be bad."

"You need some new material," I called after him.

He didn't look back, passed through the terminal, and was greeted by a small entourage. They whisked him away in a big Daimler.

The Strength Through Joy couples were boarding a bus as I caught a cab. Large rectangular signs plastered the sides of the bus. One featured the stylized portrait of an ideal worker next to the words, BLUT und BODEN, which translated: Blood and Soil. The other sign, with a stylized portrait of an ideal wife, read: KUCHE und KINDER, meaning Kitchen and Children. Welcome home, Third Reich style.

My taxi wound its way toward the heart of the city through Neukolln, a working class district. The flag makers and printers must have been leading the economic recovery. Propaganda posters were everywhere. Most delivered patriotic slogans inscribed next to heroic pictures of Hitler, idealized Aryans, or fearsome eagles. Other posters attacked the communists.

Yet others assailed the Jews who were grotesquely caricatured. Nonsense you might think. Except Germans didn't walk on the grass if the sign said, *keep off*.

The cabby spotted me for an American and couldn't stop talking about his beloved city. Founded seven hundred years before by the grandsons of Albert the Bear on an island in the Spree, Berlin was now the largest city on the continent. It was a shipping, aviation, manufacturing, and cultural dynamo. His advice: walk the Linden; see a play in the theater district; shop at the great stores on Leipziger Strasse; visit the Tiergarten and its fabulous zoo; study the treasures on Museum Island; and enjoy the cafes, cinemas, and cabarets on Kurfurstendamm. But what I really needed to do was listen to the music.

Erich Kleiber at the State Opera. Bruno Walter at the German Opera. And Wilhelm Furtwangler at the Berlin Philharmonic. The cabby spoke their names with the reverence Americans reserved for Washington and Lincoln, Ruth and Dempsey, or Armstrong and Ellington. While Louie and Duke had their admirers on the Ku'damm, Strauss, Wagner, and Orff were respectively Berlin's current, past and future kings.

For a guy with so much to say, I thought the cabby would have an opinion or two about Hitler. If he did, he wasn't sharing them. When I asked, he fell silent. He must have had an inkling of what was in store for his heros. Within a few months, the Nazis would force Bruno Walter out, and Kleiber would leave Berlin in protest. Even great conductors were expendable in the interest of racial purity.

The taxi dropped me at the Adlon Hotel on Pariser Platz at the corner of the Linden and Wilhelmstrasse. Fancy address for a Pinkerton agent. My suit needed a press but was too old to hold one. I carried a new one in my suitcase. Compliments of my boss, Humphrey.

"Ya can't see a movie mogul dressed like a bum," was part of his lecture two weeks before in his State Street office.

"I'm not right for this job. And I don't need a new suit 'cause I'm not going. You're the last one I should havta tell."

"There's a tailor from Marshall Field outside the door. You're going or you're fired."

I argued for a while but we both knew I needed my job. It was more than the money. For over six years I'd been drinking near the edge – messed up about a girl who I didn't know well enough to be sure of her name. I'd screwed up a job in Paris. If I'd done my job better, I might have brought her home. If I'd known her better or a little longer, I might not have loved her. As it was, I still did.

When Humphrey didn't have me working, I spent my time fending off memories with bootleg whisky in Chicago's speakeasies. Every month or so Hump would bail me out of some jam or other, and give me a new assignment. I would sober up and get it done. Then I'd hop off the wagon as if to prove I was in control. I was smart enough to recognize the pattern but too dumb to shake it.

The Berlin job sounded a lot like the one from '27. That's why I tried to say no.

As the cabby handed my bag to the doorman, I remembered Fix. According to Zukor he was the best barman in Berlin and one reason the Adlon was better than the Bristol. The nuances of Berlin's top hotels had been wasted on me. After all, clean sheets were a treat where I came from. From bartenders I wanted only speed and discretion. Still I owed it to Zukor to have a look at Fix as soon as possible. Besides I was thirsty.

Just then my curiosity interrupted. For once in my life I would have been better off going directly to the bar.

A hundred yards down the Linden, forty or so Brownshirts were milling around the front of a stately building. They carried signs that basically said commies were shits. They were chanting something about assholes that I couldn't make out. I'd heard that Germans were obsessed with bathroom humor but these guys weren't playing for laughs.

I nodded in their direction and spoke to the cabby, "What's that all about?"

He looked embarrassed. "Storm Troopers. The SA for short. They won but don't seem to know it. They battled the communists for years. Killings on both sides. Hard to say who was worse. But now Hitler is Chancellor and the communists are illegal. So what do they do? They harass the Russian Embassy. They want a second revolution. Hitler has not gone far enough. He's sold out to the Prussians and the industrialists. They demand real socialism. What they really want are the privileges of power. They want to play on the Ku'damm, and fuck cabaret dancers and pretty boys. They want money. Like their boss, Rohm."

"So you like these guys."

"I'm a cabby. I like everyone. Good luck to you," he said, lingering for a tip.

I give him a buck. Heck of a tip in 1934. Generosity was easy with Zukor's money.

"Moss and no shavings," said the cabby, tipping his hat approvingly as he got in his cab.

Berliners had their own slang. "Moss" was foreign currency as opposed to Reichsmarks which were "eggs". "Shavings" were change.

The doorman was dressed in a smart, pale-blue uniform and wore white gloves. He looked worried about soiling his gloves on my beat-up valise. But duty was duty.

"May I take your luggage, sir?"

I waved him off and continued to watch the storm troopers.

A lieutenant and his sergeant were attempting to get their rabble in formation. They were not having an easy time. Finally the lieutenant fired his Luger in the air. The troops settled down and pitched their signs on the embassy lawn. They assembled in a loose formation and began marching between the lime trees which lined the Linden, forcing traffic to maneuver around them.

As they came closer, I saw hard men who were accustomed to violence and loss. Superimposed on the meanness of their faces was the arrogance of new and aimless power. As the formation came abreast of the hotel, two troopers shot me the Nazi salute.

I did nothing.

"Sieg Heil!" they barked.

I gave them a *you-must-be-shitting-me* look.

The two troopers broke formation and swaggered over. They repeated their salute with another "Sieg Heil."

I should have walked into the hotel, but didn't. My *you-can't-bully-me* expression must have been easy to read.

The Brownshirt on my right called me a jew-boy. Then the trooper on my left clubbed me. Before I could react, I was on the ground, jackboots and truncheons tattooing my old suit. To them I was just another Jew getting his due. Had I the time, I might have cried that I was no Jew. The thought of that bothered me later.

I came around in the hotel manager's office. Hedda Adlon, the owner's wife, was waiving a bottle of ammonia under my nose. Behind her stood the house doctor. He never said a word but whenever Hedda spoke he nodded like a cuckoo.

"These are turbulent times, but the Fuhrer is working to curb the excesses," said Hedda reassuringly. "Things are improving. The storm troopers left as soon as our doorman came to assist you. Six months ago you would have been seriously hurt and they would have beaten our man for an offense against the healthy instincts of the people."

"Healthy instincts?" I said.

"Yes, something of a new social code. You will be fine after rest and some Bayer."

I chased the aspirin with my own prescription: a double shot of scotch. Frau Adlon let me keep the bottle she had provided. It was the least she could do.

I fell asleep thinking that it had been a hell of day. I'd seen the future, twice.

Chapter Two

I slept late only to awake stiff and sore. Fifteen hours of sleep, three ounces of scotch and a handful of aspirin weren't enough to shake the effects of an SA mugging. I took a long, hot shower that left me feeling relieved. By the time I arrived at the hotel's Lindenbaum Cafe, I was walking with a minimum of pain and was ready to eat everything in sight.

I hunkered down to a lunch that would have made a cardiologist faint. Beer kept everything lubricated and the nut cake was a perfect finisher.

After lunch I hauled myself back to my room. I flopped on the bed and dreamed the Germans lost the great war by eating yards of sausage which decomposed into hydrogen. Trim soldiers swelled, becoming obese burghers who floated from their trenches like clown balloons. In the sky above no-mans-land, they exploded and showered the front with shit.

I woke at six, showered off another layer of dead skin, dressed in my new suit, and went to see if Zukor had been right about Fix.

The Adlon Bar was a blend of black walnut and crystal. Light danced in the crystal and vanished into the wood, creating an illusion of sparkling darkness. Forest-green, linen-covered tables were tucked among lush potted plants. Two waiters worked the room from a service bar. Fix glided behind the main bar as if he had wheels for feet. His tux was perfection. His hair, slicked backed with tonic, gleamed like a perfectly cut black sapphire.

Fix put a double scotch at my hand almost before I finished ordering. He paused a second or two. When I said nothing, he moved off, leaving me to my thoughts. They drifted to my meeting with Zukor.

I arrived for my appointment at ten sharp, only to be left waiting as if I had appeared uninvited to pitch a third-rate script. Zukor's gatekeeper was an old lady who had the demeanor and heart of a drill sergeant. While I cooled my heels, I thought about Zukor.

Before studying up on him, I'd assumed that movies were a Hollywood business. It turned out movie moguls made their money in New York financing movies, and then parceling out the films of their production companies to theaters owned by their distribution companies. When the business school wizards later studied the arrangement, they dubbed it vertical integration. Zukor and his rivals, Fox and Loew, called it grabbing the brass ring.

At first Edison tried to control the industry through his patents on cameras and projectors. He filmed one-reelers that didn't tell stories. Hell, the pictures moved. What more did the immigrants want for their nickels? In 1912 Zukor imported *Queen Elizabeth*, a four-reel drama from Britain with Sarah Bernhardt playing the queen. He made a fortune distributing it. By 1927 his Paramount operation, with its Long Island studio and nationwide chain of theaters, dominated the silent film industry. Edison's movie trust had been crushed by an immigrant who had started out sweeping streets.

By 1934 Zukor and Paramount were at risk of being crushed by the depression and new rivals like Jack Warner. After the crash of '29, Paramount's chain of theaters became a financial drain. And having been the king of silent film wasn't worth a cup of coffee after Al Jolson said, "You ain't seen nothing yet," in Warner's first talkie, *The Jazz Singer*.

If Zukor was worried, he wasn't letting on that day in May of

1934 when I was finally ushered into his ninth floor office in the Paramount Building. The building towered thirty-three stories above Paramount's flagship theater. When it opened in 1926, the papers called the complex the Jewel of Times Square.

His office walls were covered with photos of Zukor with friends, stars, politicians, bankers, and family. Documents were neatly stacked on his desk. He came around and offered me his hand. For a little man in his fifties, he had a steam-shovel grip. Mostly bald, he regarded me from expressive eyes, which registered curiosity. His square face was dominated by a wide, sensuous mouth. A cigar was planted in its corner like a permanent fixture. He saw me eying his photographs.

"Not bad for a pisher who didn't speak English when he passed through Ellis Island. Most of these people helped me one way or another. Three are special."

He pointed to a photo in which he posed with an old man wearing glasses pinched on the bridge of his nose. In the picture Zukor smiled like a greedy kid who thinks he's found the philosophers' stone. Or perhaps he was happy because his wavy hair was still thick enough to attract a girl's fingers. The old man had no hair, no smile, and looked like he'd discovered the philosophers' stone years before only to learn its promise was a hoax.

"Meyer Rubel," said Zukor. "He was in dry goods. Got me started in the fur business before the turn of the century. Taught me the customer is always right. Give'm what they want - even if it's drek they want!"

He pointed at a second photo in which he posed with a young slick. They wore plaid suits and had the look of Alexanders off to conquer the world.

"Menachem Adamovski. By the time I met him, he was calling himself Mac Adams. Taught me the real money was in volume. He got me outa fur and into Nickelodeons."

Zukor pointed to a third photo. In it he reverently gazed at a handsome woman in her early sixties.

"Sarah Bernhardt. Divine. One of a kind. Showed me the

value of stars. That's a big part of what I do. I make 'em. Pickford. Fairbanks. Swanson. Bow. Valentino. You think they made it on their own? Think again! And I need even bigger stars today. Can't expect people to sacrifice lunch money for a movie ticket with a nobody playing the lead. I intend to deliver."

He walked back to his desk. When he sat, he almost disappeared behind the piles of paper.

"Sit. Sit," he said, holding out his hands as if he were offering me the paper stacked between us. "Scripts. They call the talkin' dialogue. It's harder than it was in the silent days. That brings me to you."

In a flash I pictured myself starring in a Paramount talky. What dreamers we can be.

"No such thing as a silent star today. One of my directors, von Sternberg, has found a Pickford with the voice of an angel. But such a will Pickford never had. A few months ago she convinced von Sternberg to send her to Germany to do a film at Ufa, the big, kraut studio. Insanity. With Hitler coming to power, all the talent in Germany is running here, but she insists on going there. Don't get me started. But stars who can talk aren't so easy to find. She wants to stay in Germany. I want her back. Your boss, Humphrey, says you're the man to bring her home."

"What's the girl's name?"

"Sara Potter. I may leave it. Has a nice ring."

"If everyone's leaving Germany, why's she staying?"

"The Nazis and Goebbels have taken over Ufa. She thinks Goebbels is a mensch. Here, read this ca-ca she wrote von Sternberg."

The letter was a month old. It sung the praises of the new Germany and the leadership of Hitler and Goebbels. She was going to play the sister of Horst Wessel in an epic about a young storm trooper who was murdered by the communists.

"So she likes Goebbels. What of it?"

"Hitler gives a hell of a stump speech. I've seen the newsreels. But this is an American girl. No kid from Kansas either. She's thirty if she's a day. A sweetheart on the screen but she's been to the big city. Has a mind of her own. Then this shit. So what's her angle?"

"Maybe she thinks they can make her a star. Didn't *The Blue Angel* make Marlene Dietrich a star? That's a German movie. Right."

"Bullshit. Paramount made *The Blue Angel*. We filmed it at Ufa but it was our baby all the way. Dietrich was a nothing. Von Sternberg found her in a little nothing on the Ku'damm. We made her over. Sara knows the story. She knows I'm the one who makes the stars. She should know the Germans are doing a fade-out. Ufa was in the crapper even before Goebbels started calling the shots."

"You don't like dictators who make the trains run on time?"

"Don't be a smart ass. I don't like men whose strength is their hate. That's what makes Hitler tick. Listen to his speeches. Read his book, *My Struggle*. He shoulda called it *A Lunatic's Rant*."

Zukor leaned forward, put his elbows on the desk and rubbed his forehead just above his eyebrows. I couldn't tell if he was exorcizing anger or pain.

"To him Jews are kikes - cut one open, you find maggots. With the help of their Marxist creed, the Jews are out to conquer world, and will be the funeral wreath of humanity.

"*Mien Kampf* goes on for pages and pages like that. Hitler thinks he's fighting a holy war. And he doesn't like Christians either. Calls Christianity, and I quote, 'The heaviest blow that ever struck humanity. Bolshevism is Christianity's bastard child. Both are inventions of the Jew. Christianity is a liar and will disappear.' That's word for fucking Hitler's word.

"He hates France for winning the war. He hates the Russians because they have land he wants for German expansion. He hates everyone who isn't Aryan. Listen to this. 'All of human culture, all the results of art, science, and technology that we see today, are almost exclusively the creative product of the Aryan. All those who are not of the Aryan race are chaff.' That's word for word too. So Irving Berlin and Albert Einstein are a pair of shmucks?

"So no jokes about trains running on time. This bastard is

Chancellor of Germany. He wasn't lucky. It's all in his vile little book. How to organize and win the masses. How to mold people with the power of the spoken word and the hysteria of the mass meeting. How to make a lie the truth through propaganda. How to apply brute force with persistence and ruthlessness.

"Will he start killing Jews? Will he attack France and Russia? Time will tell. But the Chancellery won't be enough. I tell you we are all threatened!"

Zukor stopped as if he'd forgotten where he was going, or was surprised by his tirade. I didn't know what to say. When he started up again his passion hadn't cooled.

"I can't do much about him. But Potter's under contract with Paramount. I don't want her in Nazi movies. I don't want Paramount tainted with a swastika. Am I clear?"

He glared at me, a bulldog protecting his turf. But even the loudest bark couldn't carry the Atlantic. I held up Potter's letter to von Sternberg.

"This says she's a believer and staying for a while. How do I change that?"

"Look, I told you before, she's savvy. Hell, at first she didn't even want the Ufa deal. She wouldn't buy their propaganda if she knew what was really going on. Make her read this."

Zukor began handing me stuff.

"Newspaper stories about the storm troopers. The English version of *Mien Kampf*. Some of Hitler's speeches. A speech Goebbels made. Look, if the stories about the storm troopers are half true, you shouldn't have to do much more than take her for a walk in Berlin. Make her see what's happening. She's probably locked in a whirlwind of Ufa parties and work. It's like that in our business.

"If that doesn't work, tell her I've cancelled her contract for not showing up. But I got a heart of gold. I'm giving her a new one. Swanson money. But here's the catch. If she's not in our Long Island studio by July fifteenth, the new contract is void. And Paramount issues a press release that will finish her. She'll wind up waiting tables at Chock-Full-Of-Nuts."

He leaned back in his chair, his anger cooling.

"You look like a nice boy. You too should come back safe. It's not so good to be a Jew's agent in Germany. I called Sime Silverman's kid over at *Variety*. From now on you are one of their reporters on assignment in Berlin. The Nazis love movies. If you run into any, gossip up a storm. The scoops behind the stories. Just don't flatter any Jews. Better yet, pretend we don't exist."

Zukor began handing me more paper.

"Everything you'll need. The new contract. The press release. Background reports and pictures of Potter. Your *Variety* credentials. The last dozen issues of *Variety* and a commemorative issue from last year that has a history of the business. Read it on the ship - all of it.

"Then see Dietrich."

Watching Fix glide along the bar to serve his well-heeled customers and listening to their buoyant talk made Zukor's words seemed unreal. A crazy man couldn't be running the show for these civilized, happy people. Then again my ribs weren't sore because the Nazis were breaking ground for Gandhi.

"Fix, what do you think about Hitler?"

He looked around, just as Gerta Oster had in Vienna.

"You are a guest at the hotel?"

I introduced myself

"The man who was beaten at our doorstep?"

"Yes."

"We must all learn to salute. I'm sorry. I must attend to another customer."

Fix moved down the bar as if I'd ask him to commit treason. I pushed my half-finished double away. A walk in Berlin's sharp, clear air would be better than scotch.

I was barely out the door when I saw two Brownshirts staggering arm-in-arm toward the Brandenburg Gate. They were singing the Horst Wessel song. They carried beer bottles in their free hands. After passing the hotel, they stopped in the middle of Pariser Platz and turned to face the French Embassy. They gestured wildly and shouted obscenities. Then they heaved their bottles at the embassy as if tossing grenades over a trench wall. The bottles shattered on the embassy's facade. The storm troopers staggered off, laughing and singing, savoring their counterfeit vengeance.

I went back to my room and poured myself a double.

Chapter Three

The next morning I hopped a cab to the suburbs. The hack was a stubby guy about the size of a hog. His sight line wasn't more than an inch or two above the steering wheel. Only divine intervention could account for his remarkable negotiation of the heavy traffic.

The Kaiser Parkway took us south into Wilmersdorf where Berlin's middle class lived in respectable apartments and small houses. Fresh paint was everywhere. There wasn't much Nazi regalia around. Apparently these folks liked the benefits but had reservations about flying the colors.

After we turned west on Wald Chaussee, the traffic thinned. Without the challenge of congestion, the porker seemed to lose interest and settled back in his seat. I figured from his new position he wouldn't be able to see anything but a double-decker bus.

"Fancy address you gave me," he said.

"It's a house. Belongs to a guy named Alfred Hugenberg."

"In Dahlem creases don't have pens, only barns."

A crease was a suit and hence a businessman. Pens were ordinary houses. Barns were mansions. He was right about the neighborhood.

Potter was staying at a villa near the Rot-Weisse Lawn Tennis Club. The posh neighborhood was six miles southwest of the Adlon. Hidden amid cherry and dogwood trees, and tucked behind white brick walls were rambling estates with swimming pools and greenhouses. Von Ribbentrop and a handful of other Nazi bigwigs had already bought out some of the merely rich who previously called Dahlem home.

Potter was staying at a guesthouse on Hugenberg's spread. He was one of the many German fat-cats who now supported the supposedly socialist Nazis. He was a financier who had used his money to buy a string of newspapers as well as UFA, Germany's foremost movie studio. As the porker slowed to stop at the gate, I told him to drive on to UFA.

"What!"

"The studio. Ufa. In Babelsberg."

"I know where it is," he said as if I'd insulted him.

The studio was eight miles further southwest, just across the Havel and about a mile east of Potsdam. The sister towns were both built on dreams. Babelsberg was Germany's Hollywood. Potsdam was the cradle of Prussian militarism. The army still called it home.

UFA's front gate was even more formidable than Hugenberg's. Dietrich had been right. Potter was ensconced behind walls intended to keep out the likes of me, even with my *Variety* credentials.

I told the porker to drive me back to Berlin. I gave him an address on Tiergartenstrasse. I had been given the address in Vienna.

Vienna may have been the home to Mozart and Strauss, but it wasn't a waltz I was whistling when Zukor sent me there. It was *Awake in a Dream*, the song Marlene Dietrich sang to Gary Cooper in *Desire*. Cooper hadn't acted like he was aroused. He acted like he was worried that his arousal would show. He should have been. In theaters across the country, audiences whispered that Cooper hadn't gotten his hands in his pockets quickly enough.

Zukor told me to visit Dietrich, explaining that she still had contacts in the German film industry who could provide me with an introduction to Potter. He bragged Dietrich would jump at the chance to help him.

Then he shuffled me into his limousine. On the ride across Manhattan to the German-Lloyd Line terminal, Zukor filled me in on Fix and recommended aquavit, claiming it was better than a vodka martini.

When I said I was partial to beer and Wild Turkey shooters, Zukor smiled uncomfortably as if I reminded him of his past.

The limo dropped me under a banner boasting the "FASTEST SHIPS ON THE SEAS." There I boarded the *Europa*, a sleek liner bound for Germany.

When the ship docked at Hamburg, I trudged under another banner that proclaimed that the *Europa* had set a new speed record for the Atlantic crossing. Just under four days. Given that my reading material included *Mien Kampf* and a contract written by a lawyer who was being paid by the word, the crossing had not been fast enough. I was greeted by a telegram from Zukor. It said Dietrich would see me three days hence in her Vienna hotel suite.

She was staying at the Sacher on Philharmonik Street near the State Opera House. In its heyday the hotel had been the stomping ground for Austrian royalty. Around the turn of the century Archduke Otto, a nephew of the Emperor, chased a friend through the lobby wearing nothing but his sword. At the time the hotel staff never spoke of Otto's dash. It was that kind of place.

By the early thirties, the Sacher had slipped a notch. The guest list was down to new money, divas, and film stars. But the hotel still maintained confidences. The front desk would not even admit Dietrich had checked in. When I started to raise cane, the desk clerk made a phone call. I expected a hard-ass house detective to appear. Instead an extraordinary old lady sashayed across the lobby on the arm of a clerk.

She was so fragile that she was either a step from death or had just risen from the dead. But there was a panatela in her mouth, rouge on her cheeks, and a smile on her face. Her Viennese was indecipherable. The clerk introduced us and translated. The biddy was tough enough to be a cop but turned out to be the hotel's owner, Anne Sacher. She cross-examined me through a haze of cigar smoke and then gave me Dietrich's room number.

I knocked on her door and was greeted by a matinee-idol type who turned out to be exactly that. I introduced myself and he invited me into a suite grand enough for a Hapsburg. The idol called Dietrich, sounding a bit peeved. A minute later she glided in. Dressed all in white, her filmy blouse and pleated pants revealed nothing and suggested everything. Like a liquid goddess she flowed to the idol, washed up his body, and gave him the kind of kiss idols expect.

"Hans, I'll see you for dinner tomorrow?" Her voice was husky and bored. Its ennui suggested the kiss had been a lie.

"Of course!" he said, anything but bored. He left, flashing a mouthful of perfect teeth.

With the idol gone, Dietrich seemed to solidify. She studied me with deep-set eyes. I wasn't sure she was pretty or even feminine. She seemed more like an androgynous carnal predator.

"Zukor said that you could help. I've . . ."

"Yes, yes. Zukor wired me. He has some nerve. A year ago he sued me and obtained a court order putting me under house arrest. He fed me bread and water while I finished *Song of Songs*. You can believe that!"

I gave her my best effort at a charming smile. I didn't have the idol's toothy grin but what the hell. How many times do you meet a movie star?

"I read that the house was in the Hamptons. The bread was caviar. The water, champagne. And you were making two grand a week. I may tell Zukor to buzz off and hope he sues me."

Something of her liquid look returned. There was a hint of interest in her voice. "You would have to be very good for that to happen. So are you good at anything?"

I turned a little red at the suggestion, if that's what it was.

"I've had some luck finding people and . . . well, I'll leave it at that."

She chuckled. "How delightful. Sternberg told me Zukor was sending a Pinkerton thug. Instead I get a nervous young man. Come with me. I won't bite."

I followed her into a sitting room fit for her rival, Garbo. She sat on an Empire couch and twisted sideways, resting her back against the couch's arm. Kicking her shoe off, she rested her right leg on the seat. She pointed to the bar.

"Get us some champagne. Then we'll talk about Sara Potter."

"Pop this open?" I said holding a bottle of Dom Perignon. I hadn't seen one since 1927.

"Yes. Then come and sit down. Right there."

She pointed to the couch, at the space just past her toes. It was nothing but a naked foot and a tad of ankle, but it might as well have been Anita Berber dancing in the buff at the White Mouse. I handed her a glass and squeezed into the opening. The foot didn't move a smidgen. It rested an inch or so from my thigh, radiating heat or so it seemed. I stared into my Champagne flute, determined not to gaze up that leg.

"How quaint. A bashful dick."

She laughed and swung the provocative leg to the floor. She rested her elbows on her knees and looked over her shoulder at me, her huge eyes amused.

"In spite of Zukor, I'm going to help you. Two reasons. First Joe von Sternberg asked me to. Second the Nazis are bad business and no one deserves to be in their clutches. So . . ."

She was cut short by a ten-year-old who bounced into the room followed by another leading man type.

"Momma, we are going to the Prater!"

"Wonderful. You can see for miles from the top of the Ferris Wheel. Mr. Temple, this is my daughter, Maria, and my husband, Rudi Sieber. Come, angel, give me a hug."

Rudi gave me a slight bow while Maria gave her mom a hug. Once Maria and Rudi left, Dietrich got down to business as if juggling a husband, boyfriend, and daughter in a hotel suite was perfectly normal.

"You won't be able to see her at Ufa. Strangers can't get on the lot without a pass. Potter is staying with Hugenberg in a guest house on his Dahlem estate. His security is better than Ufa's. You will have to meet her socially.

"Before you leave I will give you a letter of introduction to Bella Fromm. She writes a column for *Vossische Zeitung*. It's the oldest newspaper in Germany. Snobby. Condescendingly liberal. An institution. No one reads old *Tante Voss* except everyone who counts. Hmm. Make that everyone who counted before Hitler and his gang arrived. Bella is the Louella Parsons of the diplomatic corps, except everyone loves her. Well everyone but the Nazis. She's a Jew but the Nazis can't touch her. The diplomats would have the entire civilized world crying foul. She'll find a way for you to meet Potter."

"Tell me about Hugenberg. Could he and Potter be . . . involved?"

"Involved?" She looked at me like I was a relic from the Victorian age.

"I hope she would set her sights higher. He is a boring, old man who thinks he is accumulating power by currying favor with the Nazis. He may own Ufa and a dozen newspapers but Goebbels calls the shots. He has spent his money to become a Nazi puppet. If Potter wants to screw her way to stardom, she needs to bed Goebbels. That is easy enough, but she better be good because the little minister has the attention span of a rabbit. Oh my, have I embarrassed you? How sweet."

"Must be the champagne."

"Yes. Be a darling and pour us more. You could use some color. You're as white as a sheet."

"You don't let up, do you?"

"Not until I've had my fill," she said smiling pleasantly.

"Here you go."

She extended her glass, peering over its rim at me. As the bubbly filled the flute, she ran her tongue around her lips. She was outrageous.

"That's part of what I had in mind," she said.

After I sat down, she resumed her Cleopatra pose. Her toes

nibbled at my thigh. She couldn't be serious, could she?

"How do I find Bella Fromm?"

"You are all business, aren't you? At least Zukor will get his money's worth. The address will be on the letter I have for you. Anything else I can do for you?"

"I read *Mien Kampf.* Why would Potter fall for that crap?"

She continued to diddle with my thigh.

"Girls fall for the damnedest people. Hard to account for such things."

"I'm serious."

"How boring. I have not read the book. I have not been in Berlin in two years. But things are bad. Many Ufa people have fled, Paris, New York, Hollywood, even Vienna. In Germany people are afraid to talk freely, even in their homes. Everyone thinks the Gestapo is listening. Your best friend may turn out to be an informant. That's all I can tell you about Berlin.

"But Potter has made an enemy, an actress named Paula Glaise. Not so talented, except in the most primitive of ways. Was that delicate enough for you? Very ambitious. She regards Potter as a rival. Wants her to go home as much as Zukor does. In that she could be your ally.

"Paula writes me occasionally. She is calculating and cultivates anyone who might be able to help her. She praises me as Germany's greatest actress and begs me to come home. She claims Potter is mixed up in some anti-Nazi plot. I think she writes for the censors. Do you understand?"

"Yeah. She curries favor with the Nazis and stabs Potter in the back at the same time. A dangerous lady."

"Many women are dangerous, Michael."

She rose from her reclining position, put down her flute, and eased her way onto my lap. She gave me a serious kiss. My God this was Marlene Dietrich! I knew exactly how Gary Cooper felt. The Pinkerton manual didn't cover this, but I figured I could struggle through on instinct. She lifted her breasts from my chest and gave me her patented look. I can tell you it worked without a bit of trick lighting. I leaned forward to kiss her neck.

She pulled away and laughed.

"Why you handsome devil. Taking advantage of a lonely girl whose men are out. For shame. I could never do that to Hans or Rudi, in Vienna."

Before she showed me the door, she handed me an envelope addressed to Bella Fromm. The script was so bold that it looked contrived. The address was 282 Tiergartenstrasse, in the heart of Berlin's diplomatic district.

If only we hadn't met in Vienna. The thought had me smiling as I left the Sacher. I had a heck of a story for the boys back in Chicago, although they weren't likely to believe it.

Chapter Four

For the neighborhood Fromm's house appeared modest. But with ten rooms and servants' quarters in the attic, it was deceiving. Out back was a small stable where she kept two Lipizzaners for riding in the Tiergarten.

Fromm answered the door herself. She was short and unattractive, but carried herself with grace and strength. There was an air of quiet decency about her, an odd trait for a newspaper reporter who supposedly traded in gossip. But then she worked for *Tante Voss* with its old world approach to reporting. Blue blood was respected and yellow journalism wasn't.

I introduced myself and handed her Dietrich's letter of introduction. She invited me in only after surveying the street. Closing the door behind us, she read the letter standing in the foyer. When she finished, she led me through the house, out the back door, past her small stable, and through a gate that opened into the Tiergarten. There footpaths and horse trails cut through elms and black alders, looped around ponds, spilled into flowered meadows, and crossed wooden bridges spanning rivulets that flowed nowhere. We walked in silence finally stopping at a goldfish pond.

"I did so love to ride here. Often I joined government officials or staff officers who were out for exercise. It was a fine time for me, personally and professionally."

"You've given up riding?"

"No. I still ride."

She walked on, not explaining her use of the past tense.

Eventually she said, "Your German is good for an American.

Tell me about yourself."

"I work for Pinkerton, usually running down missing people. I live in Skokie, a town just north of Chicago. Big German community there. Some of the old-timers still speak nothing but German. That's where I picked it up. I'm here looking for a girl named Sara Potter. Dietrich's letter must have explained that."

"Who is the Mayor?"

"Of Skokie?"

"Yes."

"Phillip Gregg."

"Do you like this baseball?"

"Baseball? Yes. My favorite sport."

"Who are your favorite contestants? Favorite clubs?"

I told her that '34 looked like a big year for Hank Greenberg and his Tigers.

"Is Greenberg a Jew?"

"He's a first baseman."

She gave me a questioning look.

"That's his position on the team. I never thought about where he went to church."

She nodded as if she'd made a decision.

"Conversation can be dangerous these days, even in your own house. We're not walking out here because of the Hitler weather."

"Hitler weather?"

"It's a beautiful day. All good things come from the Fuhrer. So nice weather is Hitler weather."

"Making stormy days Stalin weather?"

"Something like that. You have the makings of a National Socialist thinker."

She smiled brightly. She was the most attractive homely woman I ever met.

"So is Hitler a great leader?"

"When he became Chancellor most people thought he would not last the year. Give him credit. He has prospered on the myth that we did not lose the war but were betrayed. He promotes another myth. The Aryan. Nietzsche's superman. Since Hitler is a dark-haired Austrian apparently anyone but a Jew can be an Aryan. But he's put people to work building his Reich. Government buildings, roads, and - some say - guns, tanks, and military aircraft. Jobs are good politics with the masses; and the industrialists are happy because their factories are busy, profits are high, and the Communists have been crushed."

"And the military is happy because of the new weapons?"

"Well, Goering is. But he is not the Army. It is the most important service in Germany and the last threat to Hitler. The Army is worried. The SA has become its rival. If Hitler does not curb it, the generals may run Rohm and Herr Hitler into the Spree. But the Army will not help you find Sara Potter."

"Dietrich said that you can do that."

"Marlene." Fromm laughed in a warm, quiet way. "I first met her backstage after a performance of *Two Bow Ties*. When she discovered I was a reporter, she was very solicitous. Goebbels is not the only one who knows how to use the press. I last saw her at the nineteen-thirty Press Ball. By then *The Blue Angel* had been released and the critics were saying she would become the next Garbo. Do you know about the Press Ball?"

"A party for newspaper people?"

"Only the important ones. It is quite the gala. Everyone who is anyone turns out. Soccer and tennis champions to Prussian aristocrats. Artists to industrialists. Diplomats and government officials to the military brass. The Prussians sit in their boxes convinced the movie and theater people will be the end of civilization, while the movie and theater people joke that the Prussians are so half-witted they don't realize they died a generation ago."

"I think I'd rather watch baseball."

"Oh no. They were wonderful affairs. At the nineteen-thirty ball, Marlene, Anne May Wong, and Leni Riefenstahl were quite the triumvirate, parrying the advances of eligible young men and well as older men on the prowl."

Fromm lost her smile and seemed to shift gears.

"Marlene broke away and sought me out. She was thinking

of leaving Germany. That was the year Horst Wessel was killed. Some say he was a pimp, killed by another pimp. The Nazis said he was an SA hero killed by the communists. They wrote a song about him. The Nazis have been in our consciousness ever since, like a perverted but powerful relative. You like what he can do for you but hate yourself for accepting. Marlene asked me if the Nazis had a chance to come to power. I told her no. I hope Marlene did not recommended me to you based on my predictive abilities."

"Can you help?"

"Let me make some inquiries. Call on me Thursday."

"At *Tante Voss*?"

"No, no. I have been released. Call on me here. Will ten-thirty be convenient for you?"

"Released?"

"A new law prohibits newspapers from employing Jews as writers. It was suggested that I stay and ghost write a column for my Aryan replacement. I thought not."

"Dietrich thought you were untouchable."

"I am. Unfortunately not in the manner she anticipated."

On Thursday we were back in the Tiergarten, walking trails whose splendor shamed Europe's great cathedrals. As we passed her stable, Fromm asked if I wanted to ride. I told her that boys from Skokie only rode the bus.

"In Germany a man your age would never refer to himself as a boy."

"In Chicago men are forever boys. What's your point?"

"German men have clubs for everything, bicycling to chess. They are forever joining something. But they never think of themselves as boys. Hitler's men may be buffoons, but they are deadly serious about themselves. Goebbels is among the most serious. He is running Ufa. I'm afraid he has taken an interest in your Fraulein Potter."

"So am I supposed to hightail it home?"

"I have told many of my friends to - as you put it - hightail it to the United States. But I would not presume to suggest anything to a person who has come to me for help."

"Sorry."

"I have a Press Ball invitation for you," she said handing me an engraved card. "Fraulein Potter will be attending with the Ufa contingent. I don't know her but you look as if you could be charming enough to introduce yourself."

"I thought these tickets were hard to come by."

I was looking at the invitation. It was fancy enough for a coronation.

"The Nazis are coming in numbers this year. After all they control the government. But that made available a number of tickets."

"The Jews are excluded?"

"Not entirely. The Nazis don't yet draw the invitation list. But some Jews who would have been invited have left Germany; and some, who were invited, have declined."

"Are you going?"

"It won't be the same but the Nazis will not run me off. I hope Goebbels sees me. A Jew with friendships he envies. He is smart enough to know that he is only tolerated. Petty as it is, I shall enjoy his annoyance."

"You said Goebbels has an interest in Potter?"

"He is the Propaganda Minister. Most political parties and governments operate in a world where there is an objective reality. But reality can be a bother. So Goebbels reconstructs it, creating a perception consistent with the Nazi viewpoint. He's very good at that."

"And Potter's part of that?"

"The Nazis think film is important. It is an embarrassment that Dietrich left Germany. In the new reality, Dietrich was lured from Germany by Jewish money while Sara Potter has come to Germany for the sake of art and a belief in Germany's new direction. With this beautiful American kneeling at the altar of German culture, Dietrich is nullified."

"And Potter is going along with that?"

"It is easy to be caught up in the wave of the future."

A few minutes later I left.

That night at the Adlon bar, I asked Fix about the ball. He scanned the room. Then he leaned toward me and spoke quietly.

"Rohm is such a pig he might decide to shit in the Prussian circle. The he-goat of Babelsberg is such a lecher he might decide to screw some General's daughter in the garden. And Goering may decide to appropriate a few paintings on the spot. There are many possibilities."

"The he-goat of Babelsberg?"

"Goebbels. But what are a few rough edges, if Germany is restored?"

Fix glided off to serve another patron.

Later remembering Zukor's suggestion, I ordered an aquavit. It tasted like vodka filtered through caraway seeds. Fancy stuff for a guy from Skokie. It went down smooth. I'm open-minded about booze, so ten minutes later I ordered another one.

I was looking forward to the Press Ball with the anticipation of a spectator with first turn seats at the Indy 500. If Fix was right, the ball would disintegrate into a free-for-all with wrecks galore. Surely that would help Potter see the light. Or, as it were, the darkness.

As it would turn out, I didn't see Fromm at the ball. I could have missed her in the crowd, but I wondered if she had decided not to go. After all, her friends would be putting themselves at risk by acknowledging their friendship.

Chapter Five

The next morning I was fitted for a tux. The tailor came to my room at the Adlon and promised delivery by six. I could picture Zukor choking on his cigar at the cost. If this job lasted long enough, I might finagle a whole new wardrobe.

I reviewed Zukor's files on Potter that afternoon.

Paramount's publicity file contained three glossy photos and a biographical sketch. Unless the pictures lied, Potter was a knockout. According to her bio, she was the loving daughter of a Massachusetts shoe manufacturer. She attended Smith College, majoring in theater. She left school early for the Big Apple where she made her parents proud, working her way into leading roles in a number of Broadway dramas. Zukor discovered her in 1931. The camera adored her and the public wasn't far behind. She was a cross between apple pie and the Big Apple.

The second file contained three grainy shots of Potter walking through Central Park. In them she didn't look much like a movie star. More like an ordinary a girl easily lost in a crowd.

There was also a report from the Reliable Detective Agency dated April 27, 1931. According to it, Potter's father was an old-school robber baron whose workers churned out shoes until their hands were so mangled that they couldn't tie their own laces. His workers may have been disposable chattels, but Sara was his prize possession. She loved her father but hated what he was. She quit Smith after her junior year because her dad was paying the bills. She moved to New York to pursue acting and lived in near poverty, refusing her father's offer of an allowance. Yet she wrote faithfully and visited on holidays.

By the time von Sternberg spotted her, she had become a Broadway success. It could have happened earlier. However, five days before opening night of the first play in which she had the lead, she made a discovery. Dad had paid the producer to give her the part. She walked out, despite the director's assurance that she was terrific. That earned her a reputation as a kook. She didn't get another job for five months and didn't get a second shot at a leading role for a year and a half.

Being an active member of Actors' Equity hadn't helped with producers who wanted compliant performers at low wages. Even worse she had attended a few Socialist Party meetings. She almost joined after hearing Norman Thomas champion his brand of moderate socialism.

Her personal life was no less messy. She liked men and they liked her. But their lives were never in sync. On one occasion she became pregnant while dating an actor named Paul Bennett. He received a Hollywood offer before a doctor confirmed the pregnancy. She never told Bennett. He went off to the West Coast and disappeared. She had an abortion and suffered a bout of depression.

Finally there was a report from Harry Philpot, Paramount's security chief, reviewing her time with the studio. Potter looked and sounded great in her first film. But she was flirting with socialism and had even attended a communist party meeting. That was all too common on the artistic side of the business, although flirtation alone wasn't a problem for talented actors - provided they showed up on time. Unfortunately Potter had missed some calls and was dropped from the production of *Shanghai Express*. The distraction was her family. Her father was apparently involved with a German woman but the facts were sketchy.

Before Hitler came to power, Paramount and UFA made a deal for Paramount to make movies in Berlin. Later UFA asked Paramount to lend it Potter for a role in a comedy about an American visitor who can't quite get a handle on Wagner. Potter said no, but UFA kept pressing. Eventually she agreed. Zukor predicted she would become an international star - America's gift to Europe, a Garbo in reverse.

Unfortunately the landscape changed by the time Potter reached Babelsberg. Goebbels was running UFA and the studio switched projects on her. The comedy was out, replaced by what smelled like a propaganda film. Zukor was outraged but Potter agreed. On top of that her father had disappeared and she was running around Berlin as if she might find him in some beer garden.

Philpot's report concluded that Potter was a loose cannon with whom the studio should cut ties.

I arrived at eight to find a line of cars stretching from the banquet halls. If Fromm hadn't given me a map to my table, I might have spent the night wandering in the glitter. A reception hall led to the "Main Restaurant." The center of the restaurant had been cleared for dancing. The dance floor was the size of a softball diamond and was surrounded by tables seven deep. Light from spotlights splayed off four mirrored globes that rotated above the dance floor.

Off the Main Restaurant were four large halls. One was reserved for Prussian aristocrats, military officers, and SS bigwigs. Another hall was for industrialists, old money, Nazi bigshots, and the classical music aristocracy. Another held government officials, the diplomatic corps, and newspaper elites. The fourth hall held everyone else, including the best the SA had to offer. In each hall, a banquet would be served at eight-thirty.

I was at a table in the fourth hall. There I found three beer-bellied businessmen and their wives listening to a Gauleiter from Mannheim and the new owner of a recently aryanized ball bearing factory gloat about the future. One of the businessmen seemed uncomfortable. The reason was clear. Every so often his sweet-faced, teenaged son - who was decked out in a Hitler Youth uniform - would contribute a blood-curdling remark. When the kid said something about Jews corrupting the Fatherland, his mother lost control.

"That's enough, Ernie. The only Jews you have ever known were Herr Roth and his family, and they were our friends."

Her eyes had the faraway look of a soldier charging into fire. She turned to the new ball bearing king.

"Herr Kunkel, you knew Herr Roth, didn't you?"

"Yes. What of it?"

"I remember Herr Roth telling us how lucky he was to have an employee named Kunkel. He had just promoted this Kunkel, making him a director. The first director in three generations who was not a family member. Herr Roth was proud of that. A year later Herr Roth and his family had been removed and you, Herr Kunkel, owned the business."

"I don't own it all. Other party members have an interest."

"Do you intentionally miss the point? Herr Roth was forced out. He was paid a pittance for his business. His business was stolen and his family ruined."

"Wini! Be quiet!" ordered the boy's father.

"They were our friends, Carl. I want to hear what Herr Kunkel has to say."

"Herr Becker, I will answer your wife. Frau Becker, Herr Roth was no friend to me. I earned my position. With my directorship came no ownership, no control. Jews never share that. Ball bearings are critical to the Fatherland's redevelopment. Such a business cannot be trusted to a Jew."

"I don't believe the man ever set foot in a temple. He fought in the war."

Becker put an arm around his wife, pulling her close. He whispered something to her. She blanched and left the table without speaking. Young Ernie allowed that his mother's outburst was an example of behavior detrimental to the people. Becker looked as if he were about to lose his mind. The other businessmen looked like they wanted to disappear. The gauleiter looked ready to order up a firing squad; and Kunkel looked ready to join it.

The first course of dinner arrived just as young Ernie started to brag about joining the SS. It was that or the Gestapo for men who really cared about the Fatherland. An uneasy silence spread over the table. The kid's bloodthirsty enthusiasm was too much for even the ball bearing king.

I spent the meal watching a nearby table where Sara Potter sat with some of the UFA contingent. I was not the only one watching her. Her publicity photos didn't do her justice. Unlike some beauties, she was a natural and seemed unaware that men were drooling and women were admiring.

Halfway through dessert, Potter left her table. I followed. The crowd opened before and closed behind her. I bounced around in her wake like a pushy oaf. I caught up with her as she entered the ballroom.

"Sara. Sara Potter?"

"Yes. You're American. Have we met?"

She was not a perfect Aryan. Her hair was only sandy blonde, her nose was slightly out of kilter, and her eyes were green, not blue.

"No. I'm Michael Temple. I'd like a half hour of your time, if not tonight, sometime tomorrow. Or the day after. When you have time."

"I hate to sound like a jerk, but I'm very busy over the next few days."

"It's important. I'm a reporter from *Variety* and I also have a message from Joe von Sternberg."

She raised her eyebrows. "I know. They want me home."

"Something like that."

"Zukor must have put Joe up to it. What a pair. I've already told them I'll be back when I've finished here."

"I've come a long way for nothing if you don't give me a few minutes. Besides Zukor will have my head if we don't talk. You don't want that on your conscience, do you?"

She laughed. "God forbid. Okay, you don't look like a bad guy. But I have to run now. Meet me at Ufa tomorrow at ten. Do you know where the studio is?"

"Yes. Will we have some privacy? What I have to say is - let's call it - sensitive."

"How mysterious." She waved me off. "I have to run. A bit to do. I'll see you tomorrow. There will be a pass at the gate."

I wandered through the party's restrained gaiety. The orchestra was mostly a bore. It knew every waltz but little else. Finally a mazurka brought some life to the dance floor. What the place needed was Benny Goodman and the Lindy.

What it got was the he-goat, better known as the Gauleiter of Berlin and the Minister of Propaganda. The double moniker seemed a lot for a five-foot-five clubfoot. As he limped to the conductor's microphone, Goebbels cut a figure from a black comedy. His head towered above frail shoulders like an outsize gargoyle. He looked emaciated but wasn't. He burned energy at a frantic pace, kissing Hitler's ass and fucking with everyone else. I had to remind myself that he was Germany's third or fourth most powerful citizen.

He didn't have to wait long for the applause to die down. Before speaking he stared impassively at Berlin's best, demanding silence. Once the main restaurant was quiet, he began almost conversationally, although there was a subdued passion in his words. His voice was wonderfully rich.

"Tonight we gather in these great halls, noble Germans from across a culture forged in antiquity on the principle of blood and soil and blossoming today under National Socialism to our destiny. Tonight we celebrate . . ."

Like an orchestra building to a crescendo, Goebbels fed the room's collective ego with a litany of German accomplishments. Then came references to alien forces that had betrayed Germany in the past but which would be crushed in the future. But his sermon wasn't primarily about enemies. It became a whirlwind of dreams delivered with power and style. The deformed clown became the visionary herald of a glorious tomorrow.

He finished to a sincere ovation.

Goebbels signaled for quiet. He had a special treat. The

American movie star, Sara Potter, would sing *Deutschland Uber Allies*. As Potter walked to the microphone, she cast Goebbels a fawning look. Although she was taller, her look gave him stature. He beamed like a dwarf prince basking in reflected glory.

Her eyes sparkled as she sang. She didn't sing particularly well. The crowd could have cared less; they loved it. I felt sick, as if I'd been betrayed. The look she'd given Goebbels was more repulsive than her rendition of the German anthem. Fromm was right. Goebbels had found a propaganda tool.

When she finished, they saluted each other to another ovation. Goebbels looked like he was having an orgasm. After he dropped the salute, he went to the microphone and introduced Reichsmarshall Goering. The introduction was tepid. He then escorted Potter from the podium without waiting to greet the second most powerful man in Germany.

Goering was the closest thing the National Socialists had to an aristocrat or a war hero. A fighter ace, he had succeeded von Richthofen as the commander of the Flying Circus. But Goering was no longer in fighting trim. Layers of fat were swathed in a pale blue uniform that supported a Christmas tree of decorations on his ample breast. He wore makeup that gave his face a contrived look, although to what end was unclear.

Goering looked out of sorts. "Wonderful party," was his perfunctory greeting. "We have a great surprise for you. The man who predicted that Herr Hitler would become Chancellor. A man who can see the future. The man who will preview your tomorrows. Eric Jan Hanussen!"

My flying companion walked to the microphone. He looked worse than Goering. He mumbled something about "clouded vision."

From the audience came calls to speak up.

Goering put an arm over his shoulders and steered Hanussen closer to the microphone.

"We want no clouds. Tell us about Germany's wonderful future or admit your blindness."

Goering laughed, slapped Hanussen on the back and then, as if having a premonition, he spoke again, "Minister Goebbels tells me that only you see tomorrow as clearly as he does. Prove yourself."

The self-proclaimed master entertainer seemed to have a case of stage fright.

"I see a hidden enemy exposed as the killer of his lover," said Hanussen, reluctantly leaning toward the microphone.

"A communist. Name him!" someone shouted from the audience.

"I see men who pretend to be loyal Germans who steal from the country."

"Jews. Tell us something new!" shouted a Brownshirt, causing a few people near me to blanch but even more to laugh.

Hanussen ignored the response.

"I see a girl who loses her heart to a party man."

"I've lost my heart to Adolph Hitler," called a young woman from the dance floor. Her proclamation was followed by laughter and whoops of celebration.

Hanussen wagged a finger, as if cautioning, and said, "I see people, who tell us what to believe and fill us with lies."

The Brownshirts were having fun now and began calling out the names of their favorite bogeymen.

"Communists!"

"Jews!"

"Gypsies!"

"Weimar Dogs!"

Hanussen spoke into the building din, now determined to be heard.

"Heed my words. Heed my words."

Hanussen paused. The crowd quieted.

"I see a seemingly victorious country crushed by its enemy."

An SS Colonel jumped from his chair and yelled, "France!"

The Nazi crowd began chanting, "Down with France! Down with France!"

Hanussen stepped back from the microphone. Only when the Nazis quieted, did he continue. "I see slaughter in the East."

The Nazi crowd responded enthusiastically.

"The Russians!"

"Lebensraum!"

'The communist swine!"

Some people began to leave, embarrassed by the joyful response to the prediction of bloody war.

Now Hanussen whispered into microphone, teasing the audience with words that could not be heard above the din. The Nazis settled down. Those who had been leaving stopped, unable to resist the temptation of another prediction.

Once the crowd quieted, Hanussen spoke slowly with increasing volume, "I see a new power in Europe. A rising power in Europe. A new Europe rising from the ashes of the old! A new day!"

The Nazis chanted back, "Deutschland! Deutschland! Deutschland!"

The elation was infectious. Soon most everyone joined the chant. They seemed to be begging for the victor's glory if not for war itself.

Hanussen bowed and left the podium. Goering flashed an uncertain smile and followed as if he had questions. But Hanussen was too quick and disappeared into the admiring throng.

By midnight only Nazis were left. By twelve-fifteen the crowd had dwindled to only Brownshirts, some army men, and a few men whom I took to be longtime party zealots. I stayed to twelve-thirty.

I drink more than the next guy but these were madmen guzzling with a crazed determination not to leave a drop. They reveled in their boorishness as if debauchery was a form of grace. It was enough to make me swear off booze and I was hardly a shrinking violet.

That night I dreamed of a world beaten senseless by an army of baby-faced boys dressed in lederhosen and knee socks. They goose-stepped to a march played by a band of miscreants conducted by Goering in his baby-blue uniform.

Chapter Six

As promised, Potter left a pass at UFA's front gate. The guard told me how to find her. I walked unattended through the studio's bustle. Handymen trucked scenery and lights here and there. Costumed extras milled about like refugees from other times and places, while motorized carts zipped VIPS to appointed destinations. Potter's place was tucked away from the hubbub down a street lined with Bauhaus bungalows. She was in number fourteen. Next door, at number sixteen, a red Mercedes convertible lingered long and low, its flowing lines creating a sense of motion. Across the street at number fifteen, a Maybach awaited the return of some mogul.

Potter answered almost before I knocked. She pushed past me, closing the door behind her. She looked like she was coming off a long night.

"I could use a walk this morning. Did you enjoy the Ball?"

"I'm not a ball kind of guy. Two left feet for starters."

"Well, you looked the part."

"You had some part last night."

She gave me a defiant look and then softened.

"The singing. I guess it went well enough. It was good of Goebbels to ask."

"He looks like a real sweetheart."

"Why don't you tell me what you want and cut the sarcasm."

"You're worried about sarcasm? Zukor was right. You need to open your eyes."

"And you should open yours. Zukor isn't worried about anything except making a bundle on his next movie."

This was not a promising start, but I'd come too far to skip the sales pitch. Besides I had plenty of material to work with including last night's ugly reaction to Hanussen. I let her have it.

Her response was more weary than angry.

"Just like Zukor to send a reporter to bribe me with a new contract and imply I'm an idiot because I don't see things his way. Tell him I don't intend to read his translations and that I'll be back when I'm good and ready. And tell him I'm calling Jack Warner."

She gave this little speech within earshot of a stuffed-shirt who had been watching us walk toward his motorized cart. He was on his way to us before she finished.

"Sara, is this man bothering you?"

"No, Alfred. I was just telling him why I don't intend to go back to Paramount. Michael Temple, this is Alfred Hugenberg. Alfred owns Ufa. Alfred, you won't hold Zukor against me will you?"

Hugenberg looked fit for a man in his mid-sixties. He was dressed and manicured like he owned the world but with his porcupine haircut and walrus mustache he looked a relic from the last century.

"Of course not, my dear. And who are you, Herr Temple?"

"Alfred, he's a reporter from *Variety*, the American trade magazine. He came to tell me Zukor's plans for me. I was giving him a tour. And a piece of my mind."

"Humph. These modern women. What are we to do, Herr Temple? But this one, she is delightful, no?"

Hugenberg shot me a conspiratorial look that implied we men missed the pre-flapper days when women had babies, managed the servants, and left the world to their husbands.

I smiled pleasantly and suggested, "Perhaps she could use a week in a detention camp?"

Potter's face went white. Hugenberg's face drew itself into a nasty question mark. I'd stepped over the line. Detention was acceptable for Jews and commies but publicly joking about it was in bad taste - perhaps an offense against the people's instincts.

"Americans," said Potter.

She shot Hugenberg a conspiratorial look that implied Yanks were ill-mannered children.

Before he could respond, a hysterical cry came from down the street. A maid was standing near Potter's bungalow waving her arms and yelling for help.

"It's Steffie. The girl who does my cottage," said Potter.

"Get in," said Hugenberg.

He wasn't talking to me, but Potter grabbed my hand and off we went. The VIP cart had us there in seconds.

"Steffie, what is it?" said Potter.

"Fraulein Potter, something has happened to Fraulein Glaise. It is terrible."

Behind the red Mercedes, the door to number sixteen stood open. Hugenberg dawdled like an old man who'd lost his stomach. Potter hesitated, then walked in. When I started to follow Hugenberg grabbed my arm.

"Where are you going?" he demanded, his gumption returning.

"We can't let her go in there alone."

"Humph. Yes, yes."

Hugenberg was irritated but followed me into a smallish living room. Empty wine and champagne glasses were on a coffee table. The champagne bottle was gone but an empty bottle of Riesling Trockenbeerenauslese lay on the floor. Dishes and serving plates evidenced a smorgasbord of desserts. An evening gown, silk stockings and underwear were draped over the back of a lounge chair.

A hall led from the living room past a Pullman kitchen on the left and a small dining room on the right. Beyond were a study, a bedroom and bath.

We found Potter in the bedroom mumbling unintelligibly. Her arms were crossed and she was rocking from the waist up. She might have been in shock. Hugenberg put an arm around her and pulled her from the room.

A blonde was stretched across the bed, eyes still open. Her throat was bruised. The whites of her eyes were reddened and her face had a blue pallor. But these signs of strangulation were just the start. The neck of the missing champagne bottle had been inserted in her vagina. As if that weren't enough, her chest had been cleaved open and her heart removed. At the midpoint of the bed were two yellow stains.

The gore transported me back to my days of driving ambulances - dangerous territory filled with images having the power to paralyze me. I told myself, *The here and now counts. Don't lose it. Figure out what happened in this room.*

I went to the body and wedged a finger into her left armpit. It might have been a little warmer than room temperature. Then I moved the arm. The joints were stiff but full rigor mortis had not set in. I guessed she'd been dead for six to seven hours. Dead bodies don't bleed so the lack of blood around the hole in her chest told me that she'd been killed before that insult.

So she'd died of strangulation before being screwed by a champagne bottle and having her heart stolen by some deranged fucker. Welcome to Germany. Hollywood at its worst wasn't this bad.

A pair of high heels was beside the bed. There was no other clothing around. She must have walked from the living room, naked as a jay bird, in her heels. Had she been doomed from the first sip of wine or had something triggered the killer after they'd reached her bedroom?

A fancy party pin lay across the room on the floor near a wall. Above a garland an eagle perched, wings spread for flight. Below hung a tiny placard on which was inscribed the word "Gauleiter." The pin belonged to a Nazi boss at the municipal level, not some rank and file beer guzzler.

Someone who'd been at the Press Ball? Maybe the guy who owned the Maybach? I had stepped into serious trouble. If not saluting could get a person mugged, there was no telling where this was going.

Just then, four press photographers burst in the bedroom, flash bulbs popping. They were welcome to Paula Glaise.

Hugenberg was in the living room, comforting Potter. I blew

by them. I wasn't sticking around for a game in which the killer might be a Nazi big shot. Before leaving Berlin I would take a last shot at Potter to see if this murder had changed her mind. If not, I was going home.

I walked out the front door. The Maybach was gone, replaced by three unmarked cop cars. I didn't get far before I was stopped. A guy with a face full of scar tissue ordered me held. I was cuffed and clubbed into the back seat of a car. The Gestapo.

These were Germany's real bogeymen. The SA liked to rough up people and dump them in the gutter. But if they grabbed you, chances were you would live see another day. The Gestapo made people permanently disappear.

I managed to roll into a sitting position in time to see the photographers shoved from the bungalow. Their cameras came flying a moment later. The equipment shattered as it bounced down the walk leading to the street. It didn't take the photographers long to discover their film had been confiscated.

Twenty minutes later the Gestapo motorcade pulled off. When we turned on Prinz Albrechtstrasse, my worst fear was realized. Gestapo headquarters was located on this otherwise pleasant street.

I'd been sitting alone in an examining room for ten minutes when I recalled Hanussen's bloody vision - the one he had shown me in Vienna. Then there were his words at the Press Ball. Something about a leader stealing a girl's heart. No wonder he had looked like a poster boy for stage fright. Had he actually seen Paula Glaise's future?

Bullshit, I told myself.

Just then scar-face walked in. Some of these Germans looked absurdly sinister. He was one of those. There was an unreality about him, as if central casting had been too obvious and the costume department too enterprising: black jackboots polished to a mirror finish; black uniform crisply tailored; and black hair combed back with slick perfection. Above the bill of his hat were a skull and crossbones. The emblem was a nice complement to his scars - dueling scars. One ran across his right cheek. Another ran from under his lip across his left jaw. These had been bone-deep wounds. There were other, lesser scars that on some faces would have been disturbing. On his they were almost an afterthought.

"I am Rudolf Diels. SS. Chief of the Gestapo. What were you doing in number sixteen?"

"Do you speak English? I'm an American. My German's not so good."

"We will stick to German. Answer the question," he replied.

I told him I was a *Variety* reporter covering Potter's work with UFA and that I'd agreed to bring Potter Paramount's new contract proposal. Then I told him how I came to be in Glaise's bungalow.

He asked what I'd seen in the bedroom.

"The body was naked. There was a bottle. You must have seen it. Her chest was mangled. I didn't see a knife or whatever was used to hack her open. It was bad. I didn't stay very long."

"What else did you see?"

"Nothing. No. In the living room there were glasses and some plates. And a woman's clothing. Hers I suppose. I saw that walking in. That's it."

I sure wasn't going to say anything about a party pin.

"What is this Paramount contract?" said Diels, changing direction.

I told him that Paramount wanted Potter back for a new movie and the contract was the carrot. I didn't volunteer Zukor's opinion of the Nazis.

"I think you are an American agent."

"I just told you that. I work for *Variety* and moonlight for Paramount."

"Owned by a Jew?"

"I don't know. A guy named von Sternberg sent me. He's a German, for Christ's sake. Not a Jew as far as I know."

"So it is only a coincidence that you were in number sixteen this morning?"

"That's right."

He backhanded me in the face, spinning me off the chair on which I had been sitting. Still handcuffed, I landed awkwardly on the floor. The prick stood above me, as if trying to decide whether to scuff his boot on my head. Just then there was a knock at the door. A corporal entered and whispered something to Diels who seemed perturbed at the interruption. They walked out, leaving me on the floor as if I'd ceased to exist.

Two hours later the corporal returned. They were releasing me but holding my passport, pending the outcome of the investigation. I trusted a Gestapo investigation about as much they loved Jews. I was getting out of Germany with or without a passport. I didn't care if I had to walk. Potter may have thought these guys were all right, but I believed Mien Kampf.

They processed me out. Lots of paper and rubber stamps sealing this and marking that. What would they ever do with all the paper? Confetti for the Fuhrer's motorcades?

Potter was waiting for me in the lobby, her face lined with worry. When she spotted me, her concern became relief, then delight. She seemed different, as if a mask had fallen exposing a better person. But when she spoke the mask returned.

"We're so glad to see you."

I hadn't noticed Hugenberg until she used the word "we."

"Did they have you locked up too?" I asked.

"Of course not," Hugenberg answered, indignant at the very idea.

"He's teasing," said Sara.

"American humor? Humm. Well, Sara thought that we should make sure you were released. I thought Gestapo headquarters was the perfect place for Paramount's man. Lucky for you Sara is persuasive."

"Alfred is such a joker. We both wanted to make sure you would be released quickly. Alfred made some calls."

"Who did you call?" I asked

"That is not important. Sara and I need to go. Where are you staying? If it is on our way, we will drop you."

Generosity must have been his middle name.

They dropped me at the Adlon. I hadn't lost my resolve to escape but there were good reasons to delay. First, walking out of Germany without a passport wasn't much of a plan. Second, the Gestapo might be following me, expecting me to run. Third, I couldn't shake my recollection of Sara during those few seconds when her guard fell. And fourth, she had slipped me a note as we were getting into Hugenberg's car.

Chapter Seven

While walking to the newsstand the next day later, I reread Sara's note:

> *Michael:*
>
> *Being an actress far from home isn't easy. My roles aren't necessarily the ones I would pick had I the choice. I have no right to ask for your friendship but having you for a friend would be nice. Will you meet me at Wertheim's perfume counter on Saturday at eleven?*
>
> *Sara*

Perhaps I did have a chance to save Potter for Zukor. No telling what Saturday would bring. But for now I was off to see how the German press reported Hanussen's curious predictions and Glaise's grotesque murder.

Off the Adlon's main lobby was an arcade of small shops. Max's newsstand was tucked between a tobacconist and a barber shop. Across the way was a perfumer. A jumble of aromas emanated from each shop. I lingered in the arcade, trying to place a particular smell that reminded me of some foggy yesterday. The memory eluded me. It was something pleasant from a time of innocence. From childhood maybe. Certainly from before I reached the western front, where the carnage put an end to innocence.

I turned into Max's and found lots of newspapers to choose from. If quantity counted, Berlin had been the newspaper capitol of the world. A year earlier the city enjoyed fifty morning papers and even more afternoon ones. Now the count was down by half. Leftist and left-leaning newspapers had been banned. For Hitler's National Socialists, the emphasis was nationalism, not socialism.

Three papers were prominently display. *Der Volkischer Beobachter* was the official Nazi paper. *Der Angriff* was owned and edited by Goebbels. And *Der Sturmer* was Julius Streicher's hate tract. What a choice: *The People's Observer*, *The Attack*, and *The Storm*. Three different flavors of propaganda. On any given day, the first two might actually report some real news. *The Storm* was nothing but venom. And boring to boot. There were only so may ways to report how Jews raped old women and communists swindled children.

On the front page of *The Peoples Observer* was a story about the opening of Alcatraz, a prison in San Francisco Bay. According to the *Observer*, Franklin Roosevelt intended to imprison negroes and German Americans in the new facility at the request of the Zionists. I had a good laugh at that. Roosevelt carried the negro and German vote big time. He was more likely to fill Alcatraz with the Republican wing of his own family.

I was looking for a story about Glaise's murder. There had been nothing in the papers the day before. That was odd. German publishers were no better than Hearst and Pulitzer. They all knew murder and mayhem sold. I browsed the front pages of a dozen papers before finally spotting the story in *The Ku'damm Gazette*. It ran next to an article about Hanussen. No other paper had either story.

I bought a *Gazette* and an *Observer*.

"Max, what do you hear about the murder at Ufa."

"Not a thing."

That was baloney. Max was another Adlon legend. He read everything and forgot nothing. He had an answer to every question and an opinion on every subject, but now he wasn't sharing them.

I paid him and then turned up the arcade, anticipating brunch. I folded the *Gazette* inside the *Observer*. That wasn't by chance. Max was playing dumb for a reason. I'd been in town a week, and I already knew that the *Observer* was a safe read.

I was ten feet from Max's when three storm troopers turned into the arcade. The first was on me in a flash. He snatched the papers from my hand but saw only the *Observer*. Without an apology he returned my papers and then led his cohorts to Max's. Moments later they marched out with the entire stack of *Gazettes*.

My appetite was gone. My room seemed the best place to read. The *Gazette* articles had their share of surprises.

STARLET MURDERED

Twenty-six-year-old Paula Glaise was found dead in her UFA bungalow in Babelsberg. A maid discovered the body at approximately 10.35 Sunday. The body is rumored to have been mutilated.

A rising star at UFA, Fraulein Glaise was to have attended the Press Ball gala on Saturday night with a group from the studio. However she was taken ill Saturday afternoon and was unable to attend.

The Gestapo has undertaken the investigation. Gestapo Chief Rudolf Diels would not state the cause of death nor would he confirm reports that Fraulein Glaise's heart had been removed. However he did deplore, as does this newspaper, the scandalous rumors linking Minister Goebbels to Fraulein Glaise and her death. Leader Diels stated that the Minister had been with the American actress Sara Potter at the time of Fraulein Glaise's death.

Minister Goebbels discovered Fraulein Glaise two years ago and had since promoted her career at UFA. In the last eighteen months Fraulein Glaise had appeared in . . .

HANUSSEN DENIES SPECULATION

. . . Hanussen left the stage to tumultuous applause, and immediately left the ball for his rooms at the Esplanade Hotel.

On Sunday morning Hanussen breakfasted with a number of reporters who asked him to confirm or deny the speculation that his predictions meant the following.

- The hidden enemy is Hitler because he allegedly killed a young woman named Geli Raubal who was reputedly his lover.

- It is the National Socialists who fill us with lies.

- The girl losing her heart did not lose it to a lover but to a murderer who is a party official.

- The Germans pretending to be loyal while they steal from the country are Goering, Ley, and the other little Fuhrers.

- The victorious country that will be crushed is Germany.

- The slaughter in the east will be Germans and Russians killing each other.

- The new power in Europe will be the United States.

Hanussen denied all the speculation and said the audience had correctly understood his words.

The Gazette deplores such craven speculation and demands

that these rumors be run to ground. They are a strike at Germany. The authorities must investigate the death of Geli Raubal and vindicate the Fuhrer. The authorities must investigate those accused of theft and vindicate them.

Hanussen himself has gone into seclusion. What little is known of his background comes from his agent and publicist, Walter Prinz. In the summer of 1918, Hanussen suffered a head wound during the Chemin des Dames offensive. He claimed that during his recovery he began to have visions. The visions continued, and evolved into an ability to control the minds of those around him - or so Hanussen has claimed. Extraordinary tails of Hanussen's powers began to circulate. One such . . .

The newspaper articles raised more questions than they answered. But two things were clear. Potter was in bed with the devil and someone was going to pay for the "craven speculation."

The following Saturday I felt a little like a moth circling the flame as I headed for my rendezvous with Potter.

Leipziger Strasse was seven blocks south of the Linden. For a half mile, stores and shops lined the boulevard with Berlin's two great department stores - Wertheim's and the Tietz - at either end. The street was crowded. Green taxis darted around yellow double-decker buses while cars of all descriptions searched for parking. The shoppers were eagerly spending money they hadn't had a year before. The joy of prosperity was everywhere. I scanned the shoppers' faces for a hint of uncertainty or shame. If it was there, I missed it. I heard plenty of heil-Hitlers.

Chicago's Marshall Field was a trading post compared to Wertheim's. Outside, the gigantic stone palace was lit by a 100,000 light bulbs. Inside, a four-story atrium ran the length of the store which sparkled with marble walls, crystal chandeliers and tiled fountains. Eighty elevators zipped up and down seven floors.

The perfume counter was a collection of stalls within a cosmetic department that sprawled like an Arabian bazaar across a third of the atrium floor. Potter might as well have told me to meet her in Comiskey Park on the day of a sellout. I was ready to bail out of cosmetics and buy a few ties on Zukor's nickel when Potter took my arm.

"Michael, that's a nasty scowl on you face. Are your shorts riding up?"

She wore no makeup and was dressed in a simple, lime-colored shift. The wind had ruffled her hair and there were faint bags under her eyes. Maybe it was her warm smile and the mischief in her voice. Whatever it was, she looked better than she did the night of the Press Ball. I had to remind myself that she was Goebbels' alibi.

"Well?" She insisted.

"Well what?"

"Pull the darn things down. They may be cutting off circulation."

I couldn't help but chuckle and faked a tug at my drawers.

"Much better. I was hoping we could be friends."

"My last movie star gave me the runaround. You'd dump me in a flash for Gable."

"Movie stars are boring. They can't see beyond their own reflection."

"But you're one."

"Not yet. On my way at best. Keep an eye on me. If I spend too much time looking in the mirror, you can kick me in the butt."

"How 'bout lunch? That way I can keep an eye on things."

"I'd like that. Wait a minute. Who was your last movie star? I want to hear about this."

Who was your last Nazi? I should have said something like that, but didn't. I wanted the easy banter to continue. I wanted her to be something other than what she probably was. So I raised an eyebrow and tried to grin like Dietrich's matinee idol.

"Marlene Dietrich. She's partial to champagne in the afternoon."

Sara laughed. "You make quite a wolf. Let's run before you attract a crowd."

She grabbed my hand and we zigzagged through eager shoppers to the street where we hopped a cab to Kempenski's, a nearby restaurant. In the taxi, I told her about meeting Dietrich, including her opinions about the Nazis. Sara ignored the opinions and joked that after lunch she would buy a pair of slacks, jettison her shoes, and see how good she might be at foot flirting.

I can't remember what the restaurant looked like or what we ate. I do remember trading stories about growing up. Funny ones. By the end of lunch we had laughed ourselves through high school.

After lunch, we taxied to Neumann's. She told the cabby to double-park and ordered me to stay put. An army of clothing was mustered across a giant two-story display window. The range of merchandise would have made a decisive man hesitant. I was settling in for a long wait, when Sara popped back in the cab wearing slacks and sandals, and carrying a large bag. She scooted to the far side of the seat, flipped off a sandal, rested her leg on the seat, wiggled a toe at my thigh, and gave me a patently-fake, vamp look.

"Watch out or I'll haul out my wolf routine."

"Not that!" she said with mock horror.

"Oh, yes."

I moved toward her doing a sorry imitation of a rakish bon vivant only to give her modest kiss on the cheek.

"Not exactly Gable," she teased.

"Not exactly Dietrich."

"And you said she was only a tease."

"I was being polite. Gentlemen don't kiss and tell."

"I certainly hope not. The beach?"

She pulled two swim suits and a couple of towels from the Neumann's bag. She waved them around like a kid who'd discovered a surprise.

"It's a hell of a ride to the Baltic Sea," I said.

"Driver, Wannsee Beach," she called.

The cabbie peered into the back seat through his mirror and said, "Feel free to change on the way."

"Feel free to keep your eyes on the road," Sara said, winking shamelessly at the driver.

"Another boring fare," the cabby groused, not meaning a word of it.

"Yes, yes," said Sara affecting boredom.

On the way to the beach the cabby warned us about beached whales and sharks.

Translation: obese nudists and peddlers hawking everything from bogus suntan lotion to cotton candy that turned your teeth black.

The beach sprawled along a gently curving shore of the Havel and faced Peacock Island around which the river flowed.

We avoided the peddlers, changed in the public bathhouse, steered clear of the whales, splashed each other in the shallow water near the beach, and then swam to a large raft anchored midstream, halfway to the island. Sara was a good swimmer and beat me to the raft.

"Let me give you a hand, slowpoke," she said laughing.

She extended a hand and yanked me from the water with surprising ease.

"Wow, you must be hell with a medicine ball."

"Ladies never discuss hell or the balls they work with," she answered, smiling brighter than the afternoon sun.

We sunbathed on the raft's wooden planks and then did back flips and cannonballs from its rickety diving platform. Then we swam to the island where we spotted a few peacocks and explored a small, long-abandoned castle. As the sun fell toward the island's black oaks, we swam back to the beach.

Wrapped in our towels, we gathered our clothes from the bathhouse and hailed a taxi. Sara ordered it to the Adlon. We fell asleep, her head resting on my shoulder, my head resting on hers.

The cabby woke us. I envisioned us making love. Sara suggested separate showers and a night on the town. She told me to pull out my tux while she bought some goodies in the arcade where Max sold papers.

We showered and dressed with the modesty of a brother and sister forced to share a room at a family reunion. We slipped once. She was helping me with my bow tie and her breasts came to rest on my back. Our bodies melded and I put my hands behind me and pulled her hips to mine. We briefly swayed to some primal rhythm. Then she pushed away.

"It's amazing what a tux will do for a boy from Ohio."

"Illinois."

"Is there a difference?"

"You're just an east coast snob."

By nine we were at Resi's, one of those clubs with telephones on the tables. We were early. The band wouldn't start for another half-hour. Sara explained the place's attraction.

"It's hokey but surprise, the food is good. No surprise, the place is full of jerks but they're part of the fun. The game is to see how many colors you can make them turn. Let's have a pile of oysters. And champagne. See that fat guy across the way? He's an easy one. A little dirty talk and a nasty invitation. He'll be going nuts in no time. But he won't know who's calling. He'll wind up beet red and deserve it."

Sara ate like a horse but never called the jerk. When I asked why she hadn't pulled the telephone prank, she looked a little disappointed and said that our conversation was enough fun. No reason to actually mess with the guy even if he was a jerk.

She started telling stories and soon had me in stitches about the high-jinks of acting companies from Boston to Broadway. She was scraping up the last of her Black Forest cake when she announced that the perfect finish to our day would be a Ferris wheel ride at Luna Park.

"First, you've have to see the beach," she said after the cab dropped us at the park's entrance.

She grabbed my hand and we skipped into the park like kids. Beyond the bumper cars and the Thunder Coaster was a line of artificial palm trees and fake cabanas that formed a wall. Scripted with letters formed by coconuts was a sign that read, Luna Beach.

The ticket taker didn't blink an eye at my tux or Sara's outfit. On the other side of the wall, twenty yards of sand ran to the water and stretched fifty yards in either direction. Waves rolled toward the beach from a wall forty yards out. The far wall was painted to create the illusion of a seascape with tropical islands in the distance. The slice-of-paradise theme continued down the pool's side walls. To either side of the entrance were lockers and changing rooms. With a lot of imagination, it might have been a tropical beach at twilight.

Except it wasn't. The whales were out in numbers. Some stood in the water, like pachyderms, allowing the water to lighten their burden, their blubber rolling with the water's motion. Others lay on the beach watching sleek young couples, posing to advertise their Aryan perfection. Here and there couples mated on the sand or in the water, turning love tawdry.

"Let's go, Michael. I didn't expect this. It's not like this in the day. Then it's hundreds of children laughing and splashing. Mothers and fathers with love in their eyes. This is disgusting."

Outside we drifted into the shimmer of the park's neon rainbow. Its radiance clashed with our mood. We both seemed embarrassed by the Luna Beach scene. Where had that come from? I wasn't a prude. And anyone who consorted with Goebbels had no claim to virtue.

"Where's that Ferris wheel?" I asked, trying to recapture the buoyancy of the day.

"I hate to be killjoy but we should call it a night. Okay?"

"Sure. Where to?"

"The Adlon for you and Ufa for me. I think that would be best."

"A nightcap?"

"No. I have an early shoot tomorrow. Michael, you turned out to be a swell wolf. I needed a good day and you gave me one. Marlene should have been nicer."

"I'll be around. Available for butt kicking if you start to go Hollywood."

"That's a good thought. Well here we are, and there's s a taxi. Yours or mine?"

"You take it. So I can be your voice of reason in the days ahead?"

"I'll call if I have a chance to get away. Thank you for the day. It was the nicest I've had in a long time. Sorry for running out like this. I shouldn't have . . . well, good bye."

As she stepped into the taxi, she smiled although her eyes betrayed her. She was already someplace else. A second later she was gone.

Had the day been a beautiful lie? It had been one without initiative on my part. I hadn't asked about the alibi for Goebbels. Or why Sara was playing Nazi poster girl. Or what she knew about Glaise's murder. I told myself those questions would have irritated her, making it more difficult to bring her home. Of course bullshitting yourself is a sure way to land in a ditch. The fact was I had avoided anything unpleasant to prolong the day's pleasure.

On that scale, the day had been my best since the early days with the girl whose memory still haunted me. The comparison wasn't reassuring.

Chapter Eight

She didn't call. She sent a message. I was in the Lindenbaum Cafe when the note arrived the following morning. It was waiting for me at the front desk after I finished breakfast.

> Michael
>
> Thanks for the nice day. I'm on a shoot for ten days or so. Have a safe trip home. Tell Zukor that I hope Paramount will have me back. Heil Hitler.
>
> Sara

"Shoot" my ass. Something else was going on. The Sara who skipped into Luna Park wasn't a Nazi. Nazis didn't skip, they goose stepped. That's what I told myself.

Hedda Adlon arranged for a car. It was a beat up Opal. I drove to Babelsberg and parked near UFA's front gate. Slouching down I peered through the dirty windshield like a jealous kid watching for his favorite girl who only had eyes for the campus bully. It was laughable but I wasn't laughing.

A little after four, the red convertible that I'd seen at bungalow sixteen sped through the gate. Humphrey said the question was usually this: who profited? The thought was not reassuring. Sara was driving. Had she moved up the UFA pecking order and inherited the convertible from Paula Glaise? Goebbels was her passenger. I put the Opal in gear and struggled to keep pace. She could have lost me but wasn't trying. The Mercedes eventually disappeared behind the gates of Hugenberg's estate.

I parked up the road and watched a dozen or so other cars arrive over the next half-hour. One looked like the Maybach that I'd seen at bungalow fifteen. I couldn't make out the driver in the late afternoon shade. By ten-thirty no one had left. I considered scaling Hugenberg's wall for some closer snooping. On foot I circled looking for a way over. Soon I heard dogs growling on the other side. The image of Doberman Pinschers convinced me to try something safer.

Humphrey had recommended Richard Cooper as a source of information. They had been trading information since the days when Cooper was a cub reporter for the *Chicago Tribune*. Back then he was a bad reporter and fabulous husband. His editor joked, if he had a wife like Cooper's, he would have left home late, gone home early, and wound up in bankruptcy with a smile on his face. Everything changed for Cooper when his wife died while giving birth to their first child. The baby died three days later. After that Cooper's only life was his job. His rivals sneered that his fanaticism was nothing but a defense against his pain. He agreed.

Cooper achieved star status at an age when other reporters were still looking for their first byline. It started with a tip and ended with a Pulitzer nomination.

Bill Cromwell (a New York, silk-stocking lawyer) offered Mark Hanna (a Cleveland industrialist and Republican king-maker) sixty grand to help Philippe Bunau-Varilla (a French promoter). Philippe was looking for a bailout. His canal scheme had tanked. Hanna took the money. Within months Uncle Sam bailed out Philippe and was pushing the Panamanians to secede from Columbia. They did. Cromwell wrote Panama's constitution in a New York hotel room while smoking a Havana cigar and sipping Kentucky bourbon. Then he negotiated a canal treaty with the new Panamanian government.

Cooper broke the story nine years after Cromwell and Hanna began playing geopolitics, and a year before the Panama Canal was finished - proving, according to Cooper, that mother nature was more intractable than human nature. The story garnered three inch headlines, and earned Cooper the nickname Scoop.

Cooper continued to find stories where others found nothing. He got it straight when others were confused. Unlike most reporters, he was naturally taciturn. He could spin a master line of baloney to pry a story from a reluctant witness, but was otherwise inclined to listen. He spoke through his column, *Cooper on Assignment*, which the *Trib* syndicated across the country.

Humphrey warned that Cooper would trade information but gave nothing away. "And don't call him Scoop. He's Richard to his friends and Mister Cooper to everyone else."

"Success gone to his head?" I asked Humphrey.

"He likes the trappings, but he's still a bloodhound. He thinks Hitler will be the biggest story ever. That's why he's been in Germany the last four months, Panama hat and all."

"Panama hat?"

"You bet. Cooper never set foot in the country, but he's been wearing a Panama ever since he broke the canal story. It's his trademark."

I found Cooper at the Tavern on Kurfuerstenstrasse, a couple of blocks east of the S-Bahn's Zoo Station. The Tavern was the place to be if you liked low ceilings, smoke, and air that smelled of tobacco, beer, coffee, baking bread, garlic, sausage, and tomato paste. Cooper and eight other men were sitting around a circular, oak table covered with ashtrays, beer bottles, plates of spaghetti, and baskets of Italian bread. They were a worn but animated bunch. An hour before they had wired their stories home. Now they were winding down with beer and bullshit.

Cooper was tall and elegantly dressed. With his pencil moustache and graying temples, he looked more like a British Lord than a Chicago journalist. He was wearing his Panama and listening.

I started to walk over when I noticed Diels at the table. The Gestapo son-of-a-bitch was sitting there in a business suit - just like one of the boys. I grabbed a small table positioned at Diels's back. I ordered a beer and watched. Two beers later Diels left. I walked over to Cooper.

"Humphrey told me to look you up. I'm Michael Temple. I'm with Pinkerton."

"Does that old fox have a last name?"

The question was the start of an old joke and a test.

"I thought he didn't have a first name," I said.

Cooper laughed at the old gag.

"What can I do for you?" said Cooper.

"Swap some information."

"We don't want to interrupt the rest of these fellas. Let's go over to your table."

He led the way while his pals groused about his refusal to share my information. I was impressed. Cooper had not looked my way while I sat waiting for Diels to leave. But he knew my table. He spoke as soon as we sat down.

"What's a Pinkerton agent doing in Berlin?"

I explained my assignment.

"I sure as hell would hate to be scooped by a fake reporter from *Variety*." Cooper laughed at the improbability and got down to business. "Whadayagot?"

"For starters I'll tell you why your buddy Diels handcuffed me off to Prinz Albrechtstrasse if you tell me what he was doing at your table."

"That's a hellofa lead," Cooper smiled. "Willy, bring us two beers," he called.

A large man wearing an apron brought the beer.

When he'd gone, Cooper said, "Willy is an unusual man. A loyal German but he loves his foreign correspondents. We lend the place a certain cachet. We attract diplomats and some party members looking for a chance to talk. Off the record for the most part.

"Rudy Diels is one of those. Outspoken, but always off the

record. Admits that there are abuses. Describes Goebbels and the rest of the little Fuhrers as jockeying for position to kiss Hitler's ass and grab power. Gives us nasty tidbits. Goering, for example, is a morphine addict who fancies tables with legs carved in the shape of penises. Diels says the party sometimes seems like the world of Hieronymus Bosch come alive. You ever hear of the guy?"

"I don't know Hieronymus from the Himalayas but Busch owns the St. Louis Cardinals, doesn't he?"

Cooper laughed.

"That's about what I thought. Turns out Bosch was a painter who died four hundred years ago. He painted bizarre images of a world gone mad. Hell of a reference for a Nazi to make. In spite of that, Rudy seems to think Hitler walks on water. Christ come to resurrect Germany from the tomb of Versailles. Best I can tell, Rudy thinks he's on a mission to save Hitler from his lieutenants.

"He gives us stuff to curry favor. He's good at extracting information." Cooper nodded at his colleagues. "Those guys aren't rookies. But Rudy gets them talking. Next thing you know, they're telling him stuff they wouldn't tell each other. So that's what Diels was doing at our table.

"Now whatdayagotforme?"

I told him everything. The pencil on his lip twitched when I described Glaise's body. When I was finished, I asked him to keep me and Potter out of his reporting.

"You're safe. But Potter's fair game. I knew all about little Miss Nazi before you walked in the door."

"She's not a Nazi."

"She's charmed you if you believe that. She's fucking Goebbels, isn't she?"

"Does Diels say that?"

"No. Rudy claims the crippled creep was fucking Glaise. What else you got for me?"

"I've told you everything I know. Now it's my turn. Tell me what you know about Potter."

"What, I'm Hedda Hopper? Okay look, I think she gave it to you straight about not going home. She's staying for a chance at stardom and basking in the glow of power. Power's a hell of an aphrodisiac. Anything else?"

"Yeah. Did Hitler kill Geli Raubal?"

"So you saw the *Gazette*."

"Yeah. Heck of a thing if it's true."

While we had been trading information, Cooper had been hunched over the table, whispering to keep our words from his friends. Now he sat back and spoke as if he didn't give a damn who heard what he was about to say.

"Who knows? But Hitler won't be exposed as a killer."

"Then there's nothing to the Raubal story?" I pressed.

"I didn't say that. But he's in control. Even if it's true, he'll keep it buried."

"What about the *Gazette* story?"

"It was half-clever, trying to slide in the truth as if they were exposing some anti-Nazi plot. But the Nazis aren't dumb and half-clever is usually completely dumb. The *Gazette* is a Weimar putz."

"A Weimar putz?"

"Berlin slang for a dead duck. This afternoon Goebbels appropriated its printing press and the Gestapo arrested everyone from the janitor to the publisher. They're off to Oranieburg for re-education."

"Re-education means what?"

"It's Nazi-speak for whatever happens at Oranieburg. It's a small town twenty miles north of here. The Nazis built a Re-education Center nearby. The place is growing. For the moment it has about twenty barracks behind a chain link fence. Razor wire substitutes for ivy. Students arrive but don't graduate. The foreign press can't get within a mile."

"So what was the deal with Raubal and Hitler?"

"Geli was the daughter of Hitler's half-sister, Angela. Hitler met the girl in nineteen-twenty-nine. She was twenty. He was forty. By all accounts she was a spitfire and cute to boot. He fell for her. Maybe they were lovers. There's debate about whether he can get it up."

"What is he? A homo?"

"Michael, homos can get it up. It's more like he's asexual."

"I don't get it."

"Neither do I. Do you want to hear about Geli or not?"

"What is he? Like a gelding?"

"You city boys. Geldings have had their equipment snipped. Supposedly Hitler has his, but either it doesn't work or he's disinterested in anything remotely normal. You're taking a big interest in this. You have problems?"

Cooper was smiling.

"Just trying to learn."

"Right. Anyway while Geli and Uncle Adolph were doing whatever it was that they did, she got engaged to his driver. A guy named Emile Maurice. Some say Hitler staged the engagement as a cover for his own affair. The Nazis are big on appearances and porkin' your niece ain't kosher. Apparently Geli decided to try Maurice on for size. Hitler didn't react well. Maurice disappeared for a while and Geli was forbidden to see anyone else."

"And?"

Cooper shrugged. "Geli and Hitler kept up their little dance until the summer of thirty-one when she fell for an artist from Austria. Hitler blew his cork. The artist disappeared. She threatened to leave for Vienna. She and Hitler had it out very publicly at the Cafe Heck in Munich. Lots of witnesses. They went back to her boarding house where the battle continued in her room. According to the housekeeper, Anny Winter, Hitler finally stormed out, leaving Geli crying in her room. Winter claimed she heard Geli cry herself to sleep. Next morning Geli doesn't come down for breakfast. Winter checks to see what's up. It ain't Geli. She's dead, shot in the head. There's an inquest. The authorities say suicide.

"So tell me, Temple. Did Hitler kill her?"

"Where's the artist?"

"I told you. Vanished."

"How reliable is the housekeeper?"

"Was. She's dead. She must have told her story a dozen times to reporters and the police. Never varied. Told it, under oath, at the inquest. That's not to say the Nazis didn't get to her."

"How'd she die?"

"She disappeared about a year ago. After they came to power, the Nazis announced that the Soccer Boys killed her. They were one of the ringvereine."

"Ringvereine?"

"Criminal gangs masquerading as social clubs. The Weimar government tolerated them in exchange for a nasty favor now and then. Diels claims that when Anny resisted paying protection money to the Soccer Boys, they dumped her in the Landwehr Canal. The body was never found. The Gestapo sweated a confession from one of the boys. Very convenient. Hitler's best witness becomes a victim, meaning she isn't around to change her story. And the Nazis have another excuse to wipe out the ringvereine - a popular move with the average Hans and Brunhilda."

"So Winter could still be alive?"

"And Hitler is gonna replace Goebbels with Saul Ullstein. She's dead all right. But the Soccer Boys didn't mess with housekeepers. More like a Gestapo trick. Now you see her, now you don't."

"What about the driver, Maurice?"

"He's alive. Listed in Berlin's telephone book. What's that tell you?"

"That he doesn't have anything to say?"

"Exactly."

I invited Cooper to the Adlon for a night cap. I wanted to do some drinking and preferred company.

We bought a couple of bottles from Fix and retired to the Adlon's roof to take in the night. We swapped war stories and stories about Humphrey. Eventually we watched the sunrise. As morning chased the night, Cooper was talking about Willy from the Tavern. He and his Belgian wife owned the place. Cooper called them citizens of the world. They had a certain independence most Germans never contemplated. According to Cooper, Willy was a man of many talents.

I asked what Willy could do other than make a mean plate of spaghetti,

Cooper said I would have to ask Willy. "Stop at the Tavern tonight and I'll make a proper introduction."

Then he pointed his empty bourbon bottle at the sun and said, "Nice, but I need sleep."

Cooper wobbled to his feet and stumbled off. He was so drunk that his moustache was crooked. Then again I wasn't exactly sober.

That morning I dreamed of making love to Sara. The love making was a catastrophe. I kept turning into Goebbels. The dream became the kind of nightmare Bosch must have had.

Chapter Nine

I awoke at noon, woozy and wondering why I so desperately wanted Sara not to be a Nazi. I headed for the Adlon Bar.

"Fix, what do you have that beats a Bloody Mary for a hangover?"

"You could try some food."

"Out of the question."

"Then how about a prairie oyster? Jean Ross claimed it was the perfect cure for a hangover."

"Who's she, or he, and what's in it?"

Fix turned his back and started to mix something. As he worked, he told me Ross was an American flapper who'd made a brief splash as a cabaret singer a year or so before.

A minute later, he turned and handed me a tumbler that contained about eight ounces of brownish glop.

"What's in it?" I repeated

"Jean said the trick was to gulp it down, all at once," said Fix, ignoring my question.

It went down like a hot oil slick. I thought for a moment it was coming back up.

"Worcester Sauce and what?" I asked.

"Four raw eggs and a shot of vodka."

"Ugh. What happened to Ross?"

"Disappeared. Probably burned out."

"If this stuff didn't kill her first."

The prairie oyster worked. An hour later I was feeling fine and snooping around Hugenberg's place.

A service road ran behind the estate. I parked my Opal down a bit and across from the back gate. I hunkered down and watched through the rear view mirror. Ten minutes later a DKW stopped. I couldn't make out the driver behind the car's dirty windows. Five minutes later Sara walked out and got in the car. It pulled away in my direction.

So why was Sara sneaking out the back door for a ride in a jalopy when she could have pranced out the front door to a Mercedes convertible?

I followed the car northeast toward Wilmersdorf, skirting the eastern edge of Grunewald, one of the city's great forests. The Havel flowed at the forest's western edge. Only two days had passed since Sara and I had played on one of its beaches. The memory seemed oddly remote.

The DKW passed the western edge of the Tiergarten, and proceeded into Wedding, a poor working class neighborhood that festered like a canker sore north of the park. In twenty minutes I'd driven from splendor to a hellish maze where tenement houses were built five deep from the street. Each building was a block long and seven stories high. They were separated by shadowy courtyards thick with foul air. Hell's Kitchen was decent by comparison.

The DKW stopped on Ackerstrasse in front of one of these enormous complexes. An archway was cut in the middle of the front building, providing access to the courtyard in front of the next building which had its own archway leading to the next courtyard - and so on went the architectural monstrosity. There wasn't a hammer and sickle in sight, although the place had once been a communist stronghold.

I parked further down Ackerstrasse near a bakery whose plate-glass window had been smudged by the hands of wishful children. The driver of the DKW was a tall man who folded out of the small car in segments. Sara reached out to him. Although I couldn't hear her words, she seemed to want him to stay. He pushed her away and closed the car door - carefully it seemed -

before moving off.

I followed him into the building complex. The courtyards teemed with wretched people and animals whose eyes were filled with common desperation. The courtyards were progressively gloomier and the stench thickened as I went. It was a mixture of cooking oil, garbage, sauerkraut, shit, motor oil, urine, bratwurst, and burning coal. On all but the first floor, windows stood open as if catching a wisp of fresh air was possible. From the windows came the sounds of children laughing and crying, men fighting, machinery grinding, dogs barking, spouses arguing, kettles whistling, records playing, and radios spewing propaganda.

As he passed through this nether world, people gawked at the tall man, giving him a wide berth. He was easy to follow. His gate had a lurching quality and his right elbow was tucked to his side.

He went in the fourth tenement. I followed and found myself in a modest entryway with hundreds of small, mostly-broken, unused mailboxes. A stairwell ascended into shadows. The tall man was gone. I ran the steps as best I could. They were littered with trash and slippery with god-knows-what.

On each landing I pushed through a door that opened to a corridor that resembled a dimly illuminated, endless tunnel. In the corridors the stench was nearly overwhelming, although the incessant noise was muffled by the walls and metal doors behind which Germany's lesser Aryans lived.

I found the tall man collapsed in the fourth floor corridor. Children picked at his body like vultures over carrion. One had his watch. Another had his wallet. Another, his shoes. Another, his fedora and belt. They scattered as I approached. I grabbed the kid with the shoes as he tried to scoot around me. He dug his teeth into my wrist as if he enjoyed it. I let him go and he ran. The thought of rabies crossed my mind.

The right side of the tall man's clothing was saturated with blood. I knelt beside him. His eyes had rolled up as if he were taking a peek at his creator.

"What happened?" I asked over and over.

Finally his eyes drifted toward me.

"Eric?" he said. The word was barely more than a whisper.

There was no time for explanations. I answered yes.

His lips twisted slightly. A smile? A grimace? His words came haltingly, hardly loud enough to be heard.

"Stuck my nose where I . . . found Sara . . . tried as best . . . not sure she won't . . . can't trust . . . better . . . the whole thing . . . get Emile out with . . . papers. Sorry . . . get . . ."

Then he was gone. I ripped open his vest and shirt exposing his torso. Large welts told part of the story. He'd been beaten. But it was a knife wound below his rib cage that killed him. His right hand was balled-up as if it had been clinging to life. I pried the fingers open and found a scrap of paper on which was written Hugenberg's address. A paper-trail to Sara.

I took the paper and left the body.

Once back on Ackerstrasse, I gulped the relatively fresh air in relief. I looked for the DKW, but it was gone.

As I drove from Wedding, I tore up the scrap of paper and tossed it from the car window, wondering why I had decided to destroy evidence and protect Sara.

I drove back to the Adlon. With the tall man's words fresh in my memory, I made a call.

The phone was answered on the third ring. "Heil Hitler," was the greeting. A hard voice, not the voice of a whipping boy.

Speaking German, I asked for Emile Maurice.

Whoever had answered hesitated before saying, "Speaking. Who is calling?"

Now it was my turn to think. I took a shot. Even if I was wrong, I would stir up trouble.

"You are not Maurice. This is Gruppenfuhrer Diels. Who is this? What have you found?"

My imitation was mediocre but good enough.

"Obersturmfuhrer Smoltz. Maurice is gone. We are searching the apartment now."

"Where has he gone?"

"I don't know." Smoltz sounded despondent. God forbid he should disappoint.

"Leave everything as it is. You and the men go to the Center at Oranieburg. Meet me at the front gate. Contact no one before we meet. Do not try to reach me. Understood?"

Silence. Had I pushed the charade too far?

"Smoltz! Are you deaf? Confirm the order?"

"No. Yes. We will leave immediately, Gruppenfuhrer."

"Heil Hitler!" I signed off before Smoltz could ask any questions.

Fifteen minutes later I cruised past Maurice's apartment house which was located on a pleasant square in Wilmersdorf. Nice digs for an ex-chauffeur. The building was five stories, with two units per floor. I drove around the square without noticing anything but the ordinary. Kids played on the sidewalks while their mothers gossiped from front steps. Two men were unloading a chrome dinette set from a Tietz delivery van under the scrutiny of a young couple.

I parked a few streets away and walked back, passing some boys playing soccer. The square was still a picture of serenity. Diels may have been smart but his boys were a witless bunch who had abandoned the playing field to me.

The apartment's lock had been jimmied and the door left ajar. Once inside I threw the door's dead bolt. I found a snarl of wrecked furniture, scattered magazines, and busted picture frames. The cushions from overstuffed chairs and a couch had been cut open, their stuffing strewn about like dirty snow. Even the radio was smashed as if a treasure might have been hidden among its vacuum tubes. I was standing in what had been the living room. The doors in the rest of the apartment stood open, one in splinters. That one must have been locked. Only the living room had been tossed as if my call had interrupted the search.

I started with the room with the splintered door, figuring that Maurice must have locked it for a reason. The room was unnaturally dark. Fumbling for the light switch, I felt the cold burning sensation of my fingers being sliced.

Snatching my hand from the switch. I spun from the room, backed against the wall next to the door, and waited, half anticipating an attack. Nothing happened. There wasn't a sound except for my breathing.

After a minute I went into a bathroom down the hall. A small square window was open to a brick wall not more than three feet away. The middle three fingers of my right hand were working but bloody. I doused then with Mercurochrome and wrapped them in gauze.

Back in the darkened room, I discovered the switch was surrounded by razor blades imbedded in the plaster. Avoiding the blades, I flicked the switch. The room was bathed in red light as if it were a photographer's darkroom.

Black flock wall paper covered the ceiling and walls. Black carpet covered the floor. The room was a temple. There were shrines to Hitler, Hess, and Geli Raubal. Hitler's was on the far wall, the others on the side walls. Each had a picture of its subject surrounded by Nazi regalia. On either side of the door across from the Hitler shrine was a collage of obscenities. To the right were pornographic pictures including some very rough stuff. To the left were pictures of torture.

Was Maurice a typical Nazi or a particularly vile mutation? Either way Sara needed to see this. The room needed to be photographed or filmed for the world to see. I went looking for a camera but couldn't find one. I was ready to leave when I remembered a folder that rested below Geli's picture like some sacred testament.

I fetched it and headed for the front door. Before leaving I glanced out a window to see if the square remained safe. Just then a Mercedes skidded to a stop in front of the building, joining another erratically parked car. Four uniformed Gestapo men piled out of the Mercedes.

Just then someone began pounding on the apartment's front door. Where to go? I stood in the living room, panic receding in the face of resignation. Based on Maurice's pictures, being shot on the spot was preferable to capture and torture. That got me going.

I tucked the folder in my belt and headed for the bathroom window. I squirmed out just as the front door shattered. The next building wasn't three feet away. The buildings' walls - one brick, one stone - were uneven, making climbing possible. Wedged between the walls, I began to work my way up. The goal was the roof of the adjacent building. It was less than fifteen feet above. How hard could it be? Archimedes claimed he could move the world. I had only to maneuver 180 pounds a few feet.

I had climbed to a position where my left foot rested on top of the window frame when I heard someone enter the bathroom. I stopped moving, sure that I would be heard otherwise. Someone was taking a dump. After just short of an eternity, the toilette flushed. I was looking for my next foothold when a soldier stuck his head out the window.

He surveyed the narrow walkway below.

I could almost hear the slow-witted bastard thinking. Then again how smart was I - wedged as I was between two buildings sixty feet up with a bleeding hand?

The soldier twisted his head to the right and looked up. I was inches from his sight line. He swiveled his head in the other direction, again looking up. Then he pulled his head in. He hadn't seen me.

At that moment a drop of blood fell from my hand. It landed on the window sill.

He didn't miss the tiny splash. He twisted his torso through the window so that his back rested on the sill. In the instant before my foot crushed his face, his mouth opened at the sight of me. I was equally shocked and lost my grip. Had my knee not landed on his chest, I would have fallen to the pavement below. My head was still above the top of the window so I didn't know if the bathroom door was closed. If it wasn't, I could envision the picture from the hall: a soldier on his back, half out the window with a guy straddling his chest. Charlie Chaplin doing slapstick had nothing on me.

Like a clumsy Houdini I tried to maneuver into the bathroom

by crawling over the guy. Now I could see that the bathroom door was closed. Watching the door, I wormed forward within the confines of the small opening. The folder tucked in my belt caught on the soldier's belt. To make matters worse the guy was starting to come around.

As I squirmed, he called for help. It was too feeble to carry far but I was terrified that the bathroom door would open at any moment. I yanked at the folder with my good hand and with my bandaged hand tugged on the window frame. Finally, like a logjam breaking, I toppled into the bathroom.

I pulled the trooper in with the idea of stashing him in the tub behind the shower curtain. Then he called again, this time loud enough to be heard. I punched him in the face and he fell backward. Before I could grab him, he toppled out the window. For a moment I stood in disbelief.

Then I cleaned my blood from the window and scrambled out. I was back above the window when I heard the bathroom door open. Someone cursed. The voice predicted that, if Hertz didn't turn up soon, he'd be sausage.

Without thinking, I thought, *More like scrambled eggs.*

Chapter Ten

I didn't sleep well that night. It was a lot of things.

In the split second after I hit him, Hertz extended a hand to me. I didn't react. I haven't forgotten the terror in his eyes as he realized he was falling out the window - or the sound of his body striking the pavement below. What did I know of Hertz? Would he have reached to save me had our roles been reversed? The answers were: Gestapo and who knows. Still I wasn't proud about having thought of him as scrambled eggs.

It took me five minutes to work my way up the walls and onto the roof of the adjoining apartment. I made my way into the building, down a rear stairwell, and out the back. Keeping mostly to alleys, I made my way to the Opal I'd parked just an hour before.

Shoes scuffed and suit tattered past mending, I looked like a bum who couldn't find the railroad tracks. I passed the boys who had been playing soccer. The game was over and their faces were flush with spent energy and lingering enthusiasm. They teased each other, recreating the day's play and anticipating tomorrow's.

"Mister, are you all right?" asked one boy.

He wasn't a handsome kid with his acne and uneven growth of peach fuzz. But there was concern in his eyes and sincerity in his voice.

"I'm fine," I replied with a half-ass smile.

His eyes said the he didn't believe me.

I drove aimlessly from Wilmersdorf. Fifteen minutes later

I found myself driving through Grunewald forest. It seemed gloomy and oppressive. Seen with a different frame of mind, it would have been beautiful. I parked on a bluff overlooking the Havel. I sat there for a long time, fighting the urge to hop the next train to Hamburg. Was Sara worth staying for? What kind of guy can push a man to his death and joke to himself about scrambled eggs?

Eventually the decency of the pimply kid and the grandeur of the place reassured me. I remembered the mother who had challenged the new ball bearing king. I remembered that I'd been awarded a medal at the end of the war, not for killing people, but for saving them. I remembered that the Germans hadn't actually elected Hitler. Maybe the world wasn't at the edge of the abyss.

Feeling better, I decided to read the papers from Geli's shrine. So much for decent kids and brave mothers.

The papers told a sordid story that would make potent ammunition in the right hands. Where to take them? The local cops? They were gutless, or in cahoots with the Nazis. The newspapers? Those that were not Nazi-controlled didn't have the stomach for confrontation, especially after the demise of the Gazette and so many others. The American embassy? I didn't think so. Uncle Sam's biggest problems were homegrown capitalist rot and leftist agitators. For some Americans, Hitler looked like part of the solution.

I needed to find someone with independence, balls, and circulation. Someone with either nothing or everything to lose.

Back at the Adlon, I took the service stairs to my room and cleaned up. Then I rolled my scuffed shoes in my tattered suit and took the service stairs to the basement where I dumped the roll in the incinerator. I also brought Maurice's papers to the basement. I hid them on top of a heating duct that had been accumulating dust for years.

Back in my room I ordered a bottle of scotch. When it arrived I gargled a mouthful and splashed a few ounces on my clean shirt. Having been a drunk, I figured I could easily play one. I took the elevator to the lobby and stumbled through it, bumping into a woman with an imperial manner and an attitude to match. At the door of the Lindenbaum I tripped and put my fist through a pane of glass, reopening my razor wounds.

Help came quickly. Bathed as I was in the smell of scotch, the staff exchanged knowing glances.

"I'm fine. I'll take care . . . myself . . . It's nothing. I'll pay . . ."

My slurring was interrupted by the imperial bitch.

"This oaf bowled me over. He should be arrested!"

As I stumbled to my room, the staff tried to convince the Prussian Marie Antoinette that something short of extended jail time would do.

That night I tossed and turned, taunted by images of Maurice's loathsome shrines and the beseeching look on Hertz's face as he began to fall.

At Max's the following morning I scanned the headlines for news of Hertz's death or Maurice's disappearance. Not a word about either. That surprised me at first. I figured the Nazi rags would have painted Maurice as a traitor on the run or perhaps a missing hero, while portraying Hertz as a dead hero. But the Gestapo was keeping a lid on. That meant they didn't know what was going on and so weren't sure how to play the facts.

That morning a secretive buzz spread through the streets of Berlin. From behind my *People's Observer*, I overheard this whispered conversation while riding a double-decker to the *Trib*'s Berlin office.

"Have you seen it?"

"No, but I hear it says terrible things about the Fuhrer."

"What things?"

"Oh, I couldn't say."

"They say there was a real paper called the *Ku'damm Gazette*."

"Never heard of it."

"Printed some of the same stuff a few days ago. Then it was

shut down."

"No wonder. It's what, this newsletter, one mimeographed page?"

"You've seen it?"

"No, I told you. Have you?"

"Well, yes. Slanderous. Not fit for wrapping dog shit."

"Do you have it?"

"Of course not. I threw it out. It's rubbish!"

"Naturally. The right thing to do. But what did it say."

"I would never repeat such things."

"Karl, we have known each other twenty years."

"Here read it yourself. It must be the communists."

Karl and his friend got off at the next stop, leaving the rubbish behind.

I reached over the back of the seat and picked up the first edition of the *Ku'damm Conscience*. It was a single page, printed front and back. The headline said, **We Are a Better People**. A political manifesto followed. It read something like this.

Yes, the Weimar Republic was an inefficient disgrace, led by incompetents who unintentionally wrecked the country. But Hitler's Reich was an efficient disgrace whose leaders were intentionally wrecking everything that stood in the way of their vision. Bullies - who happened to be right about the Versailles Treaty and the need to get people back to work - were nevertheless bullies. The Brownshirts were out of control. Spying on neighbors and fear went hand in hand. People could not continue to disappear. Every opposing voice did not have to be squelched. All Jews were not bad. All art did not have to mirror Nazi realism. Germany had to be reclaimed from the clutches of the little corporal. He had become a demagogue, pandering to the people's legitimate aspirations only to satisfy his desire for power. Moreover this failed painter was the incestuous killer of his niece, Geli Raubal.

The manifesto concluded with a promise, "we will return with proof," and a challenge, "you must prove our proposition. We are a better people!"

When the bus slowed at my stop, I left the *Ku'damm Conscience* to the next rider.

By now the storm troopers were out in force, accosting anyone who looked bright enough to read. I was stopped twice walking the half-block to the *Trib*'s office.

When Cooper spotted me walking into the newsroom, he held up a *Ku'damm Conscience,* grinning like a kid with a dirty magazine. "Have you seen this?"

"Yeah."

"Great stuff. Got anything for me?"

"I do and it ties right in with the *Ku'damm Conscience*."

"Give."

"I'm trading"

"That works for me. Whatdayawant?"

"A meeting. You, me, Sara Potter, and the guys behind the *Ku'damm Conscience.* At the meeting I'll give what I have to all of you."

"And where do I find these *Ku'damm* guys?"

"You're the reporter. Two more things. First, get a photographer in Emile Maurice's apartment. There's a room down the hall on the right that's worth all the film you have, provided anything's left. The Gestapo has been there, so they may have already cleaned it out. And watch out for the light switch. It's surrounded by razor blades. Second find Emile Maurice. He's nuts but he knows what happened to Geli Raubal. The Gestapo wants him and so should you."

"You've been busy. Tell me more. Give me something to work with."

"I've told you plenty. Keep my name out of it. I don't want the Gestapo on my ass."

"Plenty? Baloney. You've provided the big tease. Have you been in Maurice's apartment?"

"Yes. But that's all I'm saying for now. Get the pictures, if you can. I'll be at the Adlon. Don't call. I've heard about the phones."

"I'll be damned," Cooper said to my back as I walked off.

Chapter Eleven

Four days later Sara called, saying bad weather had forced an early end to her shoot. Could we meet for a drink?

"Where was the shoot?" I asked.

She hesitated before answering. When she did her words sounded like a question.

"Baden-Baden. In the Black Forest."

"Are you asking me?"

"You sound peeved."

"Where should we meet? When?" I worked at sounding agreeable. "You name it."

"Dinner tonight, say nine o'clock. I'll meet you at Hacker's. It's a two minute cab ride from the Adlon. Okay?"

"Sounds swell."

"Are you okay?"

"Sure."

But I wasn't. A few days before I'd been blown off with a note that assumed I was leaving town. Now Sara had called as if she knew I would be waiting. And if she'd been in Baden-Baden, how did she manage her outing to Wedding with the tall man?

Hacker's was on Karl Strasse, near four of Berlin's finest theaters. One of the theaters had been built specifically for Max Reinhardt who had been Germany's foremost stage director for over twenty years. Reinhardt's run had ended a few months before when he had been exposed as a Jew whose real name was Goldmann. To the relief of those who had been deceived by the imposter, Reinhardt fled the country.

Hacker's walls were covered with glossy black and white photos in which actors, actresses, producers, directors, singers, dancers, magicians, and comedians flashed self-congratulatory smiles. Leaning into many of the pictures was the man who greeted me at the reception station.

"How may I help you?"

"Table for two. My . . . guest isn't here yet."

I hadn't been sure what to call Sara. "Guest" seemed neutral enough.

"Impossible without reservations, sir. Perhaps another night. If you could call well in advance that would be helpful. Excuse me now."

He turned to greet a couple who had walked in behind me. "Herr Bennhof, how good to see you again. I have a booth for you."

"Excellent, Hacker," said Bennhof who steered his companion behind Hacker who led them into a nearly deserted dining room.

Bennhof was on the north side of fifty. His arm-piece was on the south side of thirty. She was as stunning, in a vacant sort of way, as he was arrogant, in a cruel sort of way. There was something familiar about her which I chalked up to wishful thinking on my part.

Hacker must have seen my irritation when he returned to the lobby.

"Ah! You are concerned about the vacant tables and whether I have fibbed. I assure you, no. All are reserved and will begin to fill as the theaters let out. Shall I see what is available another night?"

Hacker's smooth veneer masked neither his condescension nor the phoniness of his deference. He ducked behind the lectern guarding the entrance to the dining room. On the wall behind him I could see the photos had been rearranged to cover gaps left by the missing pictures of Jews like Reinhardt.

Hacker bobbed up, paging through a reservation book.

"I can reserve an excellent table two weeks from yesterday.

Shall I put you down for two at eight-thirty?"

"Nobody is safe, are they?"

"Pardon me, Herr . . . I don't believe we've met."

Hacker didn't understand my remark but was alert to potential trouble.

"Did they threaten to close the place if you didn't remove Reinhardt's photos? Or did you take them down on your own?"

Hacker and I regarded each other like culprits who wanted to be rid of each other but couldn't figure out how to disengage. Sara's arrival saved us.

"What's with you two? Albert, this is my friend, Michael Temple. Michael, meet Albert Hacker. Is our table ready, Albert?"

"Yes, of course," he said.

He didn't look at me, smiled at Sara, and led us into the dining room. He gave us a small booth not far from where Bennhof and the girl were drinking champagne.

Hacker signaled a waiter and left after asking Sara how the filming of *Horst Wessel* was going.

After the waiter took our drink order, Sara asked, "What was going on with Albert? You looked ready for a fist fight."

"Nothing."

"Well nothing bothers Albert and he was bothered."

"So ask him."

"Aren't we in a mood. If I'd wanted a grouch, I could have dinned with Hugenberg."

"Why do you live with that old man?"

"I don't live with him. I live in a guest house on his estate. Alone. For heaven sake, he's old enough to be my grandfather. And what happened to your hand?"

"I tripped and cut it on some glass. Look, I'm sorry."

I should have asked about all the things that were bothering me. Instead I had apologized - for what I didn't know. Damn near pathetic.

"That's better," said Sara. "Part of me was hoping you hadn't left Berlin. I had a wonderful time the other day."

She smiled and then fell silent.

I didn't speak, thinking she would fill the silence with an explanation. Instead she gazed silently into the dining room like a benevolent goddess surveying her realm. After the waiter brought our bottle of champagne, I asked why she had called.

"I want to ask your help."

"Well, I volunteered for butt kicking."

She smiled so sadly that my hand instinctively went to hers. She pulled it back.

"If only it were so simple," she said.

"What is it?"

"I want you to go home."

"Wait a minute. That's my job. Getting you home."

"It's not funny, Michael. They suspect you."

"Who suspects me? Of what?"

"Hugenberg warned me to stay away from you."

"So what have I done?"

"You flew into Germany with that traitor, Hanussen."

"So did a dozen good party members. Hell, Goering introduced him at the Press Ball."

"They say he put you in a trance at the airfield in Vienna."

"Bullshit."

"I've seen his act. He can make people bark like dogs and run around on all fours."

"So what am I? A danger to fire hydrants?"

We both laughed. The tension between us eased.

"They're not sure what danger you pose, but they think you're up to no good. Two days ago a Gestapo sergeant was killed at a time when they cannot account for you. They know that the Adlon has supplied you with an automobile."

"I thought driving was still legal, at least if you're not a Jew."

"Michael, you're wrong about these people. They just believe in their country. Hitler wanted to be an architect. Like so many others, his career was interrupted by the war. After the war he was jailed for wanting nothing more than a non-communist Bavaria and a prosperous Germany."

"I heard he was bitter because he couldn't get in art school.

Later when he couldn't get elected in Bavaria, he tried a putsch that failed. Then he went to jail and wrote *Mien Kampf*, which is scary, disgusting, and crazy all at once. Have you read it?"

"No, but I've seen his drawings. They're good. And now he's been elected."

"You should read the book. And Hitler hasn't been elected to anything. And what about your friend, the gimp?"

"Cheap shots are unbecoming. Goebbels is a sensitive man. He writes poetry. I've read some of it. It's not bad. I've read his novel. It's called *Michael* coincidentally. It's about a young man coming of age in Germany after the war. He's suffered. He understands."

"Understands what? He's suffered, so now he gets to be a megalomaniac's mouthpiece?"

"You are stubborn, Michael. Open your eyes. Ninety-five percent of Germans are better off today. The few who aren't were grabbing more than their fair share."

"Sorry, Sara. You know better. If the Nazis weren't exactly what I think they are, you wouldn't have to warn me. They beat people up or make them disappear, and take what they want."

My words hung between us like declaration of war. After a minute her hand came to mine and our fingers joined. We were stuck in an ugly world where the next words spoken might ordain our future. We looked at our hands as if they held a solution. Our reverie was broken by the noise around us. The restaurant had begun to fill as we argued.

Sara lifted her flute and spoke joylessly, "Here's to your good judgment."

"What?"

"They'll crush you or anyone else who gets in their way. That's why you must leave."

"Why don't I stay for a poetry reading?"

"He actually can write, but that doesn't mean he isn't ruthless."

Sara's sad eyes and ironic smile told me everything and nothing.

"Come back with me. New York has plenty of poets who aren't nuts. And Zukor will make you a star. You don't need Hugenberg.

Zukor is right. You'll be ruined by this Nazi stuff."

"Being a star. Gosh, that seemed important. Great roles. Name in lights. Photos in *Life* and the *Saturday Evening Post*."

Her eyes wandered across the room where Berlin's beautiful people were basking in self-indulgence. After a time her eyes came to rest on mine. They softened and lost focus as if her mind had drifted elsewhere. She put her purse on the table. She took out a pack of Camels and a lighter. Its tortoise shell finish was inlaid in gold. Her hands were large and beautiful. I wasn't the kind of guy who noticed hands but I did that night. It was their grace. She mistook the focus of my attention.

"A gift from Goebbels. It's nice, but they can't resist."

Sara rotated the lighter so I could see its golden swastika.

"They're everywhere, on everything," she said. "Even children's candy."

After she lit her cigarette, Sara returned the lighter to her purse. She seemed lost, unable to decide what to say or do. Resting her left elbow on the table, she held the Camel before her eyes and watched its smoke drift into the room's haze. Somewhere a piano played something classical. Absently her right hand began to respond to the music. As the piece developed, her fingers played over phantom keys.

When the piece was over, she smiled. "I never could get that right and butchered it again, even on an imaginary keyboard."

"What was it?"

"Liszt's Etude Number Three."

"It sounded difficult."

"It's a practice piece, meant to be challenging. Someday I'll get it right."

"Your playing sounded great to me."

She laughed. "You must be tone deaf."

"Don't ask me to hum along."

"I thought so."

"I'm not a Liszt guy anyway. I'll take Benny Goodman."

"Etudes aren't for you?"

It was my turn to laugh.

"Where could we hear some swing? Or is this strictly an etude night?"

She snuffed her Camel in an ashtray, took some money from her purse, and dropped sixty marks on the table.

"Let's go," she said pulling me from the booth.

A step from our table she stopped, reached back, and grabbed the unfinished bottle from our champagne bucket.

The red Mercedes, top down, slouched a few steps from Hacker's door. The dashboard and doors were trimmed in mahogany. The seats were covered with plush leather. The engine purred to life, its power muffled but palpable. Sara used it, accelerating into the night with abandon. She drove, testing the car's limits and hers. We passed the bottle back and forth. The speed and champagne were galvanizing. Danger whispered in the wind that buffeted our hair. The car sped southeast into a section of the city that seemed abandoned. Then, rounding a turn, we were suddenly on a pack of cars parked pell-mell around a ramshackle warehouse. Sara parked at the edge of the pack.

"I hope you know how to jitterbug, Mr. Etude. Let's go."

Inside, a swing band played from a makeshift stage. Two guitar players spun cords into melody; the base player and drummer hammered the beat while saxophones and clarinets countered each other with harmonized riffs. Soon Sara and the music had me dancing up a storm. No mean feat for a guy who claimed two left feet. We danced until the last note died.

Then the Mercedes took us further south to a country inn that must have slipped from the pages of a fairy tale. There we made love in a goose down bed. At first hesitantly and then recklessly. And ultimately with tenderness. We fell asleep in each others arms, her Chanel No. 5 kindling memories of Paris in the '20's when the flappers abandoned the old floral scents for Chanel's enigmatic fragrance.

The sun was up well before we woke. I had tenderness and conversation to spare. A lover with expectations to share. Sara was abrupt. An actress with a rehearsal to make. On the road back to the Adlon she talked about piano lessons, a musical review in which she'd bombed, a speedboat ride on the Spree, the price of eggs, and the color of the sky. Anything but the night we'd shared or what we might have together. She seemed as careless as a schoolgirl who had survived her first date and wasn't worried about the next one.

When we got to the Adlon, she said, "I think I'll try those New York poets, Michael. Now where's Zukor's new contract?"

She told the Adlon's valet to hold the Mercedes and instructed me to meet her in the Lindenbaum. I went to my room to retrieve the contract, wondering what had changed. Maybe her night had been as good as mine. She was finishing a glass of apricot juice as I sat down at her table.

"I intend to sign this only if you promise to be on the next ship for New York. Tell Zukor that I'll be along in about two weeks. You're on the next train to Hamburg with my signature. Do we have a deal?"

"I'll wait and go back with you."

"Don't be a dufus. Once I've signed Zukor won't pay for you to stay on. Not one extra night. The cheapskate might not even pay for your dinner tonight."

Her proposal felt more like a dodge than a deal. *About two weeks* was a fudge. And, if she intended to finish *Horst Wessel,* she might as well apply for German citizenship. This much was clear: short of being kidnapped, Sara wasn't going home on any schedule but her own.

"Deal," I said, believing a signed contract was better than an argument.

She signed and handed me the contract. "I hope we can get together when I get home."

"I'd like that."

"I'll call you at Pinkerton in Chicago."

She kissed my cheek and walked out.

I sat in the Lindenbaum, feeling I'd been through this before. Another night of lovemaking, in some indefinable way, akin to my experience with Sara. I dismissed the impression. Hanussen and his tricks had me spooked. But the notion stuck.

It came to me hours later, when I overheard Fix swapping stories with a customer about the Crillon Bar in Paris.

I'd gone to Paris in 1917 with Billy Collins, teenagers with heads full of baseball, girls, and dreams of glory. Before going to the front, we dawdled in Paris for days with two girls from Madame Constantine's. I was with Lucy. To this day I picture her as young and beautiful. In truth she was older than me and no beauty. But she was wise in ways I was not, and possessed more beauty than I deserved.

It was my last night with Lucy that reminded me of my night with Sara.

I'd been scared and needy in 1917. It had been that way with Sara. Except the roles were reversed. Sara had been the one seeking the normalcy of human contact as if she were about to be tested and was uncertain of her mettle. She had been the one whose passion embraced not the act of love but the escape it offered. What future was she avoiding by lingering through the night with me? Did she feel any more for me than I had for Lucy?

The evidence to the contrary be damned. Sara wasn't a Nazi. Yet for some reason, she was determined to stay and jeopardize her career. Why?

Chapter Twelve

After Sara left, I showered and got some sleep. When I returned to the lobby, the place was buzzing. Hitler was to give a major speech from the new parliament building. As usual it would be broadcast over the radio. Behind the excitement, I sensed concern. People hoped for good news but feared some form of domestic ugliness or saber-rattling at neighboring countries.

I left to see Cooper. The streets were nearly empty despite the Hitler weather. Everyone must have been inside, glued to their radios. But there was no escape. At each intersection, Hitler's voice boomed from speaker poles that had been erected by the Party for just such occasions.

In the *Trib*'s newsroom Cooper and a dozen others stood around a radio, their heads tilted to the speaker from which Hitler's harsh, tenor voice crackled. He varied the tempo and timbre of his words as if orchestrating for maximum effect. Throughout there was an intensity that was sustained by belief and fashioned to bewitch.

The speech was a response to Roosevelt's recent call for peaceful relations. As Hitler agreed to renounce offensive weapons, he sounded like the voice of reason. But Germany wanted equality with its neighbors. It would not be a stepchild. If Germany was denied equality it would withdraw from the League of Nations and rearm.

Hitler had thrown down a gauntlet wrapped in velvet fairness. Newsmen had an ear for this kind of thing. They swapped uncomfortable glances.

As if he could feel the reaction of his radio audience, Hitler again changed his tone. He denounced war as madness. He said German conquests would only taint the country's racial purity, making conquest unthinkable. He claimed Germany would achieve its goals by increasing its birth rate. He renounced territorial claims and suggested bilateral, non-aggression pacts with Germany's neighbors. The torrent of words seemed endless but they finally swelled to a climax.

"Whoever lights the torch of war in Europe can wish for nothing but chaos. We, however, live in the firm conviction that, in our time, we will see, not the decline, but the renaissance of the West. That Germany may make an important contribution to this great work is our proud hope and our unshakable belief."

The parliament erupted with cheering. The ovation continued until the march from Tannhauser reverberated from the radio. I could picture Hitler striding from the microphone into an adoring crowd.

Such was Hitler's gift that some of the *Trib* staff took the speech at face value. The debate was on. Liar or statesman? Peacemaker or warrior biding his time to rebuild Germany's arsenal? Even the skeptics allowed themselves hope. Cooper, ever the listener, said nothing and eventually became bored.

He spotted me and pulled me aside.

"I went out with a photographer. Maurice moved according to the custodian. It took a hundred marks before he admitted the Gestapo stripped the place clean. He also thought someone fell out a window. He wouldn't say another word. I checked the alley next to the building. It looked like there was dried blood on the cobblestones.

"Whatdayaknow about that? And what we were supposed to photograph?"

"You'll get your answers at the meeting I asked you to arrange. I'm here to see how that's going."

"Nobody can get a handle on the *Ku'damm Conscience*. They are going to be hard to invite."

"Keep trying."

"Yes, boss," he replied, doing a fair impression of Jack Benny's

Rochester.

"Where did Maurice go?" I asked.

"Dumped in the alley?"

"Don't think so. You need to find him."

"Why couldn't it have been Maurice's blood in the alley?"

"Let's just say it wasn't - for sure."

"And how do you know that?"

"All in good time."

"Don't be a hero, Temple. If you haven't noticed, the heroes dress in black or brown these days. If you know something spill it now and get your ass out of the country."

"Did I say that I knew anything?"

"If Maurice turns up, it'll probably be face down in the Landwehr. Watch that you don't join him."

"I'm a good swimmer."

"Yeah? Well, remember the old saying: it's always the good swimmers who drown."

I wasn't trying to be a hero. In the war-to-end-all-wars, I learned that heroism was usually a dead man's virtue. I'd seen too many dying heroes, scared witless by their own mortality and questioning the wisdom of their courage. Besides true heroism starts with a selflessness that few men possess.

I was in this for me. I'd come alive in Berlin. I wasn't waking up with a taste for booze and going to bed with vomit on my breath. The old nightmares were gone. The excitement was back. If there was danger, it wasn't self-inflicted. Being a player in something that mattered was part of it. Sara was a bigger part.

Hanussen's agent, Walter Prinz, was listed in the phone book. His office was at the intersection of Karl Strasse and Unterbaum Strasse across from the Lessing Theater. Down a bit on Karl was Hacker's.

The building was tucked in the wedge formed by the two

streets, Berlin's version of the Flat Iron Building in New York. Prinz shared the top floor with two law firms and an accountant.

His receptionist looked like an Aryan poster girl and had an attitude to match. When I wouldn't say why I wanted to see Prinz, she walked away miffed at my reticence. She returned unrepentant. Herr Prinz would see me - apparently against her better judgment. His office was a large triangular affair, offering the kind of panorama that gave skyscrapers a good name.

"Who are you, Herr Temple?" Prinz asked.

I told him some of my story. I left out the parts about Maurice and my trip to Wedding. More than once he seemed ready to stop me but didn't. He was over six feet tall with a youthful, athletic build. He was as dark as his secretary was fair. He might once have been handsome but was showing some age. He regarded me with languid eyes. When I finished, he seemed even older, although it was hard to say how old he really was.

"Why tell me these things and endanger me?"

"I'm not here to cause trouble."

"How do you know that I will not cause you trouble?"

"You're a Jew."

"You are a fool if you think one victim will not betray another."

"What about the Aryan who keeps your gate?"

"Viktoria? She is my cousin. No more racially pure than I, although, with the right papers, she could pass easily enough. I have the ability to arrange that. So far she refuses to repudiate who she is. At once she is braver and more foolish than most."

My eyes wandered over the interior of his office. It was furnished with stark metal and leather shapes that announced their essence - chair, desk, table, cabinet - with simple chrome lines. I sat in a construction of leather bands strapped to a single piece of twisted tubing. It threw me back at an uncomfortable angle. The tubing chafed at my shoulders and legs. Perhaps it was designed to encourage short visits. Prinz was still talking.

"My family has lived in Berlin for over two hundred years. I love the city. This office was my father's. I've scaled back some. Quite a view. I can see it all without turning to look. The Reichstag is out there, a reminder of how far we have come in the wrong direction. Incredible. Still I love my country."

Prinz grunted, pensive and bitter. "But not enough to stay now that it has decided to punish me for the accident of my birth. Most Jews want to carry on. Pogroms happen every so often, they say. I say life is too short. What do you really want, Herr Temple?"

"I told you. To find Hanussen. I need him to help convince Potter to return to the states."

"She believes in his powers?"

"Yes," I lied. "So how do I find him?"

"I don't know exactly but he's out there - someplace in Wedding."

Prinz didn't look but pointed a thumb over his shoulder in a northeasterly direction.

"Wedding is a big place," I said. "I'll never find him without more."

"Precisely. He once told me that there was a bakery on Ackerstrasse with the best asparagus strudel. He said the strudel was tasty after an apple omelet."

"Sounds terrible," I said.

"Precisely."

It took a second or two for the message to register.

"Thank you for your help."

"You have never been here. How could I have helped?"

"Precisely."

He smiled.

I extracted myself from his highfalutin chair.

"One last question. Do you believe in the powers Hanussen claims to have?"

"He's an entertainer. I know some of his tricks. Generally speaking, I don't believe. But there are things I cannot explain. Hanussen himself claims he uses the tricks only to supplement his real powers."

Prinz shrugged as if to say only Hanussen knew.

"Give me an example of the inexplicable," I asked.

"When I last saw him, he said you'd come looking for him. He gave me permission to tell you about the bakery. Said the two of you were destined to play important roles. And no, he didn't say what they might be."

Before I could speak, Prinz rose from his chair and turned to the city he loved. "If you get out alive, tell Zukor that I helped. Good day."

Viktoria appeared. She took my arm and steered me out.

There were two bakeries on Ackerstrasse. I guessed the one closest to where the tall man parked. Its window was still smudged with the fingerprints of hungry kids. **Epp Und Sohn** was stenciled on the glass. The place was closed. A sign on door gave the hours: 5:30 am to 5:30 pm. I was a half hour late.

Driving back to the Adlon, I thought about Prinz. His getting-out-alive remark bothered me. It was the equanimity with which he said it. Death and disappearance had become ordinary, like a cold or the flu. Two weeks before I might have gotten drunk. Now I had no taste for it. I decided to escape by picking up an American paper at Max's. I would get lost for a while in the pennant races. Did Mickey Cochrane have the Tigers rolling? What about Dizzy Dean and the Gas House Gang? Mickey and Dizzy verses Adolph and the he-goat. That was an easy choice.

On my way from Max's, the Adlon's desk man signaled me over to say that the Gestapo was searching my room. So much for baseball. I thought about running. Scanning the lobby, I saw trench-coated men posted at the exits. They probably wanted me to run.

"Gestapo" is an anagram for secret state police. While they didn't normally wear uniforms, Gestapo men were as covert as an undertaker at a convention of comedians. They were all the same: lean, arrogant, disciplined, ruthless, intelligent, mean, and nicely dressed in dark business suits. Most had the Aryan look.

They didn't blend in. That was the idea.

I walked to the elevators pretending I didn't have a care in the world but wondering if the sweat trickling down my spine had surfaced on the back of my coat.

The door to my room was open. Two men were inside.

"Mind if I come in?" I asked.

"Temple?"

"Who else?"

"You didn't pack much for a man who has stayed as long as you have."

The speaker pointed at my meager clothing supply which was now scattered on the floor. The other man circled behind me.

"I say, travel light. Can I help you find something?"

"Where were you Tuesday afternoon?"

"I drove down to Sanssouci. That Frederick knew how to live. Hell of a library. He was one German who loved books."

Two weeks before a Nazi student association had staged nationwide book burnings to purge the country of ideas inconsistent with Nazi beliefs or insufficiently Aryan in their origin. Darwin and Einstein. Marx, Lenin, and Trotsky. Brecht and Bebel. Sinclair Lewis and Jack London. Hemingway, Dos Passos, and H. G. Wells. Mann and Proust. Freud. Even Helen Keller. Hundreds of writers had their books reduced to ashes. The new Germany was about character and values as embodied in the Aryan ideal. Everything else had to go.

The agent at my back grabbed me by the collar and pushed me face first into the wall.

"What have we here, another morally corrupt intellectual?"

"If reading the comics and sports pages makes me an egghead, guilty."

"I'll give you sports," said the agent.

He spun me around and knocked the wind out of me with a fist to the gut.

I slid down the wall. I had no problem looking contrite.

The slugger stood above me, not at all satisfied.

"Your auto was seen in Wilmersdorf."

"Not mine. Opals are almost as common as brown shirts."

I was kicked in the thigh for that crack. The slugger's face brightened as he noticed the bandage on my hand.

"What happened there?" he said pointing.

"After I got back from Sanssouci, I got drunk and fell going into the Lindenbaum - down in the lobby. Put my hand through a windowpane. No doubt old lady Adlon will bill me for the repairs."

The slugger nodded at his pal who left the room.

"Why are you still in Berlin? Your work for the Jew is finished."

"But I still have columns to write for *Variety*. Besides von Sternberg told me to bring Potter back. She isn't ready to go. So I'm staying until she's ready. Mostly I'm staying to see as much as I can of Berlin and Germany - on Paramount's ticket."

"Paramount's ticket?"

"The studio is paying my expenses. I get a vacation and *Variety* gets a story or two. Paramount can afford it."

"You mean Zukor can afford it."

"You could look at it that way."

"The Jews always can, but seldom pay," said the slugger as if he were agreeing with something I said.

His contempt for me was fading. He was trying to decide if I was a kindred spirit or at least a hustler out to con a Jew.

"Look," I said, "stretching a job into a vacation at the expense of a fat-cat in New York can't be a crime."

Before he could answer, his pal returned and announced that I was a stumbling drunk who would be billed for the broken window.

They had a good laugh and left.

I walked into the Tavern at one-thirty that morning and found the same crew around the table. Diels sat two chairs to the left of Cooper. I approached from Cooper's right. I wanted Diels to have a good look.

"Coop! I've decided to stay. You're right. Germany is the

greatest show on earth. I'm gonna stick Paramount for a few extra weeks and take it all in."

I bent over and whispered in his ear. "Go along with this or the Gestapo may boot me out before you get your story. We're old pals from Chicago. Smile. Right now I'm telling you a story about Sally Rand tickling the mayor's ass with one of her fans."

I stood back and we acted like a couple of adolescents laughing at a dirty joke.

Then Cooper introduced me. "Fellas, this character is a *Variety* reporter. Michael Temple. Don't snicker. *Variety* ain't the *Trib* but it's better than *The Hicksville Herald*. Back home he's given me a lead or two. He was just telling me what Sally Rand did to the mayor's ass with her feathers. Introduce yourselves."

Around the table they went, starting with the guy to Cooper's right. Each reporter gave his name and newspaper until it was Diels' turn. What would he have to say for himself? Nothing but the truth as it turned out:

"Rudolf Diels, Gestapo Chief, and SS Gruppenfuhrer."

Rudy made it sound like he was a regular guy with ordinary job. I wanted to shout that a few days before he'd arrested me for nothing and that his thugs had roughed me up just hours before. But the reporters knew what he was even if they didn't know what he'd done to me.

I'm sure Diels understood my message. Cooper and I were friends. Messing with me was the same as messing with the American press. If Rudy wanted to continue currying favor with the press, he had better go easy on me.

"Michael, I'd ask you to stay but the Gruppenfuhrer favors us from time to time with his off-the-record observations. Not your turf."

"Coop, I'm only surprised you would share him with the others."

I walked out as the competitors maneuvered to find advantage amid hollow laughter and ostensible good will.

Chapter Thirteen

The following morning Berlin awoke to find the second edition of the *Ku'damm Conscience* scattered across town. One had found its way under my door. The headline read, **What To Believe? A Lifetime Of Hate Or Yesterday's Propaganda.**

There followed excerpts from Hitler's peace speech juxtaposed with excerpts from *Mien Kampf*. Nice work. Once a jackal always a jackal.

By nine o'clock the Nazis had mobilized. The SA, the SS, the Gestapo, and the Kripo were out in force. Kripo was an anagram for criminal police. The Kripo and the Gestapo constituted the Sipo which was an anagram for the Security Police. Brown, black, and green uniforms crisscrossed the city accosting pedestrians and confiscating paper. It managed to be simultaneously frightening and farcical. Kafka meets the Marx brothers. Except these Aryans weren't playing for laughs. By ten the city had been rescued from the threat posed by the latest *Ku'damm Conscience.*

I headed for Epp and Son. Inside the bakery, a beet-faced woman presided over a glass display case bursting with rolls, cakes, cookies, pies, and strudels. Behind the counter a dozen varieties of bread were stacked fifteen high. The woman greeted me warmly and asked what she could get me. The bakery was a very effective cover. Either that or I was about to make a fool of myself.

"I've just finished an apple omelet and an asparagus strudel would be tasty."

She gave me quizzical look, and took a step back as if I was nuts. But she was a good soul and gave me another chance.

"I'm sorry I misunderstood. What did you want?"

I apologized for the misunderstanding and ducked out the door. The patrons behind me stepped aside, giving a wide berth to an apparent gastronomic lunatic.

Five minutes later I was trying the absurd line in a bakery further down the street. The name on the window, National Ovens, was newly painted and flanked by Nazi flags. Very patriotic. The store's inventory was meager compared to Epp's place. The clerk was another beet-faced, bowling ball of a woman.

When I'd finished my strudel and omelet spiel, she turned and called into a back room.

"Martin. There is a man here wanting asparagus strudel."

"Give me a minute," came a voice from the back.

"You heard," said the lady to me.

She turned to a blackboard and picked up a piece of chalk. With painstaking care and calligraphy that would have made a monk proud, she began listing breads and desserts that seemed in short supply. She was still at it when a burly fifty-year-old with ham-hock forearms emerged from the back room.

"We don't get many requests for asparagus strudel. Who sent you?"

"An agent named Prinz. He said Hanussen sometimes shops here."

"We may have some in the back. Follow me."

The man was dressed in bakers' whites. He had the physique of a cook who had been sampling his work. He led me through a back room into a modern commercial bakery with six massive ovens each capable of baking hundreds of loaves or pies at a time. The operation was largely automated. On the bakery floor assistants worked five of six ovens. The sixth was down for repairs. My host impassively watched it all, occasionally calling out an instruction to one of the workers. I was getting the invisible-man treatment

"Look, Mister, I'm impressed, but I didn't come to watch bread baking."

"You are American?"

"Yes."

He switched to English. "Your Henry Ford, he hates the Jews as much as the Fuhrer."

The statement sounded like a challenge. I didn't know what to say so I went with the truth.

"Ford may be a jerk but I don't think he's for stealing their property and trying to create a master race of Yankees."

The baker went back to ignoring me and watching his workers. After another five minutes a voice called from above and behind us.

"Nothing, Ludi."

"Good," said the baker to no one in particular.

He turned and asked my name.

"Michael Temple."

"Michael, do you mind if I have you searched."

"No."

Two workers appeared and patted me down. One was an old man with fear in his eyes. He treated me like I was a snake coiled to strike. He gave my wallet to Ludi for inspection. Everything in my pockets was removed and scrutinized. When they were finished Ludi spoke to the old man with the kindness of a parent reassuring a frightened child.

"He is an American, Martin. There is nothing to worry about. Thank you for your help."

Martin and the other man moved off.

"He has lost much to the Nazis. Only death will end Martin's fear. That said, caution is the best approach to life these days. So what do you want with Hanussen?"

I told him that Hanussen probably knew something about the Glaise killing that would be embarrassing to the Nazis. I wanted to put him in touch with people from the *Trib* and the *Ku'damm Conscience* so he could tell his story to the world.

Ludi seemed amused. The plan did manage to sound both grandiose and harebrained. I added that I could also use Hanussen's help with Potter.

Ludi shook his head. "That might get him killed," he said.

He called for Martin who must have been waiting nearby. He told the old man to take me to Hanussen.

Martin led me out the back of the bakery into an alley, where a small fleet of delivery trucks huddled against a wall. I wanted to ask what happened to him. I didn't. Except for the details, I could guess easily enough.

He led me through a maze of back alleys and narrow streets, the bowels of Wedding. He moved silently, bent over as if that made him less of a target. Ferret-like, his head moved from side to side looking for danger. After a while I became lost in the twists and turns of our route.

Twenty minutes later, I was shown into a small, secret room.

"We meet again as you said we would," I said, nodding in recognition of his prediction.

Hanussen pushed himself into a sitting position as if to get a better look at me. He too nodded.

"Germany has changed you. You've become presumptuous. A man who dares to make a difference. Hitler is such a man. Chancellor, soon to be president. Yes, I see that. The people will elect him.

"I too once dared. But now I hide in a slum and see only my death. I must be insane and without free will. A sane, free man would run from the future. Except I could be wrong, confusing my nightmares for the future. If so, my sojourn here proves nothing.

"Think of your arrogance, Temple. You were shaken by a single heart that bled in my hands. Yet you suppose yourself ready to challenge a man who is prepared to bleed Europe. You are madder than I. Madder than the men who harbor and embrace me. Perhaps my madness will be their instrument of deliverance. We are all drowning men, flailing about for a life preserver in freezing water, not knowing the agony of which death is greater, yet sustained by cruel hope. What do I see for you? Aaahh! I cannot see. Darkness has become preferable to the light."

Hanussen fell back on the pillow, perspiration pouring from his body. His breath was rapid and shallow. His complexion whiter than the dirty sheet on which he rested.

The room was barely bigger than his narrow bed. The space had been walled off from a small bedroom. The passage to the cell was eighteen inches wide and less than four feet tall. It was sealed by a board painted to match the false wall. Once sealed, a small dresser was moved to conceal the opening, entombing Hanussen in a space that didn't exist in an apartment on the top floor of one of the countless tenements in Wedding. At least Hanussen had disappeared by choice.

"I told you he was delirious. A bad fever."

The speaker was a man in his forties, well dressed for a tenement resident. We stood in the main room of his two room apartment. An old hand loom filled the front third of the room. Behind it were a wooden table and two straight back chairs as well as an aged settee. At the back of the room was a sink. On the sink's counter were a hot plate and the remnants of a fine china set.

"My father was a speciality weaver. Advances in the power loom ruined him. He and his best loom wound up here. From father to son. You must go now. All of the eyes and ears in the building are not friendly."

"I have many questions."

"Not of me."

Martin pulled me from the apartment. Once we were in the hall, he surprised me by speaking.

"Theo is a driver at the bakery. His wife is a Jew. So he is with us. He keeps the safe room for us. But he has no answers. Jan spoke of you as a bold man, a man to fight the Nazis."

Poor Martin. To him Hanussen was a prophet and America was Europe's savior. Unfortunately his prophet was babbling and the U.S. was in the midst of a depression. Sometimes hope is as dangerous as alcohol.

"I will take you to Eric." Martin continued. "He may be able to help you help us."

Whoever Eric was, he was just down the hall and across from Theo's apartment. Martin hesitated before knocking. Then he rapped out a short pattern.

"Go away," was the gruff response.

"Damn silly knocking in code! I can never remember it," Martin mumbled to himself.

Then he rapped urgently on the door and whispered loudly, "It's Martin, Eric. Open the door."

I recalled the tall man had mistaken me for someone named Eric in a corridor like this one.

The door sprung open to a full-fledged Aryan. Six-two, blond, blue-eyed, athletic with a face carved from stone. The racial purity police should have put this boy to stud. The girls would have lined up to do their part.

If the Aryan was surprised by us, he didn't let on.

"Come in, Martin. Bring your friend."

I might have been Martin's grandson for all the concern Eric showed. He closed the door casually. Then, in the moment I glanced around the apartment, he was behind me with a knife at my throat.

"Who is this goon, Martin?"

I had been called worse but the knife was an attention grabber.

Martin explained. Then I started explaining. I was almost finished when the Aryan stopped me and told Martin to go to the next room. I heard Martin shuffle across the wooden floor. A latch clicked. Then silence. I felt the knife draw lightly across my neck. No pain. A cold line that became warm. He showed me the blade, keeping it inches from my neck. Etched in the silver were the words: "Meine Ehre ist Treue." A droplet of my blood wobbled, like mercury, in the Gothic script. Everything stood still, except the trembling droplet. In the blade I could see myself watching the blood. The script translated: "My honor is my loyalty." The meaning escaped me.

"Hindenburg's last breath stands between Germany and the cataclysm and you talk about movie stars? You and Goebbels."

The Aryan emitted a low growl as if in pain. "I would risk nothing for you."

The knife moved. The droplet rolled off the blade and fell into the air. Fuck this, I said to myself.

"It's more than Potter. It's exposing Hitler. You're an idiot if you keep cutting the necks of people who could help because their motives aren't pure. I don't see Hitler turning down the industrialists' money or appropriating their factories to maintain the purity of his supposed socialism. And Goebbels is no less a fanatic for all his skirt chasing. "

"So?"

"So how about putting the knife away?"

"The Gestapo won't put their knives away until they have what they want."

"And you'll slit the throat of a potential ally to prove you're as tough as your enemy? I'll tell you this, they aren't dumb enough to kill an American. No wonder they're winning."

"You are a fool to think they would not kill you, me or anyone who opposes them."

"Then we're in this together. So let's start by not slitting my throat."

The Aryan laughed. "That is a modest enough beginning."

He moved the blade away and turned me around to face him. He slouched a bit, and began to look more like a college kid facing finals-week than a warrior.

"Sorry," said the Aryan. "I'm Eric Clauss. Being a son of a bitch is harder that it looks. I've been working on it."

We both laughed, worried men trying to be stronger that we were.

"You had me going."

"So how do you help us? Hanussen is only an entertainer even if he can see the future and does move in Nazi circles. More than his visions will be needed. Besides you've seen Jan. He's sick."

Eric turned out to be good at wheedling information. I soon told him about Maurice's demented temple, the cache of papers, and Hertz. Eric was astonished by my visit to Maurice's apartment. I was feeling cocky until Eric spoke.

"Let me give you some advice. Don't ever trust anyone with that story again. You know why? Because when the Gestapo squeezes your best friend's balls, he will give you up. All you need to say is that you have documents which would prove embarrassing."

He smiled like we had reached an understanding.

I suggested giving Maurice's papers to the *Trib* for publication. Eric suggested holding off but wouldn't say why. I asked if he knew who was publishing the *Ku'damm Conscience*. He said he didn't know. I asked what was going on at National Ovens. He said baking. Apparently our understanding was this: he wouldn't give me any information and I was to give him only vague information.

"Christ, Eric, will you admit day follows night? Can we trust each other with that?"

"Perhaps, in time, we can be more candid."

"In time? Do we have time? Hindenburg isn't long for this world. Five minutes ago you said disaster arrives when the old man dies."

Eric considered his words before speaking.

"A few days ago a friend said he was going to meet a woman who was close to some Nazi bigshots. She was thought to be sympathetic to us. They were going to talk about working together. I don't know where they met. Later we found him bleeding to death in the hallway on the floor below. So trusting is not an easy thing."

"Who was the woman?"

"My friend didn't say."

Eric kept talking about betrayal but I was back in Dahlem watching Sara get in the tall man's car.

After a time I heard Eric repeating my name.

"Yes, yes," I said.

"For a second you looked like someone walked across your grave."

"You're right about trust. The person you most want for a friend may be something else altogether."

"If you and I are who we appear to be, we will become friends," said Eric.

"We can hope," I said.

I didn't tell Eric that Sara was the woman who may have betrayed his friend. Forlorn hope and sweeping doubt, what a pair

As Martin guided me back to the bakery, I brooded over who was the bigger fool: the mock tough guy who thought I wanted him for a friend even though he put a knife to my neck, or the mock reporter who was star struck over a girl who might have put a knife in the tall man's gut.

Chapter Fourteen

The next morning I was paging through the *People's Observer* when an article in the arts section caught my eye. The headline read: **Horst Wessel Comes to Life**. Remembering the boy-pimp's ongoing transformation, I anticipated something juicy. Perhaps he'd risen from the dead and been carried aloft by an exaltation of winged whores to become Odin's messenger to Hitler. Now that would have been a story.

Instead the article served up the standard palaver about Wessel's battles with the communists and some baloney about Goebbels being a behind-the-scenes creative genius. The article said the following morning a reenactment of a street battle between the SA and the commies would be filmed on location in Wedding. Many cast members would be working including Sonja Potter.

Sonja?

That afternoon I found a second-hand store on Leipziger Strasse where I bought some used clothes. Zukor's expensive suit would be too snappy for my plan.

Dressed as a laborer I was in Wedding the next morning before the crew and cast arrived and just as the Kripo was cordoning off two blocks of Rennerstrasse. I was loitering about when a wet-behind-the-ears, ascot-wearing scout grabbed me for an extra. Babelsberg, here I come.

Twenty minutes later, the scout was bellowing at thirty extras through a megaphone, explaining the scenes that would be filmed that morning. In one Horst and his brown-shirted mates would battle and defeat a band of communist brawlers while we extras, playing the ordinary citizens of Wedding, would cheer them to victory.

"Any questions?" asked the scout.

A toothless man of indeterminate age with cracked lips raised his arm. Strength Through Joy had not caught up with this guy. He spoke with a lisp and a hint of anger. "I lived in Wedding all my life. We were Bolsheviks and hated the SA. Everything is backwards."

The scout was unperturbed. His answer made perfect sense. "It's a movie. Besides this is the new Germany!"

Having said it all, the scout walked over to a newly-arrived truck to supervise the unloading of klieg lights, dollies, and cameras. Moments later two more trucks arrived, carrying the professional extras who would play the storm troopers and commies. The SA extras looked like model Aryans, a far cry from the crew of misfits from which my two muggers emerged. The commie extras looked like counterfeit Jewish thugs with their rubber noses, yarmulkes, and fake Hasidic locks.

Ten minutes later a blue Mercedes convertible pulled up with the director, Sara and Jurgen Nadel, the actor playing Horst. The director, a guy named Kerrl, walked over to us amateurs and told us where to position ourselves and how to act. He was from the sledgehammer school of acting. On his cue we were to look worried and yell, "Kill the reds!" Then when the battle was won, we were to open our eyes wide, raise our eyebrows, nod our heads, look happy, and yell, "Thank you!" and "God bless you!"

The toothless extra made a joke about how little he had to be thankful for. Kerrl was not amused. He announced with dreary sincerity that there was nothing funny about making a film for the glory of the Fatherland. Kerrl was doubly right. Neither propaganda nor glory is ever funny.

Kerrl filmed two short scenes with Sara and Nadel, and then lined up the street battle. Good verses evil. The choreography was intended to crate the impression of mayhem. It took a while to work it out. Finally Kerrl called "Action!", and the combatants engaged. Two cameras recorded the battle while a third shot over and across the battle to those of us playing citizen spectators.

As the battle raged, Kerrl gave us our first cue. We were doing our bit when the toothless extra went mad.

With a banshee scream, he hurled himself at the SA extras like they were the real thing. Three of them went reeling to the ground. Within seconds all of the citizen extras, except me, threw themselves into what was becoming a real battle. From the rooftops came a fusillade of garbage targeted at the director and camera crews. The propaganda makers were under attack.

I loved it - until the shooting started.

The Kripo intervened but were taking a beating. That couldn't last. One of them glanced down the front of his green tunic and found it blood stained. He seemed dumbfounded. Then, remembering his Luger, a *fuck-this* look crossed his face. He drew his gun and fired into the air. He was rushed, dragged to the ground, and disarmed. Seeing the problem, another Kripo officer opened fire in earnest. Anyone without a green uniform was fair game.

The farce had become a tragedy.

I ran for the equipment truck where Sara was hiding. I reached under the back axel and extended my hand to hers.

"Come on. Let's get out of here before the real SA shows up."

She didn't argue. We were off and running. My car was parked a block up and a street over. On the way out we passed a pack of storm troopers who were on the way in. Nightsticks drawn, they bashed anyone who didn't get out of their way.

I drove northwest toward Tegeler Lake. Once out of Wedding it was less than a fifteen minute drive. The lake was surrounded by primal forest. It was beautiful and peaceful. I parked in an empty gravel lot near a picnic area that on weekends was reserved for Strength Though Joy members. That's what the sign said.

Neither of us spoke for a while.

"Swastikas in the forest. They're relentless," I said, nodding at the sign.

Sara was looking out the window on her side of the car, clutching her purse. Her dress was dirty and there was an oil smudge on her cheek. I watched her chest rise as she drew a deep breath. My eyes tracked to the nape of her neck and I recalled the taste of her skin. Not even swastikas have the power to shut down human nature. I chuckled at myself.

Sara turned to me. "I don't see anything funny. Lunatics wrecked the shoot. And you. You promised you were going home."

"And here I thought I was the white knight."

"You better take me back. I'll be missed. Kerrl and Hugenberg will be frantic. I'll be answering questions forever. And just what were you doing there?"

"Hoping for a chance to ask you some questions."

"Did you know that was going to happen?"

"No. If I had, I would have warned you."

"Michael, I . . . You need to get me back."

She wasn't letting anything slip. So who was she? This time I would ask my questions.

"About ten days ago a tall, thin guy picked you up behind Hugenberg's place. What was that all about?"

"You followed me?"

"Yes."

She drew away and her hand went for the door latch. She scanned the parking lot, the picnic area, and the woods.

"Let's take a walk," she said.

"Whatever you . . ."

Before I finished my sentence, she was out the door, walking into the woods. There was no path. She worked through the forest until she came to a fallen tree. Turning to me, she sat on the trunk as if burdened with a great load. I noticed her tears. And then I saw the gun. She held it in both hands and was pointing it at my chest. Her purse was on the ground between her feet. She may have been on the brink of collapse but the gun's barrel held steady.

"Who are you, Michael?"

"Just what I told you. Zukor's errand boy, come to bring you home."

"Errand boys don't snoop around back doors."

"Look, I was a maudlin jerk when I got to Berlin. But then something happened. I started to take an interest in life. That something was mostly you. But you're mixed up with the Nazis. I want to know who *you* are. I can't believe you're one of them."

Silence. The gun began to tremble.

"Do they have something on you? Or your dad?"

"My dad? What about him? Why ask about him?"

"I read he was mixed up with a German woman. Maybe he's a Nazi."

"Hardly. Who told you that? That he was mixed up with a German woman."

"It was in a report Zukor gave me."

"And you think the Nazis are bad."

"You can't be a believer - in the Nazis, I mean."

I could hear myself begging. She must have heard it too. She lowered the gun.

"Oh yes I can. They trust me. I've sat around at three in the morning listening to them talk about the future. I believe them. Oh, yes, I do. It won't be nice."

She spoke so softly her words were almost lost in a breeze that rippled through the leaves above. Her head dipped toward the ground. She may have been looking at the gun, her purse, the ground, or nothing.

"Why not get out?" I asked.

"I can't."

"What do they have on you? Not just some contract with Ufa."

"No, not just some contract."

"I want to understand."

"When someone helps you . . . well, you want to pay them back. But when someone dies for you . . . everything changes."

She fell silent. It was almost as if she'd spoken to herself, trying to understand.

"What happened?"

She drew a deep breath as if she was about to take a risk.

"Part of it has to do with Mala," Sara began.

"When it started she was no more than a child in a woman's body. She was a gypsy, beautiful and dark. Big round eyes like almonds. A dancer in a nomad troop. Mala dancing the Kolo. She was the main attraction. The dancers in the chorus clapped and chanted ever faster while the four principal dancers vied to keep pace and still maintain the pattern of the dance. Their arms and legs flew until they were a blur. It was a contest. Who would dance the other three to submission?

"It was always Mala. She danced until even the chorus gave up. She always wore a simple white dress with only panties underneath. When it was over, her dress clung to her body, drenched with sweat. No one who ever saw her forgot her.

"In the fall of thirty-one, Goebbels came to Munich on party business. Mala was the talk of the town. When Goebbels heard about the Kolo, he wanted the gypsies run off and the elders arrested - but not until he got a look at the girl who had everyone talking. He was hooked like everyone else. Well, not exactly like everyone else. Others went home and dreamed. Goebbels went to the elders and gave them a choice. He took the girl with their blessing, and they went free. Or he took the girl without their blessing, and they would be arrested. The elders didn't take long to hand Mala over.

"Within days Goebbels set her up in a house in Treptow, just outside of Berlin. She was his mistress until Magda Goebbels got fed up. Magda knew Goebbels was a philanderer but a gypsy was too much. When Goebbels started to appear in public with Mala, Magda went to Hitler. He put a stop to it.

"Goebbels was insulted by the implication that he been consorting with a mere Gypsy. He gave her up but was determined to make her a star. Mala could act but the camera hated her.

The casting people wanted to make her a character actor. For Goebbels it was star or nothing, so he lost interest. She wound up working in wardrobe."

Sara stopped. She looked on the verge of tears.

"What happened?"

"I showed up," said Sara. "Mala was assigned to me as a kind of valet. We became friends. Then I screwed up. I'd written my mother a letter. In it I spoke candidly about the Nazis. I left the letter with the regular outgoing post. A few hours later Mala returned the letter to me. It had been confiscated by the Gestapo. Mala found a way to steal it back before the Gestapo could open it.

"That was the last time I saw Mala. She disappeared. Her disappearance was tied to stealing the letter."

"How could you know that?" I asked.

"I badgered everyone who might have known anything. There were hints that a letter was involved. Goebbels finally told me that Mala had gone back to her troop. But the Nazis don't forgive."

The story had poured from Sara as if previously trapped for want of an audience or the courage to speak. Now she had run out of steam. We were wrapped in the muted sounds of the forest. There were no more tears. She moved the gun from hand to hand, as if it were a frightening but remarkable talisman.

"It wasn't your fault," was the best I could think to say.

"Don't patronize me."

"Then humor me. Why are you staying?"

Sara bowed her head as if beaten down by the weight of events. She didn't speak.

"Do you think Mala is alive? That you can save her?"

"No," she said without looking up. "Goebbels lied. Before she disappeared Mala told me she could never go back to her family. The shame of having been with Goebbels was too much."

Sara had been slumped on the trunk like a puppet whose strings had been clipped. Now she straightened, throwing back her shoulders and raising her chin. Defiance replaced weariness as if she had tapped some deep reserve of energy or anger. She had the look of a dazed fighter, pumped up for the final round by the fear of losing.

"You won't pull it off, whatever you have in mind," I said.

She shrugged her shoulders as if she didn't care.

"Even if you do, you won't get out alive."

"I didn't think about that part until you came along."

"You don't owe Mala anything. And you're not going to save the world."

"You're better than that, Michael."

"No I'm not."

"Well, you once were."

"What's wrong with us getting out of here. You're one girl. These people intend to chew up Europe. This isn't the movies where the good guys always win."

"Michael, enough. You've made your point."

Her face softened. She gave me a half-hearted smile and stood.

"I need to get back. I really do."

During the ride back to city, Sara refused to discuss her plans although her bravado was gone. When I pressed her to go home, she shook her head. She didn't want to talk. She wanted time to think.

I recognized she hadn't answered my question about the tall man. I let it go. Just as bad, I didn't ask why she was making *Horst Wessel* for Goebbels. After all, starring in a propaganda film wasn't exactly payback for making Mala disappear. As we drove in silence, it seemed to me that the Mala story raised more questions than it answered.

I'd let Sara skate - again. That's what happens when you start to care and stop thinking straight.

Chapter Fifteen

I dropped Sara at UFA. She warned me to stay away. I would only get in the way, only complicate things. She didn't say what those things were. She said she wasn't going to do anything stupid. As she walked away, she told me not to worry. No doubt that's what the cops told Lindbergh the night his son was kidnapped.

I figured Sara was out for vengeance. Inevitably that's a fool's play. Even if she succeeded, the satisfaction would likely sour and come at too big a price.

And here I was, needing her laugh, the silkiness of her skin, and even her contrariness.

I thought about calling Diels and leveling with him. "Rudy, we have a problem. I'm falling for a girl who has a grudge against your pals for bumping off her gypsy friend. She's about to do something stupid. If that happens, you'll re-educate her or worse. Everyone loses. Here's the solution - toss her out of Germany. No one gets hurt."

Yeah. And Satchel Paige and Josh Gibson are going to the majors next year. Diels would probably order my arrest for slandering "Sonja" and then order Sara's arrest at the first sign of trouble. What a coup: he saves the day and takes Goebbels down a notch by exposing his starlet. Diels wasn't the answer.

I wanted a drink but settled for some of Fix's seltzer water with a dash of grenadine. Fix winked at me and my sissy drink. He suggested I might want to try the Pink Slip, a notorious bar on the Ku'damm.

"That's all I need. An evening with Rohm, Hess, and the rest of Hitler's sweethearts trolling for Aryan queers."

Fix glanced around the bar which was crowded with mid-afternoon drinkers.

"That kind of talk can get a man re-educated," he said, moving away as if I had the plague.

I turned to the stack of Nazi newspapers I'd picked up at Max's. Maybe I would find something that would convince Sara that it was time to get out. I wasn't sure what that would be. She already knew more than Zukor ever would.

The papers were full of standard themes: Hitler toiling for the people; Germany's neighbors grinding on the Fatherland for reparations; the need for racial purity; the sanctity of the German family; the push for larger families; the plans for a new Berlin; Jewish atrocities; Communist conspiracies; and the flowering of Nazi realism in culture.

Buried on page ten of the *People's Observer* was an article about Erwin Boehm. He was described as a tall, angular man in his fifties who was at the center of a Jew conspiracy. The conspirators were behind the publication of the seditious *Ku'damm Conscience*. Boehm had approached Sonja Potter hoping to enlist the American's help. He wanted her to retract her statement that she had been with Minister Goebbels at the time of Paula Glaise's death. Boehm's comrades had killed Glaise with the idea of pinning the murder on Goebbels. But Potter spoiled their plan. She would not be swayed from the truth. Instead she reported Boehm to the authorities. Now that the Gestapo had a name and face, it was only a matter of time before the culprits behind the *Ku'damm Conscience* would be brought to justice.

The tall man's words came back to me - the ones spoken in a dark hallway with death hovering near. Something about finding Sara and not trusting her.

An article on the same page of the *Observer* reported the Gestapo had arrested Martin Pfaff at an ink wholesaler's warehouse. Pfaff, who had no connection with any recognized newspaper, had been trying to buy printer's ink. He was a misguided former Catholic priest who broken with the church after it refused to condemn the Nazis. Unfortunately the old man died of a heart attack during his interrogation.

Was Pfaff the Martin from the bakery? If he was, I'd been wrong about his loss. It was more complicated than an appropriated business or a missing relative. He had turned on his church after a lifetime of dedication. Had he lost his faith too? I didn't think much of his faith, but understood how shattering the loss would be.

A separate article reported that Sonja Potter was to be awarded the Brotherhood Cross, the Reich's highest honor for a non-citizen. Hitler would present the award two weeks hence at a ceremony in Berchtesgaden.

Sara must have realized she was dead to Zukor the second she accepted the Brotherhood Cross. What was her game? Or was I the one being played playing for a sucker?

"These new laws are appalling," Cooper said to the Tavern's round table.

"I think they will be helpful."

The speaker was a fat man who was slopping down spaghetti like a pig at the trough. I don't remember his name but he was from the *Baltimore Sun*. Like many reporters, he was so jaded that only good news surprised him. He turned from Cooper and looked at Diels.

"Rudy, see if you agree with this. The average German doesn't have the sensitivity of the party's racial aficionados and could unknowingly develop a friendship with a Jew. After all, many Jews seem to be good Germans. How is one to know? Wearing the star of David will alert people to the danger. And the naming law is a stroke of genius. Mandatory Jewish-sounding names with identification papers to match. Every male an Israel. Every female an Esther. Very practical. A boon to understanding your neighbors and avoiding confusion. Germany is to be congratulated."

Diels squeezed a smile between his scars. It was uncomfortable to look at him and impossible to discern what his smile was all about. He spoke evenly in reply.

"My fight is with the communists. I take no credit for these racial laws. But I remind you. Your Huey Long is more a socialist than our Doctor Ley. Your Father Coughlin and the Ku Klux Klan are greater advocates of racial purity than our Doctor Rosenberg. And President Roosevelt tried to pack your Supreme Court so he could write any law he wanted. If the United States suffers run-away inflation and the American communists begin to exert power, you will have laws like these in no time. And you will be searching for your own Hitler."

The *Sun* man replied through a mouthful of spaghetti. Diels watched him with poorly concealed disgust.

"Ley, the Reich drunk, runs the German Labor Front but has crushed every union. Some socialist. Rosenberg, the Reich philosopher, is also the Reich bore. His *Myth of the Twentieth Century* is so pedantic and nonsensical it puts even Nazis to sleep."

"I think you've made my point," Diels said evenly.

The *Sun* man continued, ignoring Diels. "I tried to read the monstrosity hoping to understand the German hard-on for the Jews. Got through the first fifty pages or so. Utter horse-shit gussied up with arcane terminology and high-tone rhetoric. It couldn't be . . ."

I tuned out the conversation, daydreaming about how things worked. Sara had become Sonja because the party's new American heroine couldn't have a name that sounded Jewish. There were stories about Jews being aryanized if a party bigwig wanted it to be so. I had a vision of an operating room where Jews received transfusions of Aryan blood, and their features changed as the new blood purified their once corrupt bodies. When the procedure was complete, Hess gave the freshly-minted Aryans new documents as they goose-stepped into the Third Reich.

Hermann Goering's arrival interrupted my musings. What was the second most powerful man in Germany doing at our table? For starters he was affecting affability.

"Rudy tells me you're honest-to-God reporters and the perfect antidote for the bootlickers Goebbels has on the payroll. Now why do you think Roosevelt wants to bring Germany back into the fold of nations? I think it's the girlfriend he has tucked away in Georgetown. Mistresses are a civilizing influence. Now if we could only find Hitler a woman."

Goering winked and flashed a smile. Laughter all around. His pupils were dilated and sweat bubbled from his jowls. The stories of his drug addiction looked to be true.

Quite a gathering: a scar-face killer, a flying-ace drug addict, and eight reporters who ran the gamut from dandy to slob. Not a conscience in the bunch. The conversation swirled, full of lewd jokes, sarcasm, masked hatreds, naked prejudices, lies, innuendo, false flattery, and concealed threats.

The Cubs best hitter, Gabby Hartnett, came to mind. Now there was a name: Gabby. Baseball was full of monikers that wouldn't fly on the world stage. No Dizzy could ever be a prime minister. No Babe, a president. No Shoeless Joe, a cabinet minister. No Lefty, a Fuhrer. Perhaps oddball names should be a requirement for high office. Would you follow a Daffy into battle? Would you believe a Greasy who claimed to be from a superior race?

"Michael!" Cooper's whisper was accompanied by an elbow in the ribs.

"Yeah?"

"Whatdaya make of this guy?" he said under his breath.

"A fat fuck who has a table with penises for legs? What do you think?"

"A Falstaff with bombers," said Cooper smiling at his conceit.

"What are you two whispering about?" said Diels, ever the watchdog.

Cooper answered, "Temple here thinks the Reichsmarshall and Zukor - the American movie mogul - are both skillful promoters. Zukor makes stars of people who can't act and the Reichsmarshall has made a Fuhrer of a good actor."

The table fell silent. Comparing Goering to a Jew while making Hitler the butt of a joke was pushing it. Everyone snuck a peek at Goering. Even Diels seemed to hunker down as Goering straightened in his chair and spoke.

"Hitler is no poser and I am no king maker. He is the soul of Germany. The people respond to him as their ancestors responded to the Great Elector. He embodies the passion and leadership they want. Look at their faces when he speaks. They are overwhelmed, consumed, as am I. I have no conscience save his will. But he would have become, is, and will remain the Fuhrer apart from my efforts and despite Herr Temple's poor judgment. Or was it your judgment, Herr Cooper?"

Cooper swallowed, searching for his voice. When he spoke, a wary deference replaced his usual flippancy.

"I heard him on the radio last week. He's very good. But you are too modest, Reichsmarshall. I think Hitler stands on the shoulders of able colleagues, you being the primary one."

Goering relaxed. He raised a hand to cover the smile he permitted himself. With his smooth, pudgy cheeks and delicate lips, the forty-four-year-old sybarite reminded me of an aging ingénue basking in a bit of flattery. It was difficult to believe he had been a fighter ace and had taken a bullet for Hitler during the failed 1923 beer hall putsch. Hitler and Goering had come a long way. Making love to crowds and morphine will do it.

"If he stands on any shoulders, they are the people's," said Goering. "You need to see him in person. Next week he will speak to the people from Berchtesgaden when he awards the Brotherhood Cross to Fraulein Potter. Come with us. There are a few seats on the train for foreign journalists. Herr Cooper, bring Herr Temple. Later he can describe it to Zukor."

The other reporters were green with envy and fell over each other angling for invitations. Goering waived them off but their ass-kissing had him in an expansive mood.

"You are with me," he said, rising from his chair.

Goering swept up all the reporters but Cooper and the *Sun*'s man. He herded them to the door. As he shoved them into the night, he was laughing.

"I'll give you a tour of Carinhall. Then I'll feed one of you to Caesar. She loves reporters. Why just . . ."

The rest was lost as the Tavern door closed behind them.

"What was that all about?" I asked.

Diels answered. There was an edge to his voice.

"He's taken up Hitler's bohemian ways. They'll be up most of the night. Carinhall is his hunting lodge in the country. Caesar is his lioness. It has the roam of the place - inside, mind you. One day she will kill someone."

Diels threw a fistful of marks on the table and walked out.

"What's he pissed about?" I asked Cooper.

The *Sun* man answered, "He either wants his own lion or is not beyond redemption."

Chapter Sixteen

The *Ku'damm Conscience* was back in the streets the next morning, this time reporting that Hitler was part Jewish. Nothing wrong with that provided Hitler was willing to accept the consequences as the *Ku'damm* saw them. He should resign all party and government posts, and take Israel for his given name. Alternatively he should admit the bankruptcy of his racial policies, resign all his posts, and confess his villainy for promoting hateful laws.

As they did with the Raubal story, the *Ku'damm* teased its readers with promises of evidence.

"Behind his back, the little Fuhrers call Hitler a carpet glutton," said Cooper

"Meaning what?" I asked.

We were at the Heron Club on Karl Strasse. Cooper said it was Nazi hangout. He wanted to see if the believers were in the streets hunting the defamers, or lunching on bratwurst while ogling the girls.

The food was so-so and the strippers were down to their underwear in no time. The place was laid out to insure privacy. The tables were arranged in a five-tiered semicircle around the stage. Each table was sheltered by a pair of wings that opened to the stage but offered privacy from the rest of the room. The lighting was focused on the stage. With all the cigarette smoke, the dancer in the spotlight was a murky silhouette from where we sat. For all we could see, the room might have been full of

Nazis or nearly empty.

"When things don't go his way, Hitler flies into rages. Real nut-house stuff. Sometimes it ends with him rolling on the floor and chewing the carpet. Literally, chewing the carpet."

"That can't . . . "

"Buy a girl a drink. Share a dessert?" interrupted a tall, buxom girl who appeared at our table.

She was dressed in a school girl's pleated dress, a white blouse, and peach-colored cardigan. The horn-rims perched on her nose were a nice touch. She looked familiar but there hadn't been any girls like her at Grant High in Skokie. If there had been, I might have skipped the war.

Without being asked, she sat down as a waiter appeared.

"I'll have a Himmler," she said to the waiter.

"Sure, Helli," he replied.

Before Cooper could close his mouth, the waiter was off to get a Himmler.

"We have nicknames for the drinks," said the girl. "A Himmler doesn't look like much but has a nasty kick. Call me Helli."

She had been speaking German. I responded in kind.

"Aren't you worried that we're Nazis?"

"I know the Nazis who come here. Besides I listened from around the wing. You were speaking English. Nazis don't speak English to each other."

"I thought German girls were supposed to be married, making little Nazis."

"I'd like to marry a big shot or save enough money to reach New York. I'd rather do Broadway, but a Nazi big shot is better than becoming a Rekrutenmachen, then a Gebarmaschinen at some Lebensborn home with an SS Zeugungshelfer. So I take my chances here at the Heron Club."

"A creating recruit? Then a childbearing machine at a life spring camp with an SS procreation helper? Did I get that right?" Cooper asked in English.

"On the money," I answered.

Cooper smelled a story and turned to the girl with an

academic lust that I had to admire. Not many men could have prioritized their appetites as quickly. Unfortunately for Cooper, her knowledge of life spring camps didn't go far. As she was being processed in, an SS officer decided her assets would be wasted as breeding stock. She could contribute more as a hostess at the Heron Club.

"So here we all are," she concluded. "And just where is my Himmler?

Nazi breeding camps! Cooper was salivating with curiosity and pressed for details.

But Helli shrugged, "I've heard the words but can only imagine what happens."

Just then her Himmler arrived. She raised her glass and said, "To procreation, wherever you find it."

Cooper didn't appreciate the toast. Helli noticed his umbrage, and switched gears.

"What about that *Ku'damm Conscience*? The stories can't be true, can they?" she prodded.

True to his instincts, Cooper gave up nothing.

"Who do you think is behind it?" she pressed.

Cooper shrugged. I followed his lead.

She changed subjects, and asked if we knew any submarine routes out of Germany. She explained there might come a time when she needed one.

Cooper said he had heard stories, but nothing more.

She tried a couple other topics and then gave up in the face of Cooper's reticence.

It wasn't until she walked off that I recognized her. She had been on Bennhof's arm the night Sara and I went to Hacker's. Helli got around. Maybe she had the savvy to make New York or catch a local sugar-daddy. More likely she would wind up waiting tables for shavings in some Ku'damm dive. Cooper guessed she was Gestapo, and had been pumping us for information while seeing if we would incriminate ourselves.

Then Cooper leaned forward, drawing me in to hear what he had to say. He'd arranged for a meeting with someone from the

Ku'damm Conscience. He gave me the where and when, but not the who and how of it. As it turned out, Cooper had made a big mistake.

Two days later Cooper and I went to the movies at Marmorhaus Universal Cinema. Paramount's flagship theater on Times Square had nothing on this place. Large enough to hold half of Skokie, its walls were covered with a quarry's worth of marble. It was on the Ku'damm, a block west of UFA's Palace Theater.

Leni Riefenstahl's *The Blue Light* was showing to a packed house. Riefenstahl directed and starred, playing Junta, a chaste mountain nymph and keeper of a cave full of magic crystals. The movie was so majestically filmed that Hitler hired her to memorialize the Party's 1934 Nuremberg rally. If Riefenstahl could make a Junta a radiant goddess, she could make Hitler a thundering god. And that's exactly what she did in *Triumph of the Will*.

The Blue Light was so captivating we lost track of time. Suddenly Cooper whispered, "Shit, we're late. Follow me in five minutes."

He hustled up the isle. We had been sitting in the balcony. The meeting was to have started fifteen minutes into the film. The plan was to go separately to attract less attention. I watched the face of my old Gruen tick off the minutes in the glow of the big screen. Then I followed.

The balcony lobby was twenty-five feet deep and a hundred feet wide. The restrooms were at either end. We had been sitting at the opposite end of the balcony from the men's room in which the meeting would take place. Cooper said the walk across the lobby would give us a chance to spot any trench-coats.

I had reached the lobby midpoint when the men's room door sprang open to the stiff-arm of a running man. I got a look at his face as he sprinted toward me. Then he veered left and slammed through a pair of heavy leather doors that led to the balcony. Two men chased him through the doors.

From the balcony came the sounds of a commotion, people yelling and finally a gunshot. Then everyone panicked. The audience spilled into the lobby as if the theater's screen had exploded.

In the melee I caught a glimpse of Cooper who was ashen behind his twitching moustache. I heard his voice, an octave higher than normal, ranting about freedom of the press. Diels, who had him in tow, didn't look impressed.

I started over to them but remembered I was carrying the papers from Maurice's apartment. They were my ticket to a re-education center. I joined the stampede down the staircase to the main lobby where there was mass confusion as twenty-five hundred Berliners jammed the exits.

Once outside I walked up the Ku'damm trying to look unconcerned. A half-dozen people yelled at me. Each time my heart jumped. But they only wanted to know the reason for the commotion. I ignored them and walked on, resisting the urge to run. At Kaiser Allee I turned south and hailed a taxi.

When I told the cabby the Adlon, he scowled at the short hop and small fair. He was even less pleased when I told him to stop at the Arts Academy which was a block short of the Adlon.

I cut down an alley adjoining the Academy, hoping it would lead to the hotel's service entrance. Luck was with me. I managed to sneak into the hotel, make my way to the basement, and hide Maurice's papers. I left the way I'd come, walked around the corner, and then walked in the Adlon's front door.

I expected trouble. The Gestapo didn't disappoint. A pair of trench coats was waiting as I crossed the lobby. They reminded me of Abbott and Costello: one tall and thin, the other short and a little overweight. Costello announced "Gestapo." Abbott, whose fedora was pulled low, asked where I'd been.

"I went to see to see *The Blue Light* at the Marmorhaus. All hell broke loose. Shooting in the balcony. The whole place cleared out."

Abbott pushed his hat back and squinted at me.

"What were you doing there?" he asked.

I asked what he meant. He said he was asking the questions. I agreed. He repeated his question. I asked him if it was a trick question. He asked what the hell was so tricky.

"Well, what would one do at the Marmorhaus?" I asked.

"I'm asking the questions."

"I agree. You are"

"Are what?" Abbott asked.

The real Abbott and Costello did this sort of routine. I was starting to enjoy myself. These guys had me believing the Gestapo wasn't all it was reputed to be.

Costello put an end to the fun. He told me to shut up, grabbed my arm, and steered me from the lobby into an Opal Sterling. The car's back doors locked from the front seat and didn't open from the back.

Abbott drove west under the Brandenburg Gate onto Charlottenburger Chaussee. The road took us through the Tiergarten, Charlottenburg, Spandau, and into the countryside. There the road paralleled a new freeway that hadn't yet opened. I'd never seen anything like its four wide lanes and median strip. I couldn't imagine the traffic that would justify its expense. Abbott slowed the Sterling where the freeway turned into a construction site. Eventually he stopped, parking at the top of a rise. We were surrounded by farmland lush with barley and oats.

A wide, shallow culvert ran between the freeway and Sterling. The car was pointed down the slope, allowing its headlights to illuminate a portion of the culvert.

Costello turned around to face me. "What were you and Cooper doing at the Marmorhaus?"

"Cooper the reporter?"

"Don't play the idiot."

"Look, I don't know if Cooper was there and, if he was, what he was doing. Me, I was watching the movie until all hell broke loose."

"If that is your answer, hell is going to break loose around here, and you're the one who will be burned."

When I didn't respond, he shrugged, opened the door, and stepped into the night. Abbott switched off the engine and lights, and joined Costello. They locked the car doors behind them.

We waited. They smoked in the starlight, cigarette butts piling up at their feet. They talked and then fell silent. After a while the starlight was lost to an approaching storm and their faces could only be seen in the glow of burning ash. I was drowsy but sleep was miles away in a bed which I might never reach. Eventually the rain washed Abbott and Costello back into the car. They dozed off. In the lightening I could see puddles forming at the bottom of the slope.

I was trying to figure out how long it took for boredom to kill, when a Mercedes 770G4 pulled up. It was the kind of car favored by military brass. With the top down, they could display themselves so the hoi polloi could see who counted.

I ran a hand through the condensation that covered the window to my left. I found myself looking at a man in the back seat of the Mercedes. The darkness and rivulets of rainwater coursing down the windows obscured my view. But he wore a Panama and seemed to have a moustache.

Abbott and Costello got out. Before they closed the doors, I heard Diels speak, ". . . some night. Get him out and . . ."

The man was pulled from the 770G4 and led down the incline by the two uniformed SS men who had arrived with Diels. Then Costello pulled me from the Sterling. I stood at the top of the incline between Abbott and Costello. At the bottom of the hill, the man was forced to the ground, his knees splashing in a puddle. His panama caught the headlights of the Mercedes. Diels spoke to me.

"Cooper mistakenly thinks I will not kill a reporter. So he won't tell me about your meeting at the Marmorhaus. It is up to you to save your friend."

"Like I told these two, I don't know anything."

"Tell me about *the Ku'damm Conscience.*"

"I've seen it. I've read it. That's all I know about it."

"I don't accept that from a man who knows about carpet gluttons."

A second passed before I caught the reference. Cooper must have given Diels the runaround, feeding him all the harmless nonsense he could.

"So I've been to the Heron Club. That doesn't mean I know anything about the *Ku'damm Conscience*."

"I'm pleased you remember your lunch. Do you remember Cooper asking you to bring the papers you took from Maurice's apartment so they could see the goods."

After Helli left our table, Cooper had said something like that when he told me about the meeting at the Marmorhaus. How did Diels know? Not Cooper. If he had admitted that much, he would have told the whole story and would not be kneeling in the mud. Helli must have lingered near our table, listening. But that seemed wrong. We'd spoken quietly. The music from the stage would have drowned out our voices.

"If Cooper told you that, what do you need me for?"

"Cooper is stubborn. He told us nothing. The man is a fool. It is up to you to save him."

I was certain that both Cooper and I were dead. The calm that filled me was surprising. Maybe Diels could persuade me I was wrong.

"I can't save him. You have to kill him. If he walks up that hill, he'll report his own story. You've boxed yourself in. You have to make Cooper disappear. And if he goes so do I. So why tell you anything? If you want information, you better convince me that Cooper and I are walking out of here."

"You are right about Cooper. He's the kind of reporter for whom the story means everything. So he must die."

Diels looked down the slope and shouted, "Kill him!"

My calm vanished. I'd wanted Diels to tell me I'd been wrong, that we would live.

One of Cooper's guards looked up the hill, cupped a hand behind his ear and yelled, "What?"

"Wait," I said.

"No. You were right, Temple. Cooper has been dead for the last hour or so. In his arrogance he did not realize it."

Diels turned and shouted through the rain, "Shoot him!"

They did.

The Panama flew off as Cooper fell in the mud face first. His hat finished floating in a near-by puddle. I thought I saw Cooper move. Was he struggling for breath as he bled to death?

"He's moving. Help him," I cried.

But Diels had turned back to the car. "Come, Temple. Let's get out of the rain."

I started down the slope toward Cooper but was stopped by a shot that rang out behind me. I swear I heard the bullet whistle past my head.

"If I wanted to kill you I would have just done it. Now get in. We need to talk."

Diels held open the Sterling's back, passenger-side door. I was shaking with a combination of fear, anger, and outrage. I had to do something.

"Don't be a damn fool," said Diels. "Think of it as living to fight another day."

He was mocking me. Ridicule or not, he had a point. And the instinct for life is powerful. I got in the car. Diels closed the door, went around the car, called something down to the men with Cooper's body, and then joined me in the back seat. He offered me a cigarette.

"You're neither a fool nor a fanatic. You want Potter; and I can deliver her. But I can't just let the two of you go. You would tell your story to the first reporter you found. I cannot have that. And I want your information on the *Ku'damm Conscience*. So here is my proposal. I will film you telling what you know and transfer fifty thousand American dollars to an account in your name at a bank of your choice. I get my information and enough leverage to keep you quiet. Should you decide to talk you will be exposed as a collaborator who sold out for cash."

"How do I know you can deliver Potter?"

"I have enough to destroy her in either Germany or the United

States. She will do as I say."

"What? What do you have on her?"

"You don't need to know that."

"How would we work this exchange? Assuming I'm interested and assuming I even know anything."

"I can arrange for the money tomorrow. I know your bank. It can cable a confirmation to the American Express office in Berlin. Then you will tell me everything, including the location of Maurice's papers. Then I'll deliver Potter and let you both go. The two of you will be booked on the next available liner leaving Hamburg."

"Where do we do this exchange?"

"At the Friedrichstrasse Station if you want. Naturally I will have you watched on the train. If the papers are not found where you say, you both will be pulled from the train and returned to Berlin. Do you understand? Do we have a deal?"

I understood. It took me a while to agree.

I knew Diels was lying. I would be killed as soon as I gave him what he wanted. But for now, it was either make a deal, or join Cooper in the mud. I told myself I was buying time.

Chapter Seventeen

The general thought you would like some food," said the toady.
He placed a tray on a table near the fireplace and left, locking the door behind him. A few minutes later, he was back carrying a pile of boxes.

"The general ordered new clothes for you. After you eat, you may want to refresh yourself."

He nodded toward the bath.

"Be ready by one o'clock."

Murder and intimidation to graciousness in the flick of a switch. Diels had explained it this way. We were partners of a sort. The least he could do was put me up for a night and treat me right. I wasn't buying that. People like me were lucky to get a steel cot in Columbia Haus. So why the special treatment? Was Diels playing a game that I didn't understand? Or maybe he was just schizo.

At two that afternoon, I was sitting at a desk in a small office. A map of the German rail system hung on the wall behind me. On the desk were train tickets to Hamburg and confirmations that Sara and I were booked on the *Europa* to New York. A half hour earlier I'd received a telegram from the Continental Bank in Chicago confirming that fifty thousand dollars had been deposited in my account. That was a king's ransom in 1934. For a moment I had the sensation of being rich.

I'd seen Sara in the lobby of the station. We hadn't been permitted to speak. Her face had been an expressionless mask.

Concealing what? I hadn't a clue.

A camera zeroed in on my face. I began to perspire. It wasn't the klieg light.

Off camera Diels spoke into a microphone: "Michael Temple is at the Friedrichstrasse Station as a friend of Germany to provide information concerning a Jew conspiracy that centers around a slanderous publication known as the *Ku'damm Conscience*. Herr Temple has agreed to cooperate for a payment of fifty thousand dollars. Isn't that right, Herr Temple?"

The moment of betrayal had arrived. Rationalizing was easy. It wasn't my fight. In the end the Nazis would roll up the opposition regardless of what I did. Why get killed? Live to fight another day. Who was I saving? What did I really know? Not much. A few suspicions. A baker named Ludi who might lead them to Hanussen who in turn might lead them to the *Ku'damm Conscience*.

I would like to believe I refused to talk because certain things are just wrong. But the truth is I didn't believe Diels. The tickets and the fifty grand were window dressing. He would kill me either way. So why give in? Still, I had to find an option.

"Turn off the camera," I said.

Diels nodded at Costello who shut it off.

"We have come too far for cold feet," said Diels. "I have put the equivalent of five million Reichsmarks in your account. There is no reversing course. Turn on the camera, Gerd. We will continue."

So Costello's name was Gerd.

"Gerd, don't turn it on yet. Look, Diels, I know you're up to something. Otherwise, I would have been in Columbia Haus last night, not a nice apartment. Let's be real partners. Give me the chance to earn the money. We need to talk. We may not be so different."

"Do not mistake courtesy for weakness. We either conclude our arrangement or you die in this room. I will squelch the *Ku'damm*

Conscience with or without your help. The only difference is whether you live or die. Make your choice. I've wasted enough time."

"How do you know I haven't told others you're playing a game with a private agenda? You can't . . ."

"Gerd, on my signal, kill him."

Gerd pulled a revolver from his shoulder holster.

"Last chance, Temple," warned Diels.

I wasn't going to die sitting on my ass. I didn't have a good plan but I had a target. Costello was still behind the camera. I dove across the desk at the camera, hoping to send it crashing into Costello. If enough hell broke loose . . .

I never made it. Something knocked me cold.

I awoke to find Costello pointing the revolver at my chest. No one spoke. I was on my back. I worked myself up on my elbows. Diels broke the silence.

"We don't shoot people who are unconscious. Do you really want to die today?"

I looked past Gerd to Diels. "You will lose in the end," I said.

"Not for a thousand years. That is what Hitler says. Last chance."

"Fuck you."

I think I heard the gun go off. My chest exploded and the floor crashed into the back of my head. Then there was nothing.

When I came around, I checked the scenery. From what I could tell heaven was a disappointment or hell wasn't bad. Then again, my vision was bleary and my surroundings were in motion. Probably purgatory was my last thought before fading back into darkness.

Consciousness came and went accompanied by a headache and a throbbing pain in my chest. I dreamed that Diels and Gerd were questioning me. They stabbed me in the arm with a syringe.

I drifted but never beyond the reach of their voices. A sense of wellbeing enveloped me. I wanted to continue floating in my tranquil cocoon. But gremlins pecked at the edge of the cocoon. Diels' scars opened and smiled at me. Once a gun barrel came at me, its nozzle expanding until it swallowed me in darkness. I wanted to answer the questions but couldn't hear them over the roar of what seemed like the engines of a tri-motor.

Eventually the images faded and the nightmare ended.

When I came around for good, the headache was gone but my chest felt like hell. I was back in Diels' guest bedroom. I struggled from the bed and stood before a full length mirror that hung between matching dressers. I opened my pajama top and found an ugly welt in the middle of my chest. It was the size of an orange. The bedroom door opened. In the mirror I watched the reflection of Diels crossing the room.

"Only a bruise. Some schnapps will kill the pain," he said, holding up a decanter and two crystal snifters.

He took a chair. "Please. Join me."

He poured and offered me a glass.

"Am I supposed to say thanks?"

"Why didn't you cooperate? What were you willing to die for?"

"That stunt was a game? A sick test?"

"We are past the time for games. Drink. The schnapps will calm you."

"I'm off booze."

"Well then, Germany has done you some good."

"How about some water? And coffee too?"

"Of course." Diels looked to the door and called for Gerd.

The door popped open and in stepped the man who shot me. Diels told him bring ice water and coffee. Gerd nodded and closed the door.

"How come I'm not dead?"

"A soft rubber slug. It knocked you over. You hit your head and that knocked you out."

"You're lucky I didn't have a heart attack."

"I should think you're the lucky one."

Diels smiled as if the whole episode had gone well.

"If I'd given you what you wanted, would you have let us go, Sara and me?"

"Unfortunately I never had Potter to give you. She is in Goebbels' sphere of influence. But I would have let you go. Potter was there to encourage you to leave. Would you have gone without her?"

"I thought you had something on her?"

"This is no ordinary schnapps. A gift from Goering, a man of exquisite taste and the means to indulge it. Sure you won't join me?"

Diels rolled the liqueur in his glass and then sipped.

"Told you, I'm off booze."

"The charade at the station was intended to extract information. It didn't work. Why not? Why were you willing to die?"

"It never occurred to you that I didn't have anything to give?"

"Please. I told you, we are past games."

Diels rose from his chair and went over to a cabinet. He unfastened a false bottom and pulled out a hidden drawer. In it was a tape recorder. I'd never seen one before.

"A voice recorder, very handy," said Diels. "Let me play you something."

He pressed a button and the reels spun. He played the last part of my conversation with Cooper at the Heron club.

"Remember the swastika ornament in the center of the table?" Diels asked.

"No."

"Well, that's where the microphone was hidden. The Telefunken engineers aimed it into the booth. More important is the tape. The scientists at Farben are like proud fathers. The reproduction quality is remarkable, yes."

"So you spy on your own people?"

"I gather information that may be useful to Germany. Now you know something that only a handful of people in Germany know. And Hitler isn't one of them."

That was a provocative remark and an invitation to ask why Hitler was out of the loop. Humphrey claimed asking the invited question was usually a waste of time.

So I asked, "How can you be sure Hitler doesn't know?"

Diels smiled, more to himself than at me. He hadn't considered the possibility.

"Hitler is a demanding man. He would love the tapes for their prurient content alone. If he knew the system existed and wasn't getting the tapes, he would demand them. If he already had the tapes, he would gossip about them. I would know either way."

Diels had been thinking out loud as much as speaking to me. Now he refocused.

"I shared this with you as a sign of trust. Why? Because I want you to share with me what you were willing die for."

"Your interest is touching."

"My interest is my own safety, Germany's future, and what you may be able to do for both. And you should be interested in what I can do for you. Now once again, why?"

There was a knock on the door.

"Yes!" Diels barked, impatient with the interruption.

It was the toady with water and coffee. Diels dismissed him and poured me a cup while I guzzled a glass of water.

He returned to his schnapps, sipping like a fastidious old lady. Again he asked, "Why."

"I figured you would kill me either way. It didn't matter whether I said anything or nothing. If I was dead regardless, I wasn't about to help a Nazi."

"But you are still alive."

"So you're good at holding your options open. You couldn't scare it out of me. What's next torture?"

"Oh, please."

"Too messy? You'd spoil all this nice stuff that you probably stole from some rich Jew."

"Hitler's treatment of Jews? Is that what offends you?"

"You think it's okay?"

"Were you willing to die for that?"

"That's only one reason you guys are such assholes."

"I'm afraid that is so. Hitler has helped the Fatherland, but he has gone too far. It will only get worse. Hitler demands absolute fidelity. Devotion sufficient to follow him into war. His dream of glory will destroy us. Do not smile, American. He has most of us in the palm of his hand. We will follow. Germany will be powerful and he will be unyielding. Our industries can make more than voice recorders. The next war will be worse than the last. The democracies will burn with us. Are you willing to die to stop Hitler?"

"I'm supposed to believe you're a man of peace?"

"No. You need only believe that I am a man who does not want his country destroyed. Do you want yours in another war?"

The schnapps in his glass was vibrating, betraying what? Anger? Fear? Determination?

"You're conning me again because you think torture won't work."

"Torture sometimes works. As does sodium pentathol which produces a chemical trance not unlike the state your friend Hanussen claims he can induce with his mind. In such a trance people lose their power to resist. It is difficult to use, however. Too little, no trance. Too much, the subject passes out or dies. In that, it is similar to torture."

"I've heard about truth serum. It . . . Son of a bitch, you've already tried it on me, haven't you?"

"I wondered if you would remember."

"And I thought I was dreaming. Look whatever you're selling, I'm not buying. If you want to stop Hitler, kill him yourself."

"I might. But it would be better if he were discredited or died by his own hand. That's why the chauffeur's papers are important. Did you read them?"

He'd listened to the recording from the Heron Club. There was no point in bluffing.

"Yes."

"What's in them?"

Diels was hyper-animated, like a kid asking to open a Christmas present early.

"Why does Hitler have to be discredited?"

"If he's not and he's killed, Goebbels will make him a martyr. *Mien Kampf* will become the next book of the Bible. His legacy will require blood and land. The outcome will be the same - war. But what if he is proven to be a Jew, his niece's murderer, or a pervert? The public will turn on him. He will crumble. For all his bluster, Hitler has no core. Only hatred and dreams of Aryan glory. Force him into a corner and he will choose death. He would have killed himself after the beer hall putsch if the gun hadn't been pulled from his hand. And if he doesn't do it this time, I'll make it look like he had."

"And you become the next Fuhrer?"

"No. What are the sources of power? The party, if it can be kept unified; the army; the German people; and the industrialists. I am of no consequence in the party. As for the last three, they give me no credit for my work against the communists but full credit for the Gestapo's unpleasant methods."

"Poor Diels, so misunderstood."

"A man who responds to honesty with sarcasm forfeits the right to trust."

He glared at me, his anger barely contained. Had I hit the mark? Or was he only frustrated by my reluctance to join his professed crusade to save the world from Hitler? I glared back. I have no stomach for platitudes. Especially when the messenger is a hypocrite.

"The man who runs the Gestapo has a lot of power," I said.

"I do. But Himmler is after my job. In the turmoil after Hitler's suicide, everything will be up for grabs. But your instincts are right. If the Gestapo remains in my hands, I can influence events when the struggle begins."

"And you have the recordings."

"They will be helpful. But I've never recorded Hitler. That's why I need what you have. To start the process."

"And when the process is over who is the next Fuhrer?"

"The one man acceptable to every power center, including mine. The one man for whom there will be no tapes. Goering."

Now it was my turn to smile.

"I thought this was about saving the world from Hitler. Instead it's a power grab by Goering?"

"Goering is loyal to Hitler. He knows nothing of this. If he did, he would have my head. But when Hitler is gone, he won't permit Germany to fall into the hands of Rohm, Goebbels, Streicher, or any of the truly vile creatures in Hitler's coterie."

"If Goering is such a believer in Hitler, won't he take Germany down the same road – the one to blood and land?"

"Hermann will follow Hitler anywhere but he won't lead Germany down that road. Three reasons. First, he won't overrule the army which wants no part of Hitler's plans. Second, Hermann is too comfortable to risk what he has for the messianic vision of a dead man. Third, he will need Strasser's support and Gregor is more of a socialist than an expansionist nationalist."

"What will you do with Maurice's papers?"

Diels hesitated. The man who would make a new king didn't have the details worked out.

"It depends what they contain. That will determine how I use them."

"You can't just show Hitler the papers. He'd destroy them and you. You've got to go public. But the newspapers are controlled by Goebbels, so you can't go to them. So how do you tip Hitler over the edge? You need a voice and don't have one."

"I'll find a way."

"Why didn't you let Cooper and me have our meeting with Cooper's contact at the *Ku'damm Conscience*? Hitler would have been exposed in *Conscience* and the *Trib*."

Diels shrugged as if he might have made a mistake.

"Too late now," I said. "Cooper's dead and you fucked up."

As I spoke Cooper's name, a taste of guilt washed through my mouth like a whore's kiss. What was I doing plotting with Cooper's killer? Expediency made strange bedfellows but there had to be limits.

Diels seemed to have read my mind. "Don't worry, I didn't kill him."

"He survived? Where is he?"

"At his desk, I imagine. Killing or permanently detaining an American journalist is more than I can afford right now. I released him as soon as I had you. I bought a Panama hat for the little charade on the road. A communist agitator was shot in the rain that night. With his moustache and the Panama, you were fooled."

"You killed a man for a charade?"

"He was going to die in any case. You needn't feel guilty."

"I didn't have me in mind."

"The only thing we need to feel guilty about is not stopping Hitler."

Chapter Eighteen

Diels kept me locked in his guest bedroom with Gerd as my keeper. I figured Diels was taking a last shot at finding Maurice's papers and the *Ku'damm Conscience* on his own.

Gerd gave me some reading material from home: month-old issues of *Colliers*, *Time*, and the *Saturday Evening Post*. America had its head in the sand. Shirley Temple, Clark Gable, and Huey Long were big news. Chrysler's Airflow with its overdrive transmission and Ritz Crackers were each making a splash.

German rearmament barely rated a mention. Cooper might have thought Hitler was the big story but the state-side editors didn't seem to agree. Hitler and his crew were back page material. The only major story about German politics claimed Hitler had tempered his outlook since coming to power. It didn't look that way in Germany. Maybe the book burning would rate some headline coverage.

A few days later we took a ride. Gerd, who was in the back seat with me, said nothing. Neither did his pal, Abbot, who was driving. Eventually we arrived at a large, two-story hunting lodge located deep in the countryside.

Diels greeted me at the front door. It opened into a great hall. At the far end was a fireplace the size of a small cottage. It was surrounded by clusters of couches and chairs. The balance of the room was dominated by a heavy, rough-hewn, walnut table that could accommodate thirty or more. The walls were covered with tapestries and paintings that belonged in an art museum, and game trophies that belonged in a natural history museum. They hung between timbers that soared to an apex fifty feet above a flagstone floor strewn with Indian hunting carpets.

"Welcome to Carinhall," said Diels "Goering named it after his first wife, if you're curious. He is a sentimental man. Follow me. We're using Hermann's study,"

As he led the way to a double-door off the right side of the main hall, I looked for Caesar. Maybe the crack of jackboots on the stone floor had scared the lion off.

The study was fairly spartan. To the left of the doors, three campaign chairs faced a matching desk and credenza. A picture of Hitler hung over the credenza. To the right, five wooden chairs surrounded a small conference table where Diels and I sat, joining Cooper and another man. The far wall was a bank of windows that opened on a lawn that sloped to a snake fence beyond which rose a tree line. A gate in the fence opened to a wide walkway that cut through the trees to a lake about two hundred yards off. To either side of the study's double-doors hung photographs from Goering's flying days. On the wall across from Goering's desk was the room's major indulgence: an oil painting of a beautiful woman. She sat on a love seat, her arms flung across its back. Her head was turned slightly to the right but her eyes were cast to the left as if sneaking a look at someone interesting.

The lady in the picture had my attention. I had the odd feeling that she was looking at me.

"Sara does look a little like her," said Cooper who was seated across from me.

There was a resemblance.

Diels spoke, "Carin. They say the painting does not do her justice. Some say Goebbels brought Fraulein Potter into our midst just to torment Hermann. But he never saw the resemblance. Another of Goebbels' failed machinations. A philanderer is incapable of understanding a love that defies comparison."

"Goering is hardly Byron, and waxing nonsense is crap. Let's get to business," said the fourth man at the table.

I hadn't recognized him at first. It was Ludi, dressed in a

business suit. He was not introduced but it soon became apparent that he represented the *Ku'damm Conscience.*

"Then to the matter at hand," said Diels. "Temple can supply us with Maurice's papers. Shall we see if we can cooperate long enough to stop a disaster?"

With Carin watching, Diels outlined his plan and then asked if we had any questions.

"What about Sara and me?" I asked.

"You will be free to go. Once it's over, she'll be relieved to see you with tickets to America."

I wasn't so sure.

Ludi kept glancing at the study's doors as if he expected a firing squad to crash the party. He was holding his cards tight. He wasn't saying who was behind the paper, where its presses were hidden, or how it handled circulation. But he guaranteed the stories would be printed and distributed in Berlin. He would also deliver ten thousand of each edition to other major cities for Diels to further distribute.

If Ludi was skittish, I was worried. After all, Diels needed Ludi.

"How do I know you will let Sara and me leave? Once I turn over Maurice's papers, you won't need me anymore."

"Cooper is your first insurance policy. He wouldn't want anything to happen to you. Our friend from the *Ku'damm* is your second policy. He doesn't care if you live or die. But, if I break my word to you, I will lose his trust and I need him. And as Cooper is fond of saying, I can't mess with the American press. So, if you don't trust me, trust I have reasons to behave."

He tried a reassuring smile. Not an easy thing for a scar-faced prick.

Cooper nodded at me, "It's more than a scoop. It's a chance to make history."

He wanted to be part of the story – like Cromwell and Hanna had been.

Later back in Berlin with Gerd watching, I pulled Maurice's

papers from their hiding place in the Adlon basement. Back at Diels's apartment Gerd typed a copy with two carbons. I proof read the copy. It was make-work. In effect I was under house arrest.

Diels kept Maurice's papers and the original copy. The two carbons went to Cooper. He would pass one to Ludi. Diels also gave Cooper duplicate sets documents establishing Hitler's Jewish heritage, one for the *Trib*, the other for the *Ku'damm Conscience.*

It would be a double-barreled blast that would damage Hitler just as he was about to pin a medal on Sara. On the morning his train was scheduled to leave for Berchtesgaden, the *Ku'damm* would hit the streets across Germany. It would tell the real story of Geli Raubal's death as described in Maurice's papers. The following morning the *Ku'damm* would deliver the proof of Hitler's Jewish ancestry. Meanwhile, the *Trib* would independently report the stories.

Hitler would have to face the people of Berchtesgaden as a Jew and a murderer while the rest of Germany digested the news. Although the communist party had been banned and its activities suppressed, the commies were still around, simmering, waiting for a spark. The same could be said of others who opposed the Nazis. The two editions of the Ku'damm would provide the spark. Ordinary Germans would take to the streets and demonstrate their anger at having been duped by the little corporal. That was the theory.

Between the embarrassment and the protests, the hope was Hitler would take his own life. If he didn't, Diels would act, making it seem like Hitler had.

Diels even wrote a suicide letter for Hitler. It was long a rambling affair. An angry denial of the slanders aimed at him. A page of ranting about Jewish money and duplicity. A paragraph condemning the German people for their thanklessness. An affirmation of Aryan superiority and the need for racial purity. A final blast at the Versailles Treaty. Near the end Goering was anointed his successor. The typing was replete with the mistakes an amateur might make under pressure. The letter was signed "A.

Hitler" It was so strange that Hitler might have actually written it.

Diels also prepared a short note to be used if events played out in a manner that would not have allowed Hitler the time to type the longer piece.

I was locked in Diels's guest bedroom, anxious about how events would play out for Sara and me. Then to my surprise Dials showed up with a press pass for Hitler's train. I was going to the show as *Variety*'s reporter.

"Remember Goering invited you," Diels explained. "Besides having you along will make it easier when the time comes for you and Potter to leave. Himmler and his men will be watching, so be careful. Remember, you don't know me or any of my men. Stick with Cooper. If all goes well, within seventy-two hours, Hitler will be dead, Goering will be in charge, and you will be on a train for Hamburg. If it doesn't go well, God help us all."

"You don't sound real confident," I said, wondering if I was the designated patsy, the guy who would take the fall if the plan went south.

Diels thrust out his chin.

"The plan is good, and the objective is honorable. The train is scheduled to depart at eleven-thirty, but probably will not. The Fuhrer is not a morning person and his train runs on Hitler-time. But we can control our own actions. So be on time."

Chapter Nineteen

The locomotive was a Siemens 2-8-2 festooned with swastika running flags. I walked the length of the platform to admire the engine. It was doing better than its crew. The engineer and three firemen were lined up next to the cab. An SS man was reading them the riot act. The work-hardened railroaders stood with their heads bowed, absorbing abuse from a marionette whose authority stemmed from his uniform and the moral bankruptcy it took to wear it. Their browbeating struck me as more ominous than my ass-kicking. It's one thing to mess with a stranger. It's another to abuse your own.

I turned away to see Cooper arriving. "Hellofa a train, but not the only one. The SS will have a security train running a quarter mile ahead. They don't believe love conquers all."

"Did you talk Diels into letting me come along?"

"No, you already had Goering's invitation. And Diels thought it was a good idea all on his own."

"Any thoughts on Sara?" The idea that she might be a Nazi still haunted me.

"She's just looking to push her career."

"More likely she'll wreck it."

"She hasn't thought it through. The view from the studio isn't what we see in the street. I know you're soft on her, so don't get pissed. She's a not-too-smart blonde playing a dangerous game. But that doesn't make her a Nazi."

"You've underestimated her. Does she know what we're up to?"

"I doubt it."

Variety was my cover but I would be stringing for Cooper.

The foreign reporters were sharing a car with the Nazi press and a couple dozen hand-picked guests. Since I spoke German well, Cooper wanted me to nose around and see what the guests thought about the "doings".

"The doings?" I asked.

"The upcoming show at Berchtesgaden and this morning's edition of the *Ku'damm Conscience*."

"How'd it look?"

"Ludi laid it on thick. Hitler has trouble getting it up. Something to do with watching his father beat his mother. To the extent he has a sex life, it's abuse that gets him off."

"That wasn't exactly in Maurice's papers."

"Reading between the lines it was. The story says Geli initially put up with the weirdness because Hitler looked like he was going places. She had nothing, so she hitched her star to his. Except he wouldn't marry her. Still, he's madly possessive. Her hormones are going crazy but Hitler can't get it up. He's away from Munich more and more often. So Geli starts sneaking out to the cafes where she meets what most girls want: a dreamy guy full of romance.

"When Hitler finds out, Romeo disappears and he really clamps down. Eventually Geli accuses him of having Romeo killed. She threatens to spill the beans unless Hitler cuts her some slack and marries her. Well, slack and marriage aren't what you get when you threaten Hitler. He threatens to send her to a convent. She laughs in his face and says that would be better than being his mistress. Turns out the only thing worse than threatening Hitler is laughing at him. Hitler starts to beat her and is proud as punch - pun intended - when he gets a hard-on. He figures Geli will love the development since that's what she wanted all along. The sick son-of-a-bitch apparently thinks he's found the way to her heart. But she greets the development by laughing at it and making a tawdry comparison with Romeo. He literally and figuratively deflates with the ego pricking.

"Hitler's humiliated and worried that Geli will go public with the shameful details. He gives her another beating as a warning of what will happen if she talks.

"That evening Maurice drives Hitler to Nuremberg. Hitler's depressed and worried. Maurice gives him a *buck-up-and-win-one-for-the-Fatherland* pep talk. When they get to Nuremberg Hitler, says Geli must commit suicide for the good of Germany. Maurice is to return to Munich and help her do the deed. And so Hitler is in Nuremberg with an alibi when Maurice pulls the trigger a hundred miles away in Munich. All's well that ends well."

"Did the *Ku'damm* say how Maurice loved her too? His papers say he killed her only because he loved Hitler more. When I read that, I didn't know whether to be sick or feel sorry for the guy."

"Maybe Ludi's saving that bit for another installment. I think today's version is better. The idea is to make a bastard of Hitler, not a pitiful stooge of Maurice."

The platform was beginning to fill. Not many people were smiling. Some looked bewildered. The few who arrived in a festive mood quickly sobered without necessarily understanding what was wrong. This was Germany. If you weren't sure about the wind, assume trouble was brewing.

"Looks like most people have seen our little story," said Cooper.

"I'm surprised they would show up."

"Not sure they had a choice. Let's go. Remember you're a reporter. Get me some juicy stuff – crowd reaction. That kind of thing."

Cooper led the way to the second car behind the coal tender. An SS guard blocked the steps. We queued up. No one boarded without being searched and having their papers checked. Trust was running low in the Third Reich.

An hour later and forty minutes behind schedule, the train chugged south from the station. Hitler had been late. Cooper said he always ran early or late. It was a precaution intended to keep his enemies guessing.

Our car was shared by a dozen reporters and thirty or so civilian dignitaries. Everyone seemed nervous. It's not every day you set off for a celebration where the master of ceremonies has been accused of romancing his niece and then orchestrating her death.

I changed seats twice trying to elicit a newsworthy comment from a German dignitary.

A sleepy-eyed Gauleiter from Hanover complained that he didn't have a seat in the car reserved for party notables. He had never heard of the *Ku'damm Conscience*. When I told him about the Raubal story, he grumbled something about "ass-sucking kikes." He leaned back and within a minute was snoring.

An elderly couple from Dahlem was less sanguine. They were patrons of the opera and friends of Hitler's benefactor, Helene Bechstein, the wife of the piano manufacturer. The old lady was ready to give anyone an earful.

"Helene thought he was a German Messiah. Called him her Wolf. Tried to teach him some manners. Humph! And we're invited to lend our respectability to another show. Oh, Helene. His ideas were always too radical. Politics, peugh! Why I told Helene . . . ."

The lady's diatribe was cut short by an SS Untersturmfuhrer, meaning "subordinate-storm-leader," the equivalent of a first lieutenant in our army. He was calling for the *Variety* reporter to report.

I stood and identified myself.

"The Fuhrer wants to see you," said the lieutenant.

I looked around and found Cooper's eye.

He smiled and called, "You'd better share your interview notes, you lucky stiff."

Feeling more stiff than lucky, I followed the lieutenant out. On the platform between cars, the air rushed around us, a refreshing blast after the coach's tobacco-laden atmosphere. The lieutenant told me to keep moving. I glanced up and saw the engine's black smoke swirling in the shaft of sky visible between the cars. I followed the lieutenant through a dining car where a white-coated waiter was setting tables for a late lunch.

Some bigwigs were lounging in the next car. I recognized a

few. Hess looked like a slightly confused Neanderthal under brooding eyebrows. Rosenberg looked like a dapper but slow-witted businessman. Bormann came across as a competent organizer. Goering, dressed in a three-piece suit, could have been a self-indulgent art dealer. The short, pudgy, myopic, and balding Himmler seemed to be held upright by his uniform. At his side was Heydrich, his number-two. Heydrich was a generation younger than his boss; and, unlike most of Hitler's crew, he was decidedly in the Aryan mold. Streicher was the only scary looking guy in the bunch. He radiated arrogance and pugnacity. He was short and sported a shaved head. Something like hate oozed from his sunken eyes. His thin lips were fixed in a permanent sneer as if nothing could meet his standards. A little Hitler-styled moustache provided the only relief to his forbidding presence.

I was handed off to Heydrich who led me into Hitler's private car. We were met by Hitler's body guard, Ulrich Graf, who was drinking coffee in a small, private dining room. After Graf searched me, Heydrich spoke.

"You are about to meet the Fuhrer. He is with Sonja Potter and Putzi Hanfstaengl. Hanfstaengl studied at your Harvard and is now the Reich's foreign press secretary. He believes the Fuhrer can better understand the United States by meeting Americans. The Fuhrer selected you because of your affiliation. He watches American films with interest.

"Understand this. The Fuhrer is unaware another edition of the *Ku'damm Conscience* was distributed this morning. Do you know what I am talking about?"

"I haven't seen it. But there was talk in the train."

"Inexcusable for it to be even mentioned. You are not to say anything about that vile publication. Understood?"

"Yes."

"Finally no smoking in the Fuhrer's presence. We will go in now."

We walked past Hitler's bedroom and bath into a lounge that took up the back third of the car. Wraparound windows provided a panoramic view of the receding countryside. Hanfstaengl was humming a scherzo and his hands bounced in the air as if he were directing an orchestra. Sara and Hitler watched. Hitler seemed delighted. The sight of the six-five, horse-faced Putzi humming to the accompaniment of his bobbing paws seemed ridiculous at first. But the man had a touch of magic and could carry a tune. Heydrich was immune to his charm.

As soon as Putzi finished, Heydrich stepped forward, clicked his heels, bowed at the waist, and said, "Mien Fuhrer."

The words conveyed servitude and homage.

We were introduced. Hitler sat rigidly in an easy chair. On the table to his right was a plate of pastries. His famous lock of black hair and tiny moustache struck me as clownish. The whites of his eyes and his teeth were yellowed. His suit was badly tailored although its deep blue fabric was top drawer. His reputedly hypnotic eyes were a filmy, pale blue. They inspired nothing in me.

Hitler came off as an odd looking nonentity who at the moment seemed ill at ease.

Putzi stepped into the breach. "The Fuhrer is a Gary Cooper fan. Tell us about *Farewell to Arms*."

Luckily I'd read the back issues of *Variety*, the ones Zukor gave me. One of them had a review of the movie. I embellished it with tidbits gleaned from Zukor's other reading materials.

When I finished, Putzi asked if I thought the U.S. would go to war again. He said some of his Harvard buddies thought it would if Germany attacked France or England.

Hitler put down the éclair from which he'd been sucking whipped cream.

"Putzi, enough! The United States won't entangle itself again. It is on the brink of revolution. For now Roosevelt keeps the dogs at bay with make-work projects. But if he even hints at a European adventure, the unemployed will sweep him from power. He will be begging me for help."

Without missing a beat, Hitler switched gears, relaxed, and kept talking. His voice was conversational but his eyes wandered as if scanning a large audience. Eventually he asked what I thought of *Lives of the Bengal Lancers.* The question was rhetorical.

"Gary Cooper was excellent," he said. "A fine example of an Aryan in action. There is much in the film to admire: bravery and sacrifice for example. Sometimes at night I watch it while the others sleep. Ruthlessness is more difficult to find in film. There is some of it in *I Cover the Waterfront.* The fisherman who pushes the Chinaman overboard understands its value. The quality is unappreciated. Remember when Cooper says to Tone . . ."

For a while it was fascinating. Hitler's memory was phenomenal. Not just for the names of movies, actors, and characters, but also for passages of dialogue. He played all the parts and was more than a passing mimic. He could do Cooper's shy smile and laconic delivery. But there was an edge to everything. Even when he was joking.

"You know what a Cooper is? A Cooper is the fewest words necessary to speak an elegant thought. And what surrounds me? A Goebbels is the amount of nonsense a man can speak in an hour. A Goering is the amount of badges that can be pinned on a man's chest."

Hitler chuckled. "But they are loyal. As I am to Germany. Those who serve must be loyal to me. I once had an Alsatian. They are a fine breed . . ."

He was off again, this time telling a loyal-dog story. It was ten minutes of sentimental drivel spoken with real emotion. His performance was beyond strange.

A look of attention was plastered on Sara's face. Putzi and Heydrich displayed a vacant civility born of experience.

Hitler was oblivious. His monologue switched to a variation on the theme of loyalty. Dietrich verses Riefenstahl. Treason verses commitment. We were trapped in a torrent of lofty ideas and banal personal experiences. Even good ideas sounded odd coming from Hitler. He appeared ready to talk forever when he turned his eyes on me.

"Your comments on *Farewell to Arms* were excellent. I shall order it played tonight. Hugenberg says Cooper will never marry

Clara Bow - thinks she is a has-been. Will he?"

When he stopped talking I was caught short for a second. I recovered with an opinion stolen from *Variety*. The IT girl would indeed land Cooper. Opposites attract, bla, bla, bla.

Hitler cut me off. "Yes, yes. Very good. There is nothing nicer than an ample top and a round bottom."

He immediately gave Sara a shy smile as if he'd forgotten her presence. He apologized with old-world formality for the indelicacy of his remark. Then he turned to me, anger edging into the corners of his eyes.

"Are Putzi's university friends correct?"

"I'm sorry. About what?"

"The U.S. involving itself in another European war."

About forty minutes had passed since Putzi's comment. For Hitler it might have been a few seconds. Time flies to the sound of your own voice.

" I'm not sure," I said. "But the depression has people worn down. I don't think anyone wants part of someone else's fight."

"Exactly as I thought!"

He hopped out of his chair and sprang to my side. He actually clapped me on the back.

"Putzi, I have found a reporter I like. He knows film. He knows his country. Why I believe . . ."

"Mien Fuhrer, I apologize." Graf stood at the entrance to the lounge. "A radio cable from Herr Goebbels. Your eyes only."

"Goebbels is so dramatic," said Hitler. "Let me see it."

He held out his hand. Graf walked over and gave him the envelope. A wax swastika sealed the flap. Hitler sat down in his easy chair, took a bite of his éclair, and nonchalantly opened the envelope.

He went white reading the message. He came out of the chair enraged, the veins at his temples bulging.

"Everyone out!"

His left arm slashed horizontally through the air. "Get Goering and Hess! I order it!"

Chapter Twenty

Five hours later the reporters checked into a small hotel in Berchtesgaden. Cooper and I shared a room with a mountain view. Topping out under seven thousand feet, the peaks in the area didn't compare with the Rockies and weren't particularly rugged until the last thousand feet where the pines stopped and an outcrop of rock jutted skyward.

Fifteen hundred feet above our window, a large villa sat in an Alpine meadow carved from pine trees. This was Hitler's Berghof. A hundred yards above it and behind a line of pines was Hitler's private town of Obersalzberg. On a natural shelf in the mountainside, trees had been cleared for a post office, garage, drivers' quarters, SS barracks, servants' dormitory, parade grounds, a playhouse for kids, and a hotel called the "Platterhof."

Hitler encouraged his guests to bring their children. He enjoyed kids in small doses, almost as much as he enjoyed his dogs. In the meadow down from the Berghof, Goering and Bormann were building houses.

"Have you been up there?" I asked.

"No. But Diels described it one night at the Tavern. Hitler does pretty well for a selfless public servant."

"Will Sara be at the Platterhof?"

"Either there or in one of the Berghof's guest rooms."

Just then someone knocked at our door. Himmler's men? We fell silent as if that might cause the visitor to vanish. Through the door hissed a voice that seemed familiar.

"Open up. I know you're in there."

Cooper peered through the peephole.

"An old man with a blond beard." said Cooper. "Can't be the Gestapo. They don't have beards and don't knock."

Cooper opened the door. The man's clothing hung loosely. His beard was bushy. But the extra hair and weight loss didn't change his eyes or disguise his theatrical bearing. Facing us, he breathed deeply and swayed like a tree in the wind. He looked a little puzzled and nodded at me.

"My vision is confused. Hitler dead, yes. A suicide? Perhaps. A resurrection? Goering survives but doesn't succeed. You are betrayed. I am lying in pine needles and after that I see nothing. I knew in Vienna we would play parts. That's why I allowed you to see with me that day - so you would believe when belief was important. Now the time has come and I cannot see clearly. But if I could, all would be foreordained. Nothing is certain. Watch for betrayal."

Cooper gave me a *this-guy-is-certifiable* look.

"Hanussen, how did you find us?" I said.

He laughed.

"Nothing clairvoyant. Ludi told me. He couldn't keep me away. Viktoria drove me down in Walter's Maybach. He's fled Germany. Viktoria wouldn't leave. She's a Lutheran now. And I'm her client. She's explained to the authorities that Walter was responsible for that story the *Gazette* published. I'm to be rehabilitated. Now I must go. Remember what I've said."

"Wait. I'm Richard Cooper. A friend of Ludi. I'm with the *Chicago Tribune*. Please. Give me a half hour. The world needs to know."

Hanussen flashed a wry smile. "I think the second biggest newspaper in a city located in America's corn belt is not a world voice."

Cooper bristled. "A cogent, if inaccurate, analysis for a man who was rambling incoherently a minute ago."

"The times are incoherent. After the war everything was clear. I could sense feelings and understand causes and consequences. Now it is different. But ask your questions. Just don't publish until after my death. It will be soon enough."

"Your death?"

"You must promise."

"All right," said Hanussen nodding. "You have my word."

"So ask."

"The Press Ball prediction about a girl losing her heart - was the girl Paula Glaise?"

"A question I have asked myself. If Glaise was not the girl, the coincidence was extraordinary."

"Hanussen, don't play with me."

"The girl in my vision had no name. She was young and blond with dreams of fame."

"Okay, so who killed this nameless blonde?" Cooper spoke with the urgency of a believer although it was unlikely he believed anything but his own reporting.

"There are too many faces around the body."

"You don't know, do you? What a fraud. You and your agent scripted the whole thing for the publicity and Prinz skipped town when things got ugly. The two of you miscalculated."

Cooper was baiting Hanussen.

"Jan, what was going on at the Press Ball?" I asked. "You looked scared to death but I can't believe that Prinz would have put you up to anything so risky."

"I once told you people don't want the future I see. I cannot see the killer's face. I only see a pin. A Gauleiter's pin."

That grabbed my attention.

"What did the pin look like?"

"Fancy. A Garland. A flying eagle."

Hanussen was moving to the door, concerned about something.

"Jan, who should I worry about? You warned me about betrayal."

"Only those you trust can betray you. I must go. It is best that we are not seen together."

"I have more questions."

"And so it will always be. Farewell."

There was a troubling finality to his words. Hanussen had been standing tall in the middle of the room like an old testament prophet. Now he turned up his collar, slumped, and aged before our eyes. He tottered from the room.

Cooper was disdainful.

"He's a hellofa showman but he's not using me for publicity. 'Only the trusted can betray.' Spooky horse-shit. Dollar to a donut, he's getting ready to take his act to the States. When did I start looking like a chump?"

"He was right about the pin. There was one like that on the floor near Glaise's body. No way he could know that unless he was there. or can actually see shit."

"So add him to the suspect list."

Before I could respond, there was another knock at the door.

Cooper returned to the peephole.

"Well, speak of the devil," said Cooper, opening the door.

Diels was standing there, shaking his head.

"It's a wonder the baths don't kill these old codgers who come for the cure," said Diels. "Just passed one in the hall who made Goebbels look healthy."

Diels pointed at me and said, "Let's go, you've been invited to stay at the Platterhof."

My room was on the third floor. It offered a view across the Salzach Valley to the Austrian peaks beyond. I cranked open a casement window and drank in the cool air. The sun was sinking behind the hotel, casting long shadows across the valley floor and painting the far highlands amber. Birds were singing in the pines growing on the slope that fell from the far side of the road that skirted Obersalzberg.

Great scenery can go to your head. I imagined Sara by my side, my arm over her shoulder, her head resting on my shoulder. The two of us admiring the view.

My daydream was cut short by a 770G4 that roared by on the road below my window.

I had driven up with Diels in just such a staff car. Outside Berchtesgaden we passed through the entrance gate guarding the private road to Obersalzberg. There were twenty or so people milling around the gate on the chance Hitler might pass by. It was his custom to stop, shake some hands and have photos taken with admirers. The pictures were circulated to newspapers across the Reich.

The dash to Obersalzberg had been a taste of power. The car devoured the incline effortlessly. Luxuriating on cushy leather seats with three feet of leg room, I imagined the cheering crowd and Hitler's disdain for it. I was thinking how power could go to a man's head, when Diels leaned over and spoke.

According to Diels, Hitler was eating carpet over the Raubal story. He was grumbling about betrayal and the perfidy of the German people. He was already threatening to take his life. That would show the thankless rabble.

Diels eventually got around to me.

"Hitler likes when people tell him what he already thinks. He loved it when you told him the Americans would not involve themselves in another German war."

"Wrong answer?" I said.

"Yes. Don't encourage him. If asked, say Roosevelt would oppose German expansion and that his recent overtures were intended to keep Germany in its place. I want the pressure on."

"I would hate to lose a friend."

"We should be so fortunate. Be dressed and ready to go by nine. If you're wanted, someone will come get you. Hitler is usually up half the night so be ready for a call as late as two. Or no call at all."

"Where's Sara?" I asked as the car pulled up to the hotel.

"She is staying here, at the Platterhof. Right now she's at the parade grounds making a newsreel. American girl reviews the troops the night before the big ceremony. Thrilling for all. That sort of thing. She's scheduled for dinner at the Berghof at nine-thirty."

On my dresser was a new VE. The Third Reich would never get around to making VWs because manufacturing the people's car would slow the production of airplanes and armor. But the people's radio was a winner. It was inexpensive and could deliver propaganda to every living room.

By one o'clock I was going stir crazy. Classical music was all over the dial but with Jewish composers banned, the repertoire was thin. The joke was: "How long must we listen to *The Flying Dutchman*?" The answer: until he lands but the airport is closed for party business."

Light opera was big. There was some watered-down swing that sounded like the musicians were refugees from a string quartet playing glockenspiels and flugelhorns. In the States we could hang on the escapades of the Lone Ranger, the Green Hornet, and Jack Armstrong. The Germans were stuck with the Gebuhrs, a family trying to make babies and increase productivity. Could Dad turn out a thousand rivets a day and one more for Mom at night?

I needed some air. A burly doorman warned me not to wander far. I walked down Obersalzberg's central road toward the parade grounds. In the moonlight, I could see the small stand from which Sara must have reviewed the troops. *Moonlight, the troops, my baby, and me.* I'd send the notion to Gershwin. It felt right for the times.

Not many people were around. The few who were seemed to be in a hurry. I wandered into the garage that was on the far side of the parade grounds. Its enclosed repair shop was closed for the night. But in the open carport, I could admire the cars which had been primed and polished for the next day. And suddenly there it was: Hitler's own Mercedes, cherry red, its top down waiting for a parade. Behind its headlights, Fuhrer flags hung limp from poles attached to the engine cowling.

I got in and sat in the front seat where Hitler always rode. The seat and floor were raised six inches, elevated to lend the Fuhrer stature. I could smell saddle soap on the leather. A pouch was designed into the door. A storage pocket for the Fuhrer's convenience. I reached in, looking for a souvenir. He didn't seem like the autograph type, so this would have to do. The touch of steel was chilling. I pulled out two guns. They were covered by a light veneer of dust, as if they'd been in the pouch for a long time. I returned one and wedged the barrel of the other - a Walther - between my back and belt, under my suit coat. It was an impulsive act that immediately felt wrong. I got out of the car but didn't walk off. The guilty burden under my belt held me near the car. I might have put the gun back but just then someone asked what I was doing.

I turned to see Hitler watching me.

I surprised myself at how easily the true lie came. "I like cars and was admiring yours."

He moved to where he could better see me and began to run his hand over the car's fender like another man might have caressed a lover's thigh.

"A Mercedes-Benz seven-twenty KW one-fifty, type two. Four hundred horsepower, eight cylinders, fuel injected. The cylinder dimensions are . . ."

Hitler was a relentless bore with an encyclopedic grasp of facts. He wasn't showing off. He assumed that I would be fascinated by his recitation that ran from the thickness of the car's armor plating to a critique of British artillery. The common thread was the progress of German industry and the stagnation of England's counterpart. If I had given a damn, I might have learned something.

I almost missed the change of subject.

". . . but material advantages will not be decisive. Willpower will be the difference in the coming struggle. I am two men, an artist and a leader. I would prefer to be an architect. Even now Speer and I are planning the new Berlin. But the war, the Jews, and the Weimar Republicans have forced the leader in me to the fore. Still, my intuitive side remains central. My will and my intuition are Germany's future. My intuition tells me the Americans are weak. Otherwise, they would not vote for a man as mild as Roosevelt."

The flood of words stopped so suddenly that I missed his implicit question.

"Well, Herr Temple?" He struck a pose: one hand on his

hip, the other cocked at my face like a snake primed to strike. "Weakness breeds weakness, does it not?"

"He's a rich guy. It took guts for him to implement his social programs. I don't actually know him but I think Roosevelt is a fighter."

Hitler cut me off. "Exactly. You don't know. Only the weak don't know. Roosevelt would never think about rebuilding Washington. I have great plans for . . ."

He was off on another riff, painting verbal pictures of his new Berlin. He liked long halls and massive columns. They engendered "the essence of magnificent proportion" - whatever the hell that was. He was going to build the widest boulevard, the biggest stadium, the largest dome, and so on. Once again I almost missed the shift.

". . . Ufa. They send actresses to me. Even Magda Goebbels wants to marry me off. They had the effrontery to send me Paula Glaise. A bitch in heat. A leader cannot afford self-indulgence. But the weaker sex has its attraction. You for example have seduced this actress, Potter?"

"I don't know what to say."

"I sense these things. It comes from being around Goebbels. Sometimes he's no better than a dog in heat. You reacted like that to Potter in my railcar. Don't worry. She is a fine woman. If I were not the Fuhrer. Ha! I'll wager Hugenberg has naked pictures of her. You know these actresses - no morals. I've heard the stories."

"Naked pictures? What . . ."

Hitler didn't exactly cut me off. It was more like he was oblivious to my presence.

"Women! I am attacked over the one creature I cared for. If they only knew. Next it will be Glaise. It is the Jews of course. They continue their poisoning even as they are removed. Vermin are vermin. Today at the Mountain Road gate, I saw doubt on the faces of the people for whom I have sacrificed everything. The Germans can be ingrates. And my men! Where are they? Emile has disappeared and may be a traitor. And the rest cannot find the shits who spread lies in my streets."

He spun from me and gazed through the open walls of the carport to the night sky. He drew a deep breath. Trembling, he crossed his arms as if trying to hold himself in the absence of other human contact. He had actually stopped talking.

His back was an easy target for the gun tucked under my belt. The elimination of evil was mine for the pulling of a trigger. I'd killed before. Each time with regret. Each time I swore never again. Hollow words. For me there were few absolutes. At first it hadn't occurred to me to shoot him. Standing there, his back to me, he seemed more pathetic than evil.

But you could count on him to show his stripes. He too had oaths on the mind. He spoke still staring into the night.

"'I consecrate my life to Hitler. I am ready to sacrifice my life for Hitler. I am ready to die for Hitler, the savior, the Fuhrer.' Those are the words of the Hitler Youth pledge. Yet at the gate today, a boy waved one of those despicable leaflets at me and asked if it were true. An unthinkable question! His pledge to me was forgotten. I should have had him shot on the spot."

His words were ice. If he could kill a child for asking a question, he had no limits. Pulling the gun from my belt, I saw all the angles. If I killed him, I wouldn't get out alive. I would make him a martyr and might cause a war.

He was right. It was a matter of will and I didn't have it. I tucked the gun back under my belt, believing he would have shot me had our roles been reversed.

Hitler turned and faced me. He had the look of a cornered, petty thief who is about to do something stupid.

"I won't be the object of speculation. I won't lead thankless shits. They can return to Europe's dung heap without me. Let them weep at my grave."

Hitler walked away, the strut gone from his step. I'd ceased to exist for him. Would he have the will to do what I couldn't?

Walking back to the Platterhof and later in my room as sleep eluded me, I listened for a gunshot. I heard only the sounds of a summer night.

Chapter Twenty-One

The next day broke to a glorious sunrise. From my room I watched the mountain shadows retreat across the valley. Only a lunatic could blow his brains out on a morning like this. *So there is still hope*, I joked to myself.

At eight-thirty a waiter delivered breakfast and the day's program. Sara was to be awarded her medal at twelve-fifteen during a national radio broadcast - a lunch treat for the German people. No long harangues. Goebbels had scripted a tight line-up. Hess had a minute to open. Goebbels had three minutes. Sara would receive her medal and had a half minute. Goebbels had not only timed her remarks, he had written them. Hitler then had five minutes to close. He always had the last word.

The motorcade left Obersalzberg for Berchtesgaden at eleven-thirty. The normal crowd of believers at the Mountain Road Gate was missing. The next edition of the *Ku'damm Conscience* must have had people ducking for cover in anticipation of Nazi rage.

Berchtesgaden's streets were deserted. Shutters and curtains were drawn. In the town Square, SS troops surrounded a handful of civilians who milled around like trapped dogs. There wasn't a dignitary in sight. Hitler and his entourage mounted a stage built in front of the town hall. They had the look of street fighters who had forgotten their brass knuckles. A technician fiddled with the microphone while Goebbels flitted between Hess and Hitler like a coach pumping up his players. Sara held the text of her speech in nervous fingers.

Goebbels had begun walking Hess to the microphone, when a loose bundle of papers was tossed from a window above the stage.

A sharp-eyed SS Sergeant spotted the movement and fired his machine gun at the window. At the sound of the gunfire, Hitler hit the floor. He glanced up and grabbed a floating *Ku'damm Conscience.* As he read Hitler's face turned red and then white as if he was reading his own obituary.

The SS troops sprang to action. Some rushed Hitler's entourage to the cars that had delivered them not ten minutes before. Those who had corralled the meager audience before the stage now chased them off as if they were bomb-throwing assassins instead of witnesses to cowardice.

The latest *Ku'damm* recounted the unauthorized version of Hitler's ancestry. Hitler claimed his father, Alois, was the son of Johann Hitler. But that wasn't true. His grandmother, Maria Schicklgruber, hadn't married Johann until five years after Alois was born. The *Ku'damm* editors had a photo of the marriage certificate to prove it. The Fuhrer's father was a bastard. So who was grandpa?

When Alois was born, Maria was a cook for the Frankenbergers, a wealthy Jewish family whose randy son, Reuben, was Maria's age. Alois' birth certificate was blank where his father's name should have been written. The editors had a photo of the certificate. They also had an affidavit from the Frankenbergers' chamber maid at the time. She swore the entire household knew that Alois was Reuben's son and that Herr Frankenberger had supported Maria and Alois until he lost his fortune and the family immigrated to France leaving Alois and his mother behind.

If true, the story made Hitler a Jew according to his own racial purity laws. Just call him Israel.

After being rushed off the stage, Heydrich shoved Sara and me into his car where, to my surprise, Hanussen was already seated, clean shaven and looking like the confident entertainer of old. Heydrich seemed pleased about the traveling companions he'd assembled. Just as the motorcade was pulling off, Gerd scrambled in. He rode up front with the driver.

As we reached the edge of town a field telephone buzzed. Gerd reached back and handed the receiver to Heydrich. He listened and then handed the receiver back.

"We're going to the Eagle's Nest. The award ceremony will be broadcast from there this evening," Heydrich announced.

He had an odd, high pitched voice that didn't match his princely bearing. He asked whether we knew each other.

"Of course we do," said Hanussen. "I met Herr Temple on a flight from Vienna, and Fraulein Potter at the Press Ball. Since then Fraulein Potter has become Herr Temple's friend. How are you both?"

Sara and I nodded at Hanussen. He looked delighted as if there was nothing better than sharing a drive in the mountains with old friends. Heydrich seemed disappointed at Hanussen's frankness but held his held his tongue.

"General Heydrich here would like to gain an advantage over Leader Diels," said Hanussen to Sara and me. "Am I right, General?"

Heydrich smiled pleasantly, "Go on, Hanussen. You are always entertaining."

As Heydrich listened, he sat with his legs crossed. His hands rested on his upper thigh. They were the willowy hands of a violinist. In fact he played the instrument well. Although his face gave nothing away, Heydrich seemed content to let Hanussen ramble.

"Diels thinks the three of us are involved with the scoundrels behind the *Ku'damm Conscience* and the General wonders if that could be true. Alas it is not, General. Diels should return to mugging communists. He's proficient at that. Yet his notion may wreck my career. But I'm at your disposal, General, ready to work again. The excitement! The Fuhrer giving a medal to an American whom Diels suspects of complicity. How madly curious. I intend to convince the Gestapo and the General here that I am a friend to National Socialism. After all, who will book an enemy of the people?"

Suddenly Hanussen pointed skyward.

"Look there! A falcon," he said, seemingly elated at his discovery. "Nasty business, theirs. A true predator but no denying their grace in the air.

"Speaking of grace, General, you should tell Diels only Herr Goebbels and his propaganda machine can prove the innocent guilty. And I am a favorite of the Minister."

Heydrich raised an eyebrow and said, "In that you are certainly wrong. But do continue."

"Well then, enough of me." Hanussen shrugged and again looked skyward. "The falcon seems to have his eye on our motorcade. I thought they hunted rodents and feasted on carrion. Their small minds are beyond me.

"Herr Temple, however, is an open book. He thinks we Germans are crazy. He wants to run home to America before Germany explodes. Of course it will do no such thing. But he has fallen in love with Fraulein Potter. He's determined to rescue her from us. American naiveté. He is powerless to help or hurt anyone, except possibly himself."

Hanussen again looked to the sky. "The falcon still circles. Goering is probably taking aim as I speak. Another trophy for Carinhall."

The wisecrack almost brought a smile to Heydrich. But not quite: he was the kind of man who could deny himself.

Hanussen's show played on. "Fraulein Potter's mind is more difficult to read. She is consumed by the Glaise affair. A rival slain. A mutual alibi with Minister Goebbels. And she worries that Temple will be hurt by his love for her.

"And General, you are consumed with finding whoever is behind the little newsletter with the suggestive name. You wonder. Did Goebbels really kill Glaise? Or was her murder a frame-up to bring him down? Could Goebbels be tied to the little paper? A part of some machination to replace the Fuhrer with a leader who would bring the country actual socialism. After all Goebbels was once Strasser's man and his propaganda genius is all over the *Ku'damm*'s program. These are complicated times in which even the innocent are swept up in the tempest."

"Remarkable speculation for an entertainer who wants to work in Germany," said Heydrich. "One can not help but wonder to what end."

"Service," replied Hanussen with a bow of his head.

"We shall see about that once we reach the Eagle's Nest," said Heydrich.

Hanussen didn't miss a beat, "Ah, the new high mountain retreat. Is this your first time up? It is to be the final resting place for the Fuhrer, is it not?"

"I understand the Fuhrer wants to be interned in Berlin, nearer the people," said Heydrich. "He is one of them after all."

"Like Napoleon in Paris," Hanussen said cheerfully.

Heydrich shook his head as if disappointed in having wasted his time with an idiot. He looked at me and said, "Where have you been the last few days? Not at the Adlon."

Diels had anticipated SS curiosity about my absence from the hotel. He had provided me with a story. I repeated it.

Heydrich's index finger began to trace small circles on his thigh. He was disappointed. He hadn't anticipated a pat answer. The bulldog in him wanted to challenge my story but he lacked the information to do it. He turned to Sara.

"Fraulein Potter, were you really with Minister Goebbels the night Fraulein Glaise was murdered? I'd like an honest answer. If the Minister killed her, he is a danger to the party. The party is capable of policing its own. You will be entirely safe. The ceremony will go forward in a couple hours as planned. You may continue to provide the minister with his alibi - even if it is a fabrication. After you have returned to the United States, the Minister can be appropriately reprimanded. It is important that we know the truth. If the Gauleiter killed Glaise, he does not merit your protection."

Heydrich sounded reasonable, even truthful, proving Sara and Hanussen were not the only actors in the car. I'd never believed Sara had been with Goebbels, but sticking with her story seemed safer than abandoning it. Heydrich may have been an up-and-comer but Goebbels had arrived.

Hanussen and I spoke at the same time.

He said: "Tell him the truth, Sara."

I said: "Sara, don't let him twist you around. If you said you were with Goebbels, you were with him."

Sara seemed to be watching the falcon as if it might have the best advice to offer. Then she smiled enigmatically and said, "In Germany is not the official account always the accurate account, General?"

The crack seemed like an admission of deception masquerading as sarcasm.

Heydrich's thin lips parted slightly. He could smile after all. "I see," he said, and left it at that.

The motorcade powered up the mountain. Past the tree line the road sliced through rock and repeatedly switched back on itself. There was no further conversation in the car. The scenery was spectacular but no one seemed interested. Fifteen minutes later the road ended near two huge bronze doors that had been cut into the face of the mountain. They were framed with a princely, man-made, granite portico.

The doors opened to the sound of well-tuned motors. The motorcade pulled into a cave-like, fifteen foot wide hall. Its unpolished, ruby marble walls extended 130 yards into the bowels of the mountain. At the end was a circular room large enough to park four cars. Our caravan was greeted by a squad of SS troops standing at attention. At the far end of the room were two brass doors. As Hitler, Goebbels, Goering, and Hess approached them, they opened to reveal a brass-lined room, about fifteen feet square. Fold-down leather seats were attached to the walls.

A dog and two children came running from the brass room: Hitler's dog and the oldest Goebbels children. Hitler patted the three heads with equal affection. The kids were beautiful, as was Magda Goebbels, who waited in the room. Hitler, his inner circle, the kids and the dog piled in with Magda. As the doors closed,

Magda gave Hitler's hand a sympathetic clasp. She was pregnant. Another mother doing her bit for the Fuhrer.

From behind the doors came the sound of machinery and movement. The brass room was an elevator.

I was in the last group up. The elevator rose smoothly, four hundred feet to the Eagle's Nest. The elevator opened into a gallery formed by pillars hewn from the same ruby marble that lined the passage below, although here the marble was polished. The gallery led to a spacious hallway. On the right it opened to a large dining room with windows that offered a view across and down the mountain face. To the left the hallway opened to a men's smoking room, a lady's lounge, and a study. At its far end, the hallway opened to an expansive semicircular hall. A crescent of large bay windows looked over the top of the world. If you stood in one of the bays and scanned the panorama, you could easily imagine you were floating just below the clouds. Across from the windows was a huge fireplace trimmed in red Italian marble.

A movie camera was aimed at a table and chairs that had been arranged in front of the fireplace. Goebbels limped forward. He was all business.

"Sonia my dear, Paula's killing is still unsolved. The party has enemies who would injure it by implicating me. Ridiculous, of course. I was with you at the time of her death. But one of these days you will go home. Since we are set up to film the presentation of your medal, I thought we would film your recollection of that night. I've prepared a script based on my recollection. Reinhard, step in here. You will question her."

Goebbels pointed at the table. Heydrich balked. Goering, who had been watching with some amusement, said that Hitler approved. Heydrich looked at Himmler who nodded. Heydrich and Sara did a run through of the script. Then, with Goebbels at the camera, the interview was filmed. Goering seemed to enjoy the clumsiness of the whole thing.

The story was this. Sara was unhappy with the *Horst Wessel* script. At the Press Ball, she asked Goebbels for some help with it. Because Goebbels was not a man who enjoyed parties and since his schedule was full the coming week, he suggested that they leave the party and work on the script that night. Where they went, she never said. They worked straight through the night, finishing at seven-thirty in the morning. Sara concluded by saying that one measure of Goebbels' character was how generous he was with his time.

When the filming was over, everyone congratulated each other on a well-done job except for Heydrich and Sara. They looked as if they'd swallowed hemlock. I may have been the only person in the room who didn't know if the alibi was legit. But even I knew the he-goat hadn't spent the night editing a script.

I wasn't permitted to linger and hobnob. Two SS sergeants offered to show me to my bedroom. It wasn't really an offer. I looked at Diels who was chatting with Himmler - just a couple of cops trading stories of crime and punishment, law and order, torture and terror. Diels didn't look my way.

The sergeants led me down a circular staircase that emptied into a hallway that could have been the upper floor of a country inn. They deposited me in a fair-sized room, rustically furnished. It had a small private bath. A picture of the Fuhrer hung over the head of the bed. On the other walls were color photographs of alpine scenes. The sergeants locked me in. The room had no windows and a hint of dampness. It had the feeling of a mausoleum.

My thoughts returned to Sara. I recalled she hadn't invited me into her bungalow the morning after the Press Ball. Instead, she hustled me from her doorstep. Maybe Goebbels had been limping around inside. Then I remembered how Sara wanted Goebbels to pay for the disappearance of Mala. But if that story was true, why would she ever give Goebbels an alibi?

And why did I continue to feel love-sick over a woman who, at best, was flirting with evil; and, at worst, had already sold out? I was thirty-four. Old enough to know beauty wasn't everything, and a few wonderful hours didn't project to a lifetime of happiness. I had been burned before while running down a willful American girl in a European capital. But here I was back in Europe pressing my luck. Why take the risk?

The answer was simple. Surviving isn't living. I was full of life now because of Sara. Driving up the Mountain Road, I was tingling just sitting next to her. And she had looked at me with the trust, affection, and desire that bind two people together - I saw it in her eyes.

Now locked in a basement bedroom at the top of the world I doubted. People see what they want to see. What had I seen in her eyes? Perhaps the car in front of ours had kicked up some dust which darted over the windshield, whipped into the back seat, swirled through Sara's eyelashes, and settled in her eyes the instant before she looked at me. And there, like sand on an oyster's mantle, the dust created an iridescent luster which I mistook for love.

What are the odds, I asked myself.

The odds were I was worrying about the wrong thing.

Chapter Twenty-Two

A buzzing sound woke me. The source didn't immediately register. In a stupor I traced the noise to a telephone on the small desk across from the foot of my bed. Next to it was a pen and ink stand emblazoned with a gold swastika inlaid with mother of pearl. The thing was probably worth more than everything I owned.

"Hello?"

"Temple, wake up!"

"Diels?"

"Yes."

I switched on the desk lamp. The shade had the same striped piping that trimmed the shirts of the SA. My Gruen read three-ten. Since being locked in, my only visitor had been the waiter who delivered a tray of food hours before.

"Did the ceremony come off?" I asked.

"Yes. You must hand it to Hess. Coming here was smart. Hitler loves architecture. The place has him fascinated. The cantilevering of the building and a dozen other engineering tricks have taken his mind off his ancestry. He seems to have weathered our little storm. He is not going to kill himself without some help."

"Should we be . . . talking? On this telephone."

"I control the recorders and the telephone system. The recorder is off now. Himmler is in charge of physical security but I am in charge of intelligence. Himmler is pushing for it all but he doesn't have it yet."

"How's Sara?"

"In danger. Remember she did two films today. And *Horst*

Wessel is near completion. Soon she will be expendable. Perhaps even a liability. She could always claim that she was forced to make the films once she returns to the U.S. And Himmler thinks both of you are mixed up with the *Ku'damm Conscience*. And I agreed with him."

"Why?"

"Because Heydrich disagrees with everything I say, meaning he is off in another direction."

"Where is Sara?"

"Down the hall from you. Locked in. Safe for the night."

"Goebbels won't let anything happen to his star."

As I spoke, I remembered Mala's story.

"Not necessarily," Diels warned. "I could spend an hour telling you why but we don't have the time. Just remember, Goebbels would sacrifice anything for the power his relationship with Hitler brings."

"All the squabbling little Fuhrers. I get it. It's late. What do you want?"

"I want you to kill Hitler."

I laughed.

"Fifteen minutes from now," said Diels.

"You're crazy. Besides I thought you were going to pull the trigger if Hitler wouldn't."

"It has not worked out that way."

"I'm going to kill Hitler so you and Goering can grab power? Forget it."

"If you don't, you and Sara are dead and Hitler will take Europe to war. Besides you want to do it. You almost did it last night."

"What are you talking about?"

"In the garage down from the Platterhof."

"Bullshit."

"Then why did you point a gun at the back of Hitler's head."

"How do you know that?"

"I had you watched. You stole one of Hitler's guns. That's part of why you are perfect. You have his Walther. The very gun with which he would blow his brains out."

"If I was watched, then you know I dumped the gun in some bushes walking back to the hotel."

"Gerd picked it up. It is in your room now, under the mattress. How would it look if the gun was discovered there rather than next to Hitler's body? Remember after you shoot him, wipe your fingerprints off and put the gun in his hand. Do you know how to stage a suicide?"

"I won't do it."

"A call will be recorded ten minutes from now. The tape will prove that Hitler ordered you to his room. He is always up half the night so there will be nothing unusual about a late summons. The order will be referred to Gerd. You must have noticed the guard station at the foot of the stairs, just down from Hitler's door. Gerd and I will finesse your entry to Hitler's room and give you the suicide note. The bedroom is soundproofed. No one will hear a thing."

The idea was outrageous. I should have hung up. Instead I kept talking, "You think hearing a gunshot is the only problem?"

"Take your time arranging the scene. Read the suicide note so you have an idea of Hitler's mood. Gerd will return for you at four. As you pass the guard on your way back, remark that Hitler seemed depressed. Once back in your room, I will call you with the rest of what you need to know."

"What you need to know is that I won't do it."

"Hitler will drag the world into war. You can stop that."

"Stopping wars isn't my job description."

"Nor mine, but the moment is extraordinary. If you do not play your part, I will have your room searched. You will be shot with Hitler's Walther in your hand. Those are your options. Gerd will be at your door in five minutes. He will know what to do either way. I hope we talk later. If we do not, I will leave you with this thought. Sara will die too. Do what I ask, and you will both make it home."

The line went dead.

The gun was under the mattress, loaded. I could probably kill Gerd. Then what? Break down Sara's door, and fight our way off a mountain top? Getting away with killing Hitler seemed more likely.

So Diels would make an assassin of me. It was one thing to kill in battle or self-defense. I'd done the latter. There wasn't much to it in the doing. It happened fast with no time for reflection. If there was a moment of recognition, it was very basic. Who will survive?

According to Diels it was Hitler or me. And perhaps Sara too. But Hitler wasn't trying to kill me. Self-defense didn't apply. Hitler may have been a murderous lunatic, but there wasn't a court in the world that was about to charge him with anything, much less convict him. Then again, taking Hitler at his word, there was little doubt he would eventually bring a shit-storm of death to Europe.

I was going to do it because I didn't have a choice. Lie. I was going to do it to save my skin and because Hitler deserved it.

"What if he's awake?" I asked Gerd five minutes later.

"Or what if Eva Braun is with him? Temple, we succeed or we die tonight. If he's awake, I'll take him and hope the guard does not hear. If she is in there, he will kill her and then himself."

"You expect me to kill his mistress too?"

"If she is in there, you had better. Let's go."

"I'm not going to kill Eva Braun."

"Then you had better hope I can."

"Why are you doing this, Gerd?"

"What difference does it make? Follow me."

With that he was out the door of my room. We were met in the hall by Diels who led the way to the guard station.

"The Fuhrer wants to talk to the American. About movies no doubt." Diels's voice dripped with irritation as he spoke to the guard. "I swear he never sleeps. Let me see the room log."

The guard station was tucked in a closet-sized alcove in the hallway. Diels positioned himself so the guard couldn't see Hitler's door. As Gerd knocked on the doorjamb, I could hear

Diels asking a question about the log. Gerd unlocked and opened the door. He quickly stepped into the room. It was dark. He was back in a second.

"Alone. Sleeping." He mouthed the words silently.

"Mien Fuhrer, You wanted to see Herr Temple?" he said aloud.

"Yes. Yes. I am restless tonight. Herr Temple will tell me about Hollywood. You are dismissed," Gerd responded to himself.

He was a better mimic than Hitler. If the guard was listening, he would remember a note of ennui in the Fuhrer's voice.

Gerd pushed me into the room. The door closed behind me, cutting off the sound from the hallway. No ordinary door. It sealed with vault-like precision.

The silence was eerie. At first there was nothing. Then I heard a faint beating sound. It seemed remote, the vestige of some thunderous power muffled by distance or time. I couldn't pinpoint the source. It was constant as if it surrounded me.

Or was in me. I'd been spooked by my own pulse.

My eyes adjusted to the darkness while I procrastinated to the beat of my life. The pie-shaped room was fairly large and sparsely furnished. It was about a sixth the size of the crescent hall on the floor above. Heavy drapes covered its two bay windows. I drew open a pair of drapes allowing the room to fill with moonlight. The furniture was inexpensive, modest.

On the dresser was a framed, black and white photograph of Eva Braun - a studio shot. Hips cocked at a provocative angle, she was leaning against a cabinet while staring intently at the camera. The whiteness of her satin blouse complimented the highlights in her hair which swept from her face in graceful waves. The photograph made her seem at once glamorous, seductive, and wholesome. A neat trick for she was none of that. A snapshot of Eva was tucked into the frame of the studio shot. In it she posed sitting on a rock before a waterfall. She appeared naked, her knees pulled to her chest.

Hitler's wardrobe stood between the windows, its doors

absently open. It held a blue serge suit, a brown uniform, and five shirts. The cuffs on two white dress shirts were frayed. A desk faced one wall. Its lamp and pen set were identical to those in my room. Twin beds buttressed the opposite wall. One was empty - apparently Eva's. Rumor had it that, when Hitler was done with Eva, or she with him, he dispatched her to the adjoining bedroom.

I'd been burning time, as if something would intervene and take me off the hook. But Hitler was not going to die on his own. It was time to see if I had the will. Putting the handwritten suicide note on the desk was an easy start. I wondered how good the forgery was. It was written on Hitler's personalized stationary. A supply of the paper was stacked next to the desk lamp. The note had doubtless been written with a pen identical to the one on the desk. It was similar to the note that had been passed around at Carinhall. In a scratchy hand it read:

The forces of International Jewry have conspired to embarrass the Party and that for which we stand by slandering me. Some sniveling Germans have chosen to accept the lies as truth. I have therefore decided to remove myself so that I will not impede the building of a National Socialist state.

What little I own I leave in trust to Rudolf Hess to be used to support my brothers and sisters in their modest standard of living and to further the work of the Party. I direct that the paintings in my collection be given to the city of Linz for exhibition in a gallery to be named The Hitler Institute.

The Party's work must continue with renewed force. I appoint Reichsmarshall Goering to succeed me. It is my wish that he retain my other ministers in their present positions but the Reichsmarshall shall have the freedom to manage the Party and state in accordance with National Socialist principles and his judgement. The injustices of Versailles must be peacefully eliminated so that the Fatherland again stands at the pinnacle of nations. The racial laws must be upheld to the fullest extent. Our merciless opposition to the universal poisoner of all peoples, the Jew, must continue.

A. Hitler

Hitler was sleeping on his back, his head turned to the side. A rivulet of drool dampened the pillow. If anything he appeared to be a harmless oddity with his Fuller Brush moustache and lock of black hair, now fallen in Buster Brown bangs.

Standing over Hitler, I told myself I was going to pull the trigger in humanity's defense, knowing that wasn't the whole of it.

My dad once told me that a man was defined by his choices. He saw the world in black and white. For him right and wrong existed with splendid clarity. I knew exactly where he would come down on what I was about to do. He wouldn't see the dilemma, only the commandment: thou shall not kill. That would have been the beginning and end of the analysis. I could see his logic.

But, if rules and logic were the whole story, I wouldn't have been standing in Hitler's bedroom, a pawn in a game not of my making. I was going to do this to give Sara and me a chance. It wasn't much of one but seemed all we had. Maybe I should have refused to walk into the bedroom. Would Diels really have had me shot with Hitler's Walther as evidence that I was up to no good? No point in second guessing. The odd looking sleeper had never done anything to me but he was surely evil. That made it possible.

I put the gun to his head and tried not to picture the bullet ripping through his skull into the pillow. Suddenly I realized that would not do. No one shot himself from a sleeping position. I looked at my Gruen. Gerd would be back in less than ten minutes.

How was I going to get him in a position to make the fake suicide look credible? I thought about pulling him into a sitting position - like a nurse propping up a patient. I visualize his eyes popping open as I hauled him up, my arms under his. We would both shit in our pants.

"Damn it," I cussed aloud, too loud.

Hitler bolted upright and stared, eyes blinking, at the open drapes. I put the gun to his head. As I pulled the trigger, he turned toward the door, looking to see if anyone had entered the room. The impact of the shot toppled him off the bed. The crack of the shot and the thud of his body hitting the floor seemed thunderous. I expected the door to fly open.

Nothing happened.

I felt the surge of adrenalin and the jump in my heart rate. I was surprised to see that my arm was still extended at the point in space from which Hitler had last looked at the moon. The gun! What was I doing standing around? I wiped it clean using the bed sheet. Picking it up with my handkerchief, I carried it to Hitler's body which lay on the floor, the wounded side of his head to the carpet. Blood seeped into the fabric. *Well, they say you like carpet*, I thought. I pressed the gun into his right hand, index finger around the trigger. Should I leave it there? Surely he would have dropped it as he fell off the bed.

I was kneeling there, my hand around his, when I felt it. I yanked my hand back as if I'd mistaken a viper's nest for a rabbit hole. I stood and looked at the body. It hadn't moved but I'd felt a pulse. Had I imagined it? Had I mistaken mine for his? I knelt back down and put my fingers on his neck. Nothing. I moved them a quarter inch, and there it was. The son-of-a-bitch was alive, his pulse strong.

Five minutes later the phone rang in my bedroom.

"Congratulations. Now here is what happens next."

I cut Diels off, "We may have a problem."

I could almost hear Diels draw a breath before asking, "What problem?"

"He was alive when I left."

"What were you doing in there? Masturbating in the dark!"

"Yeah, I shot the bastard with my wad. What the fuck do you think! He turned his head just as I shot. He flew off the bed like the slug hit him square. But when I put the gun in his hand, I felt a pulse."

"Jesus!"

"Too late for prayers, Diels."

"Why didn't you shoot him again?"

"Oh, that's fucking brilliant! You ever hear of a suicide victim who shoots himself twice? 'Here we go, boys. I'll scrape myself off the floor and put a second slug in the old noggin because for some reason I've still got a pulse.' Not even Goebbels could sell that shit."

"Shut up, Temple. Pull your self together. Are you telling me you hit him but think he's going to make it?"

"I hit him all right. Blew him out of bed. Blood on the floor under his head. Maybe he'll bleed to death. But I couldn't have hit him square. A straight shot would have killed him before he hit the floor. But he turned his head away. I can't be sure how much damage was done."

Silence. Diels was either in full panic or recalculating.

"Diels, what's the plan? Don't quit on me now."

More silence.

"Diels?"

"Undress. Go to bed. Get some sleep or at least pretend that is what you did after your visit to Hitler. When asked, say Gerd called your room at three-twenty-five. The recording system will show that. Gerd and I escorted you to his room at three-thirty. The Fuhrer seemed distracted, perhaps sad, but wanted to talk about Hollywood as if he was trying to cheer himself up. It did not work. At four he asked you to leave and called us to come get you. The recording system will show that. Gerd came to get you. You went to bed."

"But what if . . ."

"Shut up! Just listen. You're going to have to repeat your conversation with the Fuhrer. He would not have talked party or state politics with you. He liked adventure movies, liked gossip, anything risqué, dirt on actresses. He asked you questions about those kinds of things as if he was trying to take his mind off of something. At one point he asked what Roosevelt might do if he was accused of being a Jew. Before you could answer, Hitler shook his head and said, 'It makes no difference now'. Get your story down. You will be asked many times. You must be consistent but not repeat yourself verbatim. Understand the difference?"

"Yes."

"One last thing. If you are asked whether Hitler showed signs of being suicidal, say that never occurred to you while you were in his room. After the fact, maybe so. Do you understand all that?"

"Yes. But what if Hitler wakes up and says someone shot him."

"Then we will all be shot."

Diels hung up. Like a good soldier, I undressed, climbed in bed, and went over my story.

Chapter Twenty-Three

"Michael, you look terrible. What's wrong?" said Sara.

"Long night."

"Me too. We're a pair of mangy dogs for sure."

We'd met at the breakfast buffet which was served between eight-thirty and ten. Neither of us was hungry. Other than Hitler and Diels, all the Nazi hotshots were milling around the dining room. Goering's appetite was commensurate with his gut. He was in an expansive mood, chatting about a new fighter that Willy Messerschmitt was designing.

"Willy will not let me test it," said Goering patting his belly. "The stresses would be too great."

Magda Goebbels and Eva Braun joined his laughter.

With a slight bow to Goering, Braun disengaged and walked over to Sara who introduced me.

"The air here is wonderful," said Eva. "I strolled outside this morning. Adolph likes to sleep in. One of these days he will learn a sunrise is worth going to bed for. You two look tired. Take a walk. The mountain air will do you good. Let me show you."

She led us to an arcade that ran the length of the Eagle's Nest. It ended at a path that led to a rocky dome, the mountain's pinnacle. The Eagle's Nest itself was perched at the end of a spur that jutted from the mountain face at the edge of the dome. We left Eva standing on the portico. She admonished us to be careful. It was a long fall from the lip of the dome.

It was chilly. The air was incredibly fresh and the panorama spectacular. It was another of those places that allowed for the possibility of God. We walked in silence for a while, each of us lost in yesterday's events.

Here and there I steered our walk to the edge. Eva wasn't kidding about the danger. A skilled climber would need a hammer, pinions, and rope to get down.

"I suppose we're too close to the sun," said Sara

"What do you mean?"

"I was picturing us flying off the mountain - like Daedalus and Icarus escaping from Crete. You remember, the father made it but Icarus flew too high and the sun melted his wings.

Sara appeared to remember something and looked away from me.

"I first heard the story from my dad," she said. "It was a lesson about the consequences of disobedience. Dad liked stories that came with a moral. Washington and the apple tree, Aesop's Fables, you name it. Turns out Dad didn't think the stories applied to him. When you're rich, the rules don't always apply. He owns a shoe factory outside of Boston. A lot of men have been mangled in that place; but according to both Dad and Aesop, an act of kindness is never wasted."

Sara hesitated and then said as if relenting, "Go figure. Still credit where it's due - Dad's advice to me was always good.

"What about your family?"

"The steel mills in Cleveland's flats were dangerous too. A lot of men were killed over the years. My dad was burned pretty bad. Mom's brother, Tom, had a good job at Swift in Chicago. He got Dad an office job there. So we moved to the windy city when I was five."

"That must have been hard."

"We were so busy getting by we didn't think about hard or easy. But some of the kids in the neighborhood knew we wanted more than the slaughterhouses had to offer. That's half the reason Billy Collins and I ran off to drive ambulances in the war. Running from the slaughterhouses. Turned out we jumped from the frying pan to the fire."

"I read *Farewell To Arms*. Did Hemingway get it right?"

"Never read it. I saw mostly kids my age who were dead, or

scared about dying, or scared about losing an arm or leg, or were so depressed they didn't give a shit one way or the other. I didn't see much courage, although I expect most of them had too much to begin with. And I don't remember a lick of glory. As for me, I still have nightmares every so often."

"I guess if you weren't there, it can't be imagined."

"Want to hear what I imagine about you?"

"That's a little scary."

"I think you're not just out to avenge Mala. You're out to stop men like your father who have no rules. And like your father, you think you can do anything you want. But this isn't Boston where the Potters get their way. This isn't Broadway where playwrights script happy endings. The boys in my ambulance started out as convinced as you that they were going to save the world."

"Who's to say they didn't?"

"Me. I was there."

"And you helped beat the Germans."

"Look, we may have a chance to get out of here this morning. If that happens, we have to take it."

"You're as bad as my father. I'm not some child to be bossed around. I'll leave Germany on my terms, not on your orders."

"Your terms? Giving Goebbels an alibi is part of your terms? I can't figure you out. Are you biding your time, courting Goebbels so you can stab him in the back later? Or is the Mala story just bullshit meant to sucker me?"

"First browbeating, now insults? I don't have to answer to your questions."

Before I could completely burn my bridges, someone shouted, "Temple, get down here immediately!"

The SS sergeants, the ones who had escorted me to my bedroom the day before, were standing at the edge of the dome. Each held a machine gun at the ready.

"They're not here to give us a lift home," said Sara.

"No. No they aren't."

"I'm sorry we fought," she said as if realizing the sand in the hourglass had nearly run its course.

"Me too. With or without me, get out if you can."

"Michael, what's happening?"

It was too late for explanations. The sergeants were clattering across the rock toward us.

They shoved me in the men's smoking room across from the dining room and said Heydrich was coming to question me.

Hitler must have come around which meant I was done for. When you're facing death with time to think, part of the mind greedily seeks to re-experience life. Part prays that there is an afterlife. Part calculates the survival odds. Part regrets. And part seeks atonement. It all seems to happen at once. So I thought about my parents, my first kiss, Billy Collins, the war, the reasons I'd stopped praying, jobs I'd done for Pinkerton, the girl in Paris, Sara, the lies I would tell Heydrich, and what I'd say if there was a God on the other side of life.

"What is so amusing?"

Heydrich must have caught me smiling over a pleasant memory. I hadn't heard him come in. There was a hint of uncertainty on his face.

"Daydreaming. A time in Paris. A beautiful girl. So why am I here? What's going on?"

"You saw the Fuhrer last night."

"Yes. The guy must never sleep. He called for me in the middle of the night. Must have been three o'clock, maybe later."

"You planned this with Diels."

There was only one way to go. Assume Hitler was dead or unconscious.

"Maybe my German isn't working. Did you say that Diels and I organized Hitler calling for me at three in the morning? I didn't organize anything. Hitler must have told someone he wanted to see me. A Gestapo guy knocks on my door and takes me to Hitler's bedroom. Half hour or so later, Hitler is done with me, picks up the telephone, and tells someone to come fetch me. What's this all about?"

"What happened when you were with Hitler?"

"Nothing much. I guess he couldn't sleep. We talked about . . ."

I went through the story that I'd rehearsed.

"What did Diels say when he came to take you from the Fuhrer's room?"

"He didn't. Some other Gestapo guy took me back to my room."

"I have reason to believe that there was an attempt to kill the Fuhrer last night."

Heydrich was fishing. This wasn't his strong suit. He liked to hammer people. But he couldn't hammer an American unless it was a forgone conclusion that the American wasn't going home. I allowed myself to hope. On the other hand, he wouldn't have used the word "attempt" if Hitler was dead. I wasn't home free.

"No wonder he seemed edgy. He must have called me for a little distraction. That's why they make movies. Did someone actually try something?"

"Don't play games with me. You were in there. You had better tell me what you know. There are those who suspect Fraulein Potter."

"Of this attempt to kill Hitler? She's damn near a Nazi. That's ridiculous."

"You don't believe that. If you did, you would not be in love with her."

"Love?"

"You are a sentimentalist. You wear your disdain for us too plainly. You could easily love one of our enemies."

"Actually I'm a leg man. But even if I were cow-eyed over Sara, that doesn't make her your enemy. And I don't know anything about this attempt you're talking about."

"That would be a shame for Potter. You will tell me what you know,` or you won't see her again. As you say, she is damn near a Nazi. It would surprise no one if she became a party member, stayed in Germany, and disappeared into the party apparatus."

The hammer had arrived. On the face of it, the choice was Sara's life for mine. I was out of cute replies.

"I see you finally understand your situation, said Heydrich. "I'll leave you to think. I want an answer in ten minutes."

He walked out acting like he held all the cards.

Chapter Twenty-Four

"Time is up. What do you have to say?"

Heydrich could have been a stopwatch. He had returned in precisely ten minutes. He was many things Hitler wasn't: punctual, tall, handsome, immaculately tailored. By comparison Hitler seemed almost clownish. Maybe the clown could save me. Heydrich was bluffing. If he knew what happened, he wouldn't be asking me. One bluff deserved another.

"I want to see Hitler. I can't believe he knows what you're doing."

Heydrich actually laughed. "You want to see the Fuhrer?"

"Yes, Hitler. You know him. The fellow I chat with while you stand at attention, waiting on the chance he might want you to run an errand."

"Silence."

"Silence my ass. You're making a big mistake. I'm not some poor Jew you can order around like a dog. Hitler calls me – not you - in the night while you sleep in your boots waiting to kiss his ass."

"Shut up. No one speaks to . . ."

I had him now. He was beet red.

I hollered over his squeal "While Hitler and I were talking about the movies, I'll bet you were polishing his boots or sucking up to Himmler."

Rage drove him toward me. He flung aside a chair. It slammed a table, toppling a model battleship that fell to the floor. The two SS sergeants swapped confused glances.

"Come on," I taunted, waving him forward.

He stopped. Was he a coward or did he remember that generals don't brawl with nobodies? My money was on coward. His next command was crazier than a fist fight.

"Shoot the bastard," he screamed at a dog-whistle pitch.

The order was too fantastic to credit. The SS sergeants stared in disbelief.

I pointed at them. "You'll get these guys shot if they shoot me. Who's going to pay for that broken ship? When do I get to see the Fuhrer? Does Himmler know about this? Where is the Fuhrer's order? What about that chair! Where is Goering? You'll all be hauled up . . ."

I was raving like an amphetamine-stoked maniac while Heydrich kept squealing his crazy order. The eyes of the SS sergeants bounced between us. They had been trained to follow orders, to kill without hesitation. They were proud of the ice in their veins. But they never imagined it this way. Hitler's mountain retreat wasn't a battlefield or a re-education center. I wasn't a Jew, commie or gypsy, but an American who visited with the Fuhrer. Heydrich's order wasn't calculated to further racial purity, promote German expansion, or redress French transgressions. More importantly, if they guessed wrong, they might be the next to die.

They began to raise their weapons as Heydrich screamed for action. I searched for cover, no less panicked than were my possible executioners. I edged behind a heavy library table covered with newspapers and magazines. If either of the sergeants took aim, I would drop to my knees, upend the table, and hope its wood was thick enough to stop the initial rounds.

"Cowards! Fire!"

"Get the Fuhrer!"

Our shouting match continued. Where was everyone? Strolling on the dome? We'd been making a racket. Someone had to have heard.

The sergeant on the left snapped. His gun jerked up. I went down. The table went over. Papers and magazines flew. A gun fired. The table twitched from the impact of the rounds.

"Get around the damn table," Heydrich screamed.

I wasn't ready to die hunkered down behind a table. *Pick a side and sprint*, I told myself. Tackle the first guy in my path, wrestle his gun away, and hope for a standoff until Diels showed up. If Diels had already been arrested, I'd take out Heydrich before I went down. I visualized my attack as an explosive, fluid dance.

Ready, set, one, two, three, go.

As I was about to spring from behind the table, Goering showed up, and bellowed, "What the hell is going on?"

Heydrich, the sergeants, and I came to a dead stop. Sara darted past Goering into my arms. Diels and Himmler followed her into the room and flanked Goering. After a quick embrace, Sara stepped back, her hands still holding my biceps, giving me a once-over.

"Checking for holes?" I said, grinning like a patient with a negative biopsy.

"Just how is this funny, Michael?" said Sara.

"Well it's not, but I'm still darn pleased to be standing."

"Speak German," Goering ordered.

He had transformed himself. The bloated art collector was gone. There were no signs that he was high on anything but ego. Dressed in fatigues, he looked like an ace pilot ready for battle. A big man with waves of windswept blond hair, he looked the part of a leader. Diels and Himmler hung back - uncertain like gamblers with inside straights to fill.

"Well, Heydrich?" Goering asked.

Heydrich regained his self-control. His words were measured. "The man wouldn't answer my questions. Insulted me. A lesson was required. I told these men to shoot him. They understood that the order was not to be executed. The American panicked, started turning over furniture, and came at me. Grosz fired warning shots to protect me."

Now that was good. It more or less fit the observable facts. It gave Grosz and the other sergeant a serviceable story and took the three of them off the hook. Goering may have been an ace in the sky, but Heydrich knew how to maneuver on land.

"What do you have to say, Herr Temple?" asked Goering.

"I think it's better to question witnesses separately."

A smile flickered at the edge of Himmler's lips. Diels stepped forward and backhanded me to the ground, cutting the inside of my mouth.

Sara cried, "No!" and was grabbed by Grosz before she had taken a second step toward me.

Diels pulled me to my feet, put his right hand around my neck, and drove me against the wall. His back was to the rest of the room and his face in mine.

"Answer the Reichsmarshall! Do you understand?" he said, followed instantly by a private shush. Then, in English he lipped the words, "Agree with Heydrich."

"Yeah, okay," I stammered, with more faith than understanding.

"My apologies, Reichsmarshall," said Diels, releasing my neck. "This American seems to have a bad effect on all of us,"

Heydrich and Himmler seemed perplexed.

"Well?" said Goering.

"It's as he says. I thought he meant for them to shoot me. I lost my head."

"And what question wouldn't you answer?"

"Ask the General," I nodded at Heydrich.

Heydrich yanked on his tunic, straightening an imaginary wrinkle. Apparently the truth wouldn't do, and a suitable lie had not yet occurred to him.

"I'm asking you," Goering said to me.

Himmler started to speak but Goering scowled him to silence.

"He said that I had conspired with Diels to visit the Fuhrer last night. I told him that as far I knew Hitler called for me. Then he asked what I knew about a plot to kill Hitler. When I said I didn't know what he was talking about, he said Sara wouldn't get out of Germany alive unless I talked. I guess I was suppose to make something up because I sure as hell don't know anything about plots."

"What plot is this, Himmler?" said Goering.

"I am unaware of any plot," said Himmler sounding like a

bookkeeper denying that the general ledger was out of balance.

"Diels, are you aware of a plot?" said Goering pushing the issue.

"Nothing specific. The party has its enemies. There are people who would like to see the Fuhrer dead. The Gestapo has hundreds of undesirables in custody. But I am unaware of anything that implicates Temple. Perhaps Himmler or Heydrich know more?"

Himmler responded. "I am sure Heydrich was only probing. It is a standard technique." He turned to Heydrich and continued. "Is that correct General? Or do you know something I don't'?"

Himmler's tone left little doubt about the answer he expected.

"Correct, sir. Probing."

"And how did you provoke the General, Herr Temple?" Goering seemed relieved, as if we were back on safe ground.

"I told him that while I was chatting with Hitler, he was standing at attention like a private waiting to run an errand."

Goering suppressed a smile and nodded. "As we all do! He is our Fuhrer. Waiting is not only our duty, it is our privilege. Our devotion should provoke pride not anger."

Goering's next advice was for me.

"You must learn some manners. General Heydrich has a job to do. Yours is to cooperate. You need to temper your cowboy impulses."

Having lectured both of us, Goering didn't seem to know how to bring his intervention to a conclusion. For a moment we all stood silent, each of us wondering what the others knew and didn't know.

Hitler must have been discovered by now. He was probably alive but unconscious. If he was awake and talking, I would have been arrested. So who knew Hitler had been shot? Surely the big dogs: Goebbels, Goering, and Hess. Heydrich had to know or he wouldn't have been asking me about plots. If Heydrich knew, Himmler knew. So why not just come out with it? The answer seemed clear. For the moment there was nothing to say that the shooting wasn't an attempted suicide. But how to play that? To keep their options open, they refused to acknowledge the obvious choices. Neither suicide nor assassination fit the idea of Nazi invincibility.

The silence was broken by a nurse who appeared at the door to the lounge. "Doctor Morell needs to know if anyone is blood type A/B-negative, or O-negative."

"Has anything happened to Hitler?" Sara blurted out, obviously surprised.

Her guess wasn't surprising. Many people knew the name of Hitler's doctor. If Morell wanted blood, it was likely Hitler who needed it.

"No, no, Fraulein," Goering answered too quickly. "A soldier was practicing his climbing and fell. Isn't that right Himmler?"

"Yes," Himmler said, annoyed at being drawn into the charade.

"I'm O-negative," said Sara.

"Excellent," Goering replied. He turned to the nurse. "Take her blood in the lady's salon. Fraulein, please follow the nurse."

He turned to me. "Herr Temple, wait here."

He turned to Diels, Heydrich and Himmler, and pointed at the door.

"Gentlemen, we all have duties."

Goering was the last to leave.

Twenty minutes later Gerd walked in.

"Let's go. I'm driving you to Berlin," he said.

"I'm not leaving without Sara."

"Yes you are," said the man who had put a knife to my neck the day I'd visited Hanussen in his hideaway.

Dressed in an SS uniform, Eric - the man I had thought of as a perfect Aryan - had followed Gerd into the room.

"And why is that?" I asked.

"We need your bedroom," Gerd answered sarcastically.

"He does not need a baker's dozen reasons to leave," said the Aryan. "Get moving Temple. We will see to it that Fraulein Potter joins you later."

The "baker's dozen" crack had to signal a message from Diels or Ludi telling me it was time to go. Common sense said the same thing.

The odds of my saving Sara, much less both of us, were about the same as the Toledo Mud Hens winning the World series. Besides, if I was going to trust anyone, why not a perfect Aryan?

Chapter Twenty-Five

Gerd and I raced from the tunnel under the Eagle's Nest in a 770 KW. He was showing off by telling me what he knew.

"Hitler is alive but still unconscious. He must have turned his head because the round only grazed his skull. Still it knocked him out and caused a lot of bleeding. Morell thinks the damage is superficial but can't eliminate a skull fracture. Goering wants to bring in his own doctor. Lucky for us the guy is a Jew. Hess and the rest won't have that. So Hitler is stuck with his quack."

"What happens if he comes around?"

"If that happens, Morell predicts a full recovery. With some clean stitching, the wound will be unnoticeable. Morell also says even with a full recovery, Hitler may not remember what happened."

"And if he does remember?"

"We'll be in Switzerland. From there you make your way home. And I wait it out until Hitler falls."

"What about Diels? Did he take off too?"

"No. He thinks he can control events from the inside."

"How can Diels let us go? Isn't he worried we'll take the story to the newspapers."

"Diels is an honorable man. He knows I would never betray him. And you . . . well, why would you betray Diels since he has taken the trouble to save you?"

Gerd didn't sound too sure about that last part. He looked across the seat at me, probably wondering why Diels let me go.

"Watch the road," I said.

He was driving recklessly. One moment the 770 flirted with

the cliff face and the next it threatened to sail over the edge. Gerd was enjoying it. He and the 770 fell into a breakneck rhythm. I relaxed a little.

"What happens if Hitler dies? A suicide won't look good for the party."

"But he may have been assassinated. Since the communists and Jews are under control, the leading candidate is Rohm."

"He's one of yours."

"The SA is too powerful and Rohm too independent. The Wehrmacht is nervous. Hitler's assassination would be the perfect excuse to eliminate Rohm."

"How is Sara getting out?"

"She had nothing to do with shooting Hitler. She can leave whenever she wants."

"She's Goebbels' alibi in the Glaise killing. You people kill alibi witnesses so they can't change their stories."

"Ridiculous."

"Do you know who Anny Winter was?"

Gerd was silent as he wrestled the car from fishtailing on some loose gravel. When he spoke, it sounded as if he didn't want to concede the point.

"I have heard the stories but there is no comparison."

"What does that mean?"

He looked at me and snorted.

"It means your girl killed Glaise to frame Goebbels."

Now it was my turn to stare at Gerd. He wasn't smiling. He was serious.

"She framed Goebbels, then gave him an alibi? That makes no sense."

"Did she tell you about Mala?"

"Yes."

"Then you know why she wants to destroy Goebbels."

"She killed Glaise to destroy Goebbels? Never. That would make her a cold-blooded killer."

"What did she tell you about her father?"

"Her father? A love-hate relationship, I guess. He owns a shoe factory. She didn't like the way he treated his workers. Otherwise a great guy. What of it?"

"In the fall of thirty-two, BSAF, a big chemical company, sent an agent to America to promote trade with the shoe industry. Artificial leather. He brought along his girlfriend for a fling. Or maybe the girl was along to help promote business. Whichever the case, she made quite an impression on a number of Americans. One of those was Tom Potter. Seven months later Potter made a trip to Germany, ostensibly on business. There were all kinds of stories. This much is certain. The girl tried to blackmail Potter, claiming she was pregnant by him. Potter refused to be blackmailed. He retained a Jew lawyer and sued to take custody of the child. I don't know what happened to the baby but the proceeding was dropped, and Potter disappeared.

"I don't know how much his family learned about the affair but for a while it was a sensation in the Berlin newspapers. If his family knew anything, Glaise would have been rotten sausage to them."

"Paula Glaise? You're telling me she was blackmailing Sara's father?"

"Yes. So Sara had two reasons to kill her. Avenge the family honor and frame Goebbels."

"So why save Goebbels from her own frame-up?"

"Hitler asked her to."

"What?"

"Goebbels didn't leave the party with Sara. He left it with Ribbentrop, the foreign minister. They went to a secret meeting at the Japanese embassy to discuss a non-aggression pact. Sara knew where he was going. She agreed to meet him later at her Ufa bungalow. She would make sure Goebbels would have time for which he couldn't account. Time to kill Glaise. All she had to say was that she fell asleep and didn't remember when Goebbels got to her bungalow. She killed Glaise while Goebbels was at the embassy.

"Hitler met with Sara shortly after she and Hugenberg bailed you out. He told her he couldn't afford to lose Goebbels to a scandal. Besides, Goebbels was actually innocent because he had been with the Japanese at the time Glaise was murdered. Unfortunately the negotiations were secret and could not be revealed. Sara needed to give Goebbels an alibi. If she didn't cooperate, she certainly was a suspect. After all she had a motive and no alibi since she left the Press Ball early and alone. Both problems could be solved if she and Goebbels provided alibis for each other. Your girlfriend outsmarted herself."

"I don't believe it. She's not a murderer. Besides she's a girl. She wouldn't have been strong enough to strangle Glaise."

As I spoke, I remembered the day we went swimming and how easily she had pulled me onto the raft that floated off Wannsee Beach.

"The frame on Goebbels was almost too well done," said Gerd. "The wine bottle, positioned as it was, pointed straight at Goebbels. He wrote a novel called *Michael.* The character, Michael, was a young man struggling to come to terms with himself in postwar Germany. The Michael character stood in contrast to a repulsive character named Kurt. While Michael wrote poetry and dreamed of a rejuvenated Germany, Kurt was a street hustler. In the story Kurt killed the prostitute who gave him syphilis. Kurt finished off his handy work by sticking a bottle up the prostitute's cunt.

"The book is long forgotten for the most part. But some of the original Nazis remembered. Diels made the connection. And there were other clues. The party pin. And the wine - the Riesling - was Goebbels' favorite."

I remembered Sara talking about Goebbels, the writer. She'd read *Michael.* Still I wasn't buying it.

"Did Kurt cut out the hooker's heart?" I asked.

"No. That is enough to make you think she was in league with Hanussen. Remember . . . What the hell!"

Gerd was pumping the brake with no result. The 770 was gaining speed and couldn't hold the road entering a turn. It slid into the cliff face, tearing off the right running board and rear fender. The car glanced off the face and careened across the road where the car's wheels spun in the gravel for traction at the precipice. From where I sat, it looked like the left side of the car was already over the edge, riding the wind before the plunge. But the tires gained traction and the car lurched back onto the road. Gerd frantically downshifted. It worked through one gear. The 770 lost a bit of speed. When Gerd popped the clutch again, the transmission blew. Free of the transmission's restraint, the grade accelerated the car. An eighth of a mile ahead was another switchback where the car would obliterate itself against the cliff face.

"Hang on!" Gerd cried.

He was grinning like an adrenalin junky who had discovered a new thrill. Scared or crazy, it was hard to tell. He swerved the 770 to the right, sideswiping the cliff face. Sparks flew and for an instant the smell of shredding rubber filled the air. The car bounced back onto the roadway. Gerd forced it back into the wall. The rear bumper ripped from the car's body. Gerd tried to hold the car to the wall. It was slowing but the cliff face at the switchback was closing fast. Gerd turned the steering wheel further right. The right-side tires seemed to be gone as the car listed into the face. A rocky prominence struck the right head lamp, hurling it across the engine cowling and through the windshield. Gerd raised his left arm but the lamp exploded into him. The seat collapsed and Gerd's body flew into the back seat.

The car edged away from the wall and gained speed. I grabbed the steering wheel, turning the car back toward the wall. The right front of the car caught something, spinning it around. The 770 looped across the road, ricocheted off a stand of pine trees at the edge of the cliff and spun down the road to the switchback where it slammed into the cliff face trunk first.

The spinning and the collision bounced me around like a pinball, finally flinging me into the canvass roof where my head glanced off a strut, knocking me cold.

I smelled gasoline before I regained my wits. My neck and head ached. I was lying on the roof of the 770 with my legs dangling in the car. I'd been hurled halfway through the car's canvass roof. Four feet away the cliff face rose above the crumpled rear of the car. The belt of my trench coat had snagged on a strut, preventing me from being catapulted into the rocky face.

I heard someone walking toward the wreck. I turned and saw Gerd's sidekick - the one I thought of as Abbott.

I thought you were alive," he said.

"Gerd is here someplace. Better look for him before this thing explodes."

Abbott stood five feet from the car, smiling behind a cigarette. He looked like a craftsman inspecting his work. He said nothing.

"Is Gerd in the car?" I said. "Watch the butt or you will blow us up."

Abbott responded without moving. "He is in the car. Looks like someone ran his head through a grinder. Can you hear me, Gerd?"

An unintelligible sound came from below me.

"Diels sent me to finish what the mountain left."

"Finish what?" I asked

"I don't know why he wanted the two of you dead but he asked me to tinker with the breaks. He knew Gerd called me a tinkerer - like I was not fit for the Gestapo. Diels knew different. He knew that in the end, Gerd would not have the balls for the dirty work."

"You're mistaken. Diels wanted us to reach Switzerland."

But I knew there was no mistake. I wanted to keep Abbott talking while I freed my belt from the strut. I had to scramble off the roof before Abbott flicked his cigarette into the gasoline.

"He set up bank accounts for us there. There is plenty of money for you, for all of us."

"Money? You insult me. I serve the Fuhrer through Diels. That is enough for me."

He was an attack dog, ready to finish off two people who might harm his master.

"What did they tell you about the Fuhrer? An upset stomach? Morell would not have come to the Eagle's Nest for that. What do you think was really wrong with him?"

There was a spark of interest in Abbott's eyes.

"Someone tried to kill Hitler last night. Gerd was investigating. If you kill Gerd it will look like you had something to hide. You're being set up as the fall guy. Diels told you to say nothing about any of this, right?"

He nodded, for the first time uncertain.

"And then he told you to hurry back to the Eagle's Nest or to Gestapo headquarters in Munich. Someplace where his men could grab you."

I had gone too far, spinning too much into the story. Abbott laughed, relieved that I didn't know more than he did.

"Wrong. I have an important package to deliver."

Abbott looked over to the Maybach in which he must have arrived.

"Look hard, Temple, and see who I have in there. It will be the last thing you ever look at."

The windows were tinted. I couldn't make out who was sitting in the car.

Abbott took a step back and looked at the gasoline on the road. He raised his cigarette to his lips and blew on the ash until it glowed. Then he extended his arm to flick the butt. From below me came the sound of a single shot. A millisecond after the slug ripped through Abbott's forehead, his finger launched the cigarette. The butt sailed high in the air and landed a foot short of the gasoline slick.

The Luger was still in Gerd's hand when I found him. His face and left arm were pulp. Otherwise he seemed uninjured. One eye was gone. How he saw to make the shot I'll never know. His lips were mangled. He was trying to talk, repeating something that I could not understand. He died after a minute or two.

We had been betrayed by a man Gerd believed to be honorable. The betrayal didn't say much for either of them.

I took Gerd's Luger and headed for the Maybach. When I was

ten feet from the car, the back door swung open. I raised the gun.

Sara stumbled out. She looked terrible - washed out, bleary-eyed. Had she really murdered Paula Glaise? Had she sat and watched Abbott try to set me on fire?

"Michael? Michael?"

She looked like she might be in shock and seemed barely strong enough to stand.

"Why are you pointing that gun at me?"

I lowered the gun.

"Where was he taking you?"

"Morell said an infirmary in Berchtesgaden. He took too much blood, said I needed plasma. He may have given me a sedative."

From the looks of her that could have been true. My anger faded.

"I passed out but came around a little. I was still in la-la land. I heard them whispering - I'm not even sure who. I think Hanussen is dead. They think we were plotting to kill Hitler. I think Hitler was shot. It was confusing."

I was tempted to leave her. Her standing with the Eagle's Nest crowd was unclear; but, if she was caught with me, it would be over for her. I explained the options and gave Sara the choice. Then I sat her down in the Maybach, and told her to think about what she wanted to do while I tied up some loose ends.

Abbott had fallen with his head downgrade. His blood had drained away, leaving his uniform unstained. I stripped him. Then I undressed. I put on his uniform and then dressed him in my clothes. His uniform didn't fit me but I wasn't going to a fashion show. I considered leaving my passport but thought I might need it later, perhaps at the Swiss border - assuming we were lucky enough get that far.

I lugged Abbott into the front seat of the 770. From the trunk of the Maybach, I pulled a five-gallon can of gasoline. The Germans were like boy scouts that way: always prepared. I spread the gas inside the 770, leaving a trail on the road. I tossed a match on the slick, crossing my fingers that the car would ignite.

I shouldn't have worried. It was a pyromaniac's dream. Even the gas can in the 770's battered trunk exploded, as it might have on impact with the cliff face. Days would pass before the forensic experts would realize that the wrong person died in the wrong kind of fire.

Chapter Twenty-Six

"Drop me at the infirmary," said Sara.

I turned to look at her. She was slumped against the door in the back of the Maybach. Her color wasn't terrific but her eyes had cleared.

"Liquids and a little light food. You'll be fine."

"Doctor Temple is it?" she said, trying to be playful.

"Remember I was an ambulance driver."

"I could go for a nice, long hold. Not much of a chance of that I suppose."

"As soon as we cross the border. Promise. Thanks for the help back there at the gate."

"Remember I'm an actress."

Coming down the mountain, I pushed the Maybach almost as hard as Gerd had pushed the 770. Just above Obersalzberg Sara suggested that I start driving like I wasn't running. We looped around the enclave and minutes later pulled up to the mountain road gate - fifteen minutes or so after leaving the scene of the accident in which I died.

The gate was down. A guard came to my window. I said that I needed to get my passenger to the hospital and to report an accident on the road above Obersalzberg. The guard wanted to see my identification. I started to hand him Abbott's papers. If he knew Abbott or paid attention to Abbott's photo, there would be trouble.

Sara spoke from the back seat. "I need to get to the infirmary in town. You remember me, don't you? Hans, isn't it?"

She gave him the smile the sick give the healthy for encouragement.

He got big eyes and snapped back, "Ja, Fraulein."

He raised the gate and we drove off.

"I signed a publicity photo for him," Sara explained. "I knew he got a kick out of it. Funny how things work out."

She was talking to herself as much as to me, maybe remembering her dad's words about kindness never being wasted.

At the outskirts of Berchtesgaden, I turned off the main drag onto a road that had more potholes than asphalt. A faded wooden sign translated, Timberline Road. We bumped uphill for a mile or so until I turned down a dirt road so weathered there wasn't a tread mark in sight. A quarter mile later I pulled behind an abandoned sawmill.

I had changed my mind about dropping Sara at the infirmary. Now I was trying to change hers.

"You'll never get out once they realize the guy who was driving you is missing. We need to get into Austria. We'll check the crossings and find one that isn't guarded. If they all are, we'll walk across. You'll have to build your strength up for that. We'll take a day or two. I'll go into town, get some food. And I need a change of clothes."

"Michael, slow down. I'm not going."

"They tried to kill me. You helped me. You've burned your bridges."

"They don't know that."

"They'll figure it out soon enough. We'll make it together, don't worry."

"Michael, you don't understand. I want to stay."

When she agreed to drive down the mountain with me, I believed she was mine. *Horst Wessel*? The tall man? Accepting the Brotherhood Cross? The Paula Glaise murder? All of that could wait. It was enough to know she had chosen me.

But she hadn't.

"Why did you come down the mountain with me?"

"I thought you wouldn't get past the Mountain Road gate without help."

It was a roller coaster ride. She loves me, she loves me not.

"Why do you want to stay? Revenge for Mala? Revenge for your family?

"What?" she shot back as if I'd walked on forbidden ground.

She shifted uneasily in the seat and gave me a hard look as if prepared to fight. Instead she softened, glanced at the sawmill, and asked if I would find her some water.

"All right but then I want answers."

I was three paces away from the car, before I went back and pulled the keys from the ignition. I felt like a dog that didn't trust his master. Sara looked as if I had insulted her.

"Fuck it," I said and tossed the keys on the seat next to her.

She threw the keys at me just as I closed the door. They banged against the window and fell to the floor.

The main floor of the mill was littered with rusting equipment. Birds nested in the rafters. The place smelled of lubricants and decaying sawdust. At the back of the mill, a hallway led to a few offices and a mess hall. Beyond the mess hall was a latrine and bunkhouse. Scattered around the mess hall were newspapers from the winter of 1932-1933. There was some canned food. Squatters must have camped here during the last days of Weimar. I imagined angry men emerging from the sawmill, liberated by the Nazis, free to become Brownshirts.

In the bunkhouse I found a doll, two wooden toy trucks, and a wagon filled with small rocks arranged with a secret logic. On a table were a spool of thread, scraps of fabric and debris from the woods: twigs, leaves, grasses, flowers, and a cat-of-nine-tails. Nearby a partially crafted doll awaited completion. Someone had been teaching a little girl how to make a doll from the stuff of nature.

I thought of Gerta Oster. It could have been her family that marched out of the mill, liberated by the Nazis with hope for a better life. That kind of hope was as dangerous as Brownshirt anger.

I walked back to the mess hall and turned the tap over a grimy sink. After five minutes the water ran clear. I washed an empty jar and filled it with water. A can opener lay on the counter near some cans of food. I pocketed the opener, and picked up the jar of water and a couple of cans of peaches.

The silent testimony of the sawmill had shaken me. The ugliness of the Nazis was easily lost in the excuses and hope Hitler offered the angry and despondent.

I found the Maybach empty, save a note, quickly scratched in a shaky hand. The keys were not on the floor where they had fallen. Both of us were fools: me for giving her the chance to run and Sara for taking it.

The keys were buried under some papers in the glove box. I drove back to the main road searching for Sara. In her condition, she could not have gone far. I slowly retraced our route, hoping that she had run out of steam and would be found at the edge of the road, ready to accept help. Nothing. I retraced the route a dozen times with no luck. Here and there, I stopped and got out of the car. Standing in the middle of the road, I called her name. Nothing. I searched the main road for a half mile in either direction. Nothing.

If she was unconscious in the woods, my chances of finding her were slim at best. If she died, I might as well have dumped her in the forest myself. I read her note again, as if it might yield her whereabouts:

Dear Michael:

I do love you. It's like one of those wartime romances where everything moves too fast because there may be no tomorrow. I think no less of my love for that.

For now you must let me go. I am dangerous to you, and you to me. The Nazis are difficult to figure out. They have done some good, yet they are capable of terrible things. I have two things to accomplish before I go home. Horst Wessel is not one of them, although I will complete it, hoping that I can live it down.

Get into Austria. Hurry! I will tell them that you forced me to help you get past the Mountain Road gate and that, when I wouldn't escape with you into Switzerland, you dumped me at the infirmary. Cad! Don't come looking for me. If you do, you will get us both killed. Give me my chance. The Nazis are not a threat to me.

I'll find you later - at the Grand Terrace Cafe listening to Fatha Hines.

Sara

P.S. I know you're not a boob, but just in case you are, destroy this. Look around for the keys, you'll find them.

Love and kisses. If we don't get killed, I'll see you in Chicago. Two things to accomplish. What were they? And for good measure why not manipulate the shit out of me: *Run, Michael, or you'll get me killed.* Very clever. That the proposition might be true was even more aggravating. She had me coming and going. I took out my lighter and burned the note.

If she made it to the infirmary, I might as well cross into Austria. But had she? It was the thought of her dying in the forest that kept me from testing the border.

I drove back to the sawmill and dumped the Maybach. Past the mill some cabins were tucked in the woods. I knocked on the door of the first one with a car in the driveway. A guy named Srbik answered. He was in his late thirties and was frightened before I even spoke. It was the uniform.

I told him that there had been a crime in Berchtesgaden and that the perpetrator had been traced to his area. I never said what the crime was or that he was a suspect. I barged through his place taking what I wanted. Srbik was so unnerved that he looked guilty of the nonexistent crime. I confiscated a heavy pewter crucifix, three changes of clothing, his shaving gear, a suitcase, his identification, and his car. Before leaving I disabled his telephone. It was simple.

I told him I was taking his stuff for "scientific testing" and that, if the results were negative, his possessions would be returned. He was to stay put and contact no one. Srbik pleaded his innocence and promised to follow orders. I had no doubt that he would.

Srbik wasn't the only one unnerved. I'd played the role of Nazi bully like it was second nature. Maybe the germ is in all of us.

Back at the sawmill, I changed into Srbik's clothes. Then I drove his car to town. It was another black Opal. They were everyplace just as the Model T once was. The car made me feel invisible. I parked near an apothecary in Berchtesgaden. I went inside and found a pay telephone hanging on a wall next to a display of elixirs. I called the infirmary. A nurse answered.

"This is Gruppenfuhrer Haider. Do you have a patient named Sonja Potter, a young woman, an American?"

"Yes, Gruppenfuhrer. She was rambling when she came in. We calmed her down and are giving her plasma. She should be fine in a day or so."

"Very good. Thank you."

I hung up and walked out of the shop. Sara had delivered herself to the Nazis and I was relieved - some world.

On the way out of town, I drove past the infirmary. A staff car was pulling up with Diels and three men whom I did not recognize.

I drove on toward the Austrian border. Sara wanted it this way. There were no good options. Hugo Srbik and I weren't cowards, just realists. That's what I told myself.

I was miserable. It had to do with Sara, left to confront Diels. And with Srbik, left to confront the terror of a false accusation. They were stuck in Germany, while the fake Srbik was left to rationalize his behavior on the road to Austria.

Chapter Twenty-Seven

The cars were six deep at the Salzburg border crossing. A pair of black uniforms was carefully inspecting the car at the gate. I drove north to the crossing at Passau. No line. No black uniforms. Only two regular border guards. I pulled up and showed my identification.

"Where are you from, Herr Srbik?"

"Berchtesgaden," I answered.

The guard was reading identification papers that said exactly that.

"Why are you crossing here?"

"I'm visiting friends near Straubing."

I'd seen the sign not a minute before: "Straubing - 60 km".

"Who?"

"Who?" I might as well have been a parrot.

"I grew up there. Perhaps we have a mutual friend."

I studied the gate, calculating the odds of breaking through it. A few yards from the guard shack was a small station house. A black uniform walked out carrying a machine gun. Bluff or run? Bluffing is an uncertain art. A second black uniform emerged from the station.

To the extent you can gun an Opal, that's what I did. The car hit the timber gate which rotated away without breaking. The Opal was underpowered and too light. It spun off the gate and rolled. I was knocked out thinking I should have bluffed.

I came around groggy and found myself strapped to a bed and

wrapped like a mummy. Where was I? My head was spinning with car accidents, gated mountain roads, movie stars, villains, masked balls, spaghetti-eating lions, and dark hallways: the residue of memories and dreams. Had hours or days passed? It wasn't long before I drifted back to sleep.

Shortly after my wits returned for good, Heydrich showed up. He was all business.

"The Fuhrer will eventually remember. For the moment he suffers from traumatic retrograde amnesia. According to Doctor Morell, his memory can return like that."

Heydrich snapped his fingers. "The Fuhrer is already on his feet. His memory will not be far behind. And you had better be out of Germany before that happens. Confess now. I'll have Diels where I want him. I don't care about you; eventually you can go."

Did I look like the all-time dumb-shit?

"We did this dance before. Last time Goering chewed your ass. This time I want to see Hitler. Or, okay, Goering will do."

"They have returned to Berlin. You are my property. I think you and Diels provided the *Ku'damm Conscience* with the lies it printed. I want to know about that too."

"You're dreaming, if . . ."

"Shut up, Temple. You are still in Berchtesgaden, fifteen minutes from freedom in Salzburg. Give me what I want and you and Potter will be there before the day is out."

Same song.

Same response, "Can't give you what I don't know."

"I will have what I want, either here, with your cooperation, or in Columbia Haus without it."

Everyone knew Columbia Haus - the place where parents and children denounced each other and no one survived.

Heydrich smiled as if to reassure me that the Salzburg option was real. He needed work on his sincerity.

"You want me to make something up? I wouldn't know where to start."

Heydrich picked up a suitcase that he had brought with him. He set it on a table, and opened it.

"This is a voice recorder. Do you know what it does?"

"Yes."

"Let me play you something."

Heydrich plugged it in, turned a knob, waited until there was a faint hissing sound, and then turned another knob. I didn't recognized the voice at first.

" . . . Some still laugh behind my back. Goering, Hess, even the chicken farmer, Himmler. But their words cannot touch me. Even as a child, I knew to stand above shallow provocation. Through my education and writing, I began to see that modern man could save humanity if he was willing to sacrifice. Like fermenting wine, the impure elements must be skimmed off, leaving the precious essence. Modern man must deny the bankrupt proposition that politics is the art of the possible and embrace the proposition that politics can be the miracle of the impossible. Yet, until I met Hitler, these ideas were abstractions that I could only struggle to articulate. Hitler is the embodiment of what modern man must be. He gave me the voice to ignite the people. And he gave me the will to crush the . . ."

Heydrich stopped the tape. "Do you recognize the voice?"

"So Goebbels thinks Hitler is Christ reborn. What of it?"

Heydrich spun the tape a tad forward and then hit the play switch.

"Can you see what I mean?" said Goebbels, pleading for understanding.

"Yes. The cruelty of kids. The mentor who unlocks the future."

The voice was all too familiar to me. I did not like the dreamy quality to it.

"Tell me your experience," said Goebbels, full of empathy.

"I stuttered when I was a kid. 'Cat gu-gu-gu-gu-got yu-yu-yu-your tongue.' That kind of teasing. I can still hear them," said Sara.

Sara went on to tell Goebbels the story of a junior high speech teacher who had worked with her, showing her how to beat her impediment.

She hadn't told me the story. I was jealous.

"And you conquered your disability," said Goebbels sounding proud of her.

One thing led to another. I tried to shut out the rest: the intimate talk and the sound of love making. How could she have accepted Goebbels' bullshit? How could she equate her affection for a kindly teacher with Goebbels' idolatry of a madman? Had she been dumb or naive?

Heydrich switched off the recorder.

"That's why she lied to save Goebbels. They are kindred, flawed spirits. Think of their offspring - stuttering cripples."

Heydrich looked at me like he had won a great victory.

"I'm supposed to confess that I'm in cahoots with Diels because Sara slept with your crippled pal? You're a sick fucking bunch."

"No. You will confess later at Columbia Haus because everyone eventually confesses there. For now it is enough that you to know the truth. Perhaps it will set you free."

Heydrich gave me an icy, little smile, then clicked his heels and walked out.

Chapter Twenty-Eight

When the Opal rolled, I had been sliced by flying glass but hadn't broken anything. Most of the bandages were gone by the time Heydrich shipped me north. The doctor who removed my stitches said that I would have a few scars, including one on my forehead. I told him that I would start combing my hair like Hitler. He wasn't amused.

Columbia Haus had been a military convalescent home for thirty years when Himmler decided that the SS needed a place in Berlin for what he called the "hard work." While few people knew the details, everyone knew it was an urban torture camp. The SS denials were perfunctory. Its ugly reputation served as a warning to those tempted to cross the lines the Nazis had drawn. The cabbies called it the "insanatorium."

I was locked up for days. The pace of time slowed as if it were shackled to my dread of what was to come. Back in 1927 when I'd been jailed in a cell under the Seine, I passed the time managing imaginary baseball games. I tried that again. It didn't work. Maybe my boozing in the intervening years had short-circuited my imagination. Or maybe, in a world where lives were being stolen, there was no place for a game in which stolen bases were important.

I spent most of my time thinking about Sara and trying to concoct a story that wouldn't hurt anyone but would satisfy Heydrich. I only managed to confuse myself. When the SS guards pulled me from my cell, I was almost relieved. They took me to an interrogation room in the basement. The cabbies said that the basement was the last stop at Columbia Haus.

Heydrich walked in.

"Last chance," he said, making the cabbies look smart.

"For what?"

Heydrich gave me his best hard-ass look which was only a twitch from his normal expression.

I hoped it would be drugs. If they cooked your brain, there was nothing you could do. There was no choice, no question of courage. On the other hand, if you had the willpower, you could fight torture and die before you talked. I vowed to die like a man and prayed that I would not give in. Pretty damn desperate since I didn't believe in prayer.

Diels and Ludi. Are they worth saving? Diels is a killer whose only redeeming feature is his desire to get rid of Hitler. And Ludi - he seems okay but do I really know his angle? And won't Himmler eventually get both of them without my help? Probably. So why am I about to go down this road?

Within seconds of my vow, I was rationalizing it away. Some tough guy.

Himmler's words rescued me, gave me some backbone. I remembered the following passage from one of the speeches that Zukor gave me to read.

"After we eliminate our communists and the Jews, you Americans will look to us for the leadership to accomplish the same in your country. The communists and the Jews are insidious. As we speak, they flee beyond our reach. There are misguided Germans who favor such immigration. That will only delay the ultimate day of reckoning and move the final denouement to your shores. When that happens, there will be retribution against the Americans who have hindered us in our work. Be one who helped."

Not me, I thought.

"Goose-stepping won't sell on Main Street," I said to Heydrich.

"What?"

"Cut me loose or get on with it. You want to anyway. The thrill is beating people down, isn't it? What's it like to look at a sadist when you shave?"

Heydrich's lips tightened as I squirmed around under his skin.

"Soon enough," he said. "But for now you have a command performance to give. After that you will be coming back here, unless you are ready to talk now."

"I thought you needed a king for a command performance."

"How perceptive."

Gerta Oster had been right. Hitler lived in a modest suite at the Kaiserhof. The hotel was a few cuts below the Adlon. It catered to provincials in town for a taste of the big city. In need of renovation, it was struggling to preserve what it had never quite been. Kitsch gone tacky was a fit description.

Across Wilhelmstrasse from the hotel, steam shovels were digging the basement of the new Reich Chancellery. It would be fit for Nordic Gods. The project was a symbol. If anyone was worried about what it symbolized, the concern was lost in the excitement of an energized present and the promise of a glorious tomorrow, flowing with racial inevitability from the Teutonic past.

That's how Goebbels might have put it.

Hitler's rooms were better suited for an aging matron than a Fuhrer. His sitting room was fairly spacious and needed to be. Goebbels, Hanfstaengl, Himmler, Hess, and Goering stood like lab technicians around a Petri dish, waiting to see how the specimen would react.

For a guy who was either suicidal or a murder target, Hitler seemed tranquil. He was munching on sliced apples and hard-boiled eggs, and drinking mineral water. A box of birdseed was next to his snacks, at the ready for feeding his pet canaries.

Himmler must have arranged this absurd drama. Who else could gain from it? The premise was evident: Hitler's memory might be uncorked by his exposure to me. So there we all stood, waiting to see if Hitler's brain would continue to misfire.

Himmler broke the uneasy silence awkwardly.

"The Fuhrer wants to know whether women in the United

States are as headstrong and frivolous as Claudia Colbert in *It Happened Last Night*."

Hitler grunted derisively. "Himmler is a good policeman but has limitations. He meant in *It Happened One Night*. The Ellie character. Are American women like that?"

Having not been able to figure out Sara, I hardly qualified as an expert. So I stole more material from *Variety*.

"It started with the suffragettes. Then came the flappers after the war. There are plenty of Ellies in Chicago and New York. But for the most part, American women aren't like that. Most are homemakers like their mothers and grandmothers. Not many girls skip their wedding to run off with a charming scamp."

"But it won the Academy Award."

"Quality escapism."

"Yes! Exactly! My intuition never fails." Hitler suddenly changed the subject, "Herr Temple, I have survived an injury whose cause is shrouded in mystery. Now Himmler thought having you with us today might help illuminate the problem of my memory. And you have."

Hitler paused and looked around the room. He could have been Hanussen priming his audience. But while Hanussen relished the expectancy he created, Hitler was amused at our anxiety. He rose from his chair and shuffled to the center of the room, his herky-jerky gate suggesting some incipient neurological disorder. He began to speak and was rolling in no time, eyes wide, his arms and hands gesturing. He could have been addressing the nation.

"From my early days in Vienna, I knew intellect and conscience could not be trusted. I have always trusted my instincts. Some of you warned me not to join Hindenburg's cabinet. My intellect agreed. Wait, and I would win the next election. My conscience said joining Hindenburg's cabinet was a betrayal of National Socialist values. But my instincts said take the post. Hindenburg is old and weak. They are giving me a platform from which to seize control. My instincts said act, seize the power and impose National Socialism. Some of you doubted. But look where we are!

"Now my instincts say the instrument of my injury is not important. It is my survival that is important. My destiny is to survive and lead. Any other man would have died. I did not. The triumph and glory of National Socialism are assured.

"I am uninterested in your squabbles or your theories. Himmler will double my SS guard. If that does not secure my safety, I will die and Germany will deserve to lose its salvation.

"My instincts tell me that a movie reporter has neither the courage nor the inclination to be a part of a plot against the Fuhrer. And, if I am wrong, let him go home and tell the world that he attempted to kill Germany's Fuhrer. Germany's rage would wash over the Atlantic. The United States would grovel at Germany's feet for forgiveness . . ."

Hitler rambled on about the genius of his instincts and the power of his Germany.

So I owed my life to a smart, little man with enormous capacities for hate, deception, self-deception, risk, and cruelty. A spellbinder who couldn't converse normally but could thrill the crowd. A man incapable of love who commanded love. A dreamer who envisioned an empire but was willing to sacrifice its citizens. A man who cared for animals but had no regard for human life.

I felt like I was selling out when I didn't debunk his vainglory by telling him that he would have been dead but for the luck of turning his head at a precise moment in the flow of time. Hell, maybe there was something to destiny.

Did he really not remember? Diels said Hitler didn't like to deal with bad news. He probably wasn't sure he hadn't pulled the trigger himself. No wonder he believed that only his survival counted. To know the agency of his injury would be to acknowledge either personal weakness or betrayal. Lucky for me: unrelenting grandiosity apparently conquered all when it came to the Fuhrer.

Heydrich had been bullshitting about me returning to

Columbia Haus. The SS dropped me at the Adlon. In four days Sara and I would be going home. I wasn't to leave the hotel. On our last night in Berlin, we would attend the premier of *Horst Wessel.* Goebbels' propaganda cameras would be rolling. Zukor's star and a *Variety* reporter would be caught hobnobbing with the Nazis and toasting a crappy movie with a deceitful message. I would go from assassin to bootlicker.

I felt like a drink but held off. I wasn't convinced we were home free. Sara's note said she had two things to do before she left Germany. I didn't think the premiere was one of them.

Chapter Twenty-Nine

"There is nothing like sharing a good bottle of whiskey on a rooftop. Tonight, shall we say?"

My words had been spoken in German without any introduction. The message was clear.

"It's tempting but no. Another time, perhaps."

I hung up believing he would come. After all we lived at a time when no could easily mean yes.

The tailor from UFA's costume department arrived just as my lunch was being wheeled in. He was hunched over. Too many years of hems and cuffs. Too many ultimatums from prima donnas. He was going to fit me for an opening night tux. Now I would have more tuxedos than suits and more bow ties than clean ties. Additional evidence the universe was out of kilter.

"I'm sorry. I'll wait in the hall while you eat. I'll be outside when you are ready for me."

He shrunk away like an old watch dog kept alive on scraps because it could still bark in the night.

After two days of house arrest, I needed some conversation. I told him to stay and asked the waiter to bring another lunch and some beer. When his lunch arrived the tailor pushed the food around like it might be poisoned. He wouldn't look me in the eye but peeked at me from beneath bushy, gray eyebrows, trying to determine how I was going to screw him. It took a while. The beer finally got him talking. His name was Walter Thiele. He was forty but looked fifty-five.

We had the Third Battle of Aisne in common and remembered the date: May 27, 1918. He'd been a young lieutenant leading a platoon of under and over aged recruits. Thiele came alive telling how they crossed two rivers in less than twelve hours, their fear becoming exhilaration. The French were on the run. By the morning of May 30, they reached the Marne. He and his troops were convinced that they were leading the decisive push. They were dog tired but invincible, driven by the frenzy of victory.

Then they ran into another army. Half his men died crossing a bridge at Chateau-Thierry. On the west bank of the Marne, the Americans held. In the late afternoon on the thirtieth, the Yanks counterattacked, cutting through the Germans and retaking the bridge as well as the river's east bank.

Thiele was reliving the battle as he spoke.

"I saw it in their eyes as they drove us back - we were that close to the Americans. They had the same crazed invincibility we had the day before. In an hour, we lost our fury to theirs.

"I hear the politicians talk about being stabbed in the back. They weren't there that day. The Americans were no better or worse than we were. But there were more of you. And you were all so fresh, eager for the fight, confident you would win. We were too tired, too few to match that. We fought like dogs. There is no shame or betrayal in that."

"No, not in that," I said.

Thiele seemed lost in the memory but shook it off as if a chill was passing through him.

"If it happens again, will you Americans come again?"

That had been Hitler's question.

"I don't know. Will Germany start another war?"

"I don't know. The Nazis have many faces."

"What happened to you? After Chateau-Thierry."

From his platoon, only eleven survived. All were wounded. Thiele spent nine months in Columbia Haus, when it was still in the business of saving lives. They stitched his insides together and fused three damaged vertebrae. It was the operation that bent him over.

"I'm going to be in a textbook. The 'Goldstein fusion' is what the procedure has been called. Goldstein was my surgeon. He said my operation made him famous. He kept in touch over the years. Got me my job at Ufa. He called me a month ago and said he was leaving and that I would be the famous one now. He had seen the proofs of the latest edition of the surgical textbook. The procedure has been renamed the 'Thiele fusion'. How about that?"

"I doubt you'll be collecting royalties."

He studied me, meeting my eyes, letting me know that he was more than he seemed.

"You are the reporter from *Variety*. A man under suspicion. A man in love with an enigma."

"How do you know such things?"

"I am a tailor. People talk in front of me. I could be the hurdy-gurdy man's monkey. But the monkey has ears."

Thiele chuckled like a man who hadn't laughed in a long time. Tentative at first, almost as if he had forgotten how. Then heartily, as if for the sheer pleasure of the act. Then the laughter slowly subsided as if Thiele was reluctant to let go of the moment.

"Sorry," he said. "I make clothes for some of the Nazi big shots too. Ufa picks up the expense. I hear them talk."

"It must be revealing."

"Mostly gossip. The Nazis fight like cats and dogs for power and position around Hitler. If we had any newspapers left, the stories I could tell. Sometimes I hear which companies will get new government contracts. In the last ten months, I have made a fortune in the stock market. And I have heard talk about you and Potter."

"What do you hear about us?"

"I'm leaving with Goldstein. We can get to France. But we want to go to America. Can you help with that?"

"I can't but I can put you in touch with people who can. When do you leave?"

"Two days from now."

I gave him Matt Thompson's name and address. Thompson

was Pinkerton's main man in Paris.

"I'll let him know you're coming and what you need. He may be able to swing it."

"Thank you."

"Now, about Sara and me?"

"They intend to let you and Potter leave. Some of the Nazis are not happy about that. Tomorrow Ufa will screen *Horst Wessel* for friendly critics and an adoring audience. After the screening there will be a party. Goebbels will speak about the importance of film to national culture. Potter will say a few words about German-American fellowship. You will attend. Goebbels will film it all. Great propaganda. You two will look like Nazi sympathizers."

"I guessed as much. Tell me something new."

"A tip on the stock market?"

"How about who killed Paula Glaise?"

"Some say it was Goebbels. He was fooling around with her and she had become demanding, wanting public recognition. But that was no reason to kill her. And if he had killed her, he is too smart to have left evidence that pointed right at him. Some say Goebbels was framed by one of the other little Fuhrers. Others say Potter framed him."

"What was Potter's motive? Revenge for Mala? Did you know Mala?"

"Yes. The official word was that she went back to the gypsies when the movie roles dried up. Some said she was sent to a re-education center. But she was not political. Who would want to re-educate her or make her disappear?"

"I thought Mala was killed during questioning."

"That story went around but Mala was not a threat to anyone but Magda Goebbels. I think Magda had her banished to the countryside. People say Potter was angry about Goebbels's treatment of Mala. But killing Paula to frame Goebbels for treating a gypsy like a gypsy? Farfetched. Besides how could Potter pull it off?"

"What about Tom Potter's battle with Glaise over Glaise's kid?"

"I know only what I read in the newspapers, but there were

rumors galore. Most people did not seem to know Glaise was even pregnant."

"What about these little Fuhrers?"

"Well, Goebbels has been accumulating power at the expense of Amann, Hugenberg, Streicher, and Rosenberg."

"Who's Amann?"

"A newspaper publisher. Each of the four had a motive to frame Goebbels. All but Rosenberg had the means to do it. Only Streicher is crazy enough to have tried. But Streicher is not smart enough to have done it."

"So you would eliminate them?"

"Yes. Then there are Goering, Himmler, Ley, and Hess. Each is smart enough and had the means. But none of them was crazy enough, and none had a specific grudge against Goebbels.

"That leaves Rohm. Some say he is a threat to even Hitler. Everyone is afraid of his SA - even the SS. Everyone agrees that Rohm must go and the SA must be tamed. But Rohm won't go peacefully. He could very well strike at Hitler by undermining Hitler's lieutenants. Ruining Goebbels would appeal to Rohm."

"What do you hear about the famous alibi? Was Sara really with Goebbels when Paula was killed?"

"You were there that morning?"

"Yes."

"Did you see a Maybach parked near Potter's bungalow?"

"Yes."

"Magda gave Goebbels a Maybach on his thirty-sixth birthday last year."

Thiele shrugged his shoulders as if the answer to my question was self-evident.

"So you think she was with him?"

"I'm just a tailor. Now I need to fit you and get back to the studio."

Cooper met me on the roof that night. I brought another bottle of scotch. He was asking questions before I had the cap off.

"There are rumors that someone tried to assassinate Hitler at the Eagle's Nest. Whatdayagotforme? You were there."

Would he believe the truth? If he did, could I trust him to hold the story until Sara and I were out of the country? I couldn't take the risk, so I lied. I told myself that I would give Cooper the story later.

"The story was Hitler tripped chasing his dog," I said.

"That's the official line."

He gave me a suspicious look but moved on to a dozen other questions about the Eagle's Nest. I answered the ones I could. He finished where he'd begun.

"You're holding out on the assassination attempt, aren't you?"

Cooper was a friend of sorts, and he was my lie away from a big story. In return for misleading him I was about to ask a favor.

"No. But I'm worried that Sara will do something stupid before she leaves Germany."

"You love the girl."

"Give it a break. I don't have to be in love to be worried."

Cooper shook his head and looked at me with sympathy. His eyes drifted away, and he spoke as if from some private place.

"I know how love works. You get to be a lost cause. It's a wonderful and dangerous thing. You only see the one you love. It's extraordinary. The rest of the world moves on while you lose contact. You don't even realize what's happened. And when she's gone, there is nothing left."

I was about to razz him about romantic drivel, when I remembered Humphrey's story about the young Cooper, a man too much in love. He was telling me how it had been for him and his wife.

"That's not me," I said.

"Denial is another symptom," said Cooper.

"Well, I'm denying denial. End of story."

"Which is love's irrefutable symptom. Anyway, I think the only stupid thing Sara is going to do is play out the string on *Horst Wessel* and hope to become a star in Germany. If it blows up in her face at home, she probably thinks she can charm her way out of the jam."

"Zukor's not easily charmed."

"Then she may need a husband."

"I'm ignoring that. Look, what about those submarine routes that Helli asked us about."

"What about them?"

"If Sara does do something stupid, is there a way I can get her out?"

Cooper raised his arms in protest. "I'm a reporter. Not an adventurer."

"I'm not asking you to go along. Just arrange it. Think of the story we'll have for you if we make it. Maybe even an attempt on Hitler's life."

Cooper took a swig of scotch. I knew I had him. We talked for over an hour. This time we didn't watch the sun rise and didn't finish the bottle. Neither of us could afford a hangover.

Chapter Thirty

UFA's version of Horst Wessel's life made a decent movie even if it was a grand lie. There were lots of dry eyes, but the crowd was tough. Nazis weren't the kind to cry at funerals much less movies. Besides, most of them probably knew the real Horst pimped his sister, and died of an overdose.

It wasn't *Triumph of the Will* but there was no mistaking its propaganda value. Except for the subtle flaw that Sara crafted into her performance. I was proud and frightened. She had some guts. In every scene a pendant hung from a chain around her neck. Only in the close-ups could it be seen for what it was and even then it could have been overlooked. Only once was it prominently on display. When she cradled the dying Horst, the pendant fell across his chest and came to rest on his bloody shirt.

The pendant was a ram's horn. Jewish tradition was full of stories about Jews celebrating Rosh Hashanah and Yom Kippur by playing such horns. Zukor had such a horn in his office, and he had given Sara the pendant.

When the curtain closed and the house lights came up the applause was generous but not tumultuous. Some of the anti-Semitic fanatics in the audience must have spotted and understood Sara's pendant.

But not Hugenberg, whose walk across the stage ended the applause.

"I am touched by the power of Horst's story and honored that Minister Goebbels chose Ufa to film it! Please join the Minister, the cast, and the director at a reception on Sound Stage B. Much of *Horst Wessel* was filmed there. Some of the sets are still in place. You will find it interesting. Follow the instructions of the pages stationed at the doors."

Only a Nazi could make an invitation sound like an order. And the pages looked more like Himmler's men than Hugenberg's boys. Under their scrutiny, five hundred of us walked from the theater to the sound stage. I listened to the crowd's chatter. Not a word about the pendant. Had I been the only one to notice?

A lavish buffet spread along one wall of the sound stage. Nearby was a set depicting the apartment that had been shared by Horst and his sister. On the opposite wall a hundred and fifty feet of Rennerstrasse facades had been constructed. At one end of the sound stage, a small orchestra played lobby music. At the opposite end, giant track doors were cracked open to the night. A boom-mounted camera soared over the crowd, its zoom lens focusing on groups of revelers who aped for the camera.

I couldn't get within ten feet of Sara who was the star of the party. I could see Cooper working the floor - probing, listening, and looking for a story. For a second I caught his eye. He nodded his head slightly. Five minutes later he walked up and made a show of asking me what I thought of the movie.

"Frighteningly effective," was my honest answer.

"Yes. Although Kerrl did take a few liberties. I think the battle with the commies was really on Vogstrasse. But what's accuracy got to do with it. Ah, to be twenty-seven and free from the tedious constraints of truth."

"Cooper, you are a jaded man."

"I'm a reflection of the times. I hear you're going home. Some night on State Street after midnight, you'll be three sheets to the wind, and I'll find out whether you held out on me."

Cooper walked off shaking his head as if disappointed in me. He had more or less scripted our conversation the night before on the roof of the Adlon. We lived in strange times. The only thing odd about talking in code was how normal it seemed.

After a half-hour, the orchestra broke and left the platform.

Hugenberg introduced Goebbels who was all modesty as he introduced Martin Eckner.

"... the distinguished film critic from the *Volkischer Beobachter*. Martin has just finished his review. There is no point in him keeping us in suspense. So, Martin, tell us, what do you think?"

Goebbels stepped back. In jest he raised his eyebrows and chewed a fingernail as if Eckner might commit career suicide with a bad review. He didn't. His review was a study in adulation and so weirdly ideological that no mere film critic could have written it. Goebbels and Rosenberg had probably been the ghost writers.

The applause for the review was perfunctory. Half the audience wasn't sure what to make of it. God forbid they should cheer a review that Goebbels found wanting. They shouldn't have worried. Faking relief, Goebbels stepped back to the microphone and thanked Eckner.

The audience roared its approval of Goebbels' approval.

Goebbels then offered his own praise and called the cast to the stage. When the applause subsided, he asked "Sonja Potter, the great American actress," to say a few words.

Sara stepped forward looking like a reluctant witness. She fumbled a paper from her clutch and read from it, giving the impression of a false witness. The audience was uncomfortable. When she finished, she turned and said, "Thank you, Minister Goebbels, your words are much better than mine could ever be."

Goebbels gave her a squinty look, but hardly missed a beat. He smiled sympathetically, put his arm across the small of her back, gave her half a hug, and looked at the audience.

"The poor girl is overwhelmed by your admiration. Isn't she wonderful?"

The audience cheered in relief. Goebbels was in control.

"Now enjoy yourselves. Eat, explore the sets, listen to the orchestra, and have your photos taken with our leading players. But hurry. In thirty minutes Hugenberg will treat you to a thunderstorm! Don't worry, he won't turn on the rain machine."

Goebbels led Sara from the platform, passing the returning

orchestra members.

"Did I imagine that Sara cringed at the Minister's touch?"

It was Heydrich. I hadn't noticed his approach. Dressed in a stylish gray business suit, he looked like a gambler on a hot streak.

"He gives me the creeps," I said.

"But he is a genius at certain things."

"No doubt." I wasn't taking the bait, if that's what it was.

"Did you notice Sara's pendant, the one she was wearing in the movie? Fascinating symbolism."

"No. Was it a gift from the Minister?"

"I admire cunning women. I could still be of help should you provide me with the information I want."

"I admire persistence, but can never figure out what you're talking about. Good-by, General."

As I walked away, he told me that we would be seeing each other again.

While Heydrich had spotted the pendant, Goebbels had either missed or failed to understand it. Heydrich was right. Sara was cunning. She seemed to have done enough to undermine her propaganda value but not enough to get arrested. Would that be enough for her?

I watched her posing with movie buffs on the Rennerstrasse set. I thought she was playing it straight until I notice that the pendant was back, hanging from her neck. Her subtle defiance had crossed the line from gutsy to stupid. I wanted to yank the thing from her neck.

I was heading for her when a pasty little man stepped in my way. I'd noticed him before. He was a bit rumpled for this crowd. It occurred to me that he might be an actual film critic.

He spoke in an urgent, hushed voice. "Herr Temple, everything is under control. Let Sara be. In the next few minutes all hell is going to break loose. We will get her out. Keep out of the way. If you interfere, you will endanger Sara and accomplish nothing. She wants you to go home. She will find you at the Grand Terrace Café listening to Papa Hines."

The reference to Sara's note was clear. The guy walked off before I had a chance to ask who "we" were and what "we" were up to. I didn't have long to noodle it.

Seconds later the sound stage's overhead lights went off, the Rennerstrasse street lights went on, thunder boomed, lightning flashed, and rain poured onto the set. Then gunshots rang out. It all seemed real, especially the shots.

A stampede was on. People ran from the fake rain and the sound of gunfire. The orchestra did not play on. Its members joined the scramble. The mob piled up at the narrow opening of the track doors. Three pages scrambled up a ladder to a control booth suspended beneath the roof. Someone was running on a catwalk away from the booth. Four other pages formed a phalanx around Goebbels and hustled him through a metal door.

In the first seconds of the man-made storm, Sara did not move from the stoop. Then I lost sight of her as the crowd swept me back. When it thinned, I dashed into the artificial rain. Sara was gone. The door behind the stoop was open. To my right a page was running toward the stoop. He carried his gun as easily as a relay racer carries a baton. The kid didn't see me until I crashed into him.

The gun didn't go flying. We rolled in the rain, his Luger the center of our small universe. I was bigger, stronger. He was younger and quicker. His finger was on the trigger. My hands were wrapped around his gun hand. His free hand clawed at my hands. The gun was above our heads. He pumped a knee into my groin. I forced the gun barrel toward his head and locked my thumb over the tip of his trigger finger. An inch or so more and I would have the angle and blow him to oblivion. Then he rammed his head into mine, a weapon now as his instinct to survive overwhelmed any inhibitions. I twisted away and saw another page level his gun at me. I rolled, pulling the kid on top of me as the second page fired. The kid went limp. I grabbed the gun from the kid's hand, aimed, and fired. The second page toppled into a puddle that had formed in the phony gutter. I pushed the kid off me. His dead eyes were still open.

I had to find Sara.

From a catwalk a page aimed his gun at me and barked for me to stay put. I ducked through the door at the stoop before he could fire. Behind the facade was a tangle of supporting two-by-fours, shrouded in near darkness. Five feet past the façade was a cement block wall. Sara wasn't in sight. A path cut through the two-by-fours in both directions. I set off toward the front of the sound stage, passing under platforms that had been constructed behind some of the upper windows of the facade.

Someone stage-whispered my name.

I turned and aimed the kid's Luger at a figure descending from one of the windows.

"It's me. Thiele. Walter Thiele."

"The tailor?"

"Yes. We've got to get out of here fast. Follow me."

"Where's Sara?"

"She headed out through . . . damn. Hurry!"

At the far end of the wooden tunnel, a door opened and two men with flashlights appeared. In seconds the beams would reach us. Thiele scampered in the other direction and stepped through a door. He looked back at me.

"Make a choice. If you want to give yourself over, fine. I'm locking this door behind me. Please don't give me away."

"Wait," I said and followed Thiele through a door marked, **Kleidverleiher**.

Thiele shut the door behind us, threw a dead bolt, and ordered me to follow him. He was enjoying this. Dozens of long garment racks were lined up like regiments from across the globe and down the annals of history. There were sections for men, women, and children. There were sections for every strata of every society. There was a large area devoted to nothing but uniforms. Then there were aisles of shelves holding hats, shoes, canes, clubs, purses, parasols, and umbrellas. Thiele nodded toward a light in an adjoining room.

"The tailor shop. My apartment is behind it. You need to hide. That door won't hold."

We cut down an aisle filled with garments from Napoleon's France. It led to a dock where a dozen large hampers were lined up, each filled with dirty costumes.

"In you go."

The pounding at the door to the sound stage convinced me not to argue. I jumped in a hamper. Thiele piled dirty clothes over me. The clothing muffled the sound of his steps as he ran off.

". . . stinks back here?" was the next thing I heard.

"Dirty costumes," said Thiele's disembodied voice. "The laundry is two buildings over. We truck the cloths back and forth every few days."

Just then my hamper shuddered as I nearly gagged.

"What was that?"

"What are you talking about?"

"A noise. Something moved. One of those hampers."

"Thiele, have you hidden a killer in the laundry?"

The question sounded like a joke.

"If someone is in there, the stink will kill them," responded Thiele.

Someone laughed then said, "What a way to die. Which one moved, Karl."

"I'm not sure."

Three quick shots rang out. The second thwacked into my hamper. I might have jumped or screaming had the shooting not ended as quickly as it had begun. With no time to react, I froze.

Nothing happened. Then more laughter.

"Well, I didn't kill the stink. Go back to sewing, old man. You have some new holes to mend. Let's get out of here before we need fumigating."

I listened to the sound of fading footfalls A minute or so later Thiele was back, tossing costumes from my burrow. I sat up in the middle of the hamper. We smiled at each other, the stink of the place forgotten in the relief of dodging a bullet.

Thiele and I were driving from Babelsberg, retreating to our respective submarine routes in a car from UFA's motor pool.

"She took off with one of the SS wunderkind," said Thiele.

"SS?"

"I saw the whole thing from a window platform. About a minute before the thunderstorm, an SS man came snooping around. I thought I would have some explaining to do. But he went straight to the door where Potter was being photographed and just waited. When the storm cut loose, he opened the door and pulled her through. They ran through the door to make-up. After they disappeared, I was about to scramble back to wardrobe when I saw you running toward the set. I stuck around to see what would happen to you."

"What did they say to each other? Sara and the SS man."

"I didn't hear them say anything but she seemed willing to follow his lead."

I figured Sara was in the hands of the perfect Aryan.

Twenty minutes later Thiele stopped the car near a U-Bahn station. It wasn't my actual rendezvous point. He hadn't wanted to know that.

"If they catch me, I would probably give it up," he explained.

"I think you're too brave for that," I said.

"Bravery has limits. Not knowing is safer."

"Call me when you get to the states. I'm in the Chicago phone book."

He nodded. He had saved my life yet he looked at me like I'd done him a favor. I extended my hand to him. He waved it off.

"Not now," he said. "Later in Chicago. Go now."

I nodded and left, not liking the odds on us both reaching Chicago.

The trolley car was a new one. In the next seat, two men were arguing in hushed tones about whether Germany was rearming.

I shut out the conversation. That kind of talk wasn't going to affect the Nazis. A few minutes later the train clattered to a stop at a station in Wedding. I got out. Five minutes later at the stroke of midnight, I walked to a neighborhood tavern located in the basement of 27 Vogstrasse.

A gust of sweat, tobacco, beer, and sauerkraut blew past me as the door opened. In near darkness men were hunched over a bar and scattered tables, mumbling and grunting like weary primitives. Being men without expectations and beyond fear, they didn't look up to see who had arrived.

I went to the bar thinking I had the address wrong. These guys would be lucky to find their way home – assuming they had one - much less out of Germany.

I thought about Fix as I ordered a beer from the goon working the bar in his undershirt. I gave myself five minutes. If the contact didn't show, I would risk going to the American Embassy - even though the Gestapo watched it for people like me and even though the embassy would probably turn me over to the Kripo for shooting the kid who had tried to shoot me on the sound stage.

"Finish up. You can stay with me for the next few hours and get some sleep. You'll need it," said a voice at my side.

I had let my guard fall and hadn't seen the man approach. I turned to the voice. I had seen the somber face before but didn't immediately place it.

"I'm Theo. The weaver. A mutual friend once stayed with me while he recovered from a fever."

Chapter Thirty-One

"There is no room on the truck. Tomorrow, you go."

Ludi was in his baker's garb, complete with a light dusting of flour. It occurred to me that he didn't know the first thing about baking.

He turned to Theo. "Off you go. Leipzig by six-thirty."

Theo hopped in the cab of a good-sized truck packed with fresh bread. The bread's aroma was lost in diesel exhaust as the truck pulled away. Ludi and I were left standing on the dock behind the bakery. He lit up. In the lighter's flame, I could see nicotine stains on his fingers.

"There is a false bottom in the trailer where we store non-bakery items," said Ludi.

"What beat me out?"

"Another addition of the *Ku'damm*. Our trucks are the perfect cover for distributing the paper. Yes?"

"Too perfect, when you think about it. Someone in the Gestapo or the SS will figure it out, don't you think?"

"Here is the beauty of it. National Ovens is a Nazi operation, ostensibly owned by Paulde Gruber. Gruber bought his rank as an SS Brigadefuhrer but he didn't really have the stomach for the work. So the Party moved him over here as their front man. The bakery puts tons of cash in the party's coffers. No one suspects it."

"How did you get your job?"

"I was the plant manager for the previous owner, Jacob Silverman. I stayed on."

He handed his lighter to me. "A beauty, gift from Gruber. The swastika is real gold."

"Instead of salary?" I asked.

"No. That's part of why the Nazis are dangerous. They pay well."

I gave the lighter back and asked if the bakery was also in the printing business.

"Yes. One of the ovens always seems to be down for repairs. It's only a shell of itself. The guts have been removed to make room for a press. Jacob bought it for to us before he left Germany. The black shirts and trench coats wouldn't find it even if they came looking."

That sounded more like hubris than fact.

"What's in the latest *Ku'damm*?"

"A story Potter gave us."

"Sara?"

"Yes. Very powerful. Last week on the twenty-eighth to be exact, Himmler and Heydrich hosted a dinner for party big-shots - including Hitler - at an old castle on the Rhine near Koblenz. It was a reenactment of a conquest banquet. According to legend, the Goths slaughtered their enemies' male children and cooked the healthy ones for dinner. The Nazis pulled a couple of three-year olds from a Jewish orphanage for their main course. If there was ever any doubt about these Nazis, this will end it.

"Sara told you that?"

"Yes. You believe the Nazis are not capable of such a thing?"

"Well, for starters Hitler is a vegetarian. It sounds more like something Streicher would write about the Jews. What day was the twenty-eighth?"

"Thursday."

"That's what I thought. I know that Heydrich was in Berchtesgaden that day. So was Hitler. Did you try to verify the story?"

"What's to verify? Even if Sara got it wrong . . ." Ludi shrugged his shoulders as if to say, who cares?

"Where is she now?"

"I don't know. She came by last night with Eric after he'd gotten her out. I expected them back this morning."

I was happy Sara escaped, but could not stop thinking.

"You have two missing people, one of whom brought you a questionable story. Maybe the story was a plant, meant to . . ."

The confidence drained from Ludi like perspiration from a liar.

"I take your point."

He flicked his cigarette into the alley and rushed into the bakery where he ordered someone to catch Theo on the road to Leipzig. Someone else was instructed to burn the *Ku'damms* that were awaiting distribution. A third man was told to seal oven four.

Ludi looked at me like I was a jigsaw piece that didn't fit.

"You killed a man last night? At the *Horst Wessel* party."

He spit on the ground, an inelegant critique of Nazi culture, I suppose.

"Yes."

He thought for what seemed like along time. Then told another of his men to put me in the safe room.

As I was being led away he called, "Temple, if we are raided, check the cabinets in the hideaway. You will find gasoline. Burn the place."

Two hours later I heard what sounded like three or four bursts from an automatic. No one came to explain but neither did anyone blast their way into my sanctuary. Later I heard muted voices. I discovered I could hear better the closer I was to the floor. I pulled back the carpet and found a piece of padding over a ventilation grate. Removing it opened a pipeline through which jumped Heydrich's falsetto.

". . . worthless swine or traitor? Which is it?"

Through the grate came the sound of weeping. Then the crack of a switch against a hard surface. More weeping. Then a snap followed instantly by a cry of pain.

"Gruber, I'll slice you to mincemeat. Where is the press?"

"I don't know."

"Don't insult me. We found the remains of that pig-shit

propaganda sheet in the incinerator."

"I swear. I . . ."

Another snap, another cry.

"I don't care how much this place earns, I'll level it. I'll rip those overs apart if I have to. For each oven, I will gut one of your children and when I'm done with them it will be your wife, your parents, your brothers, your sisters. There will be liters of blood on your hands. Do you want that?"

"But I don't . . ."

Three snaps in quick succession. Wailing, followed by a cry for mercy, followed by more snaps and the sound of a body falling to the floor.

"Get him up," said Heydrich.

A door opened. A new voice. "We found the press. It was hidden in one of the ovens."

"Take this swine to Columbia Haus. When he comes around, tell him we are rounding up his family. Now, show me the press."

The room went silent. Thirty minutes later came the sounds of the room being torn apart. When the searchers finished, one of them spoke.

"From his office you couldn't prove he was a baker much less a traitor."

"Nice pornography collection though."

"Guess we know what he was doing up here, while those so-called bakers were printing dog crap."

"The dumb shit might as well have been a Jew."

"Jews don't come that dumb."

The door closed.

I called in the fire. I hadn't planned to. However once I was outside, I realized the buildings in the neighborhood were so tightly packed there was no telling how far the blaze would spread. But for the risk of burning down half of Wedding, torching the bakery seemed perfect. The records in the secret office needed to be destroyed, so why not take a Nazi business with them?

The Nazis burned the Reichstag and blamed the communists. I burned the bakery, hoping they would blame Heydrich. The *Ku'damm* bust was his operation. He would take credit for its success. Let him duck the responsibility for the fire.

The blaze was nearly out of control when the fire trucks arrived. Before the flames died, a second fire company was called. One man was killed. Later Cooper told me the dead fireman was a casualty of war. In a way he was.

I walked out of Wedding and caught a cab. My identification papers said that I was Otto Beck. According to my business card, I was a director of Beck A. G. in Düsseldorf. The cab dropped me at Hotel Unternehmen on Friedrichstrasse. It catered to wholesalers peddling merchandise and businessmen visiting the factories near Tempelhof.

An officious desk clerk told me that the Unternehmen required reservations. He explained that since Hitler became chancellor the hotel had been booked solid. A Nazi pin sparkled on his lapel.

"The Fuhrer has blessed us all," I kowtowed back. "So much work to do. I've had a long day. I'll be happy to pay in advance."

I showed him a thousand mark note. He snatched it from my hand.

"I believe there has been a cancellation. You are in luck."

I signed the ledger and paid. We did our "heil-Hitlers" and I was off to my room. There I took stock.

The safe room had been a bonanza of sorts: Ludi's journal, twenty different sets of identification, over thirty thousand marks in cash, and enough information to send a hundred men to their deaths. Himmler would have had a field day with Ludi's list of potential allies. It contained names, addresses and the reasons the people were likely to oppose Hitler. "Jewish wife," "Man of conscience," "Friend of Gregor Strasser," and so on.

In his journal Ludi coded the names of his partisans. While

the journal entries were vague, anyone with local knowledge could have deciphered the identities and entries. I didn't have the time for the whole thing. I flipped to the back to see what was on Ludi's mind over the last few days. One passage jumped at me.

"Blintz remains an enigma. She wants to be with us but seems incapable of breaking the Wizard's spell. What is she thinking? Now I send the Angel to rescue her. The last time it was Pretzel and look what happened. I should let Blintz fall. She is isolated from us but one betrayal can lead to another and so on to us. So I risk the Angel because the alternative may be worse. I hate this. Black Forest thrives on it like a runner dashing to the finish line. Would that I could see the sport of it."

I understood Blintz to be Sara and the Angel to be Eric, the perfect Aryan. Perhaps the Pretzel was the guy I thought of as the tall man. Could Black Forest be Diels? Was the Wizard Goebbels?

With the bakery busted, it would not have been long before the Nazis found the safe room. Ludi's papers would have given the Nazis a road map to people in need of re-education. Remembering Ludi's last words to me, I checked the cabinets and found the gasoline can. I took what I might need – money and new identification - and set fire to the rest.

The cash and ID gave me some freedom of movement. I was Otto Beck. Getting out of Germany was within my reach. But for the moment I wanted to find the perfect Aryan. If I was lucky, Sara would be with him. I could think of two places he might be.

The bed in my room at Unternehmen was surprisingly comfortable. As I fell asleep, it occurred to me that the silly code in Ludi's journal perfectly captured the absurdity of Germany. It was a country under the delusion that madmen were the key to prosperity and order.

The first of the tenement courtyards had been abandoned to stray pets and mangy chickens. The same was true of the next courtyard. No people. The feel was all wrong. I felt exposed walking through the arch leading to the third courtyard. The windows above looked empty but I sensed the tenants were hovering just out of sight.

In the third courtyard, even the animals had been frightened off. Four black sedans surrounded the door to the left wing of the tenement. A single SS man stood watch as if a street pirate might high-jack one of the cars. I hung in the shadows, terrified that Sara and the Angel would be dragged from the building leaving me to . . . what?

Suddenly a woman's scream filled the courtyard - the cry of an animal clamped in a trap. I froze. A pair of SS sergeants lugged a woman from the tenement door. She twisted between them, raging to break their grip. Her dress was torn at the sleeve. Hair was wild about her face, matted here and there in bloody patches. Bloody or not, the color was Sara's blond. More black shirts followed, Heydrich in their midst looking irritated. The woman broke free, spun, and went after Heydrich, her hands raised as if to claw his face. One of the troops in Heydrich's guard smashed her ribs with the stock of his rifle.

She collapsed to one knee.

"Get up, woman," ordered Heydrich.

The woman's back was to me. Her head lifted and I imagined her eyes locking on Heydrich. She put her hands on her left knee. As she pushed herself to her feet, the guard readied his rifle to strike again.

I edged from the shadows with no clear idea of what I might do but a vague sense that my last act would likely be a futile one driven by love, not reason.

The woman drew herself up. With pride she pulled back her hair and glared at Heydrich. She spoke a single word which echoed around the courtyard.

"Pig!"

The word stopped me in my tracks. The voice wasn't Sara's. I stepped back into the shadows and watched Heydrich and the woman glare at each other.

Heydrich held out a hand, signaling the troops to leave her alone.

"Foolhardy bitch," he said.

The woman responded with passion, "My husband. These people. They are the real Germans. You disgrace them!"

She spat at Heydrich while her arms were raised to the empty windows above.

Heydrich backhanded her across the face.

"You think they will help you? You are a traitor to the values of National Socialism! They dare not help. But go, if that is your choice. Your neighbors will turn you in or they will pay the price."

She hesitated.

"Choose, woman. Run to them or comply with my orders."

Her shoulders sagged with the knowledge of defeat.

"I thought so," said Heydrich, a hint of triumph in his voice.

"You are wrong," said the woman, her back straightening. "I choose not to run to my neighbors. I choose to defy your orders for Germany's honor and for the sake of my soul."

She turned, showed Heydrich her back, and slowly walked away with more dignity than Heydrich could have mustered in a dozen lifetimes.

The troops looked at Heydrich, incredulous that he would permit such defiance. She was fifteen feet away now, her pace deliberate. She was not going to run. From the windows above a few people called, "For Germany". Heydrich pulled his sidearm and took aim at her back.

From a window above someone yelled with the fear that courage engenders in the weak, "He has a gun! Stop! Please!"

The woman walked on, her pace steady, her defiance relentless.

"Your arrogance is wasted in this petty display, madam," said Heydrich. Then he looked up, "You, hiding in the windows, know that the Reich does not tolerate criminals."

He fired. The woman lurched forward but did not fall. She steadied herself and kept walking. Heydrich blinked, anger crossing his face. The gall of the woman not to fall. He fired a three-round bust that lifted her feet from the ground. I saw her face clearly in the split second she was suspended above the paving stones. The pain she felt did not alter the defiant line of her jaw, nor steal the fire from her eyes.

Theo's wife had not only beaten Heydrich, she had earned something most of us will never have.

I took a bus to Walter Prinz' former office. It was a long shot, but Sara and Eric had to be somewhere.

As the bus approached the Lessing Theater, I could see from the marquee that *Journey To Ophir* was playing. The play's story takes place in 1917. A German naval Captain is taken prisoner on the high seas by his son-in-law, the Captain of a British frigate. They are enemies with a common bond. The two Captains debate the issues of the day. The German Captain and the audience know that the journey will take the frigate through a German mine field. The tension is in not knowing if the German will alert his son-in-law to the danger or will allow the frigate to be sunk at the expense of his daughter and grandchildren. As the frigate sinks, the German lectures his son-in-law on the honor of duty.

Up the street at the Deutsche Theater was *Peter Rothman's Maid*, a blood-and-soil tale with a eugenic twist. Peter and his wife are farmers, producing crops for the Reich but no children. The wife can't get pregnant. Hanna is a local peasant girl with an innate sense of duty. Seeing Peter's plight she offers herself to him. Duty bound to accept, Peter and Hanna make a baby for the Reich. Duty bound to step aside, the good wife kills herself. To preserve the memory of the wife, Peter and Hanna don't marry. She becomes his maid. Together they work the farm and raise little Peter for shipment to a Hitler Youth Camp.

Max Reinhardt would have gagged - culture making war on humanity while sanctifying a grotesque sense of duty.

Prinz' name had been removed from the building directory and replaced by a listing for Viktoria Veidt, Theatrical Agent. The National Socialist Actors Guild was also newly listed. I imagined the guildsmen angling to play dutiful Aryans in the mold of Peter Rothman. I couldn't imagine what they made of *Faust*, given the Fatherland's bargain with Hitler.

The freshly stenciled door to Veidt's office was locked. My knocking brought no response. I was almost relieved. I had pictured a smirking Heydrich opening the door, having anticipated my arrival.

I picked the lock. I had come too far not to nose around. I pushed the door open. The small lobby was dark but a faint light came from the direction of Prinz' former office. I remembered his wraparound windows. It was probably just the glow of Berlin at twilight.

I entered the lobby and closed the door behind me. As I stepped toward the receptionist's desk, I was clubbed on the back of the head.

Chapter Thirty-Two

I came awake with a start - disoriented and water dripping from my face. I was sitting in Prinz' chrome and leather chair. When I tried to stand someone pulled me back. Someone else was sitting behind Prinz's desk. And there was a girl, holding a glass. She looked like Veronica Lake.

"You're lucky, Temple. The Nazis are on a witch hunt but you're at the bottom of their list. They won't get to you for days. On the other hand, I wouldn't go back to the Adlon. Was it you who burned the bakery?"

Lights shimmered through the windows, wrapping the speaker in his own shadow. His suit coat hung on him as if he'd lost weight. His face seemed as hard and sad as a weathered tombstone.

"Yes," I said, instantly regretting the admission.

"So tell me, is the Potter girl a Nazi?"

The guy was changing subjects like a professional interrogator would to keep a witness off balance.

"That's hard to believe."

"It's hard to believe a man like Hitler is chancellor," he said. "Are you in love with her?"

"I've asked myself that."

"In my experience love is clear, if sometimes confusing."

"What's your point?"

"You can't bring yourself to admit you're in love with a Nazi."

"I don't believe that and I certainly don't know that."

"She needs an official party card for you to admit what she is?"

"Why ask if you've already made up your mind?"

"Tell him about the last few days."

The man standing behind me spoke. "Hanussen is dead. Beaten, shot, and buried in the forest outside of Berchtesgaden. Emile Maurice is dead. Shot at Oranieburg."

The voice belonged to Eric, the man who once put a knife to my throat and the man who probably rescued Sara from the sound stage.

"You're not saying Sara had anything to do with that," I asked.

"Tell him the rest," said the man behind the desk.

"We could not figure out whose side she was on, so we mostly kept her in the dark. For example, she didn't know about Ludi or the bakery. On the other hand Heydrich didn't trust her either. He wanted to take her down. He was going to arrest her after the *Horst Wessel* party. So we decided to pull her out.

"We got word to her. Told her to stay on the stoop when the phony rain started. We would get her out in the confusion. I went in for her. I should have known. It was too easy.

"Ludi was going to slip her out of Berlin on a truck to Cologne. From there to Belgium. We went to the bakery. She told us a story that was outlandish even for the Nazis. But Ludi decided to run with it the next day. With another *Ku'damm*, there was no room for us on the truck the next morning.

"We went to my place in Wedding. I didn't spot the tail until after we entered the building. I had forgotten something in the car. The tail was walking in as I turned around. He walked on as if nothing had happened. I grabbed Sara and we made a run for it. We got away, but by then the damage had been done."

Ignoring Eric, I spoke to the specter behind Prinz' desk. He shifted in his chair, his face emerging from the shadows. For a second I imagined him to be the ghost of the tall man. There was something familiar about him.

"You think Sara told some kraut about the plan to get her out, and then the Gestapo followed the two of them to the bakery?" I asked.

"They followed. Whether she told them the plan is the question," said the man behind the desk. "And Ludi bit on that crazy story about a ritual dinner which tied her to the *Ku'damm*

Conscience."

"Who are you?"

"Once you saved me from some pack rats and then left me for dead. Eric found me and pulled me through. So did Sara compromise us?"

"You're Boehm?"

"Long story. Tell me, Temple, did Sara compromise us?"

"I sure as hell don't think so, but I don't know for a fact."

"You should know whose side she's on. The rest follows from that. You are her lover. Lovers talk even when they shouldn't. And even if she didn't spell it out, you should have sensed the truth. Evil can't hide."

Boehm's voice was filled with desperation as if his questions about Sara went to the core of who he was. And there was something proprietary in the way he said "Sara," as if the pain she could cause was only his to receive.

"She never confessed to me. And if evil can't hide, she isn't on their side. Where is she? Here?"

"Yes, she's here."

"Hadn't you better get out of here? It's just a matter of time before Ludi or one of his people tell them about this office."

"There is no reason for anyone to connect this place with us."

"I did."

"He has a point," said Eric.

"Let me see Sara."

Boehm considered, and then nodded. "Take him, Eric. Give them some privacy."

Eric led me back to the reception area. He pulled open a wall panel behind which was a steel door that unlocked to a windowless room. Old wooden file cabinets were lined up on one wall. Across from the cabinets were stacks of half-sheets and placards, the silent record of countless theater and music hall performances dating back to the 1890s. At the far wall was a private elevator with an elaborate Art Nouveau gate.

"Michael!"

"Sara."

"You have five minutes," said Eric.

He left and shut the door behind him.

Sara stood under a ceiling fixture that cast a rainbow of color through the leafy pattern of its shade. She wore slacks and a man's shirt and tie. Her hair was piled on top of her head. There were circles under her eyes. She looked great to me.

"Need a kick in the ass, lady?"

"How? What are you doing here?"

"Zukor won't pay if I go home without you."

She smiled through tears. The smile seemed rueful and the tears joyful. Or was it the reverse?

"Even that was a lie – at least at first," she said.

"What?"

"That I needed you to stay to keep me from getting a big head."

"I hoped as much."

"It's not what you think. At first you were an option for me. I let you think . . . but not much later . . . by the time we left Wannsee Beach."

She reached out and touched my cheek with her hand as if we were lost to each other. She was remote, weary like the time at Tegeler Lake. I took her by the shoulders.

"The Nazis are on a witch hunt. And those people out there think you led the Gestapo to the bakery on Ackerstrasse. We need to convince them that you're not a collaborator."

She shook her head slowly.

"It must seem like I was. That's what I would think standing in their shoes. They can't figure out what to do with me. They are good people faced with a problem I created."

"If you helped the Nazis, it was before you realized . . . You were blinded, like the Germans, by the jobs and the bullshit. Hell, half the world thinks Hitler is good for business."

"I was worse than blind. But I didn't tell anyone Eric was coming for me. And I didn't lead the Gestapo to the bakery, at least not intentionally. Michael, don't believe that of me. Please."

"I don't but Boehm, out there, is not so sure. Still he could be convinced. Then we can make a run for it."

"Boehm," she said as if trying to match the sound of the name to something. "I was so mad at him. I haven't forgiven him yet but the anger is mostly gone."

"I followed you two into Wedding that day. When I caught up with him he was laying in a hallway beaten and stabbed. He thought I was Eric. He was mumbling about Diels, Emile Maurice and you. Hard to make out what he was saying. Did you stab him?"

"There was a time after he left us . . . Throwing Mom over for a . . . God knows what I might have done when I first got to Berlin. But by that day, I had forgiven him for Paula Glaise. And I knew Viktoria was more than a cheap flirtation. In a way that was worse. By then I had paid him back by climbing in bed with his lover's enemy. The Ufa deal was an excuse. I came to Germany to find out what was going on with Dad. At first I was blinded by the Nazis. It seemed like they were alright despite Hitler's vile book. I knew it was killing Dad and initially it seemed like he was getting just what he deserved."

"What are you taking about?"

"Don't you see he found a cause. It wasn't enough to have a wife and kids who adored him and a successful business. He wanted a great adventure. But an American businessman can't very well blend into the resistance. So he became Boehm."

Looking at her with her hair drawn up, I made the connection. It was in the line of their noses, their high cheek bones, and the sweep of their jaws.

"Boehm is your father."

"And Viktoria is his lover. If only it had been a simple affair. But Victoria isn't a mindless actress. She picked the right side of the fight before most people even knew it had to be fought. She found a hell of a man to stand by her side."

"I don't understand," I said, thinking that Glaise had been Tom Potter's lover.

"He wrote. Separate letters to each of us, trying to explain. None of us got the whole truth. I guess he tailored his letters to what he thought we could accept. He must have known we would share what he'd written and piece it together. But even then we could only guess what was really going on with Vik, as he calls her. He seemed to think he could betray us without any concern that we would betray him."

She fell silent, anger still simmering.

"So you betrayed him?"

"No. He was right. I couldn't do that. But when he told me about their plan in the car that day I said I wouldn't do it. I told him that he and his girlfriend were on the wrong side of history. He could die for all I cared. He'd already made a widow of Mom. We would see if Viktoria's grief would be as real as Mom's or whether in time she would dump him and find another sucker. I was a complete jerk."

"What plan?" I asked, feeling lost in her story.

"Diels cooked it up. He thinks Hitler will ruin Germany. Diels discovered the location of the *Ku'damm* by tracking Dad. Diels confronted him. Told him he would have to act on the information because Himmler was probably just a step behind. The safe way to cover his ass was to shut down the *Ku'damm* and arrest Dad. But that would cost him two potential allies in his secret battle to get rid of Hitler.

"The alternative was to kill Boehm who was the link to the *Ku'damm*. After all, Boehm was a fiction. My father agreed. Diels provided a corpse to play the role of the dead Boehm, and then became a silent partner in the *Ku'damm* while pretending to search for the people behind it."

"Where did you come in?"

"Diels guessed the Nazis had lost their allure for me, and that I was having doubts about playing a part just to hurt my father. Diels is a schemer. He wanted to use me and at the same time cement my position with the Party. So he decided that I would blow the whistle on Boehm.

"Dad didn't say anything about Diels but he generally put the plan to me the day when you saw us. When I told him no, that he was on the wrong side of history, he said it was like a knife in the heart."

"But you did it anyway. Blew the whistle on Boehm."

"Yes."

"Why?"

"Because the Nazis are what they are, and because I couldn't leave the knife in my father's heart. So I went along with their scheme. And now I'm a traitor because I can't explain why Eric and me were followed. Maybe Himmler and Heydrich are just smarter than Diels. Maybe it was nothing more than dumb luck. I've been a fool but I've been on Dad's side since I turned in Boehm."

A grudging smile crept across her face. "She is beautiful. Guts too. She could have left with Prinz."

"Viktoria?" I asked.

"Yes. Are you jealous of Dad? Viktoria is a woman who knows her mind. Not someone who dithers like a girl."

"I've got all I need right in front of me."

"Faker. I know you're stuck on Dietrich."

"You'll do in a pinch. But I have more questions."

How had Tom Potter gotten from Glaise to Viktoria? Was he just a serial philanderer? Who stabbed Potter? Sara's story had me confused. But just then the door opened, cutting me off before I could finish quizzing Sara.

Potter, Viktoria, and Eric scrambled into the room. Eric closed the wood panel. Then he shut and locked the steel door. Viktoria crossed to the elevator and opened a control box. From the far side of the steel door came the muffled sounds of a commotion. Viktoria inserted an old key into a slot between two switches. She threw the left switch, turned the key then threw the right switch. When nothing happened, she whispered, "Damn."

From the other side of the door came the sounds of an office being torn apart. Potter whispered an explanation. "Diels has retired, probably with a bullet in his head. He's been replace by Himmler. We heard it on the radio. Not a minute later Eric spotted a car pulling up. Gestapo by the looks of who got out."

"We never should have turned the damn thing off," Eric said to no one in particular.

I thought he meant the radio but Viktoria snapped at him.

Something about old wiring and the risk of fire. Viktoria continued to fiddle with the key and switches but the elevator refused to come alive.

Someone was barking angry orders on the other side of the door. Viktoria grimaced, vexed like someone who has forgotten the combination to a familiar lock. The sequence had become an elusive tidbit, slipping further away the harder she tried to remember it. There was now pounding on the walls that hid the door to the room we were in. Potter put an arm around Sara's shoulder, a fatherly gesture meant to comfort. Sara looked like she might cry at the gesture.

"Find some way to help her," said Sara, nodding at Viktoria.

Viktoria looked at Potter as if to apologize for dragging him into the mess of a lifetime. It occurred to me she was an informant, delaying to give the Gestapo the time to find the wall panel that would lead to us. We would all be arrested. Later Viktoria would be released to collect some Nazi badge for heroism.

The intensity of pounding increased. Viktoria's eyes lingered on Potter. He gave her a reassuring smile that was mostly in his eyes. She turned back to the controls. Without thinking she flipped the switches and twisted the key in the correct sequence. The elevator came alive. The four of us piled in, and down we went.

"They will be waiting for us on the first floor," I predicted. "We need to get off between here and there."

Viktoria answered.

"This was Walter's father's private elevator. It only stopped on his floor, the ground floor, and the basement. The ground floor exit was closed off when Walter stopped using it. If they are in the basement, we fight our way out."

Eric pulled his Luger but looked less than resolute. If the Gestapo was waiting in the basement, the odds of fighting our way out of the elevator were near zero.

As Eric pulled open the elevator gate, someone barked a command from the darkness.

"Stay right there! Lower your gun, Eric. I am here to trade as Temple's friend Cooper would say."

"I thought you had been ousted." I said, recognizing the voice.

"Ousted is one way to put it. I'll explain later. For now we need to move. Viktoria, I believe old Helmut Prinz had a private tunnel connecting to the Lessing Theater?"

"Yes," she answered.

"Do you know the way? It is only a matter of time until they discover where the elevator deposited you."

"Yes," said Viktoria.

"Then lead the way," The words were a command, not a request.

"Hold it!" I said. "This bastard tried to have me killed. I'm not going to just waltz off with him."

"Circumstances change, Temple. If I still wanted you dead, I would have just shot you. We don't have all day. Let's go."

"Screw you."

Just then the elevator started clicking.

Viktoria understood the sound. "They found the elevator and are trying to call it."

"Prop the gate open and let's go," said the voice in the darkness.

"He can't be trusted," I said.

Diels stepped into the light. "Take it easy."

He put his gun on the floor and stepped back.

"Temple, you know when Cooper trades information he never goes first. But I'm going to demonstrate my good faith."

"And Hitler's giving a sermon about love at his local synagogue."

Diels ignored me and said, "It was Hitler who killed Paula Glaise. Fair enough?"

That sounded like bullshit. Then I remembered. Hitler himself told me that Glaise was a bitch with whom he had crossed paths.

I stepped out of the elevator and picked up Diels' gun.

"We need to get out of here. Lets go," I said.

"Follow me," said Viktoria who was already on the move.

We emerged from the Lessing as the streets were beginning to fill with theatergoers. We didn't blend in very well but we made it around the corner to Diels's car.

He drove across the Spree on the bridge at the foot of Unterbaum Strasse and turned north onto Kronprinzufer. The lights of the night sparkled on the river's lazy current. A Kripo car passed us, and slowed as if to pull us over. Then it accelerated away, its flashing lights adding to the river's glitter. The road followed the Spree's northeast bend to Alsenstrasse where Diels turned south toward Siegessaule. Just short of the Victory Column that paid tribute to Germany's eighteenth century unification, we stopped at a fortress-like building.

After a few seconds, Diels pulled away and drove around the block. The next time down Alsenstrasse he stopped at an alley that ran along the north side of the building. An iron gate stood at the mouth of the alley. Diels gave Eric two keys and instructions.

Diels circled the block again. As the car approached the alley, Diels checked the mirrors and flashed the car lights. Eric pushed the gate open and the car darted down the alley.

Eric closed and locked the gate behind us. At the far end of the alley, Eric had unlocked and opened an overhead steel door. Diels drove in. Eric rolled the door down as Diels parked.

"Welcome to the Reichstag Annex," said Diels. "It's been closed since the Reichstag burned. No one has been in the place since Lubbe's conviction. I can't think of a safer place for a bunch of fugitives."

"Did he burn it?" I asked referring to Lubbe.

The twenty-four-year-old communist from Holland was such a perfect suspect that half of Berlin figured he had been framed.

"Well, the evidence was irrefutable that he wanted to," said Diels with an enigmatic smile.

Chapter Thirty-Three

Diels made himself at home behind the desk of Jarman Henst, a former Reichstag Administrator. Although it was an interior office, its appointments were first class, including a wet bar. Diels offered us brandy as if we had retired to the smoking room of a private club.

Potter was irritated but spoke with a solicitous tone - the kind people used with the potentially deranged. "Can we get down to business?"

Diels took some papers from a briefcase that had been in the trunk of his car.

"These are the Ufa gate logs from the night Glaise died. Goebbels was there. He arrived at three-fifty. When did he get to your bungalow, Sara?"

Sara hesitated, then said, "At about that time."

"Hardly time to kill Glaise, given the elaborate way it was done," Diels said looking at Sara. "I understand that you were upset when Goebbels arrived."

"I wasn't expecting him."

"No late night work on the *Horst Wessel* script?"

"No. That was just the alibi story for Goebbels."

"As well as you."

"You could look at it that way," Sara agreed.

"When Goebbels arrived, you were upset because you already knew Glaise had been killed. Isn't that so?"

There was a hard edge to Diels' voice.

"What is this?" I interrupted. "I thought you said Hitler was the murderer. Don't answer him, Sara."

"Slow down, Temple," said Diels looking apologetic, a little beaten down. The indignity of his lost stature seemed to loiter among his scars.

"The habits of an interrogator die hard. But Sara knew Glaise was dead. Goebbels said that she was ashen when she opened the door. He joked that he'd taken her breath away before but never by simply saying hello."

"Watch your mouth, or I'll shut it," said Tom Potter.

"We have all done things we regret. But back to the point. Goebbels said you looked like you had seen a ghost. Later he figured you were upset because you knew what had happened to Glaise. He said he saw a bloody towel in your bathroom."

"Did you believe that?" Sara asked with more equanimity than I was feeling.

"Not necessarily. Goebbels is a liar and a manipulator. I think he was laying the groundwork to make you a suspect."

"Why would he do that?" I asked

"He probably guessed he was a suspect from my questions, and so began to divert attention."

"So he was bullshitting you about Sara." I said.

"Only about the towel, I believe. An embellishment. I think Sara found the body before Goebbels arrived. We may never know why she went to the bungalow that night. Unless she cares to share that information. Sara?"

Sara's face was remarkably calm. "You said Hitler killed Paula. Why don't you tell us about that?"

Diels nodded.

"So I did. The logs record that at eleven fourteen Hugenberg arrived on the lot with Herr Dietrich, Herr Graf, and Herr Wolf. Sepp Dietrich is in charge of Hitler's security and now doubles as Hitler's chauffeur. Ulrich Graf goes back to the twenties with Hitler and is his personal bodyguard. Since the killing, Dietrich and Graf have been too busy to be interviewed. The guard who logged in Hugenberg's party didn't show up for work the next day. He sent a note of resignation, saying he was moving to Dresden. Unfortunately, he cannot be found in Dresden, or any place else.

And what does Hugenberg have to say? He is scared shitless, but denies he was at the studio that night. According to Hugenberg, the missing guard made a mistake with his log entry.

"I say Herr Wolf was Hitler. After all Wolf is Hitler's nickname in some circles. And Hugenberg doesn't give midnight studio tours for just anyone."

For a moment I lost track of what Diels was saying, wondering if Hugenberg had time to leave the Press Ball, hook up with Hitler and get to UFA by 11:15.

". . . a pervert," Diels was saying. "Oh, not like Rohm and his sidekicks who like the boys. Hitler fancies women. But he's not looking for a wife or lover in any normal sense. Women like Magda Goebbels, Winifred Wagner, and Helene Bechstein mother him. He charms most women in a superficial way as if to prove he can. A few stir in him a dark need to debase and a yet darker need to be debased. There was urine on Glaise's bed as if someone had urinated on someone else. That is the kind of thing that satisfies the Fuhrer. He was there that night.

"The first question is who killed her. Hitler, Graf, or Dietrich? My money would be on Graf or Dietrich. Either is capable. Hitler likes to give orders but not dirty his hands."

"But why kill her?" I asked.

"Would you trust a woman like Glaise with your secrets?"

"What's the next question?" I asked, feeling like a straight man.

"It has two parts. Who decided to frame Goebbels and who carried it out? Not Hitler. He likes Goebbels. Sara, can you tell us that?"

"No," she replied.

Over the next days we hunkered down in the Reichstag Annex. It was like living in a tomb from which the bodies had been removed. The outer offices were off limits, their doors closed. At night Diels kept the hall lights off as if their light would seep through to the street and reveal our presence. We slept dormitory style in Henst's office on couches dragged from other offices. We ate canned food taken from the basement cafeteria.

Every so often the sound of a siren would penetrate to Henst's office and fill us with dread. But Diels assured us the building was safe until August fifth when the architects were to inspect the Annex and begin planning its renovation.

"We keep to schedules in the Third Reich," said Diels. "They will be neither late nor early."

"We?" I said.

Diels missed the barb, responding, "Well, everyone but Hitler. And we may yet be rid of him."

The radio reports made that seem unlikely. Hitler had arrested and executed Rohm and his key lieutenants for plotting to seize control of the army. The SA was being disbanded. Strasser, an early National Socialist, had been arrested. Dozens of Weimar loyalists had been rounded up for plotting against the government. Their fate as well as Strasser's wasn't clear. The traitors behind the *Ku'damm Conscience* had been arrested and executed including Ludi Kohl. Hitler was consolidating his power with a housecleaning that swept away enemies as well as former friends.

On the third day in the Annex, Potter asked Diels why we were still holed-up. What were we waiting for?

"I am going to get the four of you out and then you are going to save Germany."

"How are we going to do that when you couldn't save your own job?" Potter responded.

"All in good time," said Diels.

With his scars Diels always looked a little crazy, but now the madness was in his eyes. Every so often he left Henst's office for an office down the hall that was off limits to us. Without being able to make out the words, we could hear him talking. To himself? Or was he on the telephone? Either prospect was frightening.

While Diels delayed, we talked about escaping. How and to where were the questions. The radio reported more arrests. Some SA units were standing down only at gun point. The radio warned people to stay at home until the emergency passed. The streets were crawling with SS and Gestapo as well as regular cops.

On the fifth day Diels showed us a catch of papers. "You are taking these out. With the *Ku'damm* gone there is no voice. When you reach Paris, you will see they are published. Hitler will not be able to survive. Even we Germans will be appalled."

"What are they?" Viktoria asked.

"Transcriptions of dinner conversations. Hitler and his inner circle. It's all there. From the extermination of Jewry, to the planned conquests of France and Russia."

"You told me you didn't have recordings of Hitler." I said.

"I don't. He arranged for a stenographer to take the conversations down. Saving his words for posterity. I had the transcripts copied."

"What about Goering? Isn't he in the transcripts? Won't he look just as bad?" I asked.

"I did some editing."

"Why not give them to Cooper?" I said.

"He was expelled. The foreign newspaper offices are being watched. Outgoing packages as well as the mail are being opened and inspected."

Diels looked at me like we had resumed an earlier conversation. "And it is not about Goering. It is about Germany's survival as a civilized nation."

Diels slumped in Henst's chair. His eyes fixed on a photo of Henst with three teenage boys dressed for soccer. In the picture Henst regarded his sons with pride while the boys grinned at the camera. Diels held the picture up for us to see.

"These boys may never have sons. We have allowed this to happen. God help us."

Diels fell silent. He slumped lower, consumed by sadness or guilt.

Sara seemed to take mercy on him.

"You were right about the night Glaise was killed. I did go to her bungalow."

Diels sat up, a spark of interest surfacing in his eyes.

"I knew it. But you didn't frame Goebbels on your own, did

you?"

"No."

"How then?"

"I got a little drunk at the Press Ball. As I drove up to my bungalow, I saw the lights were on at her place. We had never spoken about what went on between her and my father. At first I wasn't even sure she realized I was his daughter.

"After Dad left for Germany, a reporter from the *Globe* came to New York and asked me what I knew about my father's hunt for his German love-child. He asked Mom the same thing. I was ready to strangle the guy. The *Globe* never printed anything. Dad knew the publisher. Didn't you, Dad?"

"He did me a favor," said Potter who stood behind Sara as if unable to face her.

"I took the Ufa film for a chance to find out what the *Globe* reporter was talking about. The first opportunity I had, I went to a library near Ufa and pulled old newspapers. Quite a story: nasty custody battle between German starlet and American tycoon. But that was secondary to me. What mattered was Dad had betrayed us twice. First with Paula then with Viktoria. And how could Dad have fallen for a tart like Paula to begin with?"

Sara paused, waiting. When Potter didn't volunteer, she pushed, "Don't care to answer, Dad? We're all friends here."

"Sara, there is no simple answer, no good explanation. In the end there is only who we were. Your mother and I . . ."

Sara cut him off.

"How dare you speak as if any of this was Mom's doing. When I first got to Berlin, I tried to find you to ask why. But you had disappeared. Then you contacted me and told me to leave like I was a misbehaving child. Later you contacted me with Diels' scheme. But even then you would not answer my question.

"Maybe it was the liquor but, that night after the ball, I thought I'd see what Paula had to say. So I knocked on her door drunk and belligerent."

"You're not going to tell me that you strangled her?" said Diels, upset that his Hitler theory might not pan out.

Sara gave him an odd look, and then said, "No. You asked if I framed Goebbels."

Suddenly Sara seemed to lose the thread of her story.

"And so what happened?" Diels prompted.

"She called me," Eric answered. "Since I spoke English, I had been assigned to Sara when she arrived in Germany. Many foreigners who come for an extended stay are assigned an SS case officer. The case officer is a reminder that Germany has rules and the SS keeps score.

"With all the informants around, it is not easy to find friends if you oppose the Nazis. Sara and I danced around for a couple of weeks before we understood and trusted each other."

"Eric is being kind to me," said Sara. "At first I fell for the Nazis, especially after Dad contacted me and told me to leave. Dad said I was making a fool of myself cavorting with Goebbels. So I showed him. I cavorted even more. But I began to see Dad was right. Then there was Mala. Meanwhile, Eric dropped a few hints. I dropped a few back. We came clean with each other three days before the Press Ball.

"I knew there were people who wanted to embarrass the Party. Paula supposedly had slept with Hugenberg and Goebbels. So I called Eric thinking that something might be done."

Eric picked up the story.

"I had ways in and out of Ufa that didn't require using the front gate. But time was short. And who to embarrass? Everyone important had been at the ball and then went to some party or other. They would have alibis. I knew that Goebbels was meeting the Japanese at midnight. Since both the Japs and the Nazis would deny the meeting, Goebbels wouldn't be able to account for his time."

Eric shook his head as if slightly dumbfounded for missing the obvious. "Framing Hitler never occurred to me."

"So no one told Hanussen to make the stealing heart prediction?" I asked.

"What do you mean?" Eric answered.

"I figured the prediction was part of the effort to discredit the Nazis. But Hanussen made his prediction before Sara found Paula. He couldn't have been tipped off."

"That's right. Ludi, Vik, and I wrote most of Hanussen's script," said Potter. "But Hanussen came up with the stolen heart prediction on his own."

"He put me in a trance at the airport in Vienna. Next thing I saw was Hanussen holding a beating heart," I said.

Viktoria too was puzzled. "I always thought he was a fraud. When he told us he had one more prediction, he put on quite a show. Claimed he first saw only a beating heart. Then a blond girl with her chest cut open. Still later he saw a Nazi in the girl's bedroom, standing over her body. But he could never make out their faces. Do you remember, Tom?"

"Yes," Potter recalled. "He was laying it on thick. Prinz said every so often Hanussen would pull off something the tricks couldn't explain."

I looked at Eric. "So you cut out Glaise's heart to make the prediction seem true?"

Eric looked sick at the memory of the event. "Of course it was the prediction. She was already dead. Why not really stir things up? Five minutes later I was throwing up in the bathroom."

Eric's voice trailed off as if he couldn't believe what he had done.

I couldn't let the prophecy go. "You know what you're saying. Not just that Hanussen got lucky and predicted the future, but that he made it happen. If he doesn't predict the stolen heart, Eric never steals it."

Viktoria answered, "It seemed that way to me for a while. But you know what? Hanussen was wrong. Eric isn't a Nazi."

Viktoria was right of course. There may be self-fulfilling prophesies, but no one dictates the future by making a prediction.

Later that night as I dozed off in Henst's office, it occurred to me that talking about Hanussen's prediction had a lot in common with swapping ghost stories around a campfire. While the thought was comforting, I could not shake off another thought.

If Eric was a Nazi, then, lucky or not, Hanussen had sort of gotten it right.

Time slowed to a crawl in the Annex. The radio was our lifeline to the world. It reported that order was returning thanks to what was described as "Hitler's decisive action against the agitators who wanted to subvert the army and overturn the government."

Diels was in a funk. After one broadcast, he aired his frustrations.

"The party has purged anyone who was a threat to Hitler. He has stolen a page from Stalin. I should have killed him myself when I had the chance. And this idiot had a clean shot, twice. To think the publication of dinner conversations will mean anything. He's done exactly what he said he would do and has gotten away with it."

Diels stormed from Henst's office. We followed him down the hall, concerned that he might do something stupid. He ducked into the office with the telephone and locked the door behind him.

"Rudy, the publication of the conversations can work," Potter called through the door.

"We showed the people the truth about Geli Raubal and Hitler's heritage. They don't care. Now he has eliminated his friends Strasser and Rohm as well as the opposition. He meant what he said in *Mien Kampf* about the use of brutality. The people will do nothing. It is enough that they have jobs."

The voice behind the door fell silent.

"Rudy, you have . . ."

"Go away," said Diels in a voice whose pain would brook no further intrusion.

"It doesn't seem safe to leave him," said Tom Potter.

"Safe for who? None of us is safe," I said. "I'm going down to the cafeteria."

"Wait, I'll go with you," said Potter.

The Annex elevators had been turned off, so Potter and I walked down a back set of stairs to the basement. We had taken to calling them the secret stairs.

"Were you the idiot who had a couple of clean shots at Hitler?"

"Yes," I said, and then asked, "The day I left you for dead, how did you get hurt?"

"You haven't asked Sara?"

"I did, but didn't get an answer."

"Sara and I have made our peace. Last night we talked. I told her what happened with Paula and me. With Vik and me."

"That's a lot of explaining."

"There were no explanations. I could only tell her what happened and hope."

"For what? Acceptance? Forgiveness?"

"No. For understanding. That she would believe I still loved her and her brothers. That I hadn't set out to hurt anyone. That being foolish isn't the worst thing in the world."

"So what happen? Middle-age crazy twice? Duped twice by women young enough to be your daughters?"

"She warned me you could be sarcastic. Sara can tell you what happened with Paula and Vik if she wants. Otherwise, it's not your business. Who Sara loves is my business. I'm still her father. Are you wondering if Sara stabbed me? That's a hell of a thing to think. She thinks you love her. How you could love someone like Sara and suspect she was capable of knifing her father."

"I didn't know she was your daughter."

"You did just now when you asked me how I got hurt."

"So she didn't stab you."

"Of course not. I stuck my nose where I shouldn't have that morning. Interrupted a couple of Brownshirts who were kicking around an old man. I took a knife for my trouble, and should have gone for treatment. But it didn't seem that bad and I didn't want to miss my meeting with Sara. I couldn't do that. I had already messed up enough with her. Besides I had a favor to ask, the Boehm thing."

We had come to the basement. It stunk of spoiled food, charred timbers and mildew. An ashy grime covered the floor and the bottom inch or so of the walls.

"So, did you take a shot at Hitler?" asked Potter. "Diels won't say what happened, but there were stories about an accident at the Eagle's Nest."

"Let's just say he should be dead."

"Maybe Sara hasn't made such a bad choice."

We seemed to pair off like Tom Potter and I had. Perhaps it was easier to talk that way - one on one.

The afternoon of our sixth day Viktoria announced that she wanted to find the office of Werner Pfeffer. He'd been a Social Democrat and no fan of the Nazis. "Perhaps we will find something to go with Hitler's dinner conversations," she said.

She asked me to come along, joking she might need some muscle to crack open a file cabinet. I didn't think there was much chance of finding anything incriminating, but off we went.

While we rummaged through Pfeffer's office, Viktoria told me about her and Potter. She probably figured I would pass on to Sara what she couldn't tell her directly. She began abruptly - as if she had to speak before she changed her mind.

"I met Tom when he came to Walter's office looking for help with Paula. Later, I happened to be there when Morell told him the boy died. Crib death is what he told Tom. Tom never saw the baby, although he had been given a photo by Glaise's lawyer. Tom began to shake. Sorrow at first. Then anger.

"Tom asked what crib death was. Morell said it was a rare condition that causes infants to stop breathing. I could see Tom wasn't buying that. Morell looked at Tom without the slightest sympathy. I thought Tom was going slug him. I stepped between them, and begged Tom not to do anything.

"Tom pushed me away and asked Morell about the body. Morell said Paula had the baby cremated. He told Tom, if it was any consolation, the court would have awarded Tom custody. I think Morell was rubbing it in."

"So the baby was killed to keep Potter from getting it?"

"No. I don't think Glaise or even the Nazis are baby killers, at least not of Aryan babies. Tom suspected that the baby's death was just a ruse to prevent him from taking custody given the court did seem to be leaning his way. They just wanted him to go home. Later he got word - rumors really - that the baby had been adopted by a Nazi couple."

"How do you know all this?"

"Walter was Paula's agent. Like I said, that's how I first met Tom. We kept up."

"Walter Prinz?"

"Yes. Walter said to stay on top he needed up-and-comers as well as established performers. He thought Paula might have a future."

"Was she blackmailing Potter?"

"Paula was a conniver but I don't know about blackmail. She did want compensation for the child. She went into hiding shortly after she got back from America. We never saw her during the last months of her pregnancy."

"So is the baby alive?"

"Tom thinks so. He named the baby Seth. Seth is real to him. He even carries Seth's picture. He believes the crib death story was concocted to end the custody case so Seth could be adopted by a Nazi couple. One more kid for the Fuhrer's war machine."

"What do you think?"

"I think Seth is out there someplace. I also think Tom's dream of finding him won't come true."

Later that day Sara and I walked the halls of the Annex. I told her what Viktoria told me. Sara went numb as if there were too many emotions to reconcile. When she finally spoke, her voice sounded brittle.

"How did they get from Seth to her bed?"

I finished Viktoria's story. With her help Potter tried to prove that Seth had been adopted. But all official doors were closed.

Viktoria introduced Potter to Ludi thinking he might have a way to find Seth. Ludi was no help. But one thing led to another. Soon Potter had disappeared into Ludi's apparatus and eventually into Viktoria's arms. In Viktoria's telling, their love was born in turmoil. It might not have blossomed in normal times and might not survive their return. For all of that, it was still love.

When I finished repeating Viktoria's story, Sara cried. For whom I could not tell.

I remembered the note Sara left for me at the sawmill. The similarities in their stories - Sara's and Vik's - didn't strike me as the least bit surprising or extraordinary. Quite the opposite.

The seventh day marked the return of the old, self-assured Diels. Perched on the edge of Henst's desk, he announced that Sara and I had turned up in Belgium while Potter and Viktoria had arrived in Paris. We had escaped with transcripts of conversations among the Nazi elite that revealed not just their plans for conquest but the tawdriness of their vision. Two days ago the *Chicago Tribune* in its Paris edition printed a short excerpt. In it Hitler dismissed religion as superstition and Christianity as the most dangerous religious manifestation because it was the first to exterminate its adversaries in the name of love.

Hitler wasn't the first person to make those observations, but they would enrage a lot of people.

"How delicious," Diels paused as if waiting for a round of applause.

"Why does the world think we've escaped, when we're stuck in Berlin?" Potter asked.

"I had to get Himmler and Heydrich to call off the dogs. They weren't going to do that until you were captured or had escaped. Well, now you have escaped."

"How did you manage it?" I asked.

"I gave Cooper a few pages of the transcripts before he left Germany. That much he could hide on his way out. In order to get the rest, he agreed to help my couriers escape. You are my couriers. He helped by running the articles which reported your escape. I'm sure you won't mind keeping up my end of the bargain."

"So how do we actually get out?" asked Potter.

"Since no one will be looking for you, with some false identification, you and Viktoria can drive into France while Temple and Sara can drive into Belgium."

Diels' smugness was annoying. It was never going to be that easy.

"And what becomes of you and Eric?" Sara asked with real concern.

"I'm retired. If Hitler falls and Goering heads up a new government, Himmler and I are likely to switch places. Eric must lay low for a while. The SS is looking for him and he hasn't yet escaped."

"Don't worry. Sara, I have friends who will hide me," said Eric who didn't sound as confident as his words.

"And what happens if Hitler isn't toppled?" said Sara, pressing the point.

"Then everyone is in trouble, inside and outside Germany," said Diels. "It's only a question of when and how the trouble arrives. I presume you prefer your chances outside. You leave tomorrow morning."

Chapter Thirty-Four

"What the hell was that?"

We all heard it. Eric got the words out first. A heavy thud from the front of the Annex woke us. Eric ran from Henst's office. He was back in seconds.

"There's an SS squad on the street. They're pounding the front door with a battering ram."

"I locked and barricaded every door in the place," said Diels who was grinning like he'd been waiting for this. "It will take them a while to get in. We have a few minutes. Sara run up to the fourth floor and turn on enough lights to be noticed from the street. They will chase the light. Then meet us at the cafeteria. Take the secret stairs. Go!"

"Hold it, Sara," said Potter. "Looks like you've blown it, Diels. I'm not keen on following your orders."

"I know the building, you don't. I have a plan, you don't. Those doors are tough but they will not hold forever. You're wasting time. Go, Sara."

"He's right," said Eric.

Sara looked at Potter, a daughter deferring to her father. She went to him and they held each other. Then he gently pushed her away. Looking like he had a new lease on life, Potter kissed her on the forehead and said, "Do as he says, Bundle. I'll see you in the basement."

Sara ran off.

Diels took a key ring from his pocket, selected a key, and held the ring by the key. "Eric, the gate. You know what to do."

He handed the key to Eric who nodded and left.

“Let’s go,” he said to Potter, Viktoria and me. He led us to the office he had used as his private quarters. He unlocked the door and went in. From behind the desk he lifted two bulging satchel briefcases.

“The transcripts. One for each of you. They’re heavy. The thoughts of the Fuhrer,” he said with a wry smile.

He lifted a third satchel. “Viktoria, this one is for you. Guns, money, and identification papers. You probably will not need the guns.”

He then pulled a fourth satchel from behind the desk. “This is my bag of tricks. Let’s go.”

We took the secret stairs to the basement and met Sara and Eric at the mouth of a tunnel that led to the Reichstag.

Diels spoke. “Eric will lead you. I’m staying behind. I’ll pull the gate down behind you and lock it from this side. You should be just fine.”

From above came faint sounds of shouting and jackboots on marble.

“They’re going for the lights. Hurry. There are torches in your sack, Viktoria.”

“Diels, come with us. It’s your only chance,” said Sara.

“Then there will be no one to lock the gate behind you. There are dozens of places to hide and I know them all. If they catch me, it’s peasants’ luck. But I have to get out of this hallway first. So move. And lock the gate from the far side once you lower it.”

Diels handed Eric a heavy lock. He nodded and said thanks. There were no embraces. To his credit Diels seemed to expect none. He was a gambler making his play. Two weeks before he made a different play. Had it worked, I would have died in a car crash. As the gate rolled down, I wondered if he was sending us into a trap.

The tunnel took a number of seemingly unnecessary turns. We jogged for what seemed like more than a city block when the flashlight beams hit a mass of rubble.

"Shit," said Potter, summing up the situation. "It must be the ruins of the Reichstag fire."

Getting through would not be easy.

"Didn't you check the tunnel, Eric?" I asked.

"Diels did."

"The prick set us up," I said. "We're trapped with papers stolen on Himmler's watch. He intends to capture us with the goods and turn the tables on Himmler by recapturing what Himmler couldn't protect."

"You're wrong. Diels told me about the rubble. He said we could get through."

"Maybe if you're a snake."

"Don't argue," said Potter. "There isn't a choice. Let's see if Diels was right. Look there."

He pointed his flashlight at an opening in the ruins. "Sara and Vik follow me. You two follow us in."

Eric had a different idea. "Bad plan, Tom, you're the biggest person here, the one most likely to get stuck. And the weakest. I know you're not fully recovered. Temple and I are stronger. The smallest person with the most strength should go first. That's me."

He was right - unless taking the lead was part of a trap. Potter apparently didn't share my concern. He told Eric to lead with me second. Viktoria passed out flashlights. Eric started into the debris field, followed by me, Vik, and Sara. Tom Potter brought up the rear.

An hour later we had maneuvered sixty feet or so through rubble consisting mostly of chunks of stone and brick, portions of concrete slabs, and charred timbers. The going was tight. Early on, Eric found an iron bar, maybe three feet long. He tied his flashlight around his left wrist so he could work the bar with both hands. Now a probe, now a lever, now a ram, the bar was a godsend. We didn't walk or crawl. We squirmed like contortionists in a three dimensional maze. The density of the rubble was fairly consistent: thick, but not so thick that a way could not be found. But each foot gained was work.

I was lugging one of the satchels. A few openings were so

narrow that I had to push the satchel ahead and squirm behind it. I wondered if Potter would have the strength to maneuver his satchel. I could hear him grunting but we were all doing that.

I called ahead. "Eric, shouldn't we be working our way up?"

"I've been trying that. But the crap above seems just as thick. I've been keeping an eye on that wall off to the right. With the torch, I can just make it out through the rubble. I am afraid if I lose sight of it, we will tunnel aimlessly. It's hard to keep your bearings in this stuff."

He was worried.

"You're doing fine," I said. "We'll make it."

"The great spelunker. That's me," said Eric with a graveyard laugh. "No wonder Diels wanted to stay behind. He's probably claustrophobic."

Sara's voice came from behind me. "Or any other phobia. We have dust, rats, sharp objects, darkness, mold, and a chance of being buried alive. Pick one."

"And cute spiders," added Viktoria in the spirit of the moment.

Ten minutes and another ten feet. Then Eric came to an impasse. He worked his light into the rubble at every angle, looking for a passage. From the rear came Potter's hushed voice, demanding silence.

We all stopped moving.

"I thought I heard someone pounding on the overhead door back at the annex," said Potter.

We listened but there was nothing to hear.

"Maybe it was my imagination," said Potter. "But I'll tell you this. They'll never get to us. And if they do, I'll shoot the first SOB I see. His body will plug up this ant colony just fine. Keep moving."

Ahead Eric was jabbing at the rubble looking for an opening. I started to claw into the rubble at my left. From behind me came a crashing sound as if the debris had settled.

Sara screamed, "Dad!"

Viktoria screamed "Tom!"

Silence.

"Dad, where are you? Viktoria, he was right behind me. Now I don't see him. Just dust. Oh my God, I've got to find him."

I could hear frantic movement as Sara tried to go back.

"Sara, don't move," I called. "It might still be unstable. Stay where you are."

"I'll go," said Viktoria.

"Don't be an ass, Viktoria. You can't get past me in this stuff."

"I'm sorry, Sara. I love him too. This is not . . ."

"I've got it! An opening," called Eric. "Tight but passable."

"I'm okay," came Tom's voice. "Stunned for a second there. Rock in the head. Safest place to get hit."

"What the hell were you doing, Dad?"

"I didn't want to shoot anyone so I knocked a timber loose to close off the passage."

"Thomas, you are the dumbest man alive." It was Viktoria. "Knocking a timber loose. You probably used your head as a maillot."

Suddenly we were all laughing.

An explosion at the Annex end of the tunnel ended that. The percussion shook the rubble around us. We held our breath waiting for our tangled passage to collapse. Then came the sound of what might have been jackboots on the run. We switched off our flashlights. A minute later we heard snippets of raised voices – too faint to be understood. Then came the sound – faint but definite - of someone working his way into the rubble.

Minutes passed before we heard someone shout, "It's very tight in here, sir. I don't see how anyone could get through."

"Keep trying, Keller," came a distant shout, just loud enough to be heard from our position.

"Yes, Captain."

As he made his way, Keller grunted like a big man whose size was a disadvantage. After thirty minutes it was hard to tell how far he had come. But it was far enough for ghostly shards of light from his flashlight to briefly reach us.

"Sir, I'm getting nowhere but I think I hear something."

"What?"

"Probably rats."

"Find out how many legs, Keller."

Five more minutes of movement. Keller was right. More than Keller was moving in the darkness. The sound was elusive.

"Captain, up ahead I can see what looks like a piece of cloth snagged on a timber."

"Keep going. I'm sending Unger to help you."

More noise. The minutes dragged as the men crept toward us. Fortunately Keller's complaining seemed steadier than his progress. He wanted to quit but the voice of the Captain pushed him and Unger forward. The splinters of light from their flashlights became more frequent and were brighter.

"It's a piece of cloth. Can't tell from what. Very dirty. Probably been here since the fire."

"Find the body, Keller."

Keller and Unger coughed as they fought for breath in the dust they were stirring up. Keller was now fifty minutes into his dig and should have been nearing Potter's position. Soon he would spot Potter's legs in the beam of his light and all hell would break loose. If Potter's cave-in didn't stop Keller, Potter would have to kill the man and the scramble would be on.

Unger, backed by the rest of his squad, would hustle after us. Additional troops would be called. They would scour the Reichstag wreckage from above. A slow-motion chase in darkness with bullets ricocheting in the rubble would be a crap shoot at best. Without our flashlights to guide us, we would never find our way. But turning them on would signal our location. We needed one of those miracles in which I didn't believe.

"Sir, I can't push any farther. The rubble is packed solid."

Keller must have come to Potter's cave-in.

"Stop bitching, Keller. Noises. Bits of cloth. You said it yourself. Push on. Be a good rat."

The Captain's voice had a nasty, teasing quality. He was toying with Keller's fear. Keller began to claw at the ruins. If he could force open the passage, we would be discovered.

Then came the sound of another collapse. The splinters of light disappeared.

"Keller, are you all right?" It was Unger, whispering as if afraid to reveal himself.

"What's going on in there?" It was the Captain shouting, the sport gone from his voice.

"The rubble has collapsed on Keller," screamed Unger. "I can see his light but it's not moving."

"Unger, pull the idiot out."

It took Unger ten minutes to reach Keller. A lifetime would pass before they would be able to pull him out.

Keller must have come around because now we could hear him talking to Unger.

"Otto, I feel cold all over. Except my legs. I can't feel them at all."

"Don't worry. I'm going to pull this stuff off you. We'll make it back."

"Don't. It will collapse again. You'll kill us both."

"I'll call the Captain. We can stabilize this stuff and move that timber off your back."

Unger called for help. Then came the sound of other men working into the rubble.

"They won't get here in time," said Keller

"Hans, don't be silly. Fascists are always on time," said Unger.

They laughed - the shallow laughter of men who know they may die.

"Did we do the right thing? Joining the Party, the SS. It seemed right. But some of the things we've done."

"Hans, you are just frightened. It's the darkness, the jam you are in."

"What if we see clearer in the dark?"

"It's only fear you see in the darkness."

"You sound like my mother from when I was a child. And like me talking to my son. What if I never see Leo and Freda again?"

"Don't be silly. It sounds like half the army is on the way."

"Can you reach my wallet? Back pocket. No, the other. Yes. Open it. Hold the light to their photo. Yes. They are beautiful, aren't they?"

"Yes."

"Freda detests the SS. I never would have turned her in but I worried that her mouth would get us into trouble. My God, Otto. I thought about it. "

"Don't talk now. Save your strength."

"Otto, remember the raid on the Gold apartment."

"What of it?"

"Schmidt and some of the others raped the daughter. I ran. I can't get it out of my mind. I never told Freda."

"Hans, the girl was a Jew. She brought it on herself. That crap about her father contributing more to Germany than our whole unit. She deserved what she got."

"He was a famous man."

"He was a Jew."

"Did you know what they did? The rape?"

"Hell, I screwed her too. Right up the ass with a real German prick. Better than she deserved. You should have stayed and gotten a piece. She had a great ass, Jew or not."

"Otto. What have we done?"

"Save it, Hans. We'll get you out. Stop whining."

"Freda."

They fell silent. From the rubble came the sounds of the rescue team working deeper. It was likely that Keller and Unger were looking back, waiting for the rescuers to reach them. We needed to put some distance between our position and theirs before help arrived. I moved toward Eric, intending to whisper instructions to lead the way into the new passage.

I hadn't crawled a foot when my shoulder snagged on something. I retreated from the obstacle then advanced again, only to dislodge something. Nothing big, nothing dangerous, but in the silence it made a racket. Someone's light pierced the rubble as if to see the sound.

"What the devil! Someone is in there. Did you hear that, Hans? Are you awake, Hans? Did you hear that?"

"Yes."

"Damn. You can't see more that a meter ahead in this stuff. Wait a minute. Shit, there is something in there. Like part of a pant leg or something . . . no . . . who can tell in this mess."

Unger's lantern beam flickered in our direction. Now and then a finger of light would reach me but I was sure I was unseen. I could not say the same for Sara, Viktoria, and Tom.

"Can you see anything, Hans? I swear one minute I think yes, the next no."

"Otto, bend down here, next to me I think I see them."

"Good work. Damn. There is hardly room for the two of us."

"Closer, Otto. There. Do you see?"

"No."

"Get closer. I'll guide you with my arm. Good. There. Yes?"

We could hear Hans grunting. Then a thumping sound followed by silence. We waited. Something had happened to Keller and Unger. They no longer spoke. Their lanterns did not move. We remained frozen, convinced they were playing possum.

Then came a raspy voice, "My name is Hans Keller. My wife is Freda. I spoke of her to Otto. Did you hear me?"

Silence.

"Please speak to me. I know you are there. You made a noise."

Silence.

"I killed Otto. He would have told them you are here. He bragged about raping a girl. Freda is right about what I have become. I had to do something to make amends. Saving you was my chance. A chance to atone. Tell Freda and my son - Leo is his name - that I did not die a Nazi."

A ruse or an honest plea? Were we to expose ourselves to the disembodied voice of our hunter? Hans seemed to understand.

"I know you are afraid. I have the advantage on you. I have no more to lose. What I have is that, here at the end, I did a just, decent thing. I want to believe that you will be able to escape. That you will tell Freda she was right and that I did something good."

Keller had become weaker as he spoke, as if he was running out of steam.

"Hans, thank you," said Potter. "You've given us a chance to put many things right. We will tell Freda."

"Can't we help him?" said Sara.

"Too late," came Keller's now faltering voice. "Seventeen Baumwollestrasse. Tell Freda. Go now."

I thought I could hear Keller murmuring. To his God or to his wife, I couldn't tell. His compatriots were working noisily, moving closer but still a good way off.

Potter called ahead. "Eric, get us out of here. They're making so much noise they'll never hear us."

We had been angling our way up for over an hour when we heard the dogs and froze. They were above us. How far above was hard to estimate, although we'd come far enough to see some light from above. The barking waxed and waned as the dogs tracked back and forth across the surface of the rubble. Now and then a trainer's voice would send the dogs in a new direction.

Eventually the dogs moved off as if only the night would yield creatures from the ruins. Eric broke our silence, whispering against who knew what threat.

"Should I work my way to the top? See if it's clear?"

"And walk down the street looking like a pack of coal miners?" came Potter's voice.

"Let's at least get out of the rubble," said Sara. "Find a place to stretch out. We'll make a run for it tonight."

"What if the dogs are back tonight?" I said.

"What's to say they won't be back in an hour or so?" said Sara.

"So let's go now," said Eric.

We bickered like the tired people we were. In the end we stayed in the ruins. Trying to make the best of it, Sara and I crawled to each other. We held hands as sleep proved a powerful ally. I nodded off smiling at Sara's joke about the accommodations. Something about the mattresses being lumpy.

The dogs did not return that night. We scrambled to the surface and limped across the choppy terrain, stretching our bodies in the freedom of open space. Eric led us to a car that Diels had stashed in a garage two blocks away.

We were almost giddy as Eric drove off. Lazarus had nothing on us.

Chapter Thirty-five

It didn't take long to lose the mood. We were fugitives and I couldn't shake the feeling that we were being manipulated. I hoped it was paranoia, but knew paranoia was damn near impossible in the Third Reich.

None of us knew how the cover for Ludi's operation had been blown. Sara was probably right. Thanks to dumb luck or good work, the SS had followed Sara and Eric as they fled UFA. Unknowingly they led Heydrich to Ludi's door.

Eric drove with an eye in the rearview mirror. He wove through the streets as if he didn't know where to go. On Wilhelmstrasse a large banner hung at the chancellery construction site. Lit by floodlights the banner featured a picture of Hitler and the proclamation, **Building a New Germany**.

"What's going on Eric? No one is following us," said Potter.

"Diels was wrong," said Eric as if speaking to himself.

"What are you talking about?" asked Potter.

"Hitler was in Linz the day of the Press Ball. He went to meet the architect for his new museum. It was a spur of the moment thing. I'm almost sure he spent the night. That's why I never thought of framing him. He was four hundred miles away. How could Diels not have known that?"

"He probably knew Hitler had come back to Berlin," said Viktoria.

"Perhaps. But maybe the transcripts weren't enough for Diels. Maybe he fed us a story, hoping you would repeat it when you delivered the transcripts to the press. More ammunition."

Eric seemed reassured by the thought Diels was scamming us.

Only in Germany was there comfort in being hustled. Eric sped off, going north through Wedding into Pankow.

Upper Pankow had the feel of weary, stunted development. During the boom of the 1890s, small farms with tired soil gave way to builders who sold country villas to the new rich. When the inevitable slump followed, the real estate whizzes vanished and the farmers returned, working the soil with newly developed phosphate fertilizers, while the villa owners worked at keeping up appearances.

It was to one of those villas that Eric drove. He passed it, turned around, and passed it again before pulling in on the third pass.

Eric filled us in. "The couple who keep house are in the dark. The Glochners. They think it's owned by a lawyer named Barting who uses it for visiting clients and friends. Barting doesn't exist, but the Glochners are well paid and, for the most part, have the place to themselves. So they don't ask questions. I've got a letter of introduction from Barting. There are a couple of cars in the garage. The four of you will leave tomorrow. I'll stay for a while. Let things cool down. At least I'll be well fed. Frau Glochner is reputed to be an excellent cook."

The Glochners weren't happy with our late arrival, especially since we looked like survivors from a mining disaster. The couple was in their sixties. They seemed frightened. Eric told them that we had been in a car wreck and needed food and sleep. He handed them his letter of introduction. He introduced Sara and me as the Kochs. Potter and Viktoria were the Ritters.

Frau Glochner fixed us eggs and toast. Then Herr Glochner took the Kochs and the Ritters to their bedrooms.

Sara seemed preoccupied about what was going on in the other bedroom, although she didn't say as much. When I moved to kiss her, she gently pushed me away, saying she was one Potter who needed some sleep.

"Back at the annex, your dad called you 'Bundle'. What was that all about?"

"His nickname for me - as in bundle of joy. Corny, right? "

"A little, but I like it. Come here. I'd like to do some bundling."

"Well, if you must," she said sporting her own version of a wolfish smile.

We were arrested just before sunrise as we lay in our beds. The Glochners must have called the Gestapo as soon as we went to sleep. The couple would not meet our eyes as we were being led out in handcuffs. I heard one of the Gestapo men remind Herr Glochner that he had a "half-Jew grandchild".

I'm not sure what I would have done had I been in their shoes.

We were taken to Columbia Haus, pushed down blood-spattered steps to a sub-basement, stripped, and thrown naked in separate cells with steel doors and metal cots. How long we waited I don't know. The sound of pain came relentlessly from a door at the end of the cell block.

It's a tape recording, a mind game. All torture ends. The body's capacity to endure is limited. No. The voices change. Doors open and close. It's the process that doesn't end. The victims change.

At first I tried to block out the sound. Impossible. Then I found myself concentrating on it - as if it might hold the secret to my survival.

Who's being questioned? What's being asked? What are they saying? What will satisfy the interrogator? Anything? Is the process an end in itself, the answers irrelevant?

After a few days, it was my turn. Two uniformed men led me to the now dreaded room. It looked like a cross between a dental office and slaughter house. Eric, Sara, Tom Potter, and Viktoria were already there.

Like me, they were naked. Eric was shackled to a wall, awash with blood and fresh bruises. Next to Eric stood Heydrich dressed in a clean butcher's smock and rubber galoshes. A half dozen thugs stood at the ready. No butcher's whites for them. Their fatigues were stained.

The room had a peculiar smell. Humphrey once told me

that fear smelled like blood, sweat, and shit rolled up in filthy underwear. It was something like that.

The Potters and I slouched as if our nakedness was shameful. Viktoria stood tall as if to say she understood the game and wouldn't play. A guard made a remark about Viktoria's body. Potter spun at the man, calling him a pig.

Viktoria spoke quickly, only his name, "Tom." The warmth and strength in that single syllable were a benediction of affection and courage.

Potter looked at her lovingly and then spoke to Heydrich.

"The shame is yours. Nordic gods, my ass. You're barbarians pretending at culture and posing as honorable."

"What duty demands is never shameful and we are hardly barbarians. Besides, we live in an age of discovery and have science at our disposal."

Heydrich nodded at a bookish looking man seated at a console. Once our eyes were fixed on the man, he flicked a toggle switch. Nothing happened. He did it again and still nothing happened. Heydrich looked irritated and the operator frightened.

I should have kept quiet, but couldn't resist. "So much for science. Back to the rack and screws?"

"I hope you resist, Temple," said Heydrich. "I want to hear your last quip."

"You love this. You're exactly . . . "

Eric screamed as electricity flowed from the shackles into his limbs. The operator intended only a brief jolt, but the switch failed again. The operator flicked it back and forth but the current continued to flow. Eric's arms and legs jerked spasmodically. The screaming was over in seconds. His heart lost its rhythm and his circulation dropped. His brain began to shut down from too little oxygen and too much electricity. Then his heart stopped. Still, if the current stopped, a good doctor, acting quickly, might have saved him.

Heydrich was screaming, "Idiot, I want him alive. Shut it off!"

But the operator couldn't. Eric was dead and beyond pain before his ankles and wrists began to smoke. Heydrich didn't take a club to the console until it began to look as if Eric's body might catch fire.

The spectacle was too much. Heydrich ordered us out. Sara was retching. Viktoria's knees buckled and she was kneeling on the grimy floor as if physically wounded. Tom Potter and I were not in much better shape. Even the blood-spattered soldiers seemed shaken.

I was ready to believe that even the Germans had limits when I heard Heydrich shrieking, "Incompetent! Incompetent! Incompetent!"

I looked back. He was pummeling the operator with his riding crop to the rhythm of his words.

Two days later we were herded back to the room at the end of the hall. This time we were dressed. No one was in the shackles but a new console and operator were in place. Heydrich was in his whites. I couldn't tell if the thugs were new. They all looked alike to me: mid-twenties, clean cut, blond, buzz-cuts, and dead eyes. Because their uniforms were clean, I guessed we were the day's first project. We were strapped into what might have been dental chairs.

Heydrich spoke, sounding like a mild-mannered lawyer summarizing a case.

"Not a German among you. Viktoria, a Jew masquerading as a German. Potter, a weak, sentimental man seduced by an actress and then by a Jew. Sara, ambitious but confused about so many things. And Temple, the reluctant agent of a Jew, led astray by his fascination with the would-be movie star.

"We are inclined to deport you Americans even though there is enough evidence to convict Potter and Temple of everything from spitting on the grass to murder. Sara remains an enigma, but that won't be enough to stop her execution if necessary.

"We know everything except who killed Glaise. I want the answer to that. Glaise herself was, and remains, unimportant. Punishing her killer is not important. But solving the crime is."

I wondered why I was still alive if he knew everything but the identity of Paula's killer.

"It is up to you. Go home in exchange for the information we want, or face execution for your crimes."

"Eric told us that Hitler did it," I said.

Heydrich responded without sarcasm. He seemed to be speaking to an audience larger than our little group.

"Insulting Germany and my intelligence is not helpful. Moreover, the Fuhrer was in Linz the night Glaise was killed. There are a dozen witnesses."

"So he sent his errand boys, Dietrich and Graf."

"You are hardly one to speak of errand boys."

Potter interrupted, "We have no reason to believe a thing you say."

Before Heydrich could answer, a door opened and Goering stepped into the chamber.

"I've been watching."

Goering flicked a thumb in the direction of a mirror that was built into a wall. "From the other side, it's a window. General Heydrich wants to see you punished. But others, including me, see value in showing our compassion."

"So now we have propaganda value?" I said.

"Call it what you will. Hitler meant it when he said he wanted to rejoin the community of nations on an equal footing. If your release helps, I say fine. If you don't cooperate and are punished, justice will be served. I say fine to that too."

Goering's eyes were clear but wary. Himmler and Heydrich had him boxed in. His man Diels was in disgrace or worse. Goering himself must have been under suspicion. Heydrich wanted to sink Goering while Goering wanted to right the ship. If we hadn't been the pawns in their game, I would have been enjoying myself.

"Tell the General what he wants to know. It's up to you whether you go home."

With that, Goering left the room. He looked like an art dealer worried that he was about to be caught selling a forgery.

"What's it going to be?" asked Heydrich.

More of Heydrich's badgering produced nothing. Did they expect Goering's phony reassurances would cause us to do a one-eighty? Besides, there was no reason to think any of us knew who killed Glaise – except for maybe Sara. Why was knowing Glaise's killer so important? It must have become a bone of contention among those angling for power around Hitler.

After ten minutes Heydrich lost patience. He walked over to what looked like a table from a high school chemistry lab. There was a sink built into the table. Heydrich picked up a bar of soap and held it up for our inspection.

"Plain soap made of acids and alkalis. It will clean tender skin but its components can burn the toughest hide."

He turned to the table, tossed the soap in the sink, and picked up two glass cruets. He held them up for us to see. They were labeled but I couldn't make out the writing.

"Here we have hydrochloric acid and here sulfuric acid. Get either on your skin and you had better flush it away quickly to avoid a serious burn."

Heydrich returned the cruets to the table and picked up another vial. He held it up so we could see the clear liquid it held.

"Nitric acid. Very corrosive. If this gets on you, you'll find yourself in the hospital and potentially in the morgue."

He spoke with the detachment of a professor going through the motions - coolly flaunting his expertise. He walked toward Sara, pulling the stopper from the vial. He stopped next to her chair.

"Tilt it back," he said to one of the troops.

The chair tilted, elevating Sara's legs to Heydrich. She wore a prison smock that exposed her calves. Heydrich positioned the vial a few inches above her right calf and ever so slowly began to tip the vial.

"Just let me know who killed Glaise and this can stop," he said.

Sara cringed, her eyes, large as saucers, locked on the vial.

Viktoria and I yelled at once.

I called for Goering to stop Heydrich's sick game.

Viktoria called Heydrich an embarrassment to Germany and begged him to stop for the sake of German honor.

Heydrich didn't see honor that way. The vial kept moving. Just before the first drop would have fallen, Tom Potter yelled, "I'll tell you."

Heydrich pulled the vial up.

"Go ahead," he said.

"Eric was a part of Ludi Kohl's group at the bakery. So was I. My daughter was not. Neither was Viktoria but she worked for Paula's agent, Walter Prinz. Eric, Ludi and I knew I wasn't the only man Paula had seduced. Goebbels was another. I suggested that might make a good story for the *Ku'damm Conscience.* Ludi laughed and said, if Goebbels wasn't screwing her, that would be news.

"I didn't know what happened until a few days ago. We were on the run with Eric. He knew about Paula's fling with Goebbels and decided to frame Goebbels by killing Paula. The point was to destroy Goebbels and embarrass Hitler. Eric said he had a way to get onto the Ufa lot without logging through the main gate. He went in, killed her, then set it up to look like Goebbels had done it."

I liked it. It had a ring of truth because parts of it were true.

Heydrich thought about Potter's story, then shook his head.

"My men found a service gate with a broken lock. But you're lying. If Eric had killed Glaise he would have told us yesterday."

"Eventually he would have confessed," I said. "But your fucked-up electric machine fried him first."

"No. By the time the machine malfunctioned, Eric had already told us that he went to Glaise's bungalow to pressure her for information about Goebbels only to find her strangled. He admitted that he framed Goebbels but denied that he killed her. If he killed her, he would have told us."

Heydrich tipped the cruet. The acid oozed toward the bottle's lip. Tom Potter and I strained against our bindings as if that could reverse the flow. A drop fell on Sara's shin and coursed slowly toward her calf. Nothing happened for a time long enough to think the stunt was a cruel deception. Then every muscle in Sara's body contracted and she gasped for air as if her lungs were being sucked dry by pain. Her jaw locked as if to trap some primal wail.

We were all yelling now. Contradictory tales of Glaise's death. Viktoria said it was Hitler. Potter said that he did it. I knew what Heydrich wanted even though I knew it wasn't true. I said Diels did it.

Heydrich looked at one of the soldiers and said, "Clean it."

The soldier dumped baking soda over the burn, then hosed the area down. He finished by dumping more baking soda on the wound. After a minute Sara's body relaxed.

"My father didn't kill anyone. Don't be foolish, Dad," she said.

"Of course not, child," said Heydrich.

He was about Sara's age but looked at her like she was a misguided teenager. Then he turned to Potter, his voice shifting from feigned tenderness to steel.

"Admit you lied. If you don't, I'll pour this whole bottle over your daughter's pretty face."

Potter shook his head. "I just wanted you to stop."

Heydrich walked over to Viktoria and raised the cruet over the back of her left hand. Instinctively she tried to jerk her hand away but the leather strap that bound her wrist to the arm of the chair held fast.

"Lies have consequences," said Heydrich. "Now, what were you saying about the Fuhrer?"

Viktoria looked at Heydrich for such a long time I thought she had decided to lose a hand for the satisfaction of not backing down. Tom Potter and Sara both started to say something but Heydrich cut them short.

"It's her decision."

"It was something Eric said. I don't know if it was true," said Viktoria.

"Much better, Fraulein."

Heydrich turned to me.

"Tell me about Diels. He's behind this attempt to discredit Minister Goebbels, is he not!"

The door next to the two-way mirror opened and Goering popped out. I thought he might.

"Heydrich, your tactics are flawed. Give me the bottle," ordered Goering.

"Reichsmarshall, I thought the interrogation was mine."

Goering, the flying ace, was back. "The bottle!" he commanded with a ferocity that brooked no opposition.

Heydrich handed over the acid.

"Here is the problem with dumping acid on people," said Goering.

He walked over to Sara and told two troopers to twist her head to the side and strap it down.

"Now, Temple, I'm going to let this acid eat through your girlfriend's face if you don't retract your remarks about Diels. Do I make myself clear?"

I didn't know where this was going but Goering was right. I would have said anything to keep the acid off her face.

"You're right. It was bullshit. I just wanted Heydrich to wash the acid off her leg."

"I thought so. Your methods, Heydrich, are crude. And even worse they are unreliable. Let me show you."

He poured a few drops acid on Sara's face. Within seconds her neck muscles seemed ready to explode. Potter and I roared. We were instantly gagged. Sara groaned through her teeth as she bucked against her straps.

"I'll wash it away, Sara, as soon as you tell me that Temple killed Glaise."

The room was so quiet now that I imagined that I could hear Sara's teeth grinding and her skin burning.

"Tell me, Sara," said Goering, his voice no more than a whisper.

"No!" came the response, muffled but defiant.

Goering seemed unruffled. "You see, Heydrich, this American is not so soft as to betray the one she loves."

Goering poured another drop on Sara's face. She reacted but

not as badly as at first. Her facial nerves must have already been damaged. "Now, Sara, I want you to tell me that Viktoria killed Glaise."

Again silence.

Viktoria yelled, "Sara, for God's sake, it makes no difference. Tell him I did it."

"It does and I won't," Sara said through her gritted teeth.

This was insane. Resisting the bully was a fine thing but accepting punishment over nothing was senseless. On top of that, Goering seemed to be making the point that torture was unreliable – so why not help him make his point?

Viktoria was pleading, "Reichsmarshall, you are a lover of beauty. Surely you . . . "

Goering cut her off. "Do not preach to me."

But he looked a little weak-kneed. This wasn't aerial combat where the aces never saw their enemies' faces.

"Wash her off. Keep it from her eyes. Use the baking soda," Goering grumbled.

"Does the Reichsmarshall now have a greater respect for the work we do?" said Heydrich.

Goering snapped back, "There is a difference between courage and unproductive callousness, General." Goering's remark seemed to follow on some earlier, unfinished conversation.

Although Goering had lost his taste for the game, he wasn't ready to quit. It was Viktoria's turn again. Viktoria took the acid on her arm, up six inches from her hand.

"So tell me, Fraulein, how Potter killed Glaise."

I don't know why he thought Viktoria would be weaker than Sara. That said, he got an answer, although it wasn't what he expected.

"I did it. Clean her arm and I'll tell you," said Sara. "It's time to end this."

As she told the story, Sara seemed bewildered, as if astounded by the event she was recounting.

"After the Press Ball, Glaise called me and said that she wanted to talk about the baby, Seth. I went to her bungalow. The place was a mess. Plates, wine glasses, but you know all that. She said Seth was beautiful, that it was a shame he died. It was too bad I hadn't met my brother. There wasn't an ounce of sincerity in her voice. It was like she was mocking the whole situation. But she didn't really want to talk about Seth.

"She wanted to brag. She hadn't gone to the ball because Hitler had visited her bungalow. That's what she said. I don't know if she was lying but from the looks of the place someone had visited. She boasted that, with Goebbels and Hitler as admirers, her career would skyrocket.

"I asked about Seth, dumb enough to think she would tell me what happened to him. She laughed at me and said she knew I wouldn't have come if she hadn't used the baby as an excuse. There was no news about Seth. She was going to be the next big star. She just wanted to crow. She said I would be dumped after *Horst Wessel*. As if that would mean something to me.

"I didn't know whether to laugh at her pettiness or cry that my dad had gotten mixed up with such a bitch. I wound up laughing but not at her. Or at myself. I was laughing at . . . I don't know what. I guess I was laughing instead of crying.

"But Glaise thought I was laughing at her. She went crazy and lashed out. If I only knew the truth about Seth. Dad was stupid. I was a tramp who was giving the Nazis a propaganda coup. Once they were done using me, I'd be shipped back to Zukor as damaged goods. Mom was a frigid bitch who couldn't . . . I won't even say it. Glaise kept it up like she wanted to destroy everything that was important to me.

"I should have left. Instead I went crazy. I didn't stop choking her until her eyes rolled back. I wasn't thinking about killing her. I just wanted to shut her up. And, yes, I wanted to hurt her. Like she'd hurt my family. So I kept throttling her and didn't noticed she'd stopped struggling until her eyes were gone - rolled up. Then it was too late. I didn't intend . . . but that doesn't make any difference now."

Before Sara began talking, Goering tilted her chair upright so he could see her face, and measure it for conviction, indecision, or whatever other augury of veracity he could discern. She told the story as if reliving the event as she spoke. She almost seemed surprised that Glaise was dead. She looked at Goering without seeing him - as if she were back in the bungalow, staring at the evidence of her sin.

Goering nodded, acknowledging the truth of her confession.

Heydrich protested, "Quite a performance. I would have expected nothing less of a Jew-lover who played Horst Wessel's sister so convincingly."

Sara returned to the present, glaring at Heydrich for what he was. Heydrich was oblivious to her venomous look.

"And as shocked as you were by your actions, you still managed to arrange the scene to frame Minister Goebbels?" said Heydrich, furious the game had turned against him.

"No. I called Eric. He did it. He told you the truth about that."

"Too convenient," Heydrich hissed. "I don't believe her, not a word. I want to know what Temple was going to say."

Goering seemed angrier than Heydrich but his words were controlled and scarcely more than a whisper.

"She admitted killing Glaise to save Diels? To save Temple or her father, perhaps. To save Diels, preposterous. Would Temple hand you Diels to save Potter? Of course he would. But that would mean nothing because you display your animus toward Diels like a beacon. I am not interested in lies provoked by your ambition or your acid. We are done here today."

Chapter Thirty-Six

I sat in my cell imagining ways to escape as if the exercise could erase the image of Sara's damaged face. The idea was to reach Willie's Tavern. He would get me out through one of his submarine routes.

There was a way to escape. Each afternoon a guard entered my cell for a strip search. He would prod my ass with his baton as if I'd hidden a weapon there. But he wasn't looking for contraband. Humiliation was the point. In their arrogance the Germans allowed the guard to come alone. Prisoners by definition were broken, capable of only submission. The guard was careless. I could knock him out, exchange clothes, steal his keys, and with any luck walk out, masquerading as one of my keepers. Because dinner didn't arrive until two hours after the search, German punctuality guaranteed me a two-hour head start.

The next afternoon, I waited with the anticipation of a cliff diver poised above the sea. The guard was in his mid-twenties. But for his brown hair, he would have qualified as an Aryan prototype. That he enjoyed his work would make this all the sweeter.

"Pull them down and spread them," he said.

I obeyed. The baton probed. I gave it a chance to explore, grabbing it only when I felt it pulling away. I yanked with all I had. The guard lost his grip and his balance. I was on him in an instant, shoving the baton's business end into his mouth.

"Eat shit," I whispered with a distinct lack of imagination.

I jammed the baton deep in his throat. He was gagging now. Pain and fear drove tears down his cheeks. Hell of a way to die, choking on the wrong end of an anal dipstick.

"How do you like it? Tell me how you like it," I whispered with the intensity of ripening vengeance.

I pulled the baton out. He couldn't talk as he gasped for air; and I didn't really care to hear his answer. I shoved the baton back in.

"Tell me that you like it," I hissed.

I pulled the baton, leaving it an inch from his lips.

"Tell me you like it or I'll shove this all the way to your heart."

"I like it. I like it," he gasped.

He looked at me the same way Sara had looked at Heydrich - a Nazi with disdain for my inhumanity.

I stood, my adrenalin draining away and my anger gone with the realization that I had crossed a line.

"Get up. Get out of here."

Confusion and surprise replaced the scorn and fear which had been on his face.

I held out the baton. "Take it."

He held back, sure it was a trick.

"Take it and get out."

He reached for the baton.

I pulled it back. My self-disgust had not completely overwhelmed my will to survive.

"Remember. If you tell anyone what happened here, your career is over. You'll be cleaning latrines for the rest of your life if you're lucky. Do you understand that?"

It took a few seconds for him to work through the consequences of having been disarmed by a prisoner. "Better than you," he said after recognizing his predicament.

"You can resume searching tomorrow as if this never happened."

I held out the baton. He took it and left.

It had never been about escaping. I couldn't have left Sara, even if my plan had been more than a pipe dream. It was about proving something. In the event I came close to proving I was no better than a garden variety SA thug. The measure of my failure was the petty satisfaction I took in my moment of irrelevant power and misplaced retribution.

A month or so later an SS captain brought news.

Viktoria had been executed for treason. The captain claimed that, as the end neared, Vik begged for mercy, admitted her crimes, and swore allegiance to the Fuhrer. They may have killed her but the rest was slander.

Sara and her father had been sent home. Potter had been expelled for criminal meddling in German affairs. A diplomatic protest had been lodged with the American ambassador in Berlin and by the German ambassador in Washington. Roosevelt's state department had apologized. Sara, who opposed her father's views and continued to support the good works of the National Socialists, accompanied her father home. The captain showed me a three-day-old issue of the *Trib*'s Paris edition. It carried the story under the headline: **U.S. Embarrassed**.

Finally the captain informed me that my behavior had been the subject of a diplomatic protest by the Germans.

"And what behavior was that?" I asked.

"Shooting two pages at the premier of *Horst Wessel*. Don't bother arguing. Your government agreed you should stand trial before a Special People's Court. Both governments agreed: the less publicity the better. Your trial was a short, private one. It took place yesterday. You were convicted. In accordance with the agreement reached with your government, you will not be executed and will be eligible for parole in ten years."

Eric dead. Viktoria dead. Hanussen dead. Ludi no doubt dead. Ten years for me. Sara and Tom free in exchange for small German propaganda victories.

"Where am I to be imprisoned?" I asked, the wind just about gone from my sails.

"Upstairs, we have cells suitable for prisoners with special status."

"Special status?"

"As long as we have an interest in keeping the United States neutral, you will be special."

What a deal. If Uncle Sam ever got a backbone, my sentence would likely be commuted to death. If I was lucky, I might someday be released in a prisoner exchange. I stewed on that, not liking my prospects as a political pawn.

"Tell your boss I've got the information he wants. He gets the story, if I get out and get home."

"Tell me. I'll pass it on."

"I'm looking to make a deal. Unfortunately, Captain, you can't take a shit without permission. Pass along what I said."

Making a deal with Heydrich was a long shot. Still, having a chance seemed better than rotting away.

Nothing happened. It was as if I'd flipped a coin only to have it levitate, forever spinning in the air. It occurred to me that the Captain was Goering's man. Heydrich wouldn't visit because he didn't know I wanted to deal. Since I had nothing to offer Goering, he wouldn't be calling.

I thought a lot about Sara. There were days when I imagined that she was still in Columbia Haus, locked in the next cell. We exchanged words of comfort and love. There were other days when I believed that she had abandoned me. Still others when I knew that she had no choice about leaving. On those days I hoped that she had found someone to make her happy, knowing the sentiment was something of a lie.

After some weeks they let me read the *Volkischer Beobachter.* It was a life saver. I devoted hours to reading between the lines, trying to separate fact from fiction. Months passed. I maintained hope only because forsaking it would have given the bastards another victory. But my hope was amorphous, tied to no likely event or circumstance. It was more a refusal to admit that I would never be released and would never again see Sara.

The combination of love and anger more often than not makes for blood on the floor. In my case the combination kept hope alive.

In November a rubber-stamping Oberfuhrer came to my cell and told me I was being released. It was a humanitarian gesture to foster better relations with the United States. He gave me a new suit of nicely tailored clothes. Now I was afraid to hope.

"How am I getting home?"

"I don't know. You will be met in the lobby."

When I'd finished changing clothes, the Oberfuhrer turned to a sergeant and told him to move me out.

I immediately thought of Sara. I'd seen her in the lobby of Gestapo headquarters the day Diels first released me. She had looked great then and would look even better today.

Most of the Columbia Haus lobby was filled with a beehive of temporary offices built to accommodate the growing torture administration. Who would meet me? Someone from the embassy, no doubt. Here and there, in what remained of the lobby, were small knots of men bundled in top coats and felt hats against the winter.

"Whatdayagotforme!" said a man disengaging himself from a conversation.

For a moment I was fooled by his fedora.

"What the devil? Did you lose your Panama or just find some common sense?"

PART TWO

LIZ

1935

BERLIN AND PARIS

Chapter Thirty-Seven

The men around Cooper lifted cameras and began taking pictures as we shook hands. Cooper took me by the elbow and steered me from the building to a waiting taxi.

"What was that all about?" I asked, having a good idea of the answer.

"You're news. Evidence of Germany's magnanimity, humanity, charity, generosity, and dignity to say nothing of its mercy, clemency and decency."

"Did Hitler and his gang resign?"

"No such luck. In the next few days your mug will be on the front pages of papers from Berlin to London and New York to Los Angeles."

"Why?"

"Propaganda of course. Germany frees a murderer in the interest of building bridges. I'll tell you the rest on the plane."

The cabby dropped us at Tempelhof. Far out on the tarmac was a new DC-3, its aluminum frame shining in the afternoon sun. More photographers were gathered around the base of the airplane's gangway. When we reached the top step, Cooper told me to turn around. Pictures were part of the deal. Five minutes later the two Pratt & Whitney engines fired up. Only after we were airborne did I believe I was free.

"Your grin's as wide as the Mississippi is long."

"Damn right. Thanks. How'd you pull this off?"

"I had some help from your girlfriend and your boss."

"Sara and Humphrey?"

"Humphrey helped but I had Zukor in mind."

"Zukor?"

"None other."

"Where is Sara?"

"Paris."

"How did you guys do it?"

"Old fashion horse trading."

"Who got what from who? The deal had to be more than a few propaganda photos."

"The plastic surgeons will never be able to make Sara's face right. Even without the scar, she and her father had a hellofa story to tell. They decided to go public if the Germans didn't release you. We all knew it was risky. But we figured, even if the story ran, the Nazis would have kept you alive just to prove they weren't as bad as the story portrayed them. It was a gamble. But what the hell, I knew you would have rolled the dice."

"How'd you know that?"

"Our first night on the roof of the Adlon. You told me about being locked up in Paris. You said you'd rather die than be locked up like that again."

"I'd forgotten that."

"Forgotten, my ass. You were drunk."

"And you were sober?"

"Real reporters drink to remember."

"And I'm from *Variety.*"

Cooper smiled.

"And a fake one to boot. Anyway at the *Trib* we mocked up an article and Zukor had his boys prepare a newsreel. Zukor lent me this DC-3 and I flew to Berlin. I arranged an audience with a Goebbels lackey and showed him the article and newsreel. I told the guy they either released you or the *Trib* would run the story and Paramount would run the newsreel in the states while Pathé would run it in England and France. The guy shit a brick. Tells me to wait and hustles outa the room like I'm about to release mustard gas.

"Three hours later Wilhelm Schmidt walks in with Putzi Hanfstaengl. He's Haaavard 1909. Know who Putzi he is?"

"Yeah, foreign press secretary and court jester. I met him once. Who's Schmidt?"

"Goebbels's main flunky. Hard as nails. Shrewd, not smart. Educated in the streets, although he plays the gentleman.

"What happened?"

"Putzi started telling a story about Roosevelt. Schmidt cut him off. His proposition went like this. Germany wants good relations with its neighbors and the United States. The story and newsreel would damage that prospect. Germany would consider their publication a slanderous act of aggression by the United States that would cause Germany to see an even greater need for rearmament. Furthermore, while no one wanted you executed, your case would be reopened. The original deal with the state department would be off, and your execution would likely follow."

"So if the *Trib* reported my story, it would be responsible for German rearmament? What bullshit."

"But there was a carrot. Germany would be happy to release you if the proposed slanderous story and newsreels were quashed. Since the Ministry understood the *Tribune's* need for stories, the Ministry would be happy to give me unprecedented access if it had editorial control. And since Paramount needed films to release, it would run *Horst Wessel* for two weeks in New York. Disseminating positive information would foster mutual trust."

"So you had to write some kiss-ass columns?"

"Yes, but there was more. Schmidt wanted Sara to return to Germany to shoot an additional scene for *Horst Wessel*."

"You agreed to all that?"

"I said that I couldn't speak for the *Trib*, Paramount, or Sara. Schmidt told me to go home and get some answers. If we agreed with his terms, I should return with Sara. If we didn't agree, we would all take our chances. So I played messenger boy."

"How in the hell did you get Zukor much less the *Trib* to agree? And you're telling me Sara went back?"

"She did. They filmed a new scene. You're not going to believe this. After Horst dies, the communists come after his sister and throw acid in her face. That's the new scene. There is now an outtake showing how Sara got hurt."

"So what are they saying? That the prop man forgot to substitute water for acid and that's how her face was burned?"

"Not quite. The prop man was an evil commie who intentionally tried to wreck the film and its co-star."

"And the world is flat. Zukor hates the Nazis. Why would he agree to show *Horst Wessel*?"

"Beats me. At first he threw me out of his office. But at sunrise the next morning, he had a car at my hotel. Back in his office he says he'll go along, as long as the engagement is limited to two weeks at the Paramount on Times Square."

"And what about the *Trib*. It agreed to run propaganda?"

"No. It agreed that I could take advantage of the promised access. I would write whatever stories I saw fit and Goebbels could edit them. But the final editing as well as the decision to run a story would always remain with the *Trib*. Schmidt agreed provided there were two test articles before your release. So I wrote two puff pieces that were basically true but hardly earthshaking about Germany's economic recovery. The *Trib* and I passed the test."

"Christ, Cooper."

"Don't worry. I'm playing for access no one else has. I wrote enough namby-pamby bull to get you out. And I'm going to have great access until I start writing the truth. Meanwhile I'm on the inside or close to it. If they start to regard me as their boy, I might land a major story."

"You're going back?"

"As soon as I drop you off. Look Hitler and Germany are the story of a lifetime. They'll make the Panama Canal seem like a trout stream in Peoria."

Cooper was loving it: he had helped a pal; positioned himself for a great story; was playing the Nazis for suckers; and was flying around in a private airplane. He might as well have hit a grand slam in the bottom of the ninth to win the seventh game of the world series.

The DC-3 landed at Bourget where Lindbergh landed the Spirit of St. Louis nine years before. I'd been there that night and seen the hoopla that accompanied his exploit. The whole city celebrated, believing his flight signaled the dawn of a better, faster, new age. The Parisians had been right on two of the three.

No one greeted our arrival. On the drive into the city, there wasn't a flag or propaganda poster in sight. When I said as much, Cooper shook his head.

"The frogs are too proud by half without the trappings. It wouldn't hurt them to see what Berlin has become."

"I thought you were on top of the world."

"I'm doing just fine. It's France and the rest of the world that will be sucking hind tit if they don't wake up."

We fell silent as the cab worked its way into Paris. I was nervous about seeing Sara again. Cooper's talk of surgeons had me worried. I had fallen for a beautiful girl. How would I react?

Years before during my ambulance driving days, a badly burned and very depressed British soldier mumbled a line from a poet named Donne. It was something like, "Love built on beauty, soon as beauty, dies." At the time I missed Donne's point, thinking he hadn't given love its due.

Now I understood Donne was right. I would soon see what my love was built on.

Chapter Thirty-Eight

Cooper and I met Sara and Zukor in the Crillon Hotel's lounge. They were at a corner table off to the side. Sara's injured cheek faced the wall. They didn't look ready to pop champagne over my arrival. Zukor saw us first and nodded hello. Sara didn't turn her head as if she wanted me to see only the girl I remembered from the Wannsee beach. Then she thought better of it and looked at me straight on, defiantly, as if to say this is who I am.

It was all I could do not to gasp. Half of the skin on her left cheek had been converted to a patch of moonscape. Diels' dueling scars looked good by comparison.

Zukor stood, shoving a cigar in the corner of his mouth. He stepped away from the table and extended his hand. "Michael, I knew I picked a mensch! Welcome back."

He pulled me into an embrace, his cigar zooming by my face like a misguided roman candle. From the corner of his mouth he whispered.

"Don't be a jerk. Wipe that spooked look off your face. Smile at her like she's a person."

He let me go.

I smiled. To my relief it was real. After the initial shock, I found the scaring didn't disgust me. It made me angry because I loved Sara for reasons that went beyond beauty. I was never so certain of anything. Screw you, John Donne. Sara was still beautiful, although in a slightly different way.

Sara forced a smile but doubt registered in her eyes.

I sat next to her, and said, "I didn't realized how much I loved you until now."

Her smile softened and became genuine. "Michael, I'm so glad you're out. When we left, I felt like . . . "

"Shhh." I put a finger on her lips. "You never left me."

I kissed her. Her lips were as supple as I remembered but unresponsive. She would have to learn that the scar didn't make a difference to me.

"I do love you very much."

"I believe you, Michael," she said sounding more troubled than consoled.

"A bottle of champagne, waiter, your best," said Zukor sitting down with Cooper.

"Hello, Richard. Thanks for bringing Michael out," said Sara.

"Forget it. Reporters always stick together. Right, Michael?"

"I thought *Variety* didn't count," I said.

"But I made you a stringer. for the *Trib*."

"Then I resign. Pinkerton is easy compared to the reporting business."

"Resign? Not until I get the whole story from you. I've gotta deaf, blind kid in Munich who's produced more than you." Cooper was enjoying himself.

Just then the champagne arrived.

Zukor offered a toast. "May Cooper expose the shmucks and may the world take notice."

After our glasses were lowered, I asked Zukor why he agreed to run *Horst Wessel*.

"Like Cooper I figured a way to turn their demand against them. I controlled the audience. All the tickets were distributed in advance at synagogues around New York or were given to people of influence, friends of mine. I made damn sure they knew the real story so they would appreciate how lies are part and parcel of the German message. It opened a lot of eyes."

I made a toast to the ingenuity of Cooper and Zukor, and thanked them all for getting me out. Cooper said something about Germany hosting the 1936 Olympic games, predicting a disgusting showcase for all things Aryan. Sara seemed to be someplace else. Our little celebration quickly fizzled. Zukor pulled a key from his pocket and slid it to me.

"I'm turning in. Sara said you would want a separate room. If that's the case, you're in three twenty-three. Let's go, Cooper. I'll buy you a nightcap in the bar."

I didn't want separate rooms. We had last made love in the Reichstag Annex by sneaking off to an office with a couch. Sitting next to Sara brought back the taste of our lovemaking. I wanted one room, and soon wasn't soon enough.

But Sara wanted separate rooms, and wouldn't or couldn't explain why. I had a feeling it was more than a damaged cheek.

It was a long night for me. Once I checked the door between our rooms. It was locked from her side. I put my ear to it and thought I heard crying. I knocked but there was no response. Eventually I fell asleep on the floor next to the door.

Sara let me in the next morning. She looked to have gained some weight from our days in Columbia Haus. Room service brought breakfast. She was friendly but distant. She picked at her food as I devoured mine.

She brought me up to date without seeming the least interested in what she was saying. Her father had moved back home. Tom and his wife were trying to make a go of it. Sara didn't think the attempt at reconciliation would work. Zukor had offered her a job as an associate producer. She thought she would take it but who could say if the job would work out.

"In New York?" I asked.

"Yes."

"What about us?"

"I'm not sure there is an us. I need some time."

When I began to protest, she put a finger to my lips. As if offering a consolation prize, she asked if I would take her to the Tuileries Gardens which were across the Place de la Concorde from the hotel. Afterward we could have lunch back at the hotel.

Sure I said, feeling like a charity case.

She excused herself to change. I stayed and read the *Trib* that had arrived on the breakfast tray. I could hear a radio playing in her bathroom. The telephone rang. I answered it, thinking it had to be Cooper or Zukor.

It was Mademoiselle Saufroy from Doctor Villiot's office. The doctor wanted to change Sara's three o'clock appointment to eleven. Would that be possible? I said that Sara would call back.

When Sara came out, I told her about the call and the request. She turned and looked out the window as if her response might be found in the hieroglyphs etched in the ancient obelisk that stood in the center of the Place de la Concorde.

"We'll have to cancel our outing today," she said.

Sara went to the telephone and called Villiot's office to say she would be there at eleven. When the call ended, she said I would have to go. We would have time to see Paris later. We were flying back with Zukor, and he wasn't leaving for another four days.

"He has meetings with Pathé News," she said avoiding the subject of her appointment.

"Are you all right?" I asked.

Of course she wasn't. I figured Villiot was a plastic surgeon. Maybe there was something he could do.

"Of course. I'm fine."

She didn't seem fine, although she was maintaining a brave front. She shuffled me from her room with a promise that we would see the gardens the next day.

Back in my room, I called Pinkerton's Paris office, hoping Matt Thompson would answer. A guy named Dempsey picked up. I didn't know him but established my credentials by telling a Humphrey story.

"Call me Jack," he said. "And no jokes. I've heard then all."

"A little sensitive, slugger?"

"It's irresistible, isn't it? So what can I do for you?"

"Have you ever heard of a Paris doctor named Villiot? He's probably a plastic surgeon."

"The one I know isn't a surgeon. *Her* specialty is obstetrics.

I've followed or sent more than a few women with unwanted pregnancies to her office."

"Spell it out for me."

"She delivers babies for them that wants 'em, does abortions for them that don't, and treats the occasional case of VD - provided you're rich that is. She has an office on Rue Saint Honoré. Right between Hermès and Chanel. The ladies can visit the doc and do a little shopping without making the chauffeur drive all over town. Very convenient."

I slammed the receiver down without signing off.

VD? Impossible.

Pregnant? Possible. But Sara wasn't showing much if at all and she had to be over six months pregnant. Was she seeing a doctor to get rid of our baby? Why? Of course, I'd marry her. Hadn't I said as much last night? I remembered her telling me she wanted kids. Then I remembered the report from the Reliable Agency, the one about Paul Bennett and her abortion. I couldn't let it happen again. Not to my kid. Not over some misunderstanding. I had to catch her.

I charged into Sara's room only to find it empty.

I called Dempsey from her phone.

"I thought you just hung up on me," he said.

"Cut the shit, Jack. I don't have the time. What's the address of Villiot's office?"

"Ever hear of the telephone book?"

"Do you know it or not?"

"Two eighty-five. Two doors East of Chanel. Right at Rue Royal."

"Thanks. Bye."

I ran through the Crillon lobby offending its quiet money patrons. Once outside I raced east on Place de la Concorde, and then up Rue Royal to Rue Saint Honoré scattering pigeons and tourists as I went, to say nothing of irritating shoppers unaccustomed to being jostled as they labored through another day of consumption.

Villiot's office was above Grain de Beauté, a shop that sold astringents, washes, makeup, mud packs, mousses, softeners, curling irons, straighteners, atomizers, waxers, dyes, and more - everything but beauty itself. Most of the stuff was worthless and some of it was dangerous. All of it sold.

The entrance to Villiot's office had no sign, only a street number below which a nondescript door led to a wide hall decorated to create the illusion of an ocean liner's promenade deck. The hall ended at an elevator that looked like an ornate birdcage. It lifted me to a waiting room decorated like the ladies lounge in an elegant casino. Sara was nowhere in sight. It was 10:50. An impeccably dressed receptionist sat behind a desk that might have been a museum piece.

I asked for Sara.

With a polite but frosty tone, she asked who I was. I recognized her voice.

"Mademoiselle Saufroy, we spoke not an hour ago when you called to change Sara's appointment to eleven. She and I were to come together but I was held up on business. I've come to be with her."

"Then you should have known the appointment was at the doctor's clinic not her city office."

A stack of appointment cards rested near her left hand. I was quicker. Her hand landed on top of mine. I took a card from the stack. The clinic was in Argenteul.

I would never get there in time. This was on me. Somehow I'd failed Sara, forcing her to make the wrong choice.

At Saufroy's right hand was a telephone. She did not challenge me for the receiver. I dialed the clinic. An icy-smooth voice answered. I tried sounding businesslike.

"Mademoiselle Potter, please. She is a patient of Doctor Villiot. She should have just arrived."

"She has not arrived yet. Who is calling, please?"

"Michael Temple."

"And your relationship to her."

A good question. "Father of the kid about to be aborted" wasn't calculated to get me through. From the looks of Villiot's office, money carried weight.

"I'm her investment adviser. Immediately upon her arrival, please give her this message, 'Make no decision before I arrive. Don't proceed with the planned sale. She should hold and later purchase more. I am on the way.' Please repeat the message, mademoiselle."

She did, sounding wary.

"I understand the message is cryptic, but you must understand the information is confidential."

"I understand," she said as if she did.

Had she broken the clumsy code or accepted the message at face value? Too much seemed to be riding on a faceless voice.

Argenteul is seven miles northwest of Paris. It's famous for its white asparagus and a handful of artists who claimed its light made them better painters. Between city traffic and finding the clinic once in Argenteul, the cab ride lasted forty minutes. Too long.

The clinic was in an old chateau. The foyer had been converted to a reception area. Its refined décor varnished the nasty business conducted behind the fabric-covered walls. I introduced myself to the receptionist who told me that Sara was with Villiot.

"Did you give Mademoiselle Potter my message?"

"Yes."

"What did she say?"

"Nothing. She asked to see the doctor."

"I want to see Mademoiselle Potter immediately."

"That is not possible. Not to worry, she is not about to make any financial transactions over the next half hour or so. If you wish to wait, you may do so here or stroll outside."

"I don't want strolling. You're going to take me to Sara now or I'm going to tear this place apart looking for her."

"The garden is really quite relaxing."

"I don't want relaxing, lady!"

When she reached for her telephone, I grabbed the end of her desk and flipped it over, sending the telephone, a vase of flowers, and assorted papers flying. Behind me two women screamed. The receptionist looked at me like I'd lost my mind. She jumped out of her chair and took off running. I followed for lack of a better plan.

She bolted through a door located behind her, slamming it against me. It bounced off my shoulder and banged the wall. The receptionist raced down a hall, yelling for help. I followed, glancing in offices as I went. I was running but didn't know to where, acting for the sake of action as if that alone would produce Sara.

I was stopped in my tracks by a haughty voice that called my name with a drill sergeant's authority.

I turned to face a middle-aged woman standing in the hall, hands on her hips. She was expensively tailored. At her neck a diamond brooch pinned her blouse closed like a sparkling bow tie. She was a person accustomed to having her way.

"Where is Sara?"

"You will see her when we are finished."

"You mean when you're finished killing our child."

"You have a great deal to learn, Monsieur Temple. If your boorishness is any indication, that will take more time than I have. But start with this. Children are not killed at this clinic. Nor is Mademoiselle Potter having an abortion today; although, given your behavior, I am convinced that would be the right decision for her. Now wait in the foyer. Sara will be out in a few minutes. I cannot say whether she will speak to you. If she doesn't wish to speak to you, I will not tolerate your pestering her on my grounds. Has all that penetrated to wherever you do your thinking?"

The lady redefined haughty. I wanted to bowl her over and pull Sara from her office. I might have done exactly that if I hadn't been worried about proving her point.

"Ten minutes, Doctor. Then I'm coming, invited or not."

"If you have a brain in your head, you won't. By the way, are you at the Crillon?"

"Yes. Why?"

"I'll be sending a bill for the damage."

She dismissed me with a wave of her hand and went into her office. The door lock clicked, leaving me standing in the hall like a scoundrel unworthy of attention. I retreated to the chateau's front porch.

Five minutes later I began to wonder if I'd been had. Was the procedure underway? I'd heard stories about back alley abortions - girls dying on the spot or later from infection. I imagined the procedure was dangerous even here amid the trappings of competency and wealth. So I waited, simmering over how Sara and I had messed up.

Ten minutes later Sara walked out, eyes red and puffy. She gave me a rumpled smile that cooled my anger. She embraced me as if we hadn't seen each other since Berlin. Then she pushed me away and looked at me as if seeing me for the first time.

"I understood your message. Thank you. It meant a lot. But things are not what you think they are."

"You're not pregnant?"

"I am pregnant. But not like you think."

Just then a taxi pulled up. Sara got in, saying that she needed to be alone. The cab pulled away leaving me standing on the gravel drive.

It took two more days to pry the truth from her. She was protecting me. She felt that I would blame myself. That was true. She felt that I would feel trapped, required to stand by her. That was not true.

Chapter Thirty-Nine

Sara and I were sitting on a bench in the Tuileries Gardens.

It hadn't been easy for us to get there. Since leaving the clinic, she had been avoiding me, keeping to her room at the Crillon. From time to time I'd knock on her door or call, offering to talk or show her the city. She wasn't interested. I asked what it was that I didn't understand about her pregnancy. She put me off.

Two days later I went down to the hotel newsstand. I was browsing, killing time really, when I spotted Sara walking through the lobby. I followed, hoping she wouldn't hop a cab to the clinic.

She walked to the obelisk that stood at the center of the Place de la Concorde, stopping at the wrought iron fence that protected the hieroglyphs from the hands of curious tourists. She put on sunglasses as she looked up at the ancient writing.

After a few minutes she walked off toward the gardens, her face attracting sly glances from busybodies. She removed her sunglasses and kept walking, holding her head a little higher than normal. She walked down the gardens' central avenue to the second reflecting pond. There she turned right, passing between a terrace planted with a honeysuckle maze and another, now fallow awaiting summer's tulips.

Fathers and sons tended toy sailboats in the pond. From the maze came the laughter of kids playing hide and seek. Couples strolled with eyes only for each other. Smiling mothers pushed perambulators. Old men battled at checkers over worn boards, swapping memories as if they were current events.

On a bench overlooking the fallow terrace, Sara sat rocking to some internal rhythm. I knelt before her. She was crying.

"Sara, I love you. But I'm here not just for you. Turns out I need you - more than I can say. Now I'm going to sit down and keep my mouth shut. I'll be here if you want your butt kicked or anything else."

I sat and pretended to watch the passersby while watching Sara from the corner of my eye. A brittle smiled flickered across her face as if triggered by a warm but fleeting memory. She wiped her tears with the cuff of her blouse.

"It's not a butt kicking I need. At least not the way we joked about it."

"A lot has happened. But we're still who we were. I fell in love with the same girl who's sitting next to me now. I don't care how much shit has come down."

"I couldn't leave you in that prison," she began only to stop as if she'd said the wrong thing.

"We'll get through it, whatever it is."

"I flew to Paris with Zukor because I wanted to see you walk off the airplane at Bourget. When Cooper got off the plane without you, I thought my heart would break. We had convinced ourselves the plan would work. We underestimated them, or were fooled by wishful thinking.

"Cooper said Goebbels wanted me back in Berlin to film a new scene for *Horst Wessel*, although Goebbels wouldn't say what the scene was about. As it turned out it was about me getting acid in the face. They wanted a filmed explanation of my injury that could be blamed on a Communist prop man. Can you believe it?"

"How could Cooper and Zukor have let you go back?" I asked.

"They said I was crazy to consider it. But I didn't see the danger. What could they do? Jail me? Things would only get worse for them if they held us both. So I went."

"They should have stopped you."

"It was my decision, not theirs."

Sara drew a deep breath and then continued.

"Goebbels greeted me at Tempelhof like I was the prodigal

son. They put me up in my old Ufa bungalow. Kerrl showed up and went over the scene. They acted like it was business as usual. After Kerrl left, Goebbels asked me to dinner. I might have been just another starlet. It was unreal.

"I told the little shit that they'd ruined my face and were holding the man I loved. How could he think I was there to socialize? He acted like I'd hurt his feelings. Said he knew this was difficult for me. He was only hoping to make it easier for me. He left the bungalow, all apologetic, claiming I misunderstood him. Pathetic."

"I'd say pathological."

"The shoot was the next day. Kerrl set up the angles so that my scar would be turned from the camera at first. In the scene, a commie taunts me and I give it right back to him. Then he throws supposed acid in my face but it turns out the prop acid is real. I cry out that I'm really hurt, pandemonium breaks out on the set, the acid-tossing actor is tackled like he was a real criminal, I'm given first aid, and then rushed off to the hospital. Kerrl even had a part, coming to help me. It took about an hour to film.

"When we were done, I asked Kerrl when you and I would be leaving. He said he didn't know. He took me back to my bungalow and left. Later that afternoon I decided to take a walk across the lot. I found a guard posted at my door. He ordered me to stay put.

"Goebbels showed up that night with a fancy dinner catered from the Ufa commissary and a bottle of wine. Oh, Michael."

"What did the bastard do to you?"

She was silent.

"Tell me, Sara. It's the only way we can get past it."

"It can't be gotten around or past."

"Just tell me, Sara."

She looked away and seemed to be watching a mother who was all eyes for her daughter. The child was toddling around as if walking was a wondrous experience. Sara's right foot was tapping like crazy on the gravel beneath our bench.

"It's his baby. Not yours," she said turning to look at me.

My world crashed.

"He raped you."

"Not like you imagine."

"Get it out, Sara," I said, sounding harsh although that wasn't my intention.

"He was very mellow. He said we were kindred spirits even if I didn't realize it. He spoke of his clubfoot and how it sometimes made him feel. He said he had always yearned for a friend who could understand what a physical handicap meant. I didn't forget who he was, but it rang disgustingly true. He had been there. He did understand."

"Feeling your pain. What crap," I objected. "That's the same trick Hitler uses in his speeches - empathizing with the people."

"It's only a trick if the speaker feels no pain."

"Or uses the pain to manipulate his listener."

"I know. But when he talked about living with a deformity, he was sincere. He told me how he learned to cope. Some of it made sense."

I didn't like where this was going. I wanted to scream in protest: *He was using you. His pals did this to you.* But my face was unmarked, and I had asked Sara to tell the story. So I listened.

"Anyway we ate, or at least he ate. I listened, hoping not to make him mad. I thought to myself - no wonder I believed in these guys when I first came to Berlin. As bad as they were, there was another side to some of them, even Goebbels. And don't say it, Michael. I know he's a pig.

"After a while he fell silent. Then he pulled a photo of his kids from his wallet. All of Germany knows them. They pose with Hitler in propaganda shots. Beautiful kids. Did you see them at the Eagle's Nest?"

"I did. Amazing such a weasely bastard could have such nice looking kids."

Sara allowed herself a small, ironic laugh.

"Goebbels said just about the same thing. He went on to say that scientifically there was nothing usual about their beauty. Morell - you remember him, Hitler's quack - told him the mother controls a child's physical appearance. It has to do with her natural beauty and her health at the time of conception. Goebbels said, while his mother had been pretty enough, she had been ill when he was conceived. He and Magda were careful not to make love when she was sick since they intended to have only beautiful children.

"It was pseudo-scientific gibberish but I figured it was Goebbels way of saying that if I wanted kids I didn't have to worry about my face since I was born pretty enough.

"Then it got stranger. He said any beautiful woman who bore his child could be assured of the child's beauty. He said he was worried about his children surviving, about his bloodline ending. War was coming and the world would conspire against them. Hanussen had predicted Germany's destruction. It was all very morose, out of character.

"Then suddenly he stepped back into character. He might have started out with good intentions but after a couple of glasses of wine, he couldn't resist being himself. He said, 'Don't look at me that way. Leaders pay a price but they also have prerogatives.'"

"Prerogatives?"

"That's the way he put it. Things moved quickly from there. He knew from my medical records that I'd just ovulated and was 'ready to go' as he put it. I was going to have his baby. Even if the Jews got his family, he would have a child tucked away in the states who was unknown to the Jews. His blood line would survive."

"That's totally crazy."

"That's what I told him. I said I wasn't sleeping with him much less having his child."

Sara stopped as if she didn't have the words or strength for the rest of the story.

I continued the story for her, imagining Goebbels response. "And he said you would or I wouldn't leave Germany alive. He blackmailed you with my life?"

"He said we could both leave once the pregnancy was confirmed."

"Oh, Sara," was the best I could do.

"I told him I would abort his kid as soon as I was out of

Germany. He looked at me like I was dirt. He said I would never abort any child - including his - but if I did I'd be joining the ranks of the immoral."

"What a joke, doubly so coming from him."

"One night Morell was talking about eugenics. He said the unfit should be sterilized and the pregnancies of unfit mothers should be terminated. I called his ideas immoral. Goebbels was reminding me of what I'd said."

"It's not the same."

"Of course not. But still, should a child be responsible for the father's sins?"

"That's not the same either. Besides an embryo isn't a child."

"I had an abortion once before. Did you know that?"

"I read it in a file Zukor gave me for background."

"It was hard for me. Boston Catholics don't have abortions."

"This isn't the same."

"You're right."

Sara seemed to be watching the child, the one who was tottering around to her mother's delight. I knew Sara had already given too much, suffered too much for my freedom.

We sat in silence for a long time. I wanted Sara more than ever. Not because I owed her - although I dearly did - but because I admired her more than ever. That said, I didn't want Goebbels' child and didn't believe what was forced on a person was necessarily theirs to keep or honor.

"Look at me, Sara," I said gently turning her chin toward me. "I want to marry you because, if you do, I'll be luckiest guy in Paris."

"What about this?" she said patting her stomach.

"Don't let the prick force you to keep it with his crack about immorality. Or let the Catholic Church convince you with the guilt it loads on people."

"I wouldn't. But what about this? It'll be a baby soon."

There was something about the way she said "baby". It was as if her embryo was already a person like the toddler who cavorted not twenty feet away. Or was she haunted by another face, one that would remain forever blank, shrouded by Catholic guilt? Did she really want *this* baby? Or was she making up for her earlier abortion?

I didn't ask her any of that. I couldn't ask her to do more than she had already done.

"It's not a baby yet. So if you don't want to keep it, we go back to the clinic; there is no sin or shame in that. But if you want to keep it, we have it. I'm with you either way."

"Really?"

"One way or another we need to get a family started."

I didn't like it, but I meant it.

We named the child Elizabeth after Sara's favorite aunt. We've always called her Liz. She has her mother's dimples. Sara says I've infected her with a silly streak. That's a hell of a thing to say about a grown man. Liz loves the only father she'll ever know, and he loves her. If you knew Liz, it wouldn't seem strange at all.

PART THREE

SETH

1945

BERLIN AND NEW YORK

Chapter Forty

During the second war, I did some work for the OSS, the outfit that evolved into the CIA. Archie Hocking was my boss and a friend. He sent me to Berlin near the very end of the war.

At the time the Nazis were leading the world in rocketry. From a research facility in Peenemunde, von Braun - yes, the same guy who now works for us - spearheaded the team that produced the V-1 and V-2. The Nazis wanted to blow London to smithereens by remote control. It was a hell of an idea.

Through its Wehrmacht contacts, the OSS learned there was a staff officer in Berlin with a set of the V-2 plans. Were the Americans interested? You bet.

Arch and his pals from Yale (early on the OSS was pretty much a Bulldog club) were already planning for the next war in which our ally, Russia, would be the adversary. At the time the Reds were about to finish off the Reich by taking Berlin. The OSS wanted someone to get the plans before the Russians took the city.

I was the guy. When I came back without the plans, Arch had not been happy.

"What the devil happened?" he complained.

"I was too late. By the time I got the documents, the Russians were crawling all over the place. I couldn't risk being caught with the papers."

"I thought we landed you with enough time."

Arch was right about the timing. And I didn't like lying to him.

"Don't worry I burned the documents. The Russians didn't get them."

"That doesn't answer the question. What the shit happened?"

Arch knew my family. Other than Sara and I, he was the only person who knew for sure I wasn't Liz's real father. Cooper and Zukor must have guessed but each was too good a man to ask.

Arch and I had been trapped with some French resistance fighters just after D-day in 1944. For a while it looked like we wouldn't make it. At times like that people talk, looking for comfort, relief, forgiveness, or whatever it takes to get through the night or to prepare to die. I told him the story on one of those nights.

We hadn't spoken of it since. To have done so would have been an admission of weakness and a breach of trust. And we were men who kept brave fronts and confidences.

Arch was observant and smart. As he debriefed me about the V-2 mission, he made an educated guess.

"It wasn't a nineteen forty-five problem was it? Something happened that related back to thirties. You got waylaid by the past, didn't you?"

He almost had me.

"Not exactly. It was more about the future."

"I don't know what the hell that means but if the Russians didn't get the documents, that's good enough for me."

Chapter Forty-One

April 29, 1945 10:00 PM

The idea of flying a Messerschmitt trainer into Berlin was half good. The Germans ignored it but the Russians peppered the sky with anti-aircraft fire, somehow missing us. The intelligence was correct. The East-West Axis inside the Tiergarten had been converted to a landing strip. The Russians had so many good targets, their artillery shelled the runway only periodically. Even so my pilot, Jimmy Boyle, had to dodge two craters before bringing the trainer to a stop. I told him to take off without me if it got to be last-flight-out time.

"In that case, General, you've got five minutes to get back here," Boyle joked.

We spoke German befitting our disguise as Luftwaffe flyers.

I demanded a staff car from the young Lieutenant who seemed to be in charge of the makeshift airport. He looked at me like I needed a reality check.

"No cars. No petrol. You'll have to walk, General."

His use of "General" was an afterthought. He was more worried about the Russians than the wrath of an unknown officer.

The walk was okay except for the chance of being killed by a random incoming shell. The air was filled with smoke and the sounds of artillery and tank fire. Before 1935, the East-West Axis had been Charlottenburger Chaussee. It ran through the Tiergarten to the Brandenburg Gate where it changed character and became the Linden. Hitler had widened Charlottenburger to a sterile boulevard, stealing its character while rendering it suitable for pomp and tank movements. Now it had become a makeshift landing strip pockmarked with craters and charred vehicles.

The Brandenburg Gate stood unmarked but not a light burned at the Adlon. The hotel had taken more than a few hits and looked abandoned. Down the Linden the Interior Ministry was burning. I headed south on Wilhelmstrasse toward the Chancellery which had been completed just ten years before.

It was bomb-scarred but open. The main entrance was lightly guarded by boys and old men armed with rifles from the first world war. The lobby desk was manned by an SS Sergeant and SS Corporal who looked like they had barely survived the eastern front.

"I'm here to see General Bergdorf. Luftwaffe business."

The Corporal took my identification with his left hand and rested the papers on the stump at the end of his right arm. His review was cursory.

"Those remaining have moved to the basement. Go left at the foot of the stairs. Office B-71."

Through vacant eyes the Sergeant stared at the entrance I'd just come through. He might have been waiting for the Russians, a miracle, or nothing.

The basement smelled of putrid water and defeat. B-71 might once have been a large storage closet. Its door was missing. Inside two desks were backed up to each other, filling most of the room. A major sat at one of the desks. He dragged himself to an approximation of attention.

"At ease, Major, I'm looking for Bergdorf. You are his adjutant?"

"I'm all he has."

"Where is he?"

The major leaned forward, squinting at my name tag. I caught a whiff of schnapps.

"I'm Mueller. Bergdorf was expecting me."

"You are late."

"Difficult times. He should have waited."

"He was called to the bunker."

"The bunker?"

"Under and behind the Chancellery. Hitler had it built. He's hiding down there waiting for Wenck's army to relieve the city."

"Wenck's army?"

"A ragtag division of old men and boys. Four days ago Wenck reported he was approaching Potsdam. Three days ago contact was lost. Everyone but Hitler thinks the army - if that's what it was - it disintegrated or was overrun. No one has the stomach to tell Hitler the war is lost. So here we sit, Hitler waiting for a phantom army, while the rest of us await the Russians."

"Bergdorf has some papers for me. Did he leave them with you?"

"No."

"When is he due back?"

"Who knows? It's stranger down there than up here."

The major reached into a desk drawer, pulled out a bottle, and extended it to me.

"Just a nip," I said.

An image of Fix pouring aquavit popped to mind. I must have smiled.

"You've heard the stories?" said the major.

"The stories?"

"About the bunker."

"No."

"Bergdorf is a good man. But Hitler is living in a dream world. He's . . ."

The major filled me in as I searched the tiny office in vain for the V-2 documents. According to the major, Hitler had taken up residence in the bunker three weeks before. His last stand would be in Berlin. Living in the bunker with him were Eva Braun, his valet, his chauffeur, his secretaries, the kitchen staff, his dog, and the entire Goebbels family.

There were military briefings by Generals Keitel and Jodl, and political briefings by Bormann. The Generals reported only enemy advances. Hitler forbid retreat and ordered counterattacks by exhausted or nonexistent troops.

A few days before, what remained of the old guard had gathered for Hitler's fifty-sixth birthday. They celebrated the past. Goebbels encouraged Hitler with horoscopes showing by month end Germany's fortunes would improve.

This and more the major told me between swigs from the schnapps bottle. Then he put his head on the desk and fell asleep. In spite of the rumble of artillery, I soon followed suit.

April 30, 1945 7:30 AM

Bergdorf shook me and then his adjutant awake. He looked to have been up all night.

"These are wondrous times, gentlemen," he said with obvious sarcasm. "The Fuhrer married Eva Braun at one-thirty this morning. There followed a champagne reception in Hitler's bunker apartment. Krebs, Bormann, his secretaries, the Goebbels family, the cook, and yours truly were the guests. Hitler rambled on about the old days for over an hour, even shedding a tear at the memory of serving as best man at the Goebbels wedding.

"Then he said that it would be a relief to die because he had been betrayed by his oldest supporters. He pushed himself up from his chair and told his secretary to come with him. They went into the map room. Thirty minutes later Krebs, Goebbels, Bormann, and I were called to witness Hitler's political testament and last will. Then he and Eva went to bed.

"Bormann and I made arrangements to have the testament and will sent out of Berlin. God only knows if they will make it. We waited, figuring, Hitler might take his life. But he and Eva walked out of his apartment at seven this morning . . . damn, that was a direct hit."

The three of us eyed the ceiling, waiting for it to collapse.

When it didn't, Bergdorf turned to me.

"Too bad you were late, Mueller. I might have taken you to the Third Reich's last wedding. They both swore they were of Aryan ancestry. That may not happen for another thousand years."

"The Russians are zeroing in now," said the major.

The walls around us were trembling to exploding artillery shells.

"Bergdorf, let's get those papers," I said. "I need to get moving."

"They're in a vault down the hall. Come with me."

We walked down the corridor past the steps I had taken to the basement. People slipped in and out of offices saying little. The snappy "Heil Hitlers" of the 1930s were gone, replaced by the grumbling of defeat. At the far end of the hall three SS men were posted.

"What's with them? They look like they have some fight left," I said.

"They are guarding a bunker entrance." Bergdorf sounded critical, as if they should have been outside fighting Russians.

At the vault Bergdorf stuffed the Peenemunde documents into a leather briefcase and handed it to me.

"Get moving, Mueller. The Russian are a block from the Hippodrome. They will take the Tiergarten soon."

We returned to the hallway - and suddenly there was Goebbels walking toward us. I froze. A wave of anger washed over me accompanied by an urge to hammer the guy.

Goebbels spotted Bergdorf.

"General, where is Klint? I told you yesterday to have him here this morning. Is no one capable of complying with a simple order?"

"He will be here by nine if he isn't dead," Bergdorf replied.

"Just get him here - even if he is dead. I mean it. I want the body." There was a touch of panic in his voice.

Then he noticed me, first squinting at my face and then my name tag.

"Who are you, Mueller? I thought the Luftwaffe had abandoned Berlin."

“Still work to be done,” I replied, fighting my anger and knowing the V-2 documents were more important than settling scores.

“Very true. Have we met before?”

“I’ve seen you before. Perhaps you’ve seen me. But we were never introduced.”

“Yes, of course. So many good men. Bergdorf, don’t let me down. I want Klint here dead or alive,” said Goebbels, hobbling toward the bunker entrance.

“You too must have a double,” Bergdorf said to me.

“What do you mean?”

“Goebbels looked at you like he knew you. Since he asked about his double, it occurred to me you must have a doppelganger.”

“Klint is his security double?”

“Yes.”

“Why does he need a double in the bunker?”

“He doesn’t.”

“I don’t understand.”

Bergdorf thought awhile.

“Last night Magda said the whole family would die in the bunker with Hitler. They would poison their children, and then take their own lives. Hitler said no, said they should break out. Magda said it was not worth living in a world without him. She meant it. Hitler looked at Goebbels. What was he to say? He agreed with Magda.

“I don’t think he has it in him. You heard him say he would take Klint’s body. Seems to me there is a chance that Klint will wind up playing the dead Goebbels while the real one makes a run for it.”

The possibility of his escape was unthinkable. Not after what he’d done to Sara. And what if he showed up one day looking for Liz? The desire for retribution and the instinct to protect trumped common sense and my orders.

“How would he escape?” I asked Bergdorf.

“Do you two know each other?”

“It’s a long story.”

"Goebbels has encouraged Hitler's insanity. The army and country have taken such a beating. Beyond any measure of reason. Next to Hitler Goebbels is most responsible. I would see him in hell. But the documents are more important. You must leave now."

"Tell me how he plans to get out."

We went to his office. He dismissed the major. We argued back and forth. Finally he told me the little he knew. He kept pressing me to leave. Eventually he lost patience.

"If you are determined to stay, I'll courier the papers to your pilot. He doesn't need you to fly them out."

I agreed. Bergdorf picked up the telephone on his desk, and called for a messenger. It took him fifteen minutes to round one up. Before he was dispatched, we called the makeshift runway to let Jimmy Boyle know the plan. It was a short call. Boyle reported our trainer had just been hit. Flying out was no longer an option. He said he would come and find me.

I told him no. "The Russians are close. Find a change of clothes. You don't want to be captured dressed as a German. Go west toward our troops."

"No vodka toasts with Uncle Joe and the red horde?" Boyle joked.

"Just take care of yourself."

April 30, 1945 3:20 PM, 1945 3:20 PM

From a window in an abandoned office on the first floor of the Chancellery, I watched the bomb-ravaged garden behind the building. A concrete structure rose from the ground about thirty yards out. Hitler's bunker was buried under it. Twenty feet of dirt and fifteen feet of concrete capped his subterranean universe. Thirty rooms branched off a dining passage, a sitting passage and a conference passage. Small cement-walled boxes:

a kitchen, a pantry, a power house, a communications center, quarters for Hitler's guards and staff, Hitler's private rooms, Morell's bedroom, rooms for the Goebbels family, and a map room. Access was through the Chancellery or the Foreign Office. The concrete structure in the garden doubled as an emergency exit and ventilation shaft.

Bergdorf said if Goebbels tried to escape, his route would be the garden, and then south to Potsdamer Station where there was an open rail line to Leipzig. There the best of the remaining German troops still had some freedom of movement. From Leipzig a man could disappear.

At three-thirty the emergency exit opened. Someone started out but ducked back when a shell exploded at the back of the Foreign Office. Then came two more explosions. When it became clear the Foreign Office was the target, an SS Sergeant emerged carrying a body wrapped in a field-gray army blanket. Black trousers and black shoes protruded from the blanket. Then Bormann emerged carrying the body of a woman.

Bergdorf had given me field glasses. I trained them on the woman's face. It was Eva Braun. Goebbels and a few others completed the procession from the bunker.

The bodies were laid in a crater. A private poured gasoline over the bodies, then stood back and looked at Bormann who was lined up with Goebbels and the others. Bormann came to attention and raised his arm in a Nazi salute. The others followed suit. Then Bormann nodded at the private. He lit a wad of paper and tossed it in the crater. Flames erupted, followed by black smoke. The line of mourners held their salutes. The smoke drifted skyward, mixing with the ashes of Berlin that were already floating in the air.

As the flames subsided, the shelling stopped momentarily, only to have the next shell land within twenty yards of the exit. Bormann dropped his salute and the mourners fled underground. Only the private and Goebbels remained. The private opened another can of gasoline and threw it in the crater. Another fireball erupted. Then the private ducked down the hatch leaving Goebbels the last man standing at the inglorious cremation. He looked around the pulverized garden, anger and hate plastered on his face. He hesitated and looked toward the southern end of the garden. Then he shook his head, turned, and went underground.

April 30, 1945 7:25 PM

In the twilight the hatch opened. Joseph and Magda Goebbels emerged followed by an orderly. They embraced and briefly spoke. He took a handkerchief from the breast pocket of his suit coat and wiped the tears from under her eyes. They turned their backs to the orderly, facing the crater in which the ashes of Hitler and Eva Braun cooled. They came to attention and saluted. The orderly drew his sidearm, raised it to the back of Magda's head, and fired. She collapsed. Goebbels remained at attention.

Then another Goebbels, this one in uniform and accompanied by an SS man, walked from the Chancellery toward the crater, eventually stopping next to the real Goebbels. It was the double. He spoke to Goebbels who did not reply. The orderly raised his gun and shot Klint in the back of the head. Then the orderly poured gasoline over the bodies of Magda and Klint, and set them afire.

The orderly retreated to the bunker, reemerging minutes later dressed in a business suit and carrying a suitcase. Goebbels never looked back as he and the orderly began to walk across the garden.

I grabbed my briefcase and ran for the garden. Goebbels was not going to escape.

"Minister!" I shouted.

Both men turned. The orderly drew a gun from a holster under his jacket. I wondered how much Goebbels had paid for his loyalty. Honor was out of the question.

"I'm General Mueller. We met yesterday. I was with Bergdorf in the Chancellery basement."

They studied me, the orderly deferring to Goebbels. From the look on the orderly's face he had decided that I was trouble.

"I need to get south. I thought I would join you."

"How do you know that's where I'm going?" asked Goebbels.

"With the Fuhrer dead, that is where the work must continue."

"What is in the briefcase?" he asked.

"Scientific documents relating to reprisal weapons. They cannot fall into Russian hands. It is bad enough that von Braun has allowed himself to be captured by the Americans."

I could almost see Goebbels calculating. The papers could be invaluable, providing leverage for a man on the run.

When the orderly aimed his gun at my chest, I knew I had played the V-2 card prematurely. I was asking to be shot for the documents.

"Here, let me show you," I said.

I put down the briefcase and knelt as if to open it. Instead I hurled it at the orderly's gun and rolled to my left, drawing my own sidearm. The slug from his first shot buried itself in the flying briefcase; the second buried itself in the patch of dirt I had just abandoned. My first shot took the orderly down.

I got up and dusted myself off.

"There are traitors everyplace, Minister. We are lucky he gave himself away."

Goebbels was shaken. While he had been the spokesman for a regime that espoused violence, others had done the hands-on killing. He apparently didn't have the stomach for close combat. But he wasn't a dilettante who folded when things got bloody. In the last months, he had personally worked the streets of Berlin, exhorting its citizens in the face of terrible punishment and certain defeat. It was a measure of the man that he had achieved some success in rallying the city.

"The Fuhrer himself thought as much. About the existence of traitors that is. We had better get moving," said Goebbels.

He turned his back to me, picked up his suitcase, and headed off, waving at me to follow. The garden was surrounded by a stone wall that was surprisingly intact. Goebbels limped to an iron door for which he had a key. It opened to Leipziger Plaza, down a block from the remains of the Wertheim department store. Few people were about and no cars. Potsdamer station was on the far side of the Plaza.

"Before the war I slipped actresses through that door. The good days, when a thousand-year Reich was inevitable."

Goebbels sounded like an old man recalling the salad days of his youth.

While he wallowed in his memories, I was worried. There might be help waiting for him at the station. I might lose my chance to stop him. He deserved to be shot but I didn't see myself as an executioner, despite my run-in with Hitler. I needed to arrange for his capture by the Russians. That he would probably prefer death to capture made the idea even sweeter.

"Did you know Sara Potter? She was an actress at Ufa before the war," I asked.

He stopped, turned back, and regarded me closely. He couldn't have seen me clearly in the murky twilight.

"I had not thought of her in years. How do you . . . never mind. We can exchange stories after we get to the station. Let's go."

Goebbels turned away, stepped off the sidewalk, and started across the empty plaza. He was intrigued but not enough to indulge his curiosity.

"I heard she got pregnant after finishing *Horst Wessel*."

The pace of his shuffle only quickened.

"Later, General," he called back to me.

Why did I think Goebbels would stop for that memory? If Bergdorf was right, his children had been poisoned as part of his escape plan. The memory of another child wouldn't put a hitch in his step.

I drew my gun. It was a little like being back in Hitler's bedroom. But killing Hitler would have been a form of self-defense or at least self-preservation, and a damn good thing for the world at large. Not so with Goebbels. He was no longer a menace to anyone. The odds were a thousand to one against him turning up for Liz. But he had surely earned a bullet, and a thousand to one wasn't zero.

An artillery barrage took me off the hook. A shell exploded nearby, hurling chunks of brick from the plaza's pavement. Goebbels went down. The remaining shells found their mark, pounding the train station. When the shelling stopped, I could hear people screaming but couldn't see them. Then the dust began to settle, the smoke drifted off, and people could be seen helping the wounded.

Goebbels' was holding his once good leg, complaining about pain and the fucking Russians. I cut away his pant leg. A massive bruise was spreading over the front of his leg. The skin on the back of his thigh had been punctured by the jagged edge of his broken femur. Blood oozed freely around the exposed bone, although there was no arterial bleeding.

He would live with reasonable medical attention. Without treatment life was a dicey proposition. If he didn't slowly bleed to death, infection would likely kill him.

Goebbels wasn't talking. He was fighting his pain for self-control. He had some balls. I had seen many wounded men do worse. When he composed himself, he demanded that I get him to the station. Flames were now leaping from its roof. I told him to look. He twisted his head toward the building.

When he looked back at me, his eyes were closed in resignation. There would be no escape. Then he opened his eyes and looked at me for a long time. The muscles around his jaw worked as if to hold down the pain and sustain his dignity.

"I order you to shoot me," he finally said.

"I won't do that."

"Then give me your gun. I'll do it myself."

"You should have done it back at the bunker. Did you really kill your children?"

"Magda did it. She said there was nothing for any of us after Hitler was gone."

"And now you agree."

A spark of interest flickered in Goebbels' eyes, as if there was a last game to be enjoyed before death.

"I know you from someplace. From before the war. Your German is good but your accent is wrong."

"Heydrich thought I took a shot at Hitler one night in the Eagle's Nest."

It didn't take him long.

"The reporter? Temple?"

"Yes."

"Was Heydrich right?"

"Yes."

"And Goering was in on the plot?"

"Only Diels. He wanted Hitler dead because he anticipated all of this."

"This?"

"That Hitler would start a war and lose."

"No! Hitler was right. But there were Judases from the start. We are in ruin because of them."

"I thought that was the excuse for losing the first world war."

Goebbels' eyes lost focus as if his mind was fixed elsewhere.

"What happened to the child?" he asked

"What child?"

"You know very well. Potter's and mine."

I wasn't going to give Goebbels a last victory. "The baby died in childbirth. It would have been a boy."

"I don't know whether to believe you."

"How could you believe anyone? You made a living as the liar in chief."

Waves of pain registered on his face. It was his leg, not my words. He would not submit to either.

"As Propaganda Minister, I serve a higher truth."

Goebbels smiled as if we were sharing an insider joke. His wounded leg hadn't sapped the strength from his voice. And even as he lay in the rubble of the Reich's defeat, his eyes had an undeniable energy.

"You underestimate me," he said.

"It would be hard to overestimate you, considering you're on your ass, dying in bombed-out Berlin on what might be the Third Reich's last day."

"I am not dying. And I still have you."

"Have me?"

"Yes. You were sent into Germany to steal the plans for the reprisal weapon from under Russian noses. Am I right?"

"What of it?"

"You traded your mission for a chance at me. Now why would you do that? Not to kill me. You could have done that already. So I must know something you don't. What is it that you want to know, Temple?"

"Nothing."

"Did Sara tell you that I raped her?"

"In a manner of speaking."

"You could handle rape but not the truth."

"Don't waste your breath bullshitting me."

"The child is alive. I see it in your face."

"She lost the child. We drifted apart. I think she's back in Boston."

"Propaganda is not your strong suit." He laughed, and as he did, his leg moved. "Damn!" he groaned, fighting back a wave of pain.

I waited for the pain to subside. When it had, I said, "We don't do propaganda in the states because our higher truth isn't bullshit that needs to be draped in lies."

"How naïve. Slavery was, and segragation is, wrapped in bloody Christian cloth. The millions who toil in poverty for the benefit of the very rich are appeased by religion and the pretense of freedom. I piss on the arrogance of your deceitful higher truths.

"But you and I have business. You have my child. And I know you do not want me appearing at your door one day claiming my paternal rights."

"The Russians will finish you, if you're still alive when they get here. And if you beat the odds and show up at my door, you won't find anything but trouble."

"I'll find Sara with my child. She is too good for it to be any other way."

He said "good" as if it was a term of contempt.

"I knew that night she loved you. I wanted her to betray you by her passion. I knew the moment would come as I rode into her. We had briefly been lovers before and I would know when she yielded to the pleasure."

Goebbels couldn't resist messing with me even if his fate was in my hands.

"But she never did. She just laid there like some virgin being sacrificed. Screwing me to save you was nothing to her. I was an annoyance. You were everything. It was the possibility of pregnancy that bothered her. We both knew her Catholicism would make an abortion difficult. Oh sweet guilt.

"And you, Temple, you see yourself as a noble sort. You would marry her just to prove your worth, your willingness to sacrifice. The two of you had the child. With your bourgeoisie blood, you could have done nothing else."

"So you think you have it all figured out? Tell you what. I'll give you a chance to show up on my doorstep and see if you're right. I'm leaving."

I stood up and turned toward the Chancellery garden. I hesitated, realizing that I hadn't the faintest idea of how I would escape Berlin.

"Do you want to know about the other child?" Goebbels called. The question had a teasing, begging quality as if he could not abide my leaving.

"What other child?"

"Seth."

A breeze came up and carried the smoke from the burning train station over us.

"What about him?"

Goebbels smiled. He knew he had me.

"It started in 1933. We'd come from a private screening of the *Blue Angel* and were back in Hitler's sitting room at the Kaiserhof.

The film made Dietrich an international star. But her leaving Germany was a slap in the face. Hitler insisted she be punished. Streicher was full of crazy ideas that would have embarrassed the country. Hess shot them down for what they were. Goering took a poke at me, claiming Ufa was my province and actresses my specialty.

"Hitler said not to pick on his 'little mouse-doctor', which was what Goering and the others called me behind my back. But I was smarter than them and Hitler knew it. I understood destruction was not the solution even if destruction was what Dietrich deserved. We needed to find our own Dietrich. To recruit an American actress to National Socialism, and let her raise the swastika over the heads of those who fled Germany.

"I told them I had targeted Potter. She already had socialist leanings thanks to her beloved father. I told them, if we could get her to Germany, she would become one of us. To that end, Ufa had already made Paramount an offer for her to do a film here.

"Hitler liked the idea. Goering asked why she wasn't already in Germany. I said Zukor was preventing it. Rohm spoke up and said she needed a push. Goering asked if I was being sarcastic when I referred to her father as beloved. We talked into the night. It was like planning a practical joke."

Goebbels laughed, setting off another wave of pain. In the dirty air he could hardly catch his breath.

"What was the joke?"

"We decided - what was his name, yes - Thomas Potter would father an Aryan child. He would follow the mother to Germany. Sara would become involved in her father's plight and follow him to Germany. Her pretext for coming would be the offer Ufa had already made. Once she arrived we would convert her to National Socialism."

"How could you know they would come?"

"We trusted the family's middle class mentality. We knew he would come once Paula wrote she was pregnant by him. We hoped Sara would follow. The Ufa offer was on the table and she was a willful girl. That worked in our favor."

"How did you get Glaise to do it? How could you know that Potter would fall for the temptation?"

"Glaise would have bedded that cripple Roosevelt for a part in a movie. And she was very seductive. She even had me."

The club-footed he-goat managed the last remark without a trace of irony.

"How could you know she would get pregnant, even if she did seduce him?"

"Pregnancy wasn't the idea. What difference would it make? Morell would be her doctor and Potter would never get close enough to know."

I could see Goebbels' teeth – yellowed from too many years of cigarettes - behind what could have been a grimace or a smile.

"Morell wasn't even an obstetrician," I protested.

"Before Hitler became his patient, Morell treated many celebrated people with his famous injections. Cocktails of vitamins, hormones, and amphetamines. God only knows what else. It was not surprising that he became her doctor."

"Are you saying Seth died from one of Morell's chemical cocktails?"

"Hardly necessary. You don't see, do you?"

As Goebbels choked off a laugh, I began to see. It was all a stunt. They could manipulate people, so they did. It was a sham, a con with nothing at stake from their perspective. They would toy with a few Americans. If successful, Sara would become a Dietrich in reverse and the Nazis would score a minor propaganda victory. If unsuccessful, it would be nothing more than Hollywood and Babelsberg run amuck, their hands unseen. Scandal but not political news. And the linchpin of the scheme: a child who never existed.

"The pregnancy was a hoax. There was no Seth. Morell was window dressing."

"Now you see," said Goebbels. He looked smug, as if he expected me to congratulate him for his cleverness. "It was a delightful parlor game. And we won. Sara became our Dietrich."

"But Sara didn't become anybody's Dietrich, and with her

pendant she tried to wreck *Horst Wessel*. And Tom Potter helped put out the *Ku'damm Conscience*."

Goebbels' smugness vanished, replaced by controlled anger. He had been lying on his side, propped up on an elbow, his wounded leg resting atop his other leg. A considerable pool of blood had collected below the fracture. He glared at me through the smoke and dust that permeated Berlin's once crystal air. Goebbels didn't seem to notice. He was full of contemptuous superiority as if I were the one dying in the rubble.

"No. We touched-up the film to eliminate that puny ram's horn. And I'll wager Potter to this day carries the picture of the baby who never was - pulling it out now and then for a guilt-ridden look."

"Save it for the Fuhrer. You'll see him in hell soon enough."

I began to walk back toward the Chancellery garden. It didn't take Goebbels long to panic.

"Wait!" he called, his strength fading as the pool of blood grew. "You can't leave me for the Russians. They are barbarians."

"Show them *Horst Wessel*. Maybe they'll join the Party."

April 30, 1945 8:30 PM

I returned to the Chancellery garden through the door used by Goebbels for starlets during the Reich's glory days. I looked back and saw him silhouetted in the glare from the Potsdamer station fire. He was dragging himself across the pavement toward the garden door. Given his pace, he would need a thousand years.

I closed the door behind me and threw the deadbolt.

Chapter Forty-two

How I escaped is unimportant. Suffice it to say, I changed into civilian clothes and worked my way through the porous Russian lines west of Berlin. Three days later I met our troops a little east of Magdeburg. If I'd known it would be that easy, I would have taken the Peenemunde documents with me. But I didn't know so I burned them. There was no shortage of fires to choose from.

It is almost impossible that Goebbels escaped. The Russians say they found him with Magda in the Chancellery garden. I believe they mistook Klint for Goebbels as Goebbels intended. If the Russians had found him alive, they would have trotted him out in a propaganda game. The odds are that he died near where I last saw him, his body just one of thousands unidentified in the ruins of the shattered city.

When Arch finished grilling me, I went home and told Sara what had happened in Berlin. That violated a dozen OSS secrecy rules but Sara knew more about holding her tongue than Arch and the rest of his Yale buddies would ever know. We decided to tell her dad.

Tom and Betty Potter had been unable to patch their marriage together. Although they tried, each was more comfortable without the other. That's how they chose to put it. Tom never said as much to me but Vik would have been a hard act to follow even if Betty wasn't overly interested in the trappings of wealth.

Tom sold his shoe business for a small fortune, gave half the proceeds to Betty, and then moved to New York where he served as an unpaid administrator for the American Civil Liberties Union.

So Sara and I flew to New York. We landed at La Guardia. Although it was a spring day, it wasn't much like Tempelhof had been in 1934.

"What are you shaking your head about, Michael?"

"How lucky it is that we are here, where the air is foul and the pigeon shit looks like dirty snow."

"The chamber of commerce will love you."

"Really?"

"Of course not. If not for me, you'd be unloved and still chasing Dietrich."

"She was chasing me."

"It's your imagination I love the most."

It was the banter of messengers bearing difficult news.

As the cab entered Manhattan we fell silent. Goebbels was wrong when he said Tom tortured himself with the picture of Seth. While he was too smart for that, the picture hadn't disappeared. I'd seen it in Tom's Upper East Side apartment. Not in the living room bookcase with the nicely framed family photos. It was in his bedroom - tucked in the frame of a mirror along with other family snapshots.

When we entered the apartment, Sara and her father embraced, then stepped back to admire each other. They had long since reconciled and now possessed the special bond linking those who have been tested in the same battle.

As Tom mixed cocktails, he asked me if I thought the Russians would keep Berlin and eastern Germany.

"We're too war weary to kick them out," I said. "And they aren't going anywhere on their own."

"I'm afraid you're right. But having a divided country is a recipe for trouble."

Sara interrupted, "Dad, when Michael went to Berlin on that OSS business, he saw Goebbels. Talked to him. You should know what he had to say - about Seth."

"Seth?"

"Yes," I said.

Tom stopped mixing and almost came to attention in anticipation of the news. I told the story quickly, hoping Tom would be relieved to know he had not lost a son.

When I finished Tom said nothing. For a minute he stood there, unable to digest the story. He seemed to age before our eyes. Finally he looked at Sara with consuming sadness.

"Oh, Dad," said Sara who ran to hold him.

After a few seconds he gently broke her embrace and looked at me.

"How do you know it wasn't just another lie?" he said as if he couldn't accept losing Seth a second time.

"Goebbels was too proud of having fooled everyone. He was bragging, holding on to a small victory. I don't think he was lying. If I did, I wouldn't have told you."

Tom shook his head and dropped into a chair as if his legs had given out.

"I never would have gone to Germany. My God, everything would have . . . Your mother and I . . . We would have been spared so much."

After a few seconds of silence, Sara spoke, her voice certain and kind.

"But think what we would have lost. Seth gave you the opportunity to fight with Ludi and meet Viktoria. And Seth gave me Michael and Liz and now this one."

Sara patted her swollen belly.

Tom Potter looked at Sara and nodded. The sadness in his eyes receded without disappearing. The truth of Sara's words and the affection of her smile could only do so much.

None of us spoke of Seth again, at least not when I was around. Tom died seventeen years later. He lived those years as if he had no regrets. He was generous with his time and his money. He was a terrific father and grandfather as well as a good friend to me. After Tom's funeral, Sara and I cleaned out his apartment.

The frame of the bedroom mirror was still packed with snapshots. Over the years many pictures had been added, covering the older ones. But not the photo of the supposed Seth. The view of it remained unobstructed.

I pulled it out, tore it in quarters, and stuffed the pieces in my pocket.

End Notes

In 2009, the manuscript of this story was given to Michael Temple's grandson, John Temple, by the trust department of a Swiss bank. The turnover was in accordance with instructions given the bank by Arch Hocking in 1985. They provided for the manuscript's release only in the event Liz Gold (nee Temple) died without living decedents and only after the death of her husband.

Liz died in 2008. She survived her husband, Stuart Gold, by three years. They were married for 39 years. She suffered from endometriosis, and as a result the couple had been unable to have children. Liz taught in Chicago's public high schools for over forty years, winning many teaching awards. Over three hundred of her former students attended her funeral. It is believed that she died without knowledge of her actual parentage.

Eric Jan Hanussen was murdered in 1934. The killing was attributed to the SA, although no effort was made to solve the crime. Various motives have been ascribed to his unidentified killer(s). Hanussen claimed to be a Danish aristocrat. In fact he was a Czech Jew. After becoming a high-profile entertainer, he played a dangerous game by dabbling at the edge of Nazi Party politics with prophesies often favorable to the Nazis. He was distrusted by many party insiders who were concerned that he was gaining influence with Hitler who was receptive to occult influences. Given all that, Hanussen's connection to the *Ku'damm Conscience* was only one reason to think his murder was orchestrated by a Nazi faction.

Bella Fromm left Germany in 1938. She settled in New York City where she continued writing. In 1943 her best seller, *Blood and Banquets,* was published. The book is a diary of her years in Berlin from 1930 forward, and describes the changes occasioned by the Nazis' rise to power. She died in New York in 1972.

Fromm was not alone. Thousands of top-notch artists, designers, technicians, architects, writers, entertainers, businessmen, and scientists (most but not all Jewish) fled Germany before the Nazis completely halted immigration in 1941. The brain drain enriched the rest of the world at Germany's expense. The U.S. was the major beneficiary, particularly in the arts and sciences. Marlene Dietrich was not Jewish which was (in part) why the Nazis were so aggravated by her defection. On the other hand, von Sternberg was Jewish, notwithstanding Michael Temple thinking otherwise.

A watchmaker by trade, Emile Maurice was Hitler's closest confidant during the formative years of the Nazi party. He was the second member of the organization that grew to become the SS. (Hitler was the first.) Following the Geli Raubal affair, Maurice fell out of favor - especially so when his Jewish ancestry was discovered. However, Hitler protected Maurice from Himmler who wanted him banished from the party and the SS. Maurice was not killed in Oranieburg as Eric thought. By 1937 Maurice was in Munich serving a minor role as a craft union leader. He lived until 1972. When Hitler killed himself, he had two photos in his possession: one of Eva Braun, and one of his old friend and former driver.

Rudolf Diels escaped from the Reichstag Annex. Although banished from the Gestapo, he became a local government administrator in Cologne under the protection of Goering. There he occasionally protected local Jews and continued his covert opposition to Hitler. After the war he held various government positions in West Germany. He died in a hunting accident in 1957.

Reinhard Heydrich became a Nazi star. He held many positions of power, one of which was Protector of Czechoslovakia. His rule there was brutal. In 1942 he was assassinated in Prague by two Czech resistance fighters. Hitler gave him a Berlin funeral fit for a head-of-state. The village of Lidice was a few miles northwest of Prague. It was a hotbed of resistance. In retaliation for Heydrich's assassination, Lidice was bulldozed to the ground. One hundred and seventy-three men were killed on the spot. Two hundred and eighty-nine women and children were hauled off to concentration camps where most died.

Ludi Kohl died in Columbia Haus five days after the bakery burned. The records say he suffered a heart attack.

After the premiere of *Horst Wessel,* Walter Thiele did not return to his job at UFA. Like so many others, he simply disappeared.

Richard Cooper died in London during a V-2 attack in 1943. Two years before he had uncovered the Enigma code-breaking operation at Bletchley Park. In deference to the Allied war effort, Cooper never reported the story and took to his grave what at the time was the greatest secret - and best story - of the war.